CW00793457

So Far From God

SO FAR FROM GOD
GOD

John Harris

HUTCHINSON
LONDON SYDNEY AUCKLAND JOHANNESBURG

First published in Great Britain in 1989 by
Century Hutchinson Ltd,
Brookmount House, 62–65 Chandos Place,
London WC2N 4NW

Century Hutchinson Australia Pty Ltd
89–91 Albion Street, Surry Hills, NSW 2010, Australia

Century Hutchinson New Zealand Ltd
PO Box 40–086, Glenfield, Auckland 10, New Zealand

Century Hutchinson, South Africa Pty Ltd,
PO Box 337, Bergvlei, 2012 South Africa

Printed and bound in Great Britain by
Mackays of Chatham PLC, Chatham, Kent

British Library Cataloguing in Publication Data
Harris, John, *1916–*
So far from God.
823'.914 [J]

ISBN 0–09–173928–4

'Poor Mexico, so far from God and so near to the United States.'

Porfirio Díaz
Ruler of Mexico from 1876 to 1911

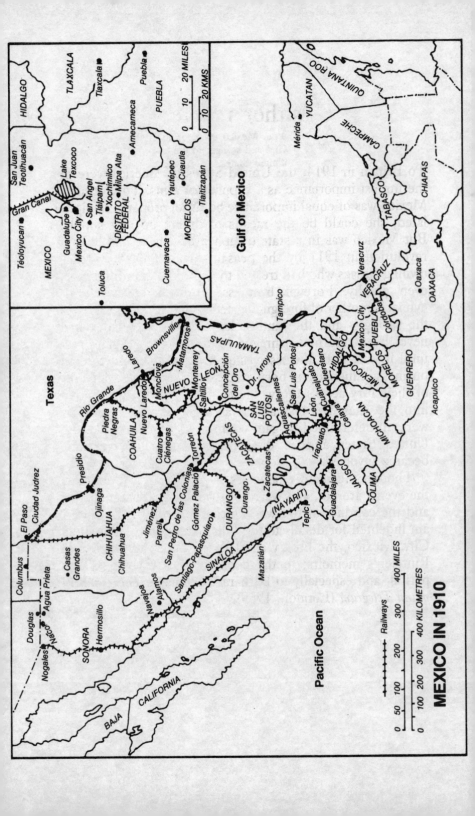

MEXICO IN 1910

Texas

Gulf of Mexico

Pacific Ocean

Railways

0   50 100   200   300   400 MILES
0 100 200 300 400 KILOMETRES

BAJA CALIFORNIA

SONORA

Douglas
Nogales Naco
        Agua Prieta
Hermosillo

Columbus
Casas Grandes
El Paso
Ciudad Juárez
Presidio
Ojinaga

CHIHUAHUA

Chihuahua

Navajoa
Álamos

SINALOA

Mazatlán

Santiago Papasquiaro

DURANGO

Durango

Jiménez
Parral
San Pedro de las Colonias
Gómez Palacio Torreón

COAHUILA

Piedra Negras
Cuatro Ciénegas
Nuevo Laredo
Monclova

Rio Grande
Laredo
Brownsville
Matamoros

NUEVO LEÓN

Monterrey
Saltillo
Concepción del Oro

TAMAULIPAS

Dr. Arroyo

Tampico

ZACATECAS

Zacatecas

SAN LUIS POTOSÍ

San Luis Potosí

Aguascalientes

Tepic

(NAYARIT)

JALISCO

Guadalajara

León
Irapuato
Cuanajuato
Querétaro

Celaya

Veracruz
Córdoba

Acapulco

GUERRERO

MICHOACÁN

COLIMA

HIDALGO

MEXICO

MORELOS

PUEBLA

Mexico City
PUEBLA

TABASCO

OAXACA

Oaxaca

CHIAPAS

CAMPECHE

YUCATÁN

Mérida

QUINTANA ROO

Gulf of Mexico

HIDALGO
TLAXCALA

Téoloyucan
San Juan Teotihuacán
Tlaxcala
Puebla
Amecameca
Gran Canal
Lake Texcoco
Guadalupe
Mexico City
Tlálpam
San Angel
Xochimilco
Milpa Alta
PUEBLA
DISTRITO FEDERAL
Yautepec
Cuautla
Tlaltizapán
MORELOS
Cuernavaca
Toluca
MEXICO

0   10   20 MILES
0 10 20 KMS

Author's Note

To Britain in 1914, the United States of America were of the utmost importance as a supplier of arms. To Germany Mexico was of equal importance because, properly manipulated, she could be the means of drying up that supply. But Mexico was in a state of upheaval. There had been a revolution in 1911 by the peasants against the hacienda-owning classes who had treated them with total indifference, even cruelty. Foreign businesses remained powerful – 'Mexico, mother of foreigners; stepmother of Mexicans' was the saying – and the land stolen by the hacendados had never been returned. Enraged leaders swore never to rest until it was, until the last vestiges of Spanish and foreign business influence had been eradicated. So, with the shadow of their fury across the whole country, Mexico descended into the anarchy of small private armies whose generals were all determined to gain control, while nations like the United States and as distant as Britain and Germany became involved.

Though the main characters in this book are fictitious the events are not, and were all part of the preparations for and the conduct of the war which broke out in Europe. I am indebted for details to the Villa Museum in Chihuahua City, Mexico; the library at El Paso, Texas; to Franz von Rintelen's memoirs; to the books of the survivors of the period; and especially to Barbara Tuchman's *The Zimmermann Telegram* (London, 1959).

Part I

1

The corpse was that of a soldier. It wore faded scraps of uniform and hung limply with a rope round its neck from the arm of a telegraph pole that was tilted to one side under its weight. Thin brown feet, bare of shoes, pointed downwards, the whole ugly shape moving slightly in the breeze.

The train had halted outside the town and the carriage had come to a stop directly opposite the swinging corpse so that it was impossible to avoid looking at it. The chatter inside died and the card games stopped abruptly. Turning in their seats, the women passengers resolutely faced the other way, trying not very successfully to keep their children from staring through the window at the horror that hung at eye level, impossible to avoid.

The train consisted of a rusty-looking engine with a large cowcatcher and a funnel like a jug, attached to a long line of battered coaches, their wooden sides splintered by bullets, their windows in some cases missing entirely. There were no first-class carriages, only the hard-seated compartments used by the peasants and, with the whole country on the move, everyone was packed in together.

Lighting a cigarette, Pierce Fitzpatrick Slattery studied the people around him. They were a colourful lot in a mixture of native charro costume, peasants' cotton and city clothes, with personal touches of gaiety here and there in the form of rebozos or bright sarapes. Until the sudden silence imposed on them by the hanged man, even an occasional burst of song had come from them as they had travelled south. There were two youths clutching sacks in which something moved, an old man with a fiddle who had been playing 'La Paloma', a leather bottle of tequila going the rounds, and two men dancing with each other, carefully avoiding a blind youth who was reciting a long heroic poem

11

about Pancho Villa, the rebel Mexican leader who was terrorizing the northern border of the country.

Now they were silent, and the heat inside the carriage increased as the sun climbed higher. The surrounding land was bare, and tawny as a lion, the distant low range of mountains like the knuckles of its spine. Slattery had read a lot about Mexico and had expected colour, flowers and music but never this emptiness, or the constant wind that rolled the dust in red clouds across the endless landscape. Opposite him a woman sat silently, trying to avoid looking at the corpse with its popping eyes and protruding tongue. She wore a cloche hat and veil and a lightweight coat and dress of dark blue that enhanced the blueness of her eyes which, in a country of black fathomless orbs, seemed to shine against the raven darkness of her hair. She sat ramrod-straight in her seat, slim, pale, her features finely boned, no longer a girl but beautiful still.

This woman, Slattery told himself, starts where all the rest leave off.

Near her an American wearing a brown derby hat and a brown suit moved restlessly up and down the centre aisle, smoking a cigar. He gestured at the corpse.

'The whole goddam country's full of those things,' he said. 'Guy here says that one's Balthasar Vásquez. He was one of General Villa's boys who was picked up by government troops.' He nodded to Slattery. 'Lidgett's the name,' he said. 'Aloysius Lidgett. You here for the same reason I'm here?'

'What reason would that be?'

'To join Villa,' Lidgett said. 'He crossed the border to start the war again.'

As Slattery well knew.

Mexico was in turmoil. Two years before, in 1911, a rebellion, raised by Francisco Indalecio Madero and supported by people as diverse as landowners and outlaws, had toppled the aging dictator, Pofirio Díaz, from the presidency he had occupied for thirty years. Elected in his place by popular vote, Madero had become president and the revolution had seemed to be over.

12

But after thirty years of dictatorship and with no followers with experience, Madero had been forced to employ many of Díaz's old supporters, so that he had been toppled in his turn by a rising backed by General Victoriano Huerta, the very man he had appointed to put it down. With Madero murdered, Huerta had become provisional president in his place and once again it had seemed the revolution was over.

'It isn't, though,' Lidgett said. 'Up north they call it the pump handle revolution. Because it goes up and down. It's just a comic opera affair.'

Slattery indicated the swinging corpse. 'I bet *he* doesn't think so.'

'I guess not. Huerta reckons he's nothing to fear, but a people in arms is more powerful than any army.'

'That's a nice phrase, Mr Lidgett.'

'I'm a newspaperman. I deal in 'em. You like nice phrases?'

'I've dealt in 'em, too, in my time.'

Lidgett smiled, a big handsome man with white teeth and features that matched Slattery's own rangy good looks. 'Call me Loyce,' he said. 'Everybody does. I decided I'd come down here and make my name. But I was with Teddy Roosevelt in Cuba in 1899 and I decided it might be more fun to be *in* the fighting than writin' about it.'

He gestured. 'Madero was often wrong, I guess,' he went on. 'But when they murdered him, armies started to appear from nowhere. Even guys who'd profited under Díaz. They're siding with peóns who've become generals leading their own goddam ragamuffin troops.'

So Slattery had heard. At the top was Venustiano Carranza, a Sonora landowner; below were all creeds, colours and conditions down to the ex-bandits, Emiliano Zapata in Morelos, south of Mexico City and a constant threat to the capital, and Pancho Villa in the north, a peasant with a genius for war and a firm base in Chihuahua, whose sphere of activity was along the Texas-Mexican border.

'Would any of them ever come round to supporting Huerta?' he asked.

13

'No.' It was the woman who spoke this time. 'Carranza will never acknowledge a régime that's not properly elected.'

Her voice was low and rich and, though she spoke perfect English, there was a trace of something harsher in it. Now that she'd joined in the conversation Slattery was determined to keep her interest.

'What about Zapata?' he asked.

'He couldn't even agree with Madero,' Lidgett said.

'And Villa?'

'He was the guy who really put Madero in power. Him and Pascual Orozco. Only Orozco decided he hadn't got enough out of the revolution so he started another to get rid of Madero. Huerta and Villa worked to get rid of *him*. But Huerta couldn't stand Villa and Villa had to bolt across the border. He's back now, though. Because they killed Madero. He came with eight men, nine horses, a few rifles, and a war chest of thirty-five pesos and a silver watch.' Lidgett grinned. 'He'll have more now.'

The train jerked and the corpse outside the window moved out of sight. As the train stopped again, they heard someone in the next coach scream as they caught sight of the man on the telegraph pole. Lidgett was busy looking out of the window and Slattery became aware of being studied by the woman opposite.

'Are you on business?' she asked. 'An American?'

'Neither. Are *you* American?'

The woman frowned. 'I'm not sure what I am,' she admitted. 'My father was a German singer who married a Mexican. I was born in Germany and taken to the States as a child. We took out naturalization papers in New York.'

'Doesn't that make you American?'

She shrugged. 'Does it work that way? Is it that simple? My father died and my mother returned to Mexico. When she died I joined my brother who has property here. My name's part German, part Mexican – Magdalena Graf. Though I am officially an American citizen, my instincts, I think, are still German – if they're not Mexican. I'm a singer.'

It explained the richness of her voice. 'Opera?'

14

'Nothing so grand. Zarzuela.'

'What's that?'

'How do I describe it? It's a Spanish creation, a special kind of stage piece with melodies from Spanish roots. But it's not operetta – though we do operetta. But operetta doesn't allow for the Spanish flavour. Zarzuela is different. It's passionate. It's - it's' – she shrugged and gave a little laugh – 'it's zarzuela. I studied at the Conservatory.'

He listened to her, enchanted. Caught up by something that interested and excited her, her face came alive, her body and her hands moved, and her eyes lit up. 'And you sing with a company?' He assumed she belonged to some small travelling troupe that went in for one-night stands in backwoods towns, with shabby sets and costumes inherited from other travelling companies.

'Of course.' She spoke proudly, almost condescendingly. 'They're on the train.'

It explained the people in city suits he'd noticed with the colourful personal additions of rebozos and bright sarapes, and the occasional bursts of song.

'We've been in Ciudad Juárez on the border,' she went on. 'We appear next in Chihuahua. I have a house there. It's handy for slipping into the United States. I've sung in El Paso and Houston. Even in Tucson. One day I'll sing in New York.'

'Are you famous?'

'People know me. Why are *you* here?'

Slattery smiled. 'That's a good question,' he said.

It was a very good question and one that Pierce Fitzpatrick Slattery hadn't yet managed to answer. Junior army captains with only one sound leg could never really expect to pursue a very active military career. The fighting in the Balkans in 1912 had drawn him as an interested but very unofficial observer, but a Turkish shell at Uskub had finished the trip rather more abruptly than he had expected. After leaving hospital back in England he had been peremptorily summoned before his commanding officer.

'You realize you've ruined your career,' he was told.

15

'I've also ruined my leg. It's a good job I'm a cavalry officer and don't have to walk.'

'I don't think you're going to be a cavalry officer much longer,' the colonel snapped. 'Not with this regiment!'

'I didn't think I would,' Slattery had responded spiritedly. 'That's why I'm resigning. I don't intend to be summoned to the War Office to be informed I've been a naughty boy.'

He had rightly assumed his career was over and his father, who had been in the Foreign Office, had suggested that he went to see a man he knew in Whitehall who might find something for him to do.

The office was on the top floor of a solid-looking block overlooking the Thames. It seemed remarkably bare. There were no files, no staff and no secretary. It contained two men, one with bushy military half-whiskers that looked as if they'd been dyed. He was a former officer from one of the British county regiments and was reputed to be the son of a regular army officer and a Polish countess. He spoke fluent German, Polish, Italian and French. His assistant was a white-haired ex-naval officer with a wooden leg which had replaced one he had lost in a train smash in Scotland. He was said to have cut off the shreds of the smashed limb with his penknife to release himself. Nobody knew who owned the office. In fact, George Bernard Shaw lived downstairs and he had no idea what was happening above him. Which, the men upstairs liked to say, seemed to indicate they were doing things right. They were busy with a discussion when Slattery arrived.

'If we're going to do the job,' the naval man was saying, 'then let's do it properly and recruit professionals. No more amateurs like Baden Powell with his bloody paint box.'

'He was good at sketches,' the military man pointed out.

The naval man sniffed. 'I always thought there was something a bit artificial about him. After all that fuss over Mafeking, when they gave him a column he hardly distinguished himself. Always seemed to be acting. Liked to disguise himself as a butterfly hunter, a journalist, a snipe shooter – things like that. Ought to have belonged to a seaside concert party.'

16

His military opposite number shrugged. 'He always prepared a detailed report at the end of every trip, all the same,' he pointed out. 'And presented it free, gratis and for nothing to the War Office.'

'Who took no bloody notice whatsoever!'

Slattery listened to them, faintly amused. He had come to the conclusion that they'd forgotten him when the naval officer suddenly asked him what languages he spoke.

'German and Serbo-Croat, which I picked up in the Balkans,' he said. 'French because my mother's French. And Spanish because I was born in Gibraltar where my father was on the staff of the Governor. My mother didn't like the place so we had a house in La Linea in Spain where I grew up.'

'We want Spanish speakers,' the naval man said. 'And you'd be no good to the army if a war came, would you?'

'Wouldn't I?' Slattery was already a little sensitive about people who liked to write him off because he had a limp.

The man behind the desk eyed him with interest. Slattery was a large man, tall and broad with blazing red hair topping a face that was commanding rather than handsome.

'That broken leg you got in the Balkans wouldn't be much good if war came,' the man with the whiskers said.

Slattery wondered just how much they knew about him but he had to agree about his leg. It had been badly set by an Albanian doctor who wore what appeared to be a velvet smoking-cap and crap-catcher trousers, and looked, smelled and behaved like a vet, and it had had to be broken again on his return to England. He certainly wasn't going to do much marching. He tried a different tack.

'*Is* war coming?' he asked.

'Of course it is,' Bushy Whiskers snapped.

'Who's going to be fighting?'

'Germany for a start. They're growing far too big for their boots.'

'And is that what this office exists for? To work out odds, choose opponents and set the number of rounds?'

Bushy Whiskers frowned at his levity. 'This office exists for counter-intelligence and combatting the efforts of difficult enemies – at the moment chiefly Irish Fenians and Germans.'

Being Irish himself, Slattery knew about Fenians and he had met a few Germans in the Balkans where they had seemed to have a finger in every pie. They were an arrogant lot on the whole, constantly crowing about *Kriegsgefahr*, Germany's strength and her future rôle in Europe. Generally speaking, he wasn't over-enamoured of them and he could remember seeing what had seemed to be hordes of them, mostly princes from Middle European states, at the funeral of Edward VII three years before. It had been a dazzling affair of bright uniforms more suited to a wedding than a wake and all somehow in bad taste, the German contingent the most tasteless of the lot. And he was well aware that Europe had been on tenterhooks for years because of the Kaiser's half-baked impulses. Algeciras. Agadir. The German fleet. The insistence on adjusted frontiers. The demands for colonies. The claims that the Belgian coast ought to be part of Germany. To anybody who read the newspapers, it had become a bit of a bore and somehow the Kaiser always managed to appear rather vulgar.

'But why Spanish?' he had asked. 'Surely the Germans haven't got their eye on Spain?'

The naval man gestured. 'They'd like to grab Gibraltar and seal off the Med. We know that. But, no, it isn't Spain. It's Mexico.'

'And you want me to be a spy?'

'We prefer to call them agents.'

'What do they do?'

'Follow each other about and report on each other's doings.'

'False whiskers? That sort of thing?'

'Not quite. But you'd be surprised what we can work out from reports.'

'Isn't Mexico where some half-baked revolution's going on?'

'More of a civil war really. Mexico's been waltzing on a volcano for years. And we're all there – Britain, Germany, the United States – all acting as partners, while the volcano prepares to erupt under us. It started rumbling when Madero appeared. Now it's really going strong. It'll be a long time before it stops.'

'Why are *we* interested?'

The naval man looked at him as if he weren't very bright. 'Because half Germany's agents seem to be going to Mexico at the moment,' he said. 'We feel we ought to send a few too.'

2

The horizon in the west turned grey beneath the coppery clouds moving up swiftly on a wind that howled out of the desert. Above, the sky looked muddy and the sun was a fading orange ball. In the distance, the mountaintops caught the last of the light, glowing pink as the fiery orb sank.

As they passed the flanks of the umber-coloured hills and rounded a curve, just ahead they saw the town of San Marino de Bravos where the train was to remain overnight. Those passengers who could afford it would be accommodated in the little town's only hotel.

As the train slowed to a stop the wind increased, lifting out of the west and sweeping ferociously along the valley of the desert to shift the hummocks and the dunes and pile the sand against the stumpy roots of the mesquite.

As the passengers stumbled down the steps from the train, two riders, hunched in their high Mexican saddles, sarapes to their mouths, hats low over eyes, plodded dumbly past with a high-wheeled cart from whose sides they were trying to obtain a little shelter. His voice hoarse with shouting abuse, the driver of the cart stumbled at the heads of the mules to prevent them turning away from the gale which struck at the flanks of the riders and punched at the brims of their hats. Powdery dust layered the clothes of the passengers from the train, parched their throats and filled their eyes with grit. Alongside the track by a hedge of prickly pear was a group of the little wooden crosses the Mexicans placed in the ground to show where someone had died, an indication of some forgotten skirmish between government and revolutionary troops during the past year.

Set well back from the track, the town was a small place of flat-roofed buildings pitted here and there with bullet holes. After two years of revolution, half the towns in Mexico seemed to be marked by bullets and graced with the little roadside symbols of violent death. The shutters of the hotel were closed, the paint seared away by the sun and the everlasting wind that blew across the northern wastes. Opposite, the twin brown towers of the church dominated the place, rising above the sparse trees. The town was still and silent and there was no sign of any of the inhabitants.

The Posada San Gabriel had been made out of an old colonial dwelling, the proprietor's family living on the ground floor, the residents in rooms opening off a balcony formed by the arches that surrounded the courtyard, where a dusty tree grew among the swathes of sand brought by the wind through the great double door. A boy, bundled to the eyes in a blanket, let the travellers in.

Aloysius Lidgett and the woman, Magdalena Graf, were among those who had decided to spend the night in the hotel. Lidgett seemed to be enjoying himself but the woman's face was strained, though as she caught Slattery's gaze on her the blue slanting eyes flashed as if to convince him she wasn't as tired as she looked.

The dining-room was thick with dust and in the centre of each spotted table-cloth was a glass containing a single wilting flower. The people from the train fell wearily into chairs as bottles of beer were brought by a waitress. She'd just been washing her hair but nobody looked twice at it. Mexican women, Slattery had begun to realize, were always washing the dust from their hair and it was nothing to have a meal served with it hanging wetly down the back. They began discussing General Villa.

'He was a rustler before he joined Madero,' Lidgett said. 'And the people who own cattle support Huerta, so that makes it okay to steal their steers. He sells them across the Rio Grande to raise money for guns.'

The wind died after dark and Slattery went to his room to wash off some of the dust. The air was stifling and as he arranged his belongings he reflected that but for a variety of circumstances he wouldn't have been there at all. There had been a few debts, but nothing much. A few enemies. A few people who were too friendly. He had been enjoying London after the Balkans and the hospital, and had been content to go on enjoying it; his presence on the wrong side of the Atlantic was really less to do with his broken leg than with women. He was a fugitive from love.

He grinned at his reflection in the spotted mirror. It sounded like the plot of a novelette. Fleeing from the attentions of two women.

Margaret Presteigne would have provided him with a safe family life, fed him well and given him sturdy children, and at the age of sixty he would have been wondering where his years had gone. Amaryllis Eade would have given him moments of wild excitement, riotous laughter and high passion, but he trembled to think what existence with her would have been like.

Margaret Presteigne was the vicar's daughter, straightforward, honest, boring, and his mother had been set on a match for years. Amaryllis Eade was a different kettle of fish altogether, and was more than willing to dispense with the inconvenience of holy matrimony. She was the author of *The British Aristocracy*, *Princely India* and a whole array of books which her relationship to an earl had not only made possible but had also helped to sell. Her brother had been at school with Slattery and he had gone through agonies in his youth when he had considered her the last word in beauty, innocence and sweetness.

That had been some years before, however, and when he had returned to England after a spell in the Middle East he had found she had sprung to fame overnight with her book on the British nobility. With her connections and the aristocracy's eagerness to read about itself, her book had been an immediate best-seller. She had written it chiefly because she had been bored but, not slow to see the advantages of fame and wealth, had immediately prevailed on her father to send her to stay with the Curzons at the Viceregal Palace in India. The book on the Indian princes had not pleased Curzon but it had sold a lot of copies.

The chances of ever meeting her again had seemed slim and Slattery had actually settled down to the desk job with the two old men in Whitehall when she had turned up again. His work had seemed to consist of writing short propaganda paragraphs for the press, reading newspapers and cutting out any items that mentioned Germany and sticking them on sheets of paper so that the man with the bushy whiskers could punch holes in them and place them in a file.

'Good training,' he encouraged. 'It'll be more exciting when war breaks out.'

Slattery was already considering giving it up when his cab had locked wheels one day in Piccadilly with another cab and he had suddenly found himself staring through the window into the face of Amaryllis.

'Paddy Slattery!'

Amaryllis had always been beautiful, with excellent shoulders and a fine bosom, green eyes surrounded by a mist of dark lashes, and a small tigerish nose which she wrinkled when she smiled. With the years, she had gained confidence and poise and she took Slattery's breath away.

The cab drivers were still cursing each other, to the delight of the newspaper sellers and small boys, and as Amaryllis' cabbie had tried to force his nag ahead, the wheel of Slattery's conveyance had been wrenched off. As it had collapsed he had been pitched into the roadway.

Amaryllis' head had appeared through the window again. 'This,' she said, 'is a very silly situation.'

'Just what I was thinking,' Slattery had agreed as he dusted himself off. 'Let's leave it and go and have lunch.'

The meal had been exciting. They were old friends meeting for the first time in years and they had discovered to their delight that at the weekend they were both heading for the same country house party in Gloucestershire.

There had been no thought of danger in Slattery's mind. But while everyone else had been engrossed in croquet, he had made the mistake of disappearing with her to the other side of the estate. They had made no bones about the attraction they still held for each other but Amaryllis had kept her head.

'Not here,' she said. 'Later.'

She appeared at his door that night. 'Why not?' she said cheerfully as she climbed into bed beside him. 'Uncle

23

George and Auntie Mabel did it on the kitchen table. I'm all for this peculiar English practice of Saturday-to-Monday house parties with separate bedrooms for husband and wife. It very much facilitates late-night visiting.' As she moved closer, she spoke cheerfully. 'I learned all there is to know about the communion between the sexes before I left school and I decided to become liberated. I'm a bit liberated already, as a matter of fact.'

'So I've noticed.'

'Love and kisses and a quiver full of children aren't for me.'

'Don't you think you'll have missed something?'

She gave a beaming smile and clutched Slattery to her. 'Don't you believe it, old Fitzpaddy,' she said. 'Shall we have another go? It's better sport than that bloody croquet.'

A week later, dressed to kill, she appeared at his flat in London. Despite the warm day, she was wearing a high-collared gown trimmed with red velvet ribbons.

'Nice of you to come,' he said warily.

She unbuttoned her elbow-length gloves and held up her hand for him to kiss. Kissing hands was always an effective curtain-raiser. Her teeth were gleaming white, her hair a dark brown, and there was a certain oriental opulence in her looks that he didn't remember from when she was younger. Perhaps it was something she had learned in India.

'The heat's brutal,' She fanned herself happily. 'I shouldn't have worn this dress. All this bloody whalebone!' She turned away from him and, dutifully, he began to undo the hooks and eyes down her back. As a youth at hunt balls he had never been granted more than a glimpse of her magnificent bosom. Now, quite casually, she unfastened the ribbon that held the neck of her chemise and allowed it to fall after the dress.

'I hope you know how to get everything back in again,' he said.

She laughed. 'I have a maid waiting in a cab outside,' she explained. 'No lady can visit a gentleman without her maid. In Paris it's quite the thing for afternoon visits.'

24

She seemed to be surrounded by acres of white cotton. 'The modern corset can be quite daunting,' she went on cheerfully. 'It must be terribly difficult for some women. What can be more humiliating than having to ask your lover to do up your reinforcements afterwards?'

She seemed to know where the bedroom was – he wondered if she'd called earlier when he was out and asked his manservant – and she led him there without blinking. Inside, she shed hair pins until her hair fell like a cascade down her back.

'Come on, old Paddy,' she said as she sat on the bed. 'Make love to me.'

She was confidently dispensing with all the preliminaries. As he took off his jacket, she reached up to unfasten his shirt. She was flushed and eager and didn't bother to unbutton it, simply wrenching it open to send buttons flying across the room.

As she wriggled out of the remainder of her clothing, flinging the garments aside willy-nilly, she held him at arm's length as if to allow him to feast his eyes on her.

'Will I do?' she asked archly.

It had been a most enjoyable experience but Slattery had a feeling he was being led into a situation that was eminently › dangerous.

Unpacking his belongings in the dusty little hotel in San Marina de Bravos, he wondered if she'd been reading Marie Corelli or Elinor Glyn – 'Would you like to sin, on a tiger skin, with Elinor Glyn?' She sometimes talked like the heroine of a novel.

It had been a sultry afternoon which had left him exhausted and more than certain that it would be a good idea to avoid her in the future. She had a reputation for getting what she wanted and he wondered if she thought he could provide her with an introduction to the foreign society she liked to write about. Perhaps she was intending to write next about Balkan tribal chiefs and thought his languages would be an asset.

As she dozed he had left her side. She was lying

25

uncovered to the knees, hugging herself as if she were cold, her splendid breasts nestled in her arms as if she were afraid she might lose them. As he had moved to the door, however, she had sighed and moved luxuriously among the welter of pillows and sheets.

'We really were very naughty, Paddy dear,' she murmured. She gave a little giggle. 'Go now,' she urged, 'and let my maid know it's time to come in. You'll find her sitting on a bench in the vestibule.'

'I'll ring the porter and ask him to pass the message.'

The porter would know exactly what to do. In the bachelor apartments where Slattery lived he had seen women sitting in the vestibule before – ladies' maids waiting to hook up their mistresses and do their hair so that they could safely be let loose on the streets again. Dressing in his study, he wondered what women did when there wasn't a vestibule or a porter or a handy means of signalling. And how did a woman summon her maid when there wasn't a telephone? A handkerchief waved from the window? A rocket?

As the maid finally disappeared and he heard the door click, he left the study to find Amaryllis sitting primly on the settee, everything, including her make-up, in place, even the vast hat she had arrived in, an affair as big as a tea-tray and decorated with cherries, flowers and a pheasant's feather long enough to poke your eye out.

'You and I,' she said, beaming at him, 'were meant for each other.'

Her words had seemed to indicate it was time to seek new pastures. Amaryllis, he decided, could become a drug and he had already grown bored with the one-legged naval officer and the man with the bushy whiskers.

Then he had remembered the interest there had been in the office in Mexico and that a lot of information had passed through his hands concerning a man called Lord Cowdray, an Englishman who owned vast oil wells at Tampico and supplied oil to the Royal Navy. It had set him thinking and, making enquiries, he had learned that the factions in the

Mexican struggle had recruiting officers out looking for just such people as himself.

It didn't take long to find a name because it was there in the files in the office. From then on it was simple because the recruiting officer was looking for men who were no longer bound by patriotic feelings to their own country but knew their job well enough to earn money as mercenaries and could provide the specialist skills the ragged Mexican armies needed to back up the untutored peasant soldiers who had no knowledge of war beyond pulling the trigger of a rifle.

'You're going where?'

Amaryllis had stared across the tumbled pillows at him, her eyes wide. She had continued to pursue him ardently for a whole month until he had come to the conclusion that his decision to leave was definitely a good one.

'Mexico,' he said.

'What on earth for?'

'There's a war going on and they need skilled soldiers.'

'But Mexico, for God's sake!'

'It's a damn sight warmer than the Balkans.'

There was a long silence. 'They have Spanish grandees there, don't they?' she said and he knew she was thinking of another book. He took pleasure in disillusioning her.

'Not any longer,' he said. 'I think they shot them all.'

'Oh!' She shrugged. 'When are you leaving?'

'Week from now. It's all fixed.'

She smiled. 'Oh well,' she said, reaching out for him. 'We've still got plenty of time, haven't we?'

3

Since the crossing of the Atlantic in the Cunarder *Lusitania*
was smooth, the weather warm and the moon at its full, he
had indulged in a shipboard romance with an American girl ·
in the next cabin called Helen Frankfurter, on her way
home to New York after a tour of Europe. She was the
daughter of divorced parents and briskly open.

'What's your name?' she demanded.

'Pierce Fitzpatrick Slattery.'

'That's romantic.'

'The Irish are a romantic people.'

'My last boyfriend was called Charley Cleaves. I don't
like Charley. Makes me think of that little guy on the movies
with the cane and funny feet.'

She insisted on calling him Fitz and spent most of the
crossing in his cabin. 'Saves opening and shutting doors
when we want to see each other,' she said. She was lusty,
full of joyous good humour, and admitted quite frankly that
she was looking for a husband.

'Not you,' she said, as they clutched each other on Slattery's bunk. '*We're* just good friends.'

She was quite prepared, however, to take a few short cuts
and claimed that any girl would want to get herself a new
name if she were called Frankfurter. 'It makes you sound
like a sausage,' she said.

When they reached New York, Slattery moved in with
her in her mother's apartment where she threw a party at
which most of the guests were German-Americans like
herself, as arrogant as ever and boasting of Germany's
growing power. Slattery avoided argument and some of
them even thought he was one of them. Among them was
a youngster from the German Consulate who told him
enthusiastically of German plans for the future. He was

engaged in building up a German following in the United States, Mexico and places like Argentina, Brazil and Bolivia.

'I can talk to you,' he said warmly. 'Germans can be relied on to keep a quiet tongue.'

Slattery smiled. He couldn't resist it. 'Actually,' he said, 'I'm British.'

The German looked disconcerted. 'I was told your name was Fritz,' he said.

'No. Fitz. It's different.'

Two mornings later, Helen Frankfurter appeared alongside Slattery's bed with his shoes and the information that her mother was due to return from Europe.

'She wired,' she explained. 'And she doesn't like Englishmen. If she arrives and finds you here, it'll be the Battle of Bunker Hill all over again.'

Thrown out on the street, Slattery still managed to enjoy himself in New York. It was a remarkable place with its tall buildings and the enormous number of cars in its streets, all with honking horns and headlights like huge staring eyes. Life seemed twice as fast as in London and twice as informal, but everybody seemed nervous about the international situation, because someone had started up a bogey about Japanese designs on America; and the fact that the Japanese were making common cause with the Mexicans who were creating so much trouble just beyond the border, seemed to unnerve people.

It was beginning, in fact, to seem as if Slattery's presence in Mexico could be urgently needed. Madero's presidency had been fraught with difficulties and the people who were against him were being backed by the hacendados, the Church, the army and the foreign investors, all of whom had a lot to gain from their support.

Within a week, Helen Frankfurter's mother had disappeared again to California and by the time Slattery moved back into the apartment with her daughter, the situation in Mexico had changed again. The Mexican army were slugging it out in the capital with what were supposed to be rebels, but it seemed that the only people being hurt were disinterested observers, and as casualties mounted up and

29

building after building was knocked down by artillery, it was becoming clear that the battle was a put-up job by the anti-Madero faction to provide the excuse that Madero had lost control and had to be removed.

Slattery was largely indifferent. It now looked as though the war wasn't going to last until he arrived, after all, and he had almost decided to give up his ideas of moving south and setting himself up in some way in business in New York when a cable arrived from Amaryllis. She had somehow acquired his address and the text was brief and to the point.

'Arriving 12th. Have booked apartment Meurice Hotel 5th Avenue.'

It was time to leave.

El Paso on the Mexican border was a long way from New York and there wasn't much to do on the long train journey except drink warm beer laced with lemonade and stretch your legs alongside the track whenever the train stopped for water or to change locomotives.

Whatever had been happening in Mexico seemed by this time to have happened. Madero had been arrested and, so it was claimed, had been shot while trying to escape.

'*Ley fuga*,' someone had explained. 'The law of flight. It's a law that allows you to shoot your prisoners. They use it a lot in Mexico.'

With Madero gone, General Huerta, the man who had deposed him, had been recognized by sixteen countries, though it was obvious that his position was still shaky because the newly-elected president of the United States, Woodrow Wilson, who regarded himself as an apostle of decency and had pledged himself to sweep away maladministration and restore integrity to United States politics, had no sympathy with usurpers.

El Paso was a bustling town, almost Mexican in appearance though the old border saloons, dance halls, brothels and gambling dens beloved of cowboys, smugglers, gunmen, rustlers, train robbers and scarlet women were disappearing. Two- and three-storey business blocks with brick fronts and false cornices were taking the place of the shanties; and anti-alcohol and purity campaigns were driving the gambling dens and saloons across the border to Ciudad Juárez in Mexico, where it was still possible to exist happily indifferent to American hygiene. Where not many years before gunfights had been common in El Paso, there were now trolley-cars and street lighting and a woman-dominated attitude of piety and order.

Slattery had been engaged in sorting out the kit he had bought – a wideawake veldt hat against the sun and a warm overcoat against the cold nights in Mexico's uplands – when a man appeared at the door of his room. He was dressed immaculately despite the flying dust from the Mexican deserts across the river that filled the air. He wore a blank look which changed from time to time to a hard alert expression. He was tall, a good six-foot-three, graceful and handsome, and there didn't seem a line or a curve in his body that had any strength in it anywhere. His hair and eyes were pale to the point of anonymity.

'Horrocks,' he introduced himself. 'Sholto Horrocks. Told to look you up.'

'Why by?'

'Oh – people. Hear you're going down into Mexico.'

'Yes, I am.'

'When?'

'Any business of yours?'

'Matter of fact, yes.'

Slattery shrugged. 'Well, I don't know yet. I'm looking for General Villa.'

'Why him?'

'He's nearest. I'm told he needs experts. I'm an expert.'

'Ever been to Mexico before?'

'No.'

Horrocks pulled a face. 'Everybody's shootin' everybody else like billy-o down there. It don't pay to let them think you're American. *They* remember the Alamo, too.'

He went on to talk about Japanese resentment against the United States and pointed out that the Japanese had sold Huerta arms and that Mexico had two thousand miles of undefended coastline and twelve hundred miles of frontier common to the United States.

'So?' Slattery said.

'I take it you've heard of the Kaiser. The German Emperor. Wilhelm Without Warning.'

'Of course I have.'

'He's a bit keen on Mexico. He tried to buy land south of California for a naval base but, as usual, he talked too much and the Americans found out and stopped it. If the Americans still had Teddy Roosevelt for a president that would have been that, but now they've got Woodrow Wilson, an ex-professor who dreams about democracy and never going to war.'

Slattery studied the other man, puzzled. 'So?' he said again.

'So Mexico is the soft underbelly of the States and if it comes to war in Europe – '

Slattery frowned. 'A lot of people keep talking to me of war in Europe.'

'Of course. There's goin' to be one.'

'You seem sure.'

'Naturally.' Like the man in London, Horrocks seemed to have no doubts whatsoever. 'The balance of power's all wrong, and the Germans are being led by the nose by the Prussian Junkers. They're shovin' their agents out everywhere and recruitin' everybody they can to work for 'em.'

'Mexicans?'

'*And* Americans. German-Americans, that is. America has several million people who were actually born in Germany. And a lot more who've not been in the States long enough to forget their German origins. There are also four million Jews, mostly Polish, who are also pro-German because they're anti-Russian, and two million Swedes who admire German *Kultur*. There are large German communities in and around places like Milwaukee, St Louis and Detroit. American politicians who are known *not* to have German antecedents would find it very difficult to push through anti-German policies.'

'And this affects me?'

32

'You *are* naïve, old boy, aren't you? Of course it does. If it comes to war in Europe, the Americans would be in the business of selling guns immediately, so all those Germans on this side of the Atlantic would be beavering away like mad to make sure Germany got more than her fair share. Stands to reason, don't it?'

'*I*'m going to *Mexico*.'

'Oh, yes, but in Mexico there's an English chap called Lord Cowdray who has Mexican oil to sell. So the Germans would need to make sure it went to them not to their enemies, wouldn't they?'

'*We* won't be their enemies.'

'You never know. So they're taking precautions. There's a German-American Bund, at least fifty naturalized Germans serving as officers in the Mexican army, and a general called Maximilian Kloss who's been made director of the manufacture of ordnance and munitions by the new President, General Huerta. German wireless operators are also being installed in Mexico City's receiving station and there are groupings of German ex-officers in Tampico, Monterrey and along the border. The Union of German Citizens has many branches and is still expanding. There's a German Minister, German consuls, German commercial agents, a German community of several thousand in Mexico City, and German-subsidized newspapers. As a result, they're not short of agents, and the whole shebang is run by a chap called Wertz.'

Horrocks beamed. 'We're watching the death of Mexico, old boy. But it's a violent death and the corpse won't lie down. So I'd advise you to make sure your powder's good and dry. You don't carry a pistol in your pocket to accompany a body to the grave, but with that sort of funeral, you have it more accessible – up your sleeve.'

Slattery studied him. He had identified him as ex-army. You could tell it from the confidence, the way he carried himself, the casual way he spoke, the fashionable slang picked up from London cabbies by young officers on leave. But Slattery still wanted to know more and he suddenly had suspicions. 'Look,' he said. 'Who are you?'

Horrocks looked pained. 'Just a chap,' he said. 'Sort of Foreign Office type. Here to look after our nationals.'

'I've never needed anybody to look after me before. Who sent you?'

'Well, the boss, of course.'

'Who's that? That old stringbag with the dyed whiskers in London?'

Horrocks sniffed. 'We do better these days than those two old jossers in Whitehall.'

'Same limited company, though?'

'I suppose you'd say so.'

'Well, I've finished with the old jossers, so I'm finished with the company, aren't I?'

Horrocks sighed. 'Our people never "finish with" us,' he pointed out. He seemed politely determined to be stubborn. 'Thought we might have a meal together. Not that the meals here are anything to write home about. Might even have a little chat.'

'I'm not interested in little chats,' Slattery said. 'And if that chap with the whiskers in London told you to get in touch with me to be an agent, you can tell him I'm not interested in that either.'

With the meal and the chat rejected, Horrocks vanished quietly into the woodwork. 'I'll be back.' he said cheerfully as he drifted away. 'I wouldn't dream of letting you go now.'

4

So here he was, in San Marina de Bravos, with a bunch of total strangers, looking for someone he didn't know in a country he'd never seen before.

The wind died during the night, and as Slattery woke at first light so did the rest of San Marino de Bravos. Children started to shriek in the street outside, cockerels crowed, dogs barked, burros brayed.

The town lay among scattered little fields, and on the road the dust was a foot deep. To the west and north lay the lower slopes of the Sierra Madre, desolate, red flinty hills covered with scattered mesquite. To the south the country fell away to the valley, motionless and silent in the brassy sunshine. Although it was still early in the year, the heat was already rising from the earth.

A mangy goat wandered down the street, a piece of rag hanging from its working mouth. In front of the church, chickens scratched round a somnolent long-haired sow suckling her litter against the steps. A peón's wife, bowed under a load of sticks, shuffled past, her bare brown feet kicking up little puffs of dust. There was a smell of urine in the air and the whole atmosphere was one of brooding silence under the harsh sunshine.

As Slattery appeared, a group of raisin-eyed urchins, their skins so coated with dirt they looked as if they hadn't been washed since the day of their birth, held out their hands. He dropped a few centavos in each. Immediately, an old woman in black rags stuck out her hand, too.

Magdalena Graf appeared soon afterwards and they drank their coffee together on the patio of the hotel. Once or twice he caught her watching him with interest, studying his face with its rocky planes and humorous mouth, and the high beak of a nose.

'What are you doing here?' she asked suddenly.

35

'I'm going to join General Villa,' he said.

'To fight?'

'I'm a soldier.'

'Are you a Catholic like me?'

'Why?'

'It helps in Mexico. They're a devout people.'

Slattery shrugged. 'Yes, I am. But a poor one. The British army's full of Irish Catholics.'

'So what is a British Catholic soldier doing in Mexico?'

'He's not a British soldier any more. He's just terminated his agreement.'

'Cashiered?'

'Resigned. We didn't see eye to eye about things. I believe there are plenty like me with Villa.'

As they talked, the other passengers from the train began to appear, among them a tall, good-looking, weak-chinned blond man whom she introduced as Hermann Stutzmann, the owner and leading tenor of her zarzuela company. Finally, Lidgett appeared, his mouth working as though his tongue was cleaved to his palate. He seemed to have been doing a lot of drinking.

As they ate their sugary rolls on the patio of the hotel they heard shouts and a cavalcade of horsemen appeared. Women screamed, snatched up children and threw stones at the pigs and chickens to clear the street. Shutters and doors were still slamming as the horsemen swept in.

'Federals,' Lidgett said, 'Government troops. Huerta's boys.'

The soldiers wore uniforms that looked like something from the French Second Empire, probably left behind by the French commissariat after their attempt to put the puppet emperor, Maximilian, on the throne in the middle of the previous century. Riding in the middle of the cavalcade was a young man in shirt-sleeves, his hands tied to the pommel of his saddle, his ankles lashed together beneath the horse's belly. A black dog was following the cavalcade close to the prisoner's mount. Its tongue was hanging out and it looked exhausted.

As the cavalcade stopped, the lashings were cut and the

36

man was wrenched from the saddle. It was only as he was dragged across the wide dusty street that it dawned on the people on the verandah of the hotel what was about to happen.

'Oh, María Madre de Dios!' Magdalena Graf's words came in a gasp. 'They're going to shoot him!'

Opposite the hotel at the side of the church was an open space and the man was slammed up against a wall, his back against the stone. The dog immediately took its place at his feet. The officer commanding the soldiers kicked out at it and it dodged away, but as he moved to a position alongside his squad it returned to squat in front of the condemned man.

The travellers on the verandah of the hotel were staring with wide eyes as the soldiers began pushing townspeople into a line to watch the shooting. A low moan escaped the crowd and a few women began to weep. As the people on the verandah of the hotel rose to go, the officer, who was dressed in a uniform that looked German in origin, shouted at them to stay where they were. Magdalena Graf turned away and automatically Slattery, who happened to be standing alongside her, put his arm round her. Just as automatically, she turned to him and hid her eyes.

The officer took his place in front of the firing-squad. The man standing with his back to the church wore no blindfold but his head was erect and the dog was still at his feet, occasionally looking round at him in a questioning way as if wondering what was happening. As the officer's arm swept down, the crash of the rifles filled their ears. Slattery saw little explosions of plaster leap from the stone as if several shots had gone wild and, in the same instant, the young man, his chest and face a bloody mass, was flung back against the wall. At the crash the dog leapt up, its tail between its legs, and bolted into the crowd.

As the dead man slid down the wall, leaving a smear of red on the stone, Magdalena Graf cringed in Slattery's arm. For a long time after the thunder of shots had died away there was silence in which Slattery could hear the sobbing of women. He could feel Magdalena Graf shaking, her face

37

buried deep in his shoulder. The officer turned to the watching people. 'You may go,' he said coldly.

For a long time the crowd stood silently as though they didn't understand, then the officer pushed at those at the end of the line and they began to shuffle off. The people on the verandah of the hotel returned to their places. No one wanted breakfast any more.

A woman moved to the body and crouched over it, sobbing. The dog crept back, belly to the ground, and lay down near her, its head on its paws. The soldiers climbed back into their saddles and, at a command from the officer, cantered out of the town. It had been short and sharp but, with the corpse he'd seen hanging from the telegraph pole the day before, to Slattery it brought home that this revolution he had been told was merely a comic opera affair was anything but.

As the train travellers waited in silence in the hall of the hotel, keeping out of the sun and away from the sight of the body across the road, another group of horsemen appeared. They were primitive, young, unruly, and full of braggadocio, and they carried rifles of every age and type. On their hats they wore that traditional addendum of all Mexican revolutions, a picture of the Virgin of Guadalupe.

Reining in with a flourish outside the hotel, their huge hats straining at the chin-cords, the foaming horses dragged back on to their haunches, they looked round aggressively for someone to bully. A man ran towards them and pointed across the road. They followed him, walking with a swagger in their high-heeled boots, to stare at the corpse. Returning, talking loudly, they demanded beer.

The proprietor sullenly produced bottles, and as the men drank they slapped at their clothes until they were surrounded by clouds of dust. They came from the Carbayales district, they said, and were looking for the rebel army.

'Villa?' Slattery asked, hoping for an indication of the whereabouts of the man he was seeking.

Not particularly, they said. Just anybody who was willing to fight. Carranza, Villa, Zapata – it didn't matter so long as there was some shooting. They didn't know much about

Madero or Huerta but they'd heard that the revolution had started again and were anxious to be in it. They were in San Marina de Bravos because they'd heard there was a rebel recruiting officer in the town who would pay for them to ride on a train to Chihuahua.

'I've never been on a train,' one of them said.

'What about Federal agents?' Slattery asked. 'They're looking for rebels, and men with horses and guns are bound to interest them.'

There were a few shifty looks. 'There's a fiesta at Chihuahua,' they explained. 'A bullfight and rodeo. They won't question us.'

As they left, in a riot of noise, colour and dust, the proprietor of the hotel stared after them, blank-faced. No money had been handed over and he had had enough sense not to demand it.

Eventually a message arrived that the train was due to leave and everybody set off for the station in a straggling group. Attached to the train now were two freight cars for horses, the owners, the men they'd seen at the hotel, squatting on the roofs. Greetings were shouted back and forth and cigarettes were tossed up. As the passengers found seats, the engine began taking on water and they were still motionless an hour later. No time of departure had been fixed because bridges ahead had been reported destroyed and there was a rumour that bandits were waiting with dynamite somewhere *en route*. The engineer and the conductor were nervously filling up with Dutch courage at a nearby bar.

Two hours later the train was still motionless and the vendors of flowers, fruit, and lethal-looking sweetmeats had begun to grow bored. The small boys who marched backwards and forwards through the carriages, shrilly offering hand-made toys, walking-sticks, pulque, cheese, even a small white pig, appeared less often. As midday approached, women along the track came to life and moved alongside the coaches calling softly – 'Tamales! Tamalitos!' – and messes of meat and corn, with a hot seasoning of green and red peppers to hide the fact that the meat was not as fresh as it might be, were handed up in maize-stalk wrappings. The dogs seeking discarded food under the coaches doubled in number. A newspaper seller appeared with oranges, pear drops, beer and lemonade. The wind got up again as the sun rose higher and the dust began to settle everywhere.

Eventually, when they were all growing weary, the engine whistled. People who had climbed down to stretch their legs began to run and the townspeople, who had gathered to see the train leave began to look interested again. The dust was sweeping down on them in thick red clouds now, but they seemed to regard it as a perfectly normal element to breathe and didn't even turn their backs to it.

Finally the train began to move, slowly at first in short jerks, then it picked up speed, the wheels clacking, the faint breeze stirred by its passing cooling the interior of the compartments. The coach was filled with peóns in sombreros and coloured sarapes, Indians in blue work clothes and cowhide sandals, and square-faced women with shawls and crying babies. People were talking, eating, spitting and singing as the conductor came past. A little drunk now, he embraced everyone he knew and a lot he didn't.

Eventually, the plump, handsome man whom Magdalena Graf had introduced as Hermann Stutzmann appeared from further down the carriage where he had been playing cards with other members of the zarzuela company and soon they all started singing. The two youths who had been clutching sacks opened them to produce fighting cocks. Moving between the seats they asked for bets on the roosters which were now wandering up and down, pecking at the crumbs and cigarette ends. Within minutes, with the coaches swaying from side to side, a whirling mass of feathers and flashing steel barbs was surging about in the aisle. The old man with the fiddle played 'La Paloma' again, then, as the fight finished and the argument over winnings started, someone spotted a coyote among the mesquite and the dispute stopped abruptly as the men on the roofs of the freight cars began blazing away at it. Immediately every

40

other man with a weapon dived for a window and enthusiastically added his share of lead to the fusillade.

The sun climbed higher and, just as predicted, as they approached Asarco the train was attacked. It was passing a low hill covered with scrub when a troop of horsemen, firing from the saddle, charged out from among the rocks alongside the track. A window fell in and women began to scream as they imagined the train stopping and grimy hands pawing their bodies for concealed valuables.

Magdalena Graf, Slattery noticed, continued to sit stiffly in her seat, her face expressionless, the only sign of fear the tightening of her lips; when he suggested she should lie on the floor she refused point-blank.

'I'm not afraid,' she said.

The attackers hadn't noticed that the men camped out on the roofs of the freight cars were armed and two of the saddles were emptied at once. Whether they were genuine rebels or merely bandits taking advantage of the uncertain conditions of the revolution it was hard to say, but they didn't press the attack; and the driver of the locomotive, bold in his drunkenness, was holding the throttle wide open. There was no arguing with the fifty-ton iron monster charging past, its smoke-stack roaring and whistle shrieking, and the horsemen scattered.

They clattered into Asarco, the engineer only managing to stop after they had passed the station. As they shot through, Slattery was aware of what seemed to be petticoats being waved in the air and, as the train halted, it was besieged by the women members of a troupe of strolling players. They were a drab lot, very different from Stutzmann's company, and their faces were smudged with tears. The male members of the troupe had abandoned them and ridden off to join the revolution on the horses that had dragged the props van. They had no money and begged the conductor to let them travel free. Still a little drunk, he was prepared to argue but Magdalena Graf stepped forward.

'Let them aboard,' she said. 'I'll pay.'

It was an imperious gesture and as the women recognized

41

her, snatching her hands and kissing them, Slattery realized
she was better known than she had led him to believe.

Nobody had been hurt in the attack and only one or two
windows had been shot out. The men on the roofs were
claiming they had driven off a band of hundreds, and the
story grew with every retelling until it sounded as if they
had defeated an army.

Now that it was over, no one seemed upset by the attack
but, as the train started again, Slattery noticed that the
townspeople of Asarco were busy driving their livestock out
of sight, putting up shutters and barring doors.

The power of the sun was intense as they drew into
the station at Chihuahua. Nearby workshop chimneys were
belching smoke and you could hear the thump and whirr
of machinery. From the pens alongside the track came the
smell of cattle dung and a haze of dust where bawling steers
were being loaded into box cars.

The station forecourt was crowded. Indians, campesinos
and their families, charros from the haciendas – everybody
who could find a horse, a cart or a donkey to carry them –
were pushing in to watch the rodeo. The horsemen had
climbed down from their perch on the roofs of the freight
cars and were unloading their animals in a tornado of dust,
shouts and flying hooves. There were no cabs so Slattery
found a bar nearby, full of small dark men wearing large
hats, where they could wait, and sent one of the waiters out
to find transport.

'You don't have to look after me,' Magdalena Graf said,
amused by his attention. 'You are kind but I have a house
here.' She paused. 'You can stay the night if you wish,' she
ended.

He looked at her steadily. 'I'm grateful.'

She returned his stare with equally steady eyes. 'This is
a hospitable country.'

There were noisy farewells to the rest of the zarzuela
company who were scattering to various parts of the town,
and a few shrill tenor cries from Stutzmann. The elderly
violinist from the train watched them for a while then he
started to play 'O Sole Mio'.

42

'Apolinario Gomez García, señor,' he introduced himself to Slattery in strangely cultured Spanish. 'At your service. I play other tunes. *"The Blue Danube Waltz,"* *"La Paloma"* and *"Mama Carlota"*. You would like to hear?'

Slattery shook his head and tossed a peso into the hat.

'I hear great things are afoot,' the old man said. 'There was a bullfight yesterday. I play outside to get the entrance fee.' He jerked his head towards three young men sitting at the far end of the bar. 'There they are – the toreros. On their way to Juárez. Serengito Ramez. He calls himself Gito. Eufemio Estrada. Virgilio Kloster.'

The young men were silently staring at their beers.

'They look as if the crowd threw the cushions at them.'

'They aren't Fuentes, or Bombita or Mechaquito, and they certainly aren't Juan Belmonte.' The old man kissed his fingertips and struck a chord on his violin. 'I saw him once, señor. In Mexico City. What grace! That lot are no more than matadors' cloak carriers. They'd be afraid of *anything* with horns – even snails. It's a wonder they haven't beards. Belmonte – el Gran Juan – says the beard grows twice as fast on the day of a corrida because of the fear.'

He struck another chord. 'When I was young I thought I might fight the bulls, but I broke my ankle falling off a horse and I knew I could never turn quickly without falling over.' He sighed and played a few chords of '*O Sole Mio*'. 'For the señorita,' he pointed out, indicating Magdalena. 'I know her and have heard her sing. It is my best tune. Much better than '*La Paloma*', which was the song of the Empress Carlota, who tried with Maximilian of Austria to steal Mexico from us. I've just come from Guerrero. Huerta's soldiers are at Casas Grandes. They think they have nothing to fear from Carranza and his generals because they've been beaten too often to be dangerous.'

He seemed remarkably well informed and, as he drifted away, Slattery glanced at Magdalena Graf. She was staring at her drink, pretending an indifference he knew was not genuine. Eventually, a carriage appeared and the bullfighters started throwing bags and equipment into it. As they climbed in after them, the old violinist played a few quick chords of what was obviously a derisive tune because one of the bullfighters leaned over the back and shouted at him. The old man put down his fiddle, snatched off his ragged sarape and with it performed a clumsy veronica.

A cab drove them out to Magdalena Graf's house in the Avenida Pacheco, in a quiet area up the hill from the centre of the town. It was a good-sized house with a high railed fence round it and a lot of scrubby land filled with clumps of maguey at the back. They were greeted by a fat woman with eyes like plums whom Magdalena Graf introduced as Victoria Casado, her housekeeper.

They sat outside on the stoop with a drink, under a tree that was purple-black against a crimson sky. The night was still, and full of the heady smell that came from the desert to the south.

Magdalena Graf looked at Slattery curiously and he noticed the imperiousness had gone. There was no fear, though, just a wary respect, and he smiled with his yellow fox's eyes, suspecting that all the old subterfuges, the old dodges that had won women round on previous occasions wouldn't work with her.

'Are you married?' She tossed the question at him unexpectedly.

'Not me.' He grinned. 'Women marry you for what you are, then try to mould you into something else. When you're so mouldy nobody else will look at you, they finally decide they never liked the look of you anyway, and run off with the man next door.'

It was an answer he had used many times and she laughed.

'You don't know much about women,' she said.

'Are *you* married?'

'No.'

'You should be. A woman like you. Has nobody ever asked you?'

'There's always Hermann Stutzmann.'

'Why don't you marry him?'

She looked at him in an amused way. 'I could always say I'm wedded to my profession but that would be an untruth.'

44

'Surely you've often been asked?'

'*Ach, ja.* But that's where the answer lies. Never by anyone who interested me.'

'Sounds like a line from one of your operettas.'

She studied him for a moment then she laughed. 'It is. *Dolores Ruíz.* Act II.' She started to collect her belongings. 'I'm going to bed,' she went on. 'And I need a bath. Another night in my clothes would have been one too many. There's a pump in the yard you can use.'

She was standing close to him, her body almost touching his, and he was aware of the femininity she exuded. For a second he thought she might be throwing out an invitation, but the moment passed and as she halted at the door she turned. 'If you want General Villa,' she said, 'try San Andres.'

'How do you know?'

'I learn a lot of things travelling about. San Andres is where they go when they're after cattle. Plenty of deep valleys where they can corral stolen steers, and plenty of high hills overlooking the plain, so they can see what's coming.'

'What about you?'

'I have to go to Mexico City.'

'Is Mexico any place for a woman alone these days?'

She answered him coolly. 'It's all right for a Mexican.'

'I thought you were American.'

'I told you. I don't know what I am.'

He gave her a wolfish grin that made her feel naked. 'I'm grateful for your hospitality.'

'There is more grace and love of God in Mexico than in any other nation on earth.'

'How did you know you could trust me?'

'I didn't. I still don't.' She reached out to where her travelling bag still lay on the floor. Opening it, she took out a small pistol. 'But most people don't argue with this. Not even in Mexico.'

45

5

During the night, Slattery heard horses outside the house and then loud male voices. They seemed to be angry but he drifted off to sleep again and woke later to hear what appeared to be the same man still talking. This time he realized the conversation concerned him. It was in German.

'He's English,' the man's voice was saying.

'So?' Magdalena Graf's answer was hostile. 'Mexicans are always hospitable. That's why we set an extra place at table. In case a stranger comes and in case he turns out to be God.'

'But he's *English!*' The man's whisper was as loud as it was possible to be without shouting.

'Germany's not at war with England.'

'*Mein liebe Kind,* she will be soon.'

As they drank their coffee at breakfast, Slattery enquired who the visitors had been. Magdalena Graf avoided his eyes and busied herself with her roll.

'There was a raid on a hacienda,' she said. 'Bandits. They're always appearing. They set fire to a grain store, ran off cattle and snatched up two of the servant girls. A posse went after them.' She paused. 'They didn't catch them.'

'And the man who called here?'

'The owner of the hacienda.'

'He didn't seem to like me. Who is he?'

She put down her cup and looked steadily up at him. 'My brother,' she said. 'Fausto Graf.'

'He sounded more like a German than you.'

'He's lived here ever since he was a youth and he's married to a Mexican woman. But he still thinks of himself as German. He stayed the night.'

'What's his objection to *me?*'

'You're English.'

She seemed unwilling to discuss her brother further and

46

when he appeared Slattery, who was prepared for an ill-tempered confrontation, was surprised at the warmth of his greeting.

He was as unexpected as his sister, tall like her, blue-eyed and just as good-looking. His hair was cropped and he wore a neat upturned moustache and carried himself erect like a military man. As he shook hands he asked Slattery's business in Mexico.

'I'm looking for Pancho Villa. I understand he needs experienced soldiers.'

Graf smiled. 'An experienced soldier would have done better to stay in England, Herr Slattery,' he said. 'There's going to be a war.'

Slattery had heard this one before. 'Oh?' he said.

'I suspect it will be with Germany.'

'If it came to a war—'

'It *will* come to a war.'

' – would you fight for Germany?'

Graf's smile widened. 'I have always fought for Germany,' he said briskly. 'I am German now and was German in the past. I will always be German. German history prevents me ever being anything else.'

He left shortly afterwards and almost immediately Slattery heard Magdalena Graf singing. She was sitting at a piano, and her voice was a lyric soprano which she used with consummate skill, even now when she appeared not to be concentrating. It was much richer, much fuller than he had ever imagined, and he began to realize why she had such confidence in herself, why lesser singers were a little awed by her, why even troubadours like the old man at the station recognized her.

'Practice,' she said. 'Always one must practice. It is like drawing, or playing a game – even shooting. As soon as you stop, you lose your skill.'

He suspected she was using it as an excuse to prevent him asking questions, but she was a beautiful woman and he enjoyed watching her and listening to her voice.

Towards midday, a big blue Studebaker slid to a stop in the road outside with locked wheels and a cloud of drifting

47

dust. It had thick spokes like the wheels of a dray and huge brass headlamps, a folding hood and a grid at the rear for carrying luggage. Attached to the driver's door, alongside the brake, was a spare wheel. The man who climbed out conceded nothing to Mexican fashion. He was short and square with a red face and he wore an enormous flat cap, a high celluloid collar and a clip-on bow tie. As Slattery appeared he introduced himself in a strong West Country accent.

'Atty Purkiss,' he said. 'I heard about 'ee, me dear.'

'Where did you hear about me?'

Purkiss gestured, his face blank. 'Havin' a drink near the station. Told you were around. Enquiry or two. Found 'ee. Dead easy. I'm Cornish. From Redruth way. I hear you're looking for Pancho Villa. So'm I.'

'Why are *you* looking for him?'

'Same as you, I expect. I'm an expert.'

'What at?'

'Machinery. You'll have seen my motor. Nobby, ennit? Can't miss it even if you try. Villa could use a good mechanic. Only thing the Mexes know to do with a motor that won't go, 'tes kick it.'

'Do you know where Villa is?'

'Sure. Sixty miles from here. In the hills near Adama. Raisin' men.'

'How many has he got?'

'Not a lot. But they keep comin' in.'

Atty Purkiss, it appeared, had arrived in Mexico years before with other men from a tin-mining area in Cornwall to help the Mexicans dig for gold. Unfortunately the gold had not been there in sufficient quantity to keep them busy and he had discovered that a knowledge of motor cars, acquired by working in his spare time on vehicles owned by the local gentry back in England, was standing him in far greater stead than his ability as a miner.

'Some fellers say Villa's nobbut a gunman,' he argued. 'Others say he's a patriot.'

'Which is right?'

'Take your pick, me dear. Both probably.'

48

Villa's name was one to be conjured with. He had been forced into outlawry and liked to indulge in savage reprisals against those he considered had enslaved his class.

'All the same,' Purkiss said, 'he's one of the best leaders of troops Mexico's ever thrown up.'

Villa had never forgotten his humble origins, it seemed, and had never been slow to hand over a few centavos to help with a wedding feast or to celebrate a birth. Men who had never tasted meat since their wedding day had eaten it again with his help, and now they were responding to the magic of his name, coming in from the villages, stealing away from the haciendas, leaving the mining camps, sometimes on a horse or a mule but mostly on foot, sometimes armed, sometimes not.

'Mostly the poor,' Atty Purkiss said. '*Los de abajo* – the underdogs, with nothin' to lose and everythin' to gain. The State Governor offered him two hundred thousand pesos and the rank of divisional general if he'd join Huerta. He wrote back that he could keep his money because he was already the supreme commander of free men.' Atty grinned. 'Eight he had at the time.'

Atty appeared to be intelligent and knowledgeable and it seemed a good opportunity to learn a few facts. 'What about the others? Venustiano Carranza, for instance.'

Atty grinned. 'Don Venus. Old Moses down from the mountain. Head of the Constitutionalist Party. There's Zapata, of course, but he's south of Mexico City and he never moves north. And Orozco. Villa loathes him because he betrayed Madero. Up here it's all Villa.'

'Fine,' Slattery said. 'We'll find him tomorrow.'

With the Studebaker garaged in Chihuahua, they left on horses Atty Purkiss had bought. Neither was much to write home about and Slattery's had a tendency to rear up and try to flick him over its tail at the slightest excuse. Magdalena Graf watched them leave. She looked lonely and curiously vulnerable.

Winding upwards into the sierra along a stony trail, they rode slouched in the saddle. At noon, with the sun high in the heavens, they came to a patch of green with a spring in the middle, shining under the heavy shade of a few black-barked trees. They watered the horses and allowed them to nibble at the grass.

'Nasty country here, me dear,' Atty advised. 'Y'ought to wear a gun.'

'Don't believe in 'em,' Slattery said. 'Except when it's official. If I start pulling one of those things out, so will the other chaps and then we'll all be at it, like ticks on a mad dog.'

As they pressed on through the cactus, the Spanish bayonet and the mesquite, the narrow track spiralled round a canyon and coiled round buttresses of rock. There was no sign of humanity, only the bones of horses and mules lying starkly in the arroyos where they'd fallen.

The sun was sinking at the end of a long ride when they were halted by a cry.

'*Alto!*'

The voice echoed and re-echoed among the crags. Immediately Atty dragged his mount to a stop and flung up his arms.

'Don't fancy getting shot, me dear,' he explained calmly.

For a long time nothing happened and Slattery sat quietly, waiting in the immense silence. Overhead a vulture wheeled. Then there was a rattle of stones behind them and, turning their heads, they saw a horse emerge from among the rocks. It was ungroomed, shaggy and scarred by cactus. The man in the saddle was small, dark, large-moustached, his face almost hidden by a sombrero whose brim sagged over his features. He wore striped city trousers and a ragged sarape. In his hands he held a rifle.

For a while he sat grinning at them, then he gestured at them to ride on. Kicking the horses' flanks, they moved forward, hooves scattering the stones. As the path descended, another man appeared, this time on foot but similarly dressed and armed. He pointed and they moved between two huge buttresses of sand-coloured rocks into a narrow valley which gradually opened out into a wide bowl. Cattle were huddled in a group under trees, fires were burning and the smell of woodsmoke was in the air. Men rose to their feet and came towards them, all of them armed and grinning murderously. One of them, obviously the leader, reached for the money-belt Slattery wore.

'Leave it where it is!' Slattery spoke in Spanish. He had spoken it all his life and it was brisk, exact and authoritative. Immediately the Mexican heaved out a revolver that looked as big as a cannon. 'Since you speak Spanish,' he snapped, 'you'll understand what I'm saying. Your money.'

Slattery smiled. 'Leave my money alone.' From the corner of his eye he could see Atty's pale eyes flickering about them. 'Who are you?'

'What's it to you? You're a gachupín and you'll soon be dead. Under the circumstances, there's no harm in knowing that I am Orácio Cerofilas and these are my friends, while those' – he jerked a hand in the direction of the cattle – 'are gachupín steers.'

'I thought they might be.' Slattery's smile was as fixed as if it were wired to his back teeth. 'So where is General Villa?'

The snout of the revolver, like a blank eye staring at him, moved slightly. An expression of suspicion crossed Cerofilas's face. 'What do you know of General Villa?' he asked slowly.

'I'm a friend of General Villa. My country admires General Villa and I've come to join him. I've been looking for him and I think I've found him. If those are gachupín cattle, you're probably rounding them up for him to exchange over the border for guns.'

Cerofilas's face changed. The grin became friendly and the revolver was lowered. 'The General doesn't like to be interrupted. He won't welcome strangers.'

Slattery's smile remained set. 'He'll welcome me,' he said.

Cerofilas gestured to one of the other men. 'Take him to the General.' He looked at Slattery. 'You will be safe,' he said. '*Vaya con Dios.*'

'Sure,' Slattery agreed. 'Have a banana.'

*

San Andres was hard to get at and easy to defend and it was full of Villa's men. They stood in groups in the street, a few of them cleaning weapons, a few arguing over a horse, a few in a circle round a cockfight. The air was thick with the smell of woodsmoke, coffee and gun oil.

They didn't look much like an army. Most of them were in work-worn clothes, even rags, with no uniform but the ubiquitous sarape. A few carried rifles and were swathed from head to waist in bandoliers of ammunition so that their dark eyes peered out of a narrow gap between the topmost bandolier and the sagging brim of a sombrero. But the rest seemed to be armed only with weapons of ancient vintage and carried their ammunition in their pockets. Some had no weapons at all and on the whole they looked more like the participants at a beggars' festival than a fighting force. Slattery began to wonder if he'd picked the wrong man.

Among them were their women with their pots, pans and bedding, ready to forage for food and care for their men if they were wounded, following them through the heat of the day or the bitter chill of the night, gathering wood for fires, humping great loads, making camp, giving birth as the armies moved on, then getting to their feet and plodding after them. One or two of the younger unattached ones carried rifles and wore bandoliers of ammunition. Their skirts were dusty, their shoes broken, but the wild turkey feathers in their hats gave them a jaunty air of confidence.

Villa had taken over the only hotel, a bat-haunted derelict run by an old woman, and slept in a room at the back, well guarded by his men. It was lit by a solitary lamp. Saddles were piled outside and alongside the wall were ammunition boxes and rifles.

As Slattery entered, the rebel leader rose, his hair on end, blinking against the light, a bear-like figure with a barrel-chest, shuffling forward with the inturned toes of a man more used to a saddle than his own two feet. But his eyes were alert and there was an air of hostile vitality about him.

'Who're you?' he demanded.

'My name's Slattery. I'm a soldier. The British army doesn't want me any more. I thought *you* might.'

'Why?' Villa frowned. 'Has your King been asking about me? How does the world regard us? We are the only people here who are fighting Huerta, you know. Carranza doesn't. All *he* does is run away. Huerta's soldiers call him *Pocapena* – not much trouble. You are a good soldier?'

'I think so. I understand weapons. *All* weapons. I'm an expert horsemaster. I can handle men.'

'My men?'

'You'll notice I speak Spanish.'

Villa was studying him with narrowed eyes. 'Do you know anything about staff work?'

'I've worked on the staff.'

'Can you fight?'

'I fought in South Africa and in the Balkans.'

It was obvious Villa had no knowledge of either place. He gestured. 'Well, we'll soon find out,' he said. 'We can try you against Huerta's people.'

'Where *are* Huerta's people.'

'Around.'

'And Carranza?'

'On the Sonora border.' Villa peered under his eyebrows at Slattery. 'Do you play cards, inglés?'

'Yes.'

'Piquet? The game the French brought over with Maximilian. Or skat like the Germans?' Villa grinned and gestured. 'This lot play as if they were fighting bulls. *Pues*, if you're a soldier, I'll give you a regiment. Your compañero can be your second-in-command. Or you can be my adviser. I meet important people these days – newspapermen and officials from over the border – and I need someone to tell me how to behave like the chocolatero officers who fight for Huerta. I'll make you a staff colonel. You can keep your ears open in places where I can't go.'

'You want me to be a spy?' It seemed everybody wanted Slattery to be a spy.

'Does it offend your English fair play?' The vigilant topaz eyes were amused. 'The whole business of fighting a war

53

is training and knowing what's going on at the other side of the hill. You can be my telescope. You can also talk to the reporters. The Norteamericano newspapers have discovered we have enough excitement here to fill their pages every day, so you can make sure they get their facts right, and sometimes more than right. You can tell them about us. How brave we are, how gallant, how we show mercy to our enemies, how we're winning the war. I expect you know how to do this.'

Slattery smiled. 'I'm not a newspaperman, mi General.'

Villa smiled back. 'You don't have to be. But this is a new way of fighting a war. I think it's called propaganda. You have to tell the world what fine fellows you are; and you're just the man, with your education, to do it for me. You will be my envoy. You don't have to know much about it. The newspapermen will sort things out. All you have to do is tell them the lies.'

6

As a staff colonel, Slattery was provided with a servant. He turned out to be a boy called Jesús. He didn't know his father, or even his surname, and had never been inside a church. He carried an ancient rifle taller than himself, wore incredibly ragged clothes and looked as if he had never taken a bath in his life. Despite his wails of protest, Atty stuffed him into the fountain in the town square and made him soap himself all over before finding him clean cut-down garments.

'Now you'm fit to prepare our food, me dear,' he said.

Every day more men came in, lean horsemen on gaunt, ill-shod, sore-backed mounts, sometimes with no other uniform than a cotton shirt and trousers and a straw sombrero, but usually carrying an old and battered carbine and a few cartridges.

The first of them were charros, cowboys used to fending for themselves, then came the miners from the lonely camps and villagers who had seen in the revolution a glimpse of a future for their children after generations of slavery under the hacendados. Finally there were men from the towns – labourers, shop assistants, teachers, a few boys who knew a little about politics and were determined their country should never go back to the old days of corrupt governors and greedy generals.

They came in ones and twos and groups, bringing in volunteers from the settlements they passed through, arriving in an aura of dust, leather, horse sweat and excitement. The revolution that had been halted during Madero's year of power was moving again and, as the growing groups cantered up, they scooped in others who had waited by the roadside with their weapons and the cry of '*Qué viva Villa!*'

It was bitterly cold in the hills, with flurries of snow and the frost making stars of the puddles. The Villistas kept themselves warm with mock bullfights. As one of them dragged a plunging steer into the square on the end of a rope to be killed for food, fifty or sixty others, ragged and muffled to the eyes with sarapes and sombreros, started waving their blankets, shouting 'Olé' and 'Hé, Toro!' in the approved fashion. They were like excited children and, to get the infuriated animal into the right spirit, one twisted its tail, another beat it with the flat of his sword and, instead of banderillas, they jabbed at its shoulders with daggers until the blood spattered them as it charged. It was the same every time they collected their rations, because in every village street you could see some ragged urchin playing at being a bullfighter with a red square off a table or a shawl stolen from his mother.

The minstrel, Apolinario García Gomez, turned up again. How he had reached Asunción from Chihuahua on his own two feet it was impossible to tell, but there he was, surprisingly articulate, beaming and bowing gracefully. To Slattery, he performed a slow veronica. '*Olé, Torero,*' he said. 'Soon, your honour, we shall be fighting more than bulls.'

'You, too?'

'Not I, your honour. Playing tunes for the warriors. All armies have their troubadours.' He lifted his violin and played a catchy little jingle. 'I've found a new one. It's about a cockroach.'

He attached himself to the little group round Slattery as if he considered a staff colonel had need of a personal musician, and was always around when the mock bullfights started, performing clumsy veronicas with his ragged cloak, knocked over a dozen times either by the infuriated steer or a running man. It never seemed to worry him.

'What a profession, your honour,' he said. 'What grace! All men drop on one knee to a bullfighter. When the British Minister was asked to leave Mexico City, he found the train surrounded by cheering people and he smiled and bowed and waved, thinking how popular he must be. But it wasn't for him, señor. It was for a bullfighter in the next compartment.'

56

The training intensified as the peóns began to learn the trade of war.

'From now on,' Villa said, 'we behave like night animals. *Como gatitos*. Like little cats. We see but we're not seen. We catch but we're not caught. We kill but we're not killed. We help ourselves like the cat in the pantry.'

It was a policy of which Slattery thoroughly approved and two days later Atty, heading for the telegraph station at Chavarria, stumbled on unexpected information.

'There's a train due in,' he told Slattery as he arrived back in camp. 'It's pulling a sealed military car. And it's full of silver bars.'

When they passed the information on to Villa he looked at Slattery suspiciously. 'Why didn't you steal if for yourself?' he asked.

'That's not why I'm here,' Slattery said.

'Nobody else knew about it. You would have been rich. You could have gone home, married a beautiful woman, had many children, bought yourself a rancho in London.'

'I didn't come to rob Mexican coffers.'

Villa shrugged. 'At least you are different, inglés. Mexicans usually grab what they can when they see it – against the day when it's not there and they are poor. I think you must be honest.' He grinned. 'It makes a change. Nobody else is.'

Within minutes he was heading out of camp, his men yelling like Apaches. When they returned their saddle bags contained a hundred and twenty-two bars of pure silver.

'That was good information, inglés,' Villa said, grinning with triumph. 'You are a better soldier than I thought. It will buy many guns. I think from now on we can trust you. We hanged the paymaster who was guarding it from a telegraph pole.'

'That will win you a lot of friends,' Slattery commented dryly.

Villa rounded on him. 'You are telling me how to behave, inglés?'

'Isn't that what I've been hired for?'

Villa glared at him, his eyes aflame, then his gaze

57

dropped. 'Perhaps you're right, inglés,' he growled. 'But a dead man's dead for keeps. If you let one go, he could come up behind you next time with a gun. Get yourself ready. The general in Chihuahua City's been asked by Huerta where I am. The operator at Chavarria told me. He said I am in all parts but in none in particular. I'm going to show him just what a man who can be in all parts yet in none in particular can do. There are four hundred of Orozco's men in Casas Grandes. They won't be there when I'm finished.'

Casas Grandes was on the site of a pre-Columbian settlement and, believing that Villa was nowhere in the vicinity, the garrison had grown careless. Villa's plan was for what he called a '*golpe terrifico*', a tremendous blow.

'We'll attack as the sun is coming up,' he said. 'It will dazzle them.'

'It wouldn't dazzle me,' Slattery said bluntly.

Villa frowned. 'You don't like my plan, inglés? Perhaps you can think of a better one.'

'You'll never succeed in full daylight. Wait until the sun's gone down.'

'Mexican soldiers don't like fighting after dark. Dark is for food and drink, for music, for women, for sleep.'

'They might think we're twice as many as we are if they see us gathering at dusk. Let every man have two hats. One to wear. One to prop up beside him. It's a trick I saw in the Balkans.'

'What is this Balkans? A city in England? We're short of rifles. The only way to do it is in daylight, so that when a man is hit the man behind can see to pick up his gun.'

'Suppose we make them think we *all* have guns. Let every man have two hats and a rifle and a stick. If he hasn't a rifle, he has two sticks. In the dusk they'll look like guns. The Orozquistas might not even wait for us. They might bolt.'

Villa stared at Slattery with a new interest. 'You have ideas, inglés. Perhaps we'll try this idea of yours.'

He moved with incredible swiftness and as the sun sank a terrifying army of conical hats appeared behind every bush

58

and rock outside Casas Grandes. And alongside every hat was the long straight shape of a weapon. As daylight faded, scattered shooting broke out to wild yells of '*Qué viva Villa!*' and '*Qué viva la revolución!*'

The Villistas moved forward warily, knowing how weak they were, but as darkness fell they found the reply to their firing was only half-hearted and they pushed into the main street to find only a token resistance. As they had come in at one side, most of the Orozquistas had slipped out at the other.

In only one area did they come up against any resistance, in the shape of an enormous barricade. In front of it Villistas sprawled like broken dolls, their faces hidden by the wide brims of their sombreros. With the houses built hard up against each other, there was no shelter for the attackers and there were men on every flat roof. Peering round the corner of a doorway, Villa had to withdraw his head as one of them took a pot shot at him.

'We can't get past that,' he said.

'So let's go through the houses,' Slattery suggested. 'That's what they did when they entered Khartoum.'

Villa's head jerked round. 'This Khartoum? It is another city like the Balkans, I suppose, where we can learn a lesson?'

'The walls are only mud. We can hack our way through.'

Villa grinned. 'I have a better idea. We will blast our way through.'

Dynamite was brought forward and men started hacking at the mud walls of the houses with picks, knives and bayonets. Holes were knocked in them so they could pass through to the next house, and where the walls were of stone they used dynamite. The explosions filled their eyes with dust and grit and sent smoke puffing through the windows in yellow clouds.

Wall by wall, they cut their way past the barricade until they reached a cross-street behind, then at Villa's signal the attackers rushed forward. The Orozquistas fought desperately in a whirling mêlée of guns, bayonets, swords, fists and boots. They were led by a tall, handsome young officer

59

who seemed to be everywhere at once, indifferent to the flying bullets. His clothes torn and bloody, one arm hanging limp, he continued to encourage his men long after they were surrounded.

'Throw down your arms, man,' Slattery yelled at him. 'You've done enough. You can surrender with honour.'

The sky was already full of vultures as the prisoners were herded together. The looting had already started and men were running in and out of shops, snatching at the debris to see if there was anything worth having. One man pushed a perambulator away. Another, grinning with delight, was dragging one coloured shirt after another over his blood-splashed clothes. A third was pulling on the boots of a dead man.

A breeze was moving the flames as Villa appeared through the smoke. Seeing the young officer Slattery had taken prisoner leaning on the arm of one of his sergeants, he drew his pistol and shot him almost without bothering to look at him. As he sank to the ground, Slattery's infuriated shout made Villa whirl.

'What happened?' he said. 'What did I do?'

'We don't fight that way in Europe,' Slattery snapped.

'There's a different way?' Villa said. 'Fighting is killing. What other way is there?'

Fires were lit and a captured band started playing patriotic airs as the dead were lifted into mule carts for burial. Down the street there was the crash of musketry, drowning the thump of the band, then another and another. As Slattery lifted his head, Villa gestured.

'It's nothing, compadre. We're getting rid of the prisoners. I had them lined up three deep because we're short of ammunition. That way we can polish off three men with every bullet. They're only Orozquistas.'

The victory at Casas Grandes had been unexpectedly easy. Villa's men were cock-a-hoop at their success and García, the old troubadour, stood in the street playing his fiddle for dancing. It didn't take much to set the Villistas dancing.

60

When there wasn't a woman handy, they danced with a boy or even with each other, and the drink flowed freely until the night was noisy with singing and shouting. The morning found huddled shapes, half-hidden under their sombreros, slouched in the street, stinking of drink, trying to sleep off their excesses.

Villa himself didn't celebrate. He was a non-smoker and almost a teetotaller and he seemed indifferent to his success. But he enjoyed the dancing, watched cockfights or played a hand of cards, and for food nibbled titbits from other people's plates.

'I'm not one for banquets,' he said.

He had moved north again when Carranza's envoys arrived to talk with him. There were three of them and Villa was eating a meal of fried beans and eggs and playing a lazy hand of cards when they were announced.

'The Magi,' he said contemptuously. 'Come to pay homage. They amount to nothing and they'll get nothing.'

He didn't bother to rise and was still sitting under the flaring naphtha lights outside a cantina, his face greasy from the food he was eating. Carranza's envoys were well-dressed men with none of the dust and dirt of the camp on them. Behind them stood three more men who to Slattery looked subtly different.

'I know why you're here,' Villa said at once through a mouthful of food. 'Carranza wants me to set things going against Huerta.'

Carranza's spokesman shifted from one foot to the other. 'Don Venustiano is the First Chief of the Constitutionalist Army,' he said.

Villa wiped food off his moustache with his sleeve and tossed down his cards. 'All Don Venus does is put out rallying calls and demands for greater effort.'

There was a murmur of laughter from the Villista officers behind him and the envoys looked uneasy. Expecting to find a dull-witted peasant flattered by Carranza's offer of an alliance, instead they had found a man with a well-organized, well-equipped army newly flushed with victory. They shifted their position, and as they did so, the light fell on

61

their faces. The rearmost of them looked familiar and, as he turned his head, Slattery saw it was Fausto Graf.

What was he doing there, he wondered immediately. And with envoys from Carranza? Unwillingly, he found himself remembering the words of the old naval man in the office in Whitehall. 'Half Germany's agents seem to be going to Mexico at the moment.' It seemed he might be right and that Graf might be one of them.

Villa was pointing with his knife. 'Your First Chief,' he was saying, 'has been beaten too often. Now he's been run out of Coahuila into Sonora.'

The three envoys looked at each other. 'The First Chief's trying to unite all loyal revolutionary forces under one command,' the spokesman said.

Villa's head jerked up. 'Carranza's?'

'The First Chief's willing to offer himself for the job.'

Villa was cleaning his plate with a rolled-up tortilla. 'When I came back to Mexico he didn't want to know me because he was a lawyer and I was just a peasant. But it's different now. I've captured Casas Grandes. You tell Don Venus that round here I have the Federals running in circles.' He paused, wiping his moustache again. 'On the other hand, perhaps something could be agreed. Do you have artillery?'

The envoys were delighted to concede something to gain support. 'The First Chief has four French 75s but no crews.'

Villa showed his teeth in a grin. 'Well, I have crews and no cannons,' he said. 'I'll make a bargain. Send me the 75s and I'll recognize Carranza.'

The new insurrection south of the Rio Grande was raising considerable interest in the United States and news-papermen were crossing the border in dozens. For the most part they were loud-mouthed, harsh-tongued, gum-chewing rumour-mongers, ignoring truth for sensation, their lurid stories slotting easily among the columns of brothel raids in New York, the exposure of love nests in California, the doings of the notorious in Chicago. They had been hanging round the bars in Chihuahua waiting for someone to make a move and now, after Villa's victory at Casas Grandes, they drove in on horses, in buggies and cars, dressed in Norfolk jackets, celluloid collars and wideawake hats. They carried typewriters and film equipment and they pounced on Slattery at once.

'When's Villa goin' to move?' they asked. 'Casas Grandes was peanuts. Torreón's where he should go for. Torreón's a railroad centre and with Torreón he could dominate the north.'

They brought news of Mexico City and what Huerta was doing.

'He's gettin' rid of the opposition,' they said. 'That's what he's doin'. He shot about twenty guys who objected to him and seized a lot more at a banquet. That guy don't want colleagues. If he looked in the mirror he'd see the whole of his government.'

With them came Carranza's guns and men who preferred the bustling activity of Villa's headquarters to the political wine-and-dine atmosphere that surrounded Carranza. Some had been sent as civil advisers, some even as plain spies. Three of them caught the attention at once because they were young, good-looking and eager to prove themselves. Known immediately as the Holy Trinity, they were Segismondo Monserrat, who had an English mother and fair hair, had been educated at the Jesuit College at Stoneyhurst in Surrey and spoke excellent English; Onesimo Preto, a professional soldier who looked a little like Slattery and had changed his allegiance because he loathed Huerta; and Florentino Vegas, a smooth-looking type who seemed to be attached to no one in particular. 'Used to be mayordomo at a ranch outside Chihuahua,' Atty said.

To Slattery's surprise, with them also came Magdalena Graf. She brought medicines, bandages and surgical instruments.

'Why?' Slattery asked.

A half-smile parted her lips and her eyes lit up with mischief. 'The Hermann Stutzmann company have to live. We can't get south of Torreón because the line is packed

63

with troop trains, so Hermann has arranged for us to remain in Chihuahua for another month.'

'So why the medicines and bandages?'

'Because many of Villa's men are still only boys, and some of them I taught to sing.'

'Are you backing Villa for the presidency?'

She smiled again. 'Villa hasn't the education to be anything but a rebel.'

'Your brother was here.'

'My brother's a very busy man.'

'Is he working for Carranza?'

She shrugged. 'I expect that above all he's working for Fausto Graf.'

She refused his suggestion that they had dinner together, with the excuse that she had to return to Chihuahua, but she agreed to have coffee with him at a bar in the Avenida Santa Ana. She seemed happy and excited to have run into him again and her smile transformed her.

'Is Hermann another German?' Slattery asked.

'There's nothing wrong with being German!' The smile vanished and she answered sharply. 'And Hermann's a kind man.'

'Are all zarzuela singers German?'

'Mostly they're Mexican but a few came from Europe.'

Enchanted by her smile, Slattery's servant, the boy, Jesús, had switched his loyalty to run errands for her, '*A los pies de Usted, Doña Magdalena*' – 'At your feet, Doña Magdalena,' – always on his lips.

'*Ein freundlich Kind*,' she said in the stiff Germanic way that often seemed to intrude into the warmth of her character. 'A nice child.'

Before they saw her into the big Stutz that was to take her back to Chihuahua she bought the boy new clothes, questioned him about his background and started to instruct him in the Catholic Church's teachings she had learned as a child on the banks of the Rhine.

'You've got to believe,' she told him earnestly. 'If you don't, God will know.'

Jesus looked puzzled. 'God is here?'

64

'God is everywhere.'

'In the cornfield?'

'Yes.'

'In the street? In the square?'

'Yes.'

His eyes flickered. 'In the yard of the orphanage where I grew up?'

'Yes.'

He grinned. 'He was very clever, Doña Magdalena. The orphanage where I grew up didn't have a yard.'

As the Stutz vanished, a wad of letters arrived for Slattery, brought from Chihuahua by Atty Purkiss who had been to collect the Studebaker. One was from Amaryllis but, as Atty handed it over, Monserrat, one of the new aides from Carranza, arrived with instructions for Slattery to report to headquarters. Stuffing the letter into his pocket unopened, he found Villa walking up and down talking to his officers. They crowded round him, dark-skinned men hung about with weapons and wearing breeches, leggings and American stetsons Villa had bought as a job lot from a travelling salesman. As Slattery appeared, he swung round.

'I have a job for you, inglés,' he said briskly. 'You are a good soldier but you talk too much and you're more use to me as a spy.'

Slattery frowned. 'I know nothing of Huerta.'

'It's not against Huerta. It's against Carranza. It's a job you can do better than anyone. Carranza is in Nogales and he's behaving as if he's God. He's set up a headquarters there and issued a political manifesto. It doesn't do much except tell us he's the First Chief of the Constitutionalist Party and we know that already.'

He was still walking up and down, a man who could barely read or write but was blessed with a tremendous driving energy and a great deal of peasant cunning.

'In spite of his guns,' he said, 'he would willingly stab me in the back. So I need to know what he's up to. Somebody soon will have to have a go at Huerta and I don't think it will be any of that chocolatero lot in Nogales. They're only concerned with making laws. Go there, inglés. Ask the questions newspapermen ask. Find out what Don Venus is doing. Because there's a war on in Mexico and it's time somebody started winning it.'

7

Nogales was a big straggling town where the boundary between Mexico and her northern neighbour ran down the middle of the street. Humorists liked to put one foot across the imaginary line of demarcation and observe that they'd been on a visit to the United States, and, while Americans crossed the border to eat cheaply, gamble and dance, the Mexicans hurried the other way to avoid the attentions of the police. The station was the usual ugly shed lined with wooden seats covered with the dust that blew in from the surrounding desert. Yaqui Indian women huddled inside, their children asleep on spread sarapes. At the Customs House a few ragged sentries were smoking.

It was late as the train arrived, and an army of newspapermen were collecting luggage under flaring lights when Slattery saw Magdalena Graf standing in the shadows. She was dressed in the blue that matched her eyes so well, the waist of the outfit high so that her figure seemed more elegant and slender than ever, in a way that roused in him a sharp sense of excitement.

'What are you doing here?'

She gave him a long unfathomable stare, and gestured at a poster stuck on the wall of the customs shed.

La Verbena de la Paloma, it announced. *Con Magdalena Graf y Hermann Stutzmann.*

'First Chief Carranza enjoys the theatre,' she smiled. 'And when we finished in Chihuahua Hermann decided to bring us here. He has a house here, for the same reason I have a house in Chihuahua. It's easy to cross the border and there have been times when it's been a good idea. I'm staying there.'

'Have dinner with me, Magdalena.'

She hesitated only a moment. 'Why not? The day after

tomorrow the First Chief is holding a conference so there's no performance.'

The only sizeable hotel was full of pressmen clamouring for accommodation. But most of Carranza's cabinet and political hangers-on were already there, sleeping four to a room, on cots in the corridors, on the stairs, on the floor, under and on the billiard table.

Despite the hour, the newspapermen were still occupied in trying to acquire cars and, finding them not as plentiful as in the States, were settling for carriages, spiders, ancient buggies, even saddle horses. They were far from filled with admiration for the new American president, Woodrow Wilson, who was determined, they claimed, that Latin American countries should be shown how to run their affairs without murder. They didn't give much for his chances.

Among the yelling crowd was a girl. She wore a stetson, breeches and a leather jacket and, seeing Slattery on his own, she took his arm.

'Pretend you know me,' she said quickly. 'The little guy over there keeps pestering me.'

The man who followed her was small and wore a dark suit and a boater with a pink ribbon. He had a straggly moustache and a lot of gold teeth.

'Scheele,' he introduced himself. 'Doctor Walter Scheele. I am German and I am here to sell the First Chief my secret weapon. Vill I show you?'

Slattery managed to brush him off and the girl smiled her thanks. 'I'm representing *Colliers* magazine,' she said. 'I'm Consuela Lidgett. Consuela Doyle as was. I speak a bit of Spanish so they sent me to find out what Mexican women are doing. What *are* Mexican women doing?'

'Keeping their heads down and praying, I imagine,' Slattery said dryly.

She was small and delicate with an innocent expression, fair hair and lost-looking blue eyes that made the breeches and stetson seem out of place. She appeared to know little about news gathering and in the end she confessed.

'Actually,' she said, 'I'm not from *Colliers*. I'm from the *Gordonsboro Herald*. Gordonsboro's in Colorado. The

68

editor's my uncle and I persuaded him to send me. My husband's here somewhere. Loyce Lidgett – Aloysius, that is. He's a local boy so he's news. I haven't heard of him for some time and I thought I'd better go look.' She managed a tired smile. 'I decided that gettin' myself made an official correspondent was the best way to do it. My uncle said he'd pay me. But it doesn't amount to much and I'm not much of a hand at gettin' news. *You* haven't heard of Loyce, I suppose?'

'I travelled to Chihuahua with him.'

'He'd got a story?'

'I don't think it was a story he was after.'

She sighed. 'I guess not. I heard he'd joined Villa's foreign contingent. He could never resist being near a fight. Are you a newspaperman?'

As Slattery smiled, she looked up at him, a little awed by his size. 'No,' he admitted. 'I can't resist being near a fight either.'

Most of the correspondents weren't very interested in Carranza. They were far more concerned with finding Villa, who was a much more colourful figure and of far greater interest to the newspaper-reading public. They had expected to find him with Carranza and, since all Carranza appeared to do was talk, they were having to fall back on stories about Huerta. There were plenty. He seemed to do the business of government in the oddest places about the capital so that foreign envoys had to scour saloons, cafés and parks for him. He preferred tea rooms and bars to offices, and did what little business he chose to do sitting with a secretary in a motor car.

To look after the noisy crowd of correspondents was a member of Carranza's staff who said they should see the First Chief at once, despite the hour. Slattery joined the crowd as they set about finding a man who would take them to headquarters. But everyone had gone to sleep and the proprietor of the hotel, dragged from the chair where he was dozing because he had given his bed to someone else, didn't know where anyone was. They kicked on doors and woke sleeping figures, most of whom turned out to be Carranza's *pro tem* cabinet officials.

Eventually they found a man who agreed to take them to the office of the First Chief, which was in a large house where sentries in huge hats presented arms as they entered.

'The First Chief's very busy,' they were told. 'There are two thousand Federals and Orozquistas at Torreón, and we must have Torreón before we can advance on Mexico City. Questions will have to be put in writing to be answered tomorrow.'

Returning to the hotel, Slattery noticed Consuela Lidgett sleeping in an armchair. With the aid of a large denomination note, he persuaded the night clerk to find a cot for her.

Atty turned up with the Studebaker at first light and at breakfast a message arrived that the press interview with Carranza would be held in the evening. When the pressmen presented themselves once more, they found headquarters crammed with people carrying portfolios and bundles of papers; Americans seeking concessions; arms smugglers; ammunition salesmen dishing out praise for their wares, among them a man offering crayon enlargements from photographs at five pesos each; and once again Dr Scheele, trying to hawk his secret weapon. The feeling of watching a comic opera was remarkably strong.

Waiting in the ante-room was a large group of men who were clearly Europeans. They were straight-backed, with high starched collars and upswept moustaches, and once again Slattery was reminded of the words he'd heard in the office in Whitehall. Mexico seemed to be knee-deep in Germans, and the background of these men seemed to shout itself out loud.

A door opened and the military-looking men were beckoned forward. The man who beckoned them was Magdalena Graf's brother, Fausto.

'Who *are* those guys?' one of the newspapermen asked. 'They aren't Mexes and they sure aren't Americans.'

When Carranza finally condescended to see the newspapermen, he was accompanied by a whole host of hangers-on. He remained standing, surrounded by the pressmen, shaking hands and peering at them through the blue-tinted spectacles he wore, a big man with a big belly and a big nose. As the room filled with smoke from the photographers' flash guns, the questions began. The American correspondents allowed nothing to slip past. They had a good grasp of the situation and had already spotted things that needed explanation.

'Why is your government here in Nogales, First Chief,' the *New York Times* man asked, 'when all the action is over in Chihuahua?'

'We direct operations from Nogales,' Carranza said stiffly.

Another man lifted his hand. 'I'm George Wiley, of the *Post*, First Chief,' he said. 'My editor says you're doing nothing here but hibernate. Wouldn't it be better to go over there and help?'

Carranza clearly didn't like the way the interview was going and he began to talk to stop the barrage of questions. There were few interruptions. Just Carranza's views. Stubborn and dogmatic, he was undoubtedly knowledgeable but was lacking in any spark of personality.

They were introduced to a man called Obregón, a smiling moustached farmer from Sonora who had become Carranza's general in the west, and more photographs were taken. All the time the group of Germans round Fausto Graf watched in silence, standing in one of the corners out of the light, their backs to the room, showing their faces only when they turned to glance at a newspaperman asking a question. With them now was a new man, young, vaguely effeminate and ginger-haired, looking like one of them but somehow apart. He was speaking German but his accent was different.

Finally, with an expansive gesture, Carranza invited everybody to join him at dinner and the theatre. Someone handed him a wide-brimmed, light-coloured felt hat so that, with his quasi-military dress, he looked like a Confederate general left over from the American Civil War, and there was a clatter of arms and equipment as the guard of honour came to untidy attention. In the street a band started to play

71

and, surrounded by his retinue, all jostling to hold a place near to him, Carranza began to march in step to a lively version of '*La Paloma*'. Other men joined the procession, officers in uniform and civilians in evening dress. Among them was Fausto Graf, with a girl who looked no more than seventeen on his arm.

Atty Purkiss stared after them all, his face blank and cynical. 'Mucho Pomposo heads for the munchies,' he said. 'That's not a leader, me dear. It's a walking monument.'

More intrigued by Magdalena Graf than he cared to admit, Slattery found his way to the theatre and sat quietly at the back of the pit stalls in an atmosphere of peeling gilt and dusty red plush.

The operetta was a tuneful piece set in the French Revolution, many of its lines adapted to what was happening in Mexico, and Magdalena's rich pure soprano seemed too good for the lightweight part she was singing. With her blue eyes she stood out from her dark-eyed, dark-skinned fellow-performers. Her opposite number, Stutzmann, had a soft-looking body, a face that radiated good humour, and an ability to reach a wavering high C.

There were several smartly-dressed young men holding roses standing near the bar and when the show finished there was a rush for the stage door. Pushing his way past, Slattery lifted the doorman off his feet and, placing him behind him, dropped coins in his hand.

'The Diva's expecting me,' he said. 'Hold that lot off!'

Magdalena's face lit up at the sight of him but she was nervous and worried.

'Not tonight,' she said, speaking breathlessly as she pleaded with him to understand. 'Tonight there is so much to do. The orchestra was terrible. We have to sort it out and it will take until midnight. Tomorrow, though, I promise. I'll be in the lounge of your hotel.'

As the theatre emptied, Nogales quietened quickly. Slattery had managed to bribe his way into a small room hardly bigger than a cupboard, which he was sharing with

Atty Purkiss, and he had just fallen asleep when he was awakened by bells. Atty sat bolt upright.

'Hotel's on fire, me dear,' he said placidly.

Half-dressed, they headed into the street. People were appearing from all directions, shouting and pointing. The fire was not in the hotel but in a small warehouse nearby where a few old saddles had been stored. One end was well alight and the fire brigade was struggling to get water to it. Their hose consisted of ill-fitting lengths, all of them punctured so that jets were hissing in all directions. Wearing brass helmets as big as hip baths, the firemen were shouting frantically at each other when suddenly the water pressure disappeared. As the taut pipes became limp and the miniature fountains sagged, the men holding the solitary nozzle stared at it in bewilderment.

Someone went off to have the pressure restored. As it returned, one of the firemen had his finger down the nozzle, trying to make out if it were blocked. The jet hit him full in the face and knocked him flat on his back while the hosepipe leapt free, to writhe like a wounded snake and saturate everybody within reach. By the time they had everything under control the end of the shed had fallen in.

Watching the uproar near Atty was the little German who had introduced himself as Dr Scheele. He was smiling and rubbing his hands. There was a girl with him. Atty gestured at him.

'This feller here,' he pointed out, 'says he started it.'

8

Slattery stared down at the little German. He was perspiring heavily, mopping his face with a violet handkerchief. The girl watched without much interest.

'He says what?' Slattery asked.

Atty shrugged. 'That he set light to it.'

Slattery stared at the German again. 'Well, what's he want us to do? Inform the police? Help him escape? Give him money? Was he *seen* setting light to it?'

'*Ach, nein, nein!*' Scheele seemed to regard Slattery as half-witted. 'I am not such a *dummkopf*. I do not use a match.'

'A bomb?'

Scheele smiled proudly and introduced himself all over again. 'I am a chemist,' he said. '*Sehr geschickt*. My credentials are excellent.' He gestured at the sagging shed. 'I set fire to draw attention to what I haf. You vill vant to know.'

'Will I?'

'You haf an automobile. I vill meet you here tomorrow und I vill demonstrate.'

The following morning they were climbing into the Studebaker outside the hotel when Scheele appeared with the girl. He was dressed in a sugar-pink blazer with white piping and the straw boater with the pink ribbon. He carried a brief-case and appeared to think they were waiting for him.

'Iss difficult to explain,' he said. 'It vill be better if I show you. Tell your chauffeur to drive us out of town.'

Atty stared indignantly but Slattery shrugged. 'Do as he says, Atty,' he advised.

They drove out to where the desert sagged into a series of folds. Among them were clumps of mesquite and cactus. While the girl remained in the car holding a sunshade, they walked a few yards from the road where Scheele scraped

74

up the dried scraps of mesquite into two piles several yards apart. Opening the brief-case, he took out two short lengths of metal tubing. In the middle of each, with the aid of a pencil, he inserted a disc of copper, then he put on gloves and, taking two square-shouldered chemist's bottles from his bag, filled the separated halves of the tubes from them and plugged the ends with sealing wax round an airtight cap. Atty began to grow bored. He clearly didn't like Scheele.

'Soon it iss finished,' Scheele said.

Laying the two lengths of tube on the piles of mesquite, he removed his boater and fanned himself with it. He was bald, with wisps of hair plastered to his head with perspiration.

'Perhaps ve move back a little,' he suggested, gesturing at the tubes.

They waited for several minutes, their eyes on the tubes. When nothing happened, Atty began to grow restless.

'He's having us on,' he said.

'*Nein, nein*,' Scheele said. '*Bitte*. Please. Be patient.'

'What do they do?' Slattery asked. 'Explode?'

'*Ach, nein.*' Scheele looked shocked. 'They are not bombs.'

'How do you set them off?'

'I haf set them off. Nothing vill stop them now.'

After half an hour Atty lit a cigarette and wandered off to talk to the girl, his interest lost. Slattery looked at his watch.

'How much longer?'

'*Ein moment, bitte.*'

Slattery was just about to give up when there was a soft pop and a hiss, and a searing white flame a foot long leapt from the end of one of the cylinders. A few seconds later more flame burst from the other end. The brightness was dazzling and Slattery could feel the heat that was given off. The twigs had caught fire and were crackling as the flames devoured them.

Atty had come back at a run. The tube burned fiercely for several minutes, the flames vivid and intense. When they went out the pile of twigs had gone and in their place was a small shallow baked trough in the earth that was still smoking. As Slattery moved forward, Scheele held his arm.

'*Achtung, mein Herr!* Take care!'

There was no sign of the metal tube beyond a small flattened silvery shape where it had melted. Slattery looked at the second tube.

'What about that one?'

'Another half-hour. I haf arranged it so.'

Prompt on time, the second tube burst into flames. By this time Slattery was intrigued.

'How safe are they?' he asked.

Scheele beamed. 'Iss no danger at all. I call them my cigars. Do you like them?'

'How's it done? A fuse?'

'*Nein, nein.* My tubes are of lead, und in the middle is a copper disc. In vun half of the tube is sulphuric acid. In the other half picric acid. Both ends iss fit mit a vax plug und a lead cap. The sulphuric eat through the copper disc und ven the two chemicals come into contact mit each other, they burst into flame. *Sehr heiss.* Very hot. It melt the tube und, as you see, it leave no trace. The copper disc, you understand, iss the timing device. The thicker it iss, the longer the acid take to burn through it. Iss very simple, iss it not?'

They dropped Scheele back in Nogales and watched him strut away with the girl on his arm, a small plump figure full of its own importance carrying a lethal briefcase.

Slattery's eyes were narrow and his mind was working fast as they sat outside the hotel with a beer. Introduced into a waggonload of flammable material, one of Scheele's 'cigars' could do immense damage.

Atty was thinking the same way. 'I reckon,' he said slowly, 'that we should be roundin' him up and whippin' him along to Villa.'

But they were already too late. When they started searching they found Scheele had vanished and his girl-friend was on the verge of tears.

'He went off with the German gentlemen in a motor car,' she said.

Slattery frowned. 'They don't miss much, do they?' he said.

When they returned to the hotel, Consuela Lidgett attached herself to them at once, petite, fair, pretty and eager to talk. She was full of information about Carranza who, she said, was in a bad temper and refusing to hand out snippets of news.

'You ask me,' she said, 'he's only interested in cameramen.'

Pushing her over to Atty, Slattery went in search of Magdalena. As she had promised, she was waiting in the crowded foyer. She was wearing blue again and had clearly taken a lot of trouble with her appearance. As Slattery drew nearer, her brother rose, smiling, from behind a palm alongside her and rested his hand on her shoulder. She shrugged it off but he put it back.

'I gather you're dining,' he said. 'Perhaps I should join you.'

Slattery's features were expressionless. 'I'm sure the First Chief's need is greater than ours. You must have papers to sort out, facts to gather, enemies to set up, chemists to drive to the station.'

Graf's smile slipped a little but it soon returned. 'Dr Scheele is German,' he said. 'A man with his gifts belongs to the Fatherland, not to Don Venus.'

'How much did you pay him?'

Graf smiled. 'I always thought Englishmen were noted for their good manners.'

'Some are noted for their rudeness.'

Graf's smile didn't falter. He shrugged and clicked his heels. 'You'll be late for your meal, Herr Slattery. Enjoy your food.'

Magdalena's face was expressionless as she collected her cape. 'I wish you hadn't goaded him,' she said. 'He's a bad enemy to have.'

'What did he want?'

'To preach at me.'

'Preach what?'

'What he always preaches: *Deutschland über alles.*
Germany's place in the sun. *Deutsche Politik in Mexiko.*'

They found a restaurant down a side street. It was in a
courtyard where there was wrought iron at the windows,
palms and a bougainvillaea dripping rusty leaves into a fountain. Somewhere out of sight someone was softly plucking
at a guitar.

'This is how I always thought Mexico would be,' Slattery
said. 'Most of the time it isn't.'

Magdalena smiled. 'When God made the world,' she
said, 'I think Mexico was last on the list and He was tired
and wanted to put His feet up. He gave her too much dust
and, above all, put her next to the United States.'

Slattery took her hand and she didn't withdraw it. 'I
enjoyed the show last night,' he said.

Her fingers tightened on his, pleased at the compliment.
'I sang badly. All I did was get the right notes in the right
places.'

'You looked superb. You look superb now.'

She gave a little laugh. 'When the Almighty created me,'
she said, 'He could have paid me a lot more attention than
He did. And my face has as many cracks on it these days
as an antique vase. I am not as young as the one in the
hotel with the leather coat.'

He hadn't realized she'd noticed Consuela Lidgett. 'She
claims she's representing *Colliers*,' he said. 'She wants to
know what Mexican women are doing.'

Magdalena's eyes glowed with unexpected heat. 'They're
grieving because their men are dead or about to die and
the politicians do little to set things in order. Tell her that
Colliers should print that. She is very pretty.'

He affected not to have noticed and she laughed.

'Of course she is! You know she is! And she has her eye
on you!' There was a new admiration in her voice and a
friendliness that made him feel warm.

As they ate, they heard loud voices in the entrance and
Slattery saw it was a group of the Germans he'd seen the
previous evening at Carranza's headquarters. Graf was not

78

among them this time and they had several women with them. As they sat down at a table out of sight behind a group of potted plants, they were all discussing Carranza at the tops of their voices. With them again was the ginger-haired young man, his voice louder than any.

'Your brother's friends,' Slattery pointed out.

'I know them,' Magdalena said calmly. 'The blond one's a German general, Maximilian Kloss. He's director of Mexico's munitions and ordnance. His picture's been in the papers often. It seems he's gone over to Carranza. The good-looking one says his name is Franz von Raschstadt but I'm not sure it is. I met him at an Embassy party a year or two ago. I heard he was a naval officer but that he'd left the navy and gone into banking.'

Slattery wondered if he had. 'And the others?'

'Probably from Huerta's army. There are many German officers. It looks as if they've gone over, too.'

He nodded at the ginger-haired young man. 'And that one?'

'Axel Sjogren. Assistant to Folke Cronholm, chargé d'aff-aires at the Swedish Embassy in Mexico City. He's more German than the Germans and complains that Sweden is lacking in glory. Fausto calls him Alexandrine. They laugh at him but he's useful.'

'Mexico seems full of Germans.'

She gave a little laugh. 'A German minister. German consuls. German commercial agents. German wireless operators. German-subsidized newspapers. German admirers. German singers even, like me. Germans work very hard.'

The Germans had been drinking and they were singing now – arms linked with the women's and swaying together – a wine cellar chorus that ended '*Eins – zwei – g'suffa!*' There was a lot of laughter and noise and the Mexican waiter was growing confused.

'I think we should slip out before I'm seen,' Magdalena said. 'Or they'll try to get us to join them and make it a party. I don't like their parties. They enjoy making me homesick.'

'You surely don't remember Germany?'

'Germans always remember Germany.' She laughed. 'And they are always homesick. They are a very sentimental people. When we do Strauss or Lehar in Mexico City the house is always sold out. They hold balls and dance old German dances and sing old German songs. They have wine-tasting evenings when the wine is always German, and sing *"Die Wacht am Rein"* and *"Deutschland über Allies"*. Don't the British sing partriotic songs?'

'It's not a British habit.'

'It's part of our heritage.'

'Since you took out American papers,' Slattery pointed out quietly, 'so is the Statue of Liberty.'

She was silent and he knew he had offended her. He paid the bill and rose. 'Let's go,' he said.

As they left, one of the Germans was singing a solo – *'Hamburg ist ein Schönes Städtchen'* – and there was a burst of applause and the banging of glasses on the table.

Taking Magdalena's arm, Slattery led her to the centre of the town where a band in the purple-painted bandstand was banging out music. The tune was *'La Golondrina'*, a Mexican melody of farewell that dated back to the last century and was regarded as safe. Revolutionary ardour being what it was, it was considered highly dangerous to play in the camp of one side any tune that was popular with the other. The wrong tune, a tune associated with Huerta, could mean death.

They sat in silence for a while on a bench in the shadows and Slattery took Magdalena's hand again. Under the jacarandas groups of people were taking their evening stroll, the girls arm-in-arm to eye the boys, the boys arrogant and bold, making eyes at the girls. Nearby a group of youths in coloured shirts wearing the big old-fashioned sombreros were drinking brightly-hued drinks they bought from a stall under the trees. Suddenly there was a squabble and a glass of crimson liquid was flung in an angry face. Immediately the little knot broke apart and a knife appeared. Stepping calmly among the scuffling group, Slattery hit the boy with the knife on top of the head with a fist as big as a maul. As the boy collapsed, he took the knife and threw it into the bushes. As the boy was dragged away, the spectators clapped and he removed his hat and bowed. Magdalena laughed delightedly and he leaned over and kissed her gently on the cheek. But, as he did so, the group of Germans appeared again, striding aggressively homewards through the moving crowds and, turning to watch them, he missed the pink flush that appeared as her head swung quickly towards him.

'I think I'd like to go home,' she said. 'To Hermann's house. He won't be there. Only my maid. Hermannn has a woman he visits on the American side of the road.'

She insisted on taking a cab. It was lopsided, battered and smelled of horse, and the animal that pulled it looked as if it were about to drop dead at any moment. Stutzmann's house was on the edge of the town, surrounded by trees.

'There was a Carranza general in here with his woman when we arrived,' she said. 'Hermann had to go to Carranza to get rid of him. Madero always tried to keep things legal.'

'Perhaps that's why he's dead,' Slattery pointed out. 'Revolutions themselves are illegal.'

'Carranza will make things legal when he becomes president.'

'Perhaps he won't become president. The man who becomes president of Mexico will be the man Washington wants for president.'

'It's nothing to do with Washington. Too many people are trying to interfere in Mexico.'

'When there are murky waters, *everybody* likes to fish in them. Didn't you hear those friends of your brothers? They were talking about naval bases. They said that, properly exploited, the civil war here could end in a United States invasion.'

He knew she must have heard but she pretended to be surprised. 'They were joking. Surely you can't believe that?'

Slattery hadn't really believed anything he'd been told in London or by the languid Horrocks in El Paso, but now, in Nogales, he found he was beginning to.

'What *is* your brother?' he asked.

'He raises cattle.'

'Not all the time, it seems.'

81

She shook her head silently. 'He's head of the North German Bund in Mexico. They're pledged to help the Fatherland. Some of them are third-generation Mexicans or Americans but they're still Germans.'

'Is your brother a German agent?'

She stared at him for a long time before she spoke. 'Why do you want to know? Are you a *British* agent? There are known to be a lot of *them* in Mexico, too.'

He smiled and patted her hand. 'I'm exactly what I said I was.'

She was silent as she let them into the house. There was no sign of the maid and she moved quietly about, finding him a drink. Slattery watched her with interest. Underneath her guarded manner, he suspected, was a full-blooded woman with a determined vitality and a luxurious, healthy capacity for living. There was something alive about her that appealed to his rebellious spirit and, as she lit the lamp with long fine-skinned hands, he found himself face to face with her.

She was suddenly shy with him, as if she understood the bold appraisal in his eyes. For a long time neither of them moved, then, as he gently put his arms round her, she seemed to melt against him, her face in the curve of his neck. For a moment, she clung to him, holding up her mouth to be kissed, then, as his hands moved, she pushed him away as if she were afraid of her own emotions.

'No,' she said, her breath coming quickly. 'No!'

Releasing herself, she leaned against the wall. A wisp of hair had fallen over her nose and the look in her eyes was suddenly full of doubt. 'No,' she said more calmly. 'You and I can never make anything together.'

'Why not?'

'Our paths are too wide apart. They can never meet. You'd better go now. Before Hermann comes. He might misunderstand.'

The door slamming behind him was like a clap of doom. As he headed for the hotel, his mind was still full of her perfume, the warmth of her body in his arms. Perhaps, he thought, he should take her to Cuernavaca south of Mexico

City. The country was supposed to be softer there than in these harsh northern plains, and Cuernavaca was said to be beautiful and haunted by the ghosts of the Emperor Maximilian and his wife and a great many other lovers. Bougainvillaea and a guitar or two playing softly in the background could make a lot of difference. Perhaps even, he decided, he should be on the doorstep the following morning early, with flowers. Mexicans liked flowers and she had lived long enough in the country to have absorbed the trait.

The hall of the hotel was full of chattering men when he arrived, and a great many more were trying to sleep in chairs, in corners, under tables. As he entered the lobby, the desk clerk called him over and handed him a letter. It was sealed and he tore it open, his mind still full of the events of the evening. The note inside immediately shattered his plans.

It was from Atty Purkiss and its message was cryptic. 'I've gone for the motor,' it said. 'Villa's on the move and heading for Torreón. The balloon's gone up.'

Part II

1

All the way across the desert from Bermejillo to Torreón, men were gathering like swarming bees, in a dusty, colourful, shabby pageant that seemed to belong to another age. All the former peóns, waggonmasters, farmers, shop-keepers and bandits who now called themselves generals and ran their own ragtag armies began to collect in a noisy, teeming mass of men, boys, waggons, horses, motor cars, cannon, camp followers, flags and tents, all coming together in swirling dust clouds of their own making.

They were a formidable, loosely-knit force, no longer the guerrilla fighters of Madero's rebellion but also by no means a formal military force either. With them were their women and children and the air over the whole area was blue with the smoke of burning mesquite as fires were built for cooking or the shoeing of horses. Some of them were trained, some were not, and they were hard to control when they fired their weapons into the air out of sheer excitement, or filled the day with the high-pitched Apache yells of vaqueros herding cattle.

Villa was pleased to see Slattery back. 'The boys are coming in,' he said cheerfully. 'Ortega's arrived with a hundred men. Tómas Urbina's on his way. Herrera's gath-ered nearly five hundred and Calixto Contreras another two hundred. Benavides is due, as well as Quijano, Robles and a few more, and they're all bringing their gente with them. Things are working well, inglés, and those three who came to me from Carranza are pulling their weight. Vegas is a doubtful quantity but Monserrat's already a good Villista. What did you find at Nogales?'

'Show, Don Pancho,' Slattery said. 'Carranza hasn't much but he dresses it up well.'

Villa laughed and Slattery went on earnestly.'Also Germans, Don Pancho.' A lot of Germans, he thought. He hadn't really believed the stories of German infiltration into Mexico but there they had been, clearly scheming and clearly heavily involved. 'They were talking to Carranza. About arms, in exchange for bases in Mexico.'

Villa shrugged. 'Arms are what we need, compadre. What about the enemy? Did you learn how many they have at Torreón?'

'Two thousand, stiffened by Orozco's men and all well equipped and well dug in.'

'And we are short of ammunition.' Villa's heavy face set in a frown. 'It haunts me, inglés.'

One after the other, the regiments and brigades began to assemble, all bearing flags with death-defying names. The Brigada Juárez. The Brigada Victoria. The Cazadores de la Sierra. The Cuerpo de Guias. The Brilliant Thirteen. The Red Two Hundred. Last of all, moving in leisurely fashion, came Tómas Urbina, Villa's bandit friend from the days before the revolution. He was a small ugly man who was unable to read or write and signed his reports with the drawing of a heart, but he had brought six hundred men and waggonloads of loot from Durango which he had just captured and sacked, leaving it full of the burned or dyna-mited homes of anyone associated with Huerta.

'They know me now in Durango,' he said as he gave Villa a bone-cracking abrazo. 'I picked out a man in every saloon I visited and asked if he supported Huerta. If he said yes, we shot him as a traitor. If he said no, we told him he was a liar and deserved to die for it, so we shot him, too. I brought a man called Fierro with me – Rodolfo Fierro – to handle the railways when we have them. He's an expert. You can now rest easy. The Lion of the Sierras has arrived.'

As he swaggered away, limping from the rheumatism he had acquired from hiding out in the mountains as a bandit, Villa stared after him with stony eyes. 'It's a crippled lion these days,' he growled. 'Tómas is past his best, and he's too fond of wine, women and loot.'

Despite the reinforcements, they were still only half an army. Apart from the 75s Carranza had sent, their artillery consisted of five home-made cannon and two machine guns, and Slattery struggled in a lean-to garage to make an old Hotchkiss fire. Eventually, he got it working sporadically, but they remained desperately in need of ammunition. Transport was also in short supply and Atty Purkiss was sweating blood trying to make old motor cars and trucks go. The Mexican mechanics, quick to give up, always considered a kick would work wonders, and it was far from unknown for an infuriated man to fire his revolver at a recalcitrant engine.

Eventually, however, the great mass began to crumble, first one corner, then the next, breaking into groups and columns, swinging round, regiment after regiment, to face south and follow the rails to Torreón. They were the same men who had put Madero in power in 1911, peóns, farmers, charros, engineers, a sprinkling of American and European daredevils to whom it was all just a lark, a few professionals and mercenaries who knew no other trade but war and had fought in Cuba and the Philippines, in North and South Africa, in Latin America and the Balkans, all of them willing to exchange their skills for money.

Among the camps, Consuela Lidgett searched constantly for her husband. But Loyce Lidgett seemed to have sunk without trace and Slattery could only imagine he had carved some niche that suited him in one of the minor armies – often little more than regiments - of some obscure 'general' and was enjoying himself enough to stay there.

Because he had captured Torreón in 1911 during Madero's rising against Díaz and been there again under Huerta during Orozco's rising against Madero, Villa knew their objective well. It was an ugly place built on an arid stretch of land for no other reason than that there the railway lines to the north, south, east and west came together. It lacked water and drainage, its streets were deep in dust and the most its inhabitants could hope for was a wire mesh screen against the flies during the day and the mosquitoes after dark. But it was important because it lay astride the line that ran from the American border to the Mexican capital, and it was wealthy because it was in the centre of a heavily-populated cotton-growing area. In rebel hands, it would isolate Huerta's garrisons in the north by blocking the passage of reinforcements from Mexico City.

As they approached Jiménez, a junction of the vital railway line, they were met by a Federal force under Orozco and swung aside to meet it. The news that his old enemy was in front of him darkened Villa's brow. He claimed – none too truthfully – that he had never killed in cold blood, but a loathing for the traitors who had murdered his hero, Madero, left him willing to match them grave for grave, atrocity for atrocity, and his hatred drove the Huertistas out of Jiménez towards Camargo, and from Camargo to La Cruz, where he defeated them again, his cavalry tearing the fleeing groups to pieces as they tried to make a stand. As it became a rout, the horsemen pursued the flying splinters towards Chihuahua City.

'*Por Dios*,' he raged, as he stood alongside the pink-painted bandstand under the jacarandas in the square at La Cruz. 'If we had ammunition, I could drive into the capital itself.'

It was as he caught up with Villa again that Slattery discovered Amaryllis's letter in his pocket. It had lain there ever since Nogales and was crumpled but, written on pale blue paper as expensive and thick as a board, it made clear her intentions.

'I'm coming to Mexico,' she wrote. 'You've been too long among the savages and need to be taken in hand and taught how to live like a gentleman again. It won't be yet, of course, because I can hardly miss the London season. They tell me April's a good time so perhaps next year would be suitable for a visit to New York and a trip to Latin America to see what it is that holds you.'

She obviously thought Mexico was south of Panama but that it was possible to reach it by a day-trip on a train.

Scenting the coming battle, Atty Purkiss turned up a few days later from his workshop, his clothes smeared with grease, his fingers scarred with work. He had got most of Villa's motor transport moving and he arrived driving the Studebaker, sitting up in the high front seat like a millionaire arriving for a horse show. He brought letters and a bundle of newspapers, both Mexican and American. Though the censored Mexican press had little to say, the American journals had it all. When Huerta had been denounced from the floor of the Chamber of Deputies in Mexico City and the speech privately printed and circulated as a pamphlet, the Senator responsible had been found shot. The American newsmen had reported it widely and President Wilson had followed their denouncement with a furious accusation of his own.

'It don't seem to have worried Huerta much, me dear,' Atty said dryly. 'He dissolved Congress and carted off a hundred and ten congressmen to jail.' He gave a hoot of laughter. 'In tramcars,' he ended. 'Because his transport's all up here in use against Villa.'

The final move to Torreón began, the ragged army like the exodus from a stricken city after a disaster.

Here and there groups of well-equipped, well-mounted men rode together, some of them even in old American khaki with Stetson hats, but for the rest it was the same raggle-taggle mob of coloured shirts, Indio scarves, sarapes and sombreros. They were a primitive-looking horde, some of them still bearing the scars of recent fighting, and all smelling of sweat, grease, horses and gun oil, all moving eastwards in a snake-like coil across the desert, surrounded by a vast cloud of red dust.

Among them were rickety carriages, spiders, buggies, carts, even old stage-coaches dating back to the war against Maximilian in the 1860s, which had been dug out of dusty stables to provide the wheels Villa so desperately needed. There were Atty's motor cars and trucks, ox waggons, pack trains, mules and donkeys, their drivers illiterate villagers determined to get something for themselves out of the vast upheaval that was taking place. For the third time in two years armies were on the march and everybody had decided to be with them, noisy, boastful, drunk, the apathy of their poverty discarded as they saw a new attempt to provide that ideal of dignity – freedom to own land – that their rulers had always failed to produce.

Moving ahead with Preto, the former Carranza aide, who had so taken to Slattery he tried to dress like him, they picked up information at Dolores Satero that enemy forces were taking advantage of Villa's presence near Torreón to move into his base in the San Andres valley.

The news set Villa whirling in his tracks with a picked column that included Slattery, to begin an incredible forced march. Jaded by thirst and galled by flying dust, they headed for days across the desert. Horses failed and men were left on foot to find their own salvation. As they halted, exhausted, their lips chapped, their skin worn by the flaying wind, to allow the stragglers to catch up, it was Slattery, pushing forward, who learned there were eighteen hundred men in and around San Andres and that a military train full of supplies was expected.

Villa was on his feet at once, reaching for his weapons. '*Vamonos ya!* Let's go! *Un golpo terrifico*. A tremendous blow. That should do it.' He grinned at Slattery. 'And because you found it, inglés, you can be part of it. Try not to get shot.'

The chances of failure were high because they were hungry and their horses were worn out, but in the heavy darkness just before dawn the regiments were drawn up, ragged untidy lines of dusty soldiers in large hats, swathed to the eyes in as much weaponry and ammunition as they could carry. Officers waved swords they didn't know how to use and a cheer went up as they moved off in a cloud of dust.

Flags were unfurled and the few guns Villa possessed opened the attack. A company of men trotted away from the main body, clattering off in commandeered country carts with ancient French machine-guns that looked like rifles mounted on tripods. They bounced over the ground at top speed, flinging up stones and dust, the men clinging to them for dear life. A crackle of musketry broke out, a few men were hit and a horse crashed down, overturning a cart and flinging its passengers sprawling. A little mountain gun went away ahead of them, bounding over the ruts in approved

Royal Horse Artillery style, and within minutes sharp cracking explosions showed that it was in action.

Coming on a raised road leading to the town, Slattery saw men pouring forward in a swarm and, heading after them with Monserrat and Preto, found himself riding between the houses surrounded by wild-looking horsemen triumphantly discharging rifles into the air. Federal soldiers were fleeing ahead of them to disappear round the backs of buildings, and a saddle emptied as its owner disappeared backwards over the horse's rump to land flat on his back with a crash of equipment.

For a moment the attack seemed to be out of control but Slattery managed to get it moving again and eventually they began to hear the unmistakeable sounds of success – bugle calls and cheers and the wild sound of horses' hooves. Skirmishing was still going on ahead and there were corpses lying like dead rats in the streets with the carcases of horses still in the shafts of halted supply waggons. One of them had been overturned and the driver lay in the road, his blood congealing among the scattered flour from the burst sacks he had been carrying.

At the sound of the bugles, the civilians had come out of their houses and were clapping, cheering, and offering cigarettes and money. Looking for Villa, Slattery found him near a crackling fire in the middle of the square where orderlies held steaming horses. A man was cooking and a second was up-ending a bottle of beer. A sombreroed cavalryman was honing a vast captured sabre to the sharpness of a carving knife and it glittered redly in the firelight as he bent over it with a dedicated expression on his face. The smell of horses filled the air with the smoke and the smell of coffee. The unexpectedness of the attack had driven the Huertistas from their trenches, and as the horsemen began to round them up they found they had wiped out a force outnumbering them nearly three to one.

As the excited Villistas surged through the town, Slattery headed for the station with Preto. Every station was connected to the next by telegraph wires and the operator's log book was always a sure source of information. The

93

windows of the houses around had been broken and the floors fouled by horses ridden up steps and through front doors. Here and there a body was propped against a wall.

Inside the telegraph office, a Federal officer was trying to get off a warning, and before Slattery could intervene Preto's men had beaten him across the face and head until they were a smother of blood.

'You don't understand, mi Coronel,' Preto said indignantly when Slattery protested.

It was pointless arguing that the officer was only doing his duty, and he was lumped together with all the other prisoners and swept outside to his death. At the door he halted, removed his shoes and handed them to one of the bare-footed peón soldiers. 'I shan't need them any more,' he said.

The telegraph operator's log book indicated that the military train they had expected was still due, so they smashed the set and headed towards the outskirts of the town. The body of the officer was already suspended from the crossbar of a telegraph pole near the station forecourt; a vendor of sticky sweets and candied fruits was setting up a portable stand alongside and, with a fly-whisk working overtime, was looking for trade among the gaping townspeople.

Near the edge of the town, they stumbled on a pilot engine and tender standing with steam up, half-hidden by trees. As they were examining it, Monserrat arrived with more men on horses. With Preto's troop clinging like flies to the engine, they steamed to a small halt a mile outside the town and, as they backed the engine into a siding, Monserrat caught up again. Sending him along the track to attack the train from behind, Slattery got Preto's men placing logs across the rails to stop it.

Eventually a pilot engine steamed slowly into view, pulling a flat car on which a machine-gun was mounted. As it stopped for the barricade, there were nervous shouts between the driver and the officer with the gun, then, as the driver tried to put it into reverse, Preto's men appeared from cover and swarmed over it. As they brought it to a halt again, Villa appeared.

94

He slapped Slattery's back. 'Well done, inglés,' he said. 'Now we wait for the supply train.'

There wasn't one train but four, and they steamed up quite unaware of what had happened. Within minutes they were surrounded by yelling Villistas and the Huertista defenders threw down their weapons and changed sides at once. The trains were crammed with ammunition and military supplies, as well as a complete battery of field guns.

'Artillery!' Villa crowed. 'Now we can start for Torreón.'

2

Torreón was protected to the north by the river and beyond that by tumbled hills and deep ravines and the garrisoned towns of Gomez Palacio and Lerdo, with the hill towns of La Loma and Aviles blocking the route from the west.

As they waited for the final orders to move, Villa summoned his leaders to elect a man whom everybody would follow without question. Most of those present had enough sense to realize that Villa himself was the only one with the personality to command, and preferred not to provoke his fluky pistol by disputing it, but there were a few who considered themselves more fitted for the job. Inevitably it was Villa who was voted into the position and Urbina went off sulking.

Villa shrugged. 'Tómas is brave and clever,' he admitted. 'But sometimes he can't walk for rheumatism. Then he drinks too much aguardiente and pretends to shoot his mother. He *always* pretends to shoot his mother. He never hits her, of course, because he has a great regard for her. But he doesn't think of the revolution as the fight of the poor against the rich but as a means of filling his own coffers.'

As the meeting broke up, the ragged host gathered round its fires for the last night before the attack. They were singing the new marching song introduced by Gomez García, the old troubadour. It started as a whisper over the flames and in the shadows, then it grew until half the army was roaring it.

> 'La cucaracha, la cucaracha,
> Ya no puede caminar;
> Porque le falta, porque no tiene
> Marijuana que fumar...'

It was a typical army song, jibing at the singers themselves,

96

big-hatted, bandoliered and surrounded by the rattle of wheels and the thump of hooves. It spoke of soldiers and their women, and everybody took it up, pale-faced city men, brown-skinned peóns, white-clad Yaqui Indians and Tara- humaras who could run like stags. Guitars picked up the catchy melody, mouth-organs whined and fiddles squealed.

Strutting between the fires with his fiddle, invariably accompanied by Jesús, the boy who had been given to Slattery as his body servant, old Gomez García had become familiar to everybody. The butt of the camp, he was known as the Captain General or the Picador's Horse Boy, but he was cleverer than he seemed and in his element as the man who had brought a new song to the north.

'Soon,' he told Slattery, 'the whole of Mexico will be singing it.'

As the army roared its delight, Carranza himself arrived, surrounded by his staff, all immaculately dressed and showing only the wear and tear of the debating chamber. He was clearly irritated by the way Villa did what he thought best without consulting headquarters, and was anxious to stamp his personality on the coming battle so that when victory came he would be able to claim some of the credit. As he talked he produced a parchment. 'Your commission as general and commander-in-chief of the Revolutionary Forces of the North,' he announced.

Villa stared at it, unimpressed. 'I've never asked for anything from the revolution,' he said slowly, crumpling the parchment indifferently. 'It's for educated men like you, First Chief, to handle the official part of things; and so long as you give back to my men and their families the land the hacendados took, I'm with you all the way. But –' he paused, gesturing with the parchment, his yellow eyes glittering with ill-disguised contempt '– I don't need this. I *already* command my army.'

It was a scorchingly hot day as the final move began, but a low roll of thunder came across the plains, and during the afternoon heavy clouds started to bank up on the surrounding high ground. The long serpent of animals,

97

vehicles and human beings struggled on in the oppressive heat, sweating under their equipment, the weary horses plodding on with lowered heads. As the weather grew more threatening, the colour of the day seemed to fade, the sky changing from blue to steel and from steel to bronze, so that the hills looked pale and washed out. Then nervous flurries of wind began to raise the dust in whirls, and the atmosphere became hot and brooding and made the tramping men and beasts irritable. Finally a breathlessness seemed to make the lungs struggle for air as the sky darkened further.

The wind began to come in squalls, short frenzied gales that roared in from every direction at once to lift an opaque wall of red dust. Then the stillness came again, ominous and frightening, while new clouds, yellow and muddy-looking, marched over the mountains. The sky became as black as pitch, and an electric storm started with an ear-splitting clap of thunder that battered at the shuddering earth in drumrolls of noise, while violent forks of purple lightning played along the horizon in an incessant flashing of unearthly light.

The first heavy drops of rain spattered the earth, then it came in a drenching downpour that almost hammered the trudging column into the earth. A vast shout of anger and discomfort rose – even here and there a little laughter – backgrounded by a shrill wail of despair from the women. But it didn't last long and Jesús sullenly wrapped himself in his sarape while the women and children about them hunched against the discomfort in a stubborn Indian stoicism.

For three hours a solid wall of water descended, so thick, so heavy, you could almost stare at yourself in it as if in a mirror. Then it stopped dead, leaving the air like that of a Turkish bath and everybody drenched and wretched. Mexicans never took kindly to rain but Villa rode up and down the long column, cursing and slapping at his men with his riding switch, encouraging them as they dragged their feet through the mud which an hour or two before had been thick dust.

'Keep going, compadres,' he kept saying. '*Por Dios*, don't stop for a drop of rain!'

Coming up behind the army, Slattery found it fighting in a growing morass to drag waggonloads of ammunition through knee-deep quagmires where the water had gathered. The ground was churned up by feet and hooves and wheels, and everybody seemed to be covered with wet red mud. Nearby, Atty was struggling under a stalled truck, with a dripping Jesús standing alongside, holding his tools and an oil can.

But there was no stopping. Villa had set a time limit for the arrival at Torreón and the army fought on against the swamp the rain had made, cursing, panting, exhausted and despairing.

The whole world looked pale and rubbed out now, and over the plain a wet haze drifted like a ghost. For a while a weak sun came out again, thin and casting no shadows, but it started a steam bath that increased the mist to cotton wool. Eventually it lifted and the sun poured down again, but almost immediately the clouds came together once more and another downpour burst on them, shutting out the horizon with its weight and fury.

When they halted for the night they were all soaked and more than willing to concede the victory – any victory – to Huerta. There were no fires because it was impossible to light them and they had to eat what was left of their last meal, cold tortillas and beans and, for those who had it, meat out of tins. More rain came in the night so that when the column dragged itself to its feet again the following morning to tramp the stiffness out of their bones, the gulleys which had been full of dust the day before were now swirling rivers. Carts had to be dragged across by sweating men and wild-eyed horses and mules. What couldn't be heaved forward had to be left behind. Their wet skirts clinging to their legs, women carried children across, then their equipment and cooking pots, and finally tramped off again after their men.

La Loma fell after a two-day attack then, after confused fighting in the foothills, the Federals were driven back on

Aviles, and again to the gates of Torreón. Villa was cock-a-hoop at the booty. 'Two cannons, five hundred rifles, three hundred shells and a hundred and fifty thousand rounds of ammunition,' he grinned.

His armoury replenished, he set his men against Torreón itself. Bringing forward his artillery, he flung in his force in a mass assault at night against three sides of the city at once. Knowing their fate if they lost, the Federal officers put up a stubborn defence.

Slattery found Villa outside a small house he had made his headquarters. Cooking fires were burning nearby and, though his staff were eating, Villa himself, showing his usual indifference to food, simply moved among them, helping himself to a few beans from one plate, a little meat from another. Nearby was a group of men totally different from Villa's ragtag soldiers. In Norfolk jackets, breeches and leggings, they were smart and clean and clung closely together. Slattery recognized them at once as the Germans from Nogales. There were four of them and three of them stood aside whispering together while the fourth moved up and down just behind Villa. It was Fausto Graf and he was wearing a revolver, leggings and a military-style cap and was trying to make Villa listen to him. Villa seemed disinclined to pay attention but Slattery knew he was taking in everything that was being said. Occasionally, he flung a word over his shoulder and Graf leaned forward to explain something, earnest, urgent and anxious to be understood. As he finally moved away with a frustrated expression to confer with his friends, he came face-to-face with Slattery.

For once there was no smile. 'What are you doing here?' he demanded.

Slattery grinned. 'Same as you, I suspect. Looking after General Villa's interests.'

Graf scowled then, suddenly, the devastating, disarming smile came. 'Let's not fight each other, Englander,' he said. 'There is enough fighting going on in Mexico without us starting another war. Have you seen my sister? She's here somewhere. They've been doing *The Merry Widow* at Monterrey and were to put it on in Torreón. But Torreón's

100

a little too preoccupied to enjoy Lehár just now and they can't get through the lines. Come along to our tent for a drink. We have some excellent Mosel.'

As the group moved away, Slattery stared after them. Horrocks was more right than he had believed.

Villa was indifferent to his warning, however. 'Sure,' he said. 'Germans. He told me Huerta's proposing to hold elections. He said there are at least four candidates, one of them Porfirio Díaz's nephew.' He grinned. 'But *he*'s decided to run his campaign from Veracruz so he can bolt to the American fleet if there's trouble.' The grin vanished, to be replaced by a frown. 'I should be in Mexico City. That's the only place where the election will count. The German said so.'

'His name's Graf, Don Pancho. He's the leader of the German-Mexican Bund.' Slattery was struggling to convince Villa of some obscure danger he wasn't sure of himself and it occurred to him he was doing exactly what Horrocks and the men in Whitehall had wanted him to do. 'He may be Mexican, but his interest isn't Mexico. The blond one's name is Kloss. He's a German general.'

Villa gestured. 'I know him. He was in charge of munitions and ordnance. But not any longer. Who are the others?'

'One of them's called Von Raschstadt. He claims to be a banker but I think he's a German naval officer. I think they're all German officers and all German agents.'

Villa nodded placidly. 'I thought they might be.'

'They work for Germany, not Mexico, Don Pancho.'

'Sure. I know this, too. What he didn't tell me I guessed.'

'What do they want?'

Villa grinned. 'What you said they'd want. To supply us with arms. He talked about concessions when we'd won. But when we've got the arms, we just forget the concessions.'

'Don't you believe it, Don Pancho.'

'Germans can't interfere with Mexico.'

'They'll try.'

Villa scowled. 'Well,' he conceded. 'Perhaps we can leave

it for the time being. There are plenty of arms in Torreón. I'll tell them I'm not interested.' He put an arm round Slattery's shoulder and gave him a bear hug. 'All right, compadre, I'll do as I'm told.' He winked. 'This time, anyway.'

The shooting swelled to a roar and wounded began to trickle back, some on foot, dumbly clutching their injuries, some helped by friends, some carried in bloody blankets that left a trail of dark drops on the ground. Moving up with Atty and Jesús and, as often as not, the strange old fiddler, Gomez García, Slattery found the Villistas sheltering from the firing behind the hills. They were hiding among the rocks on either side of the road, only their tall hats showing. Because Villa always put arms before personal comfort, they were still in a picturesque state of poverty – some in store suits, some in coveralls, some in the white peón cotton, but all with the all-purpose sarape that served as coat, blanket and makeshift shelter from the rain. The flop-brimmed sombreros were decorated according to taste with flowers, sprigs of brush, ribbons, a woman's scarf, or pictures of the Virgin of Guadalupe. They were cleaning guns, grooming horses, playing cards or dice, their women blowing at smouldering twigs to heat water for coffee.

Women from the towns around had arrived in dozens at the prospect of fighting, some to sell themselves for money, some to set up hospital tents and dressing stations in the scattered farmhouses. Nearby was a large marquee with a home-made Red Cross flag flying from a pole and the words *Brigada Sanitaria* on a poster. A few lightly wounded men were waiting outside for a cart to take them to the rear. Moving in and out of the tent were women who were more flamboyantly dressed than the local women and there were men helping with stretchers. A high tenor voice started.

'– *Venimos todos con gusto*
Y placer a felicitarte'

– and immediately a chorus rose –

102

Then Slattery recognized the plump shape of Hermann Stutzmann, and it dawned on him the Red Cross tent was being run by his company of singers and actors from Monterrey. As he approached, Stutzmann smiled.

'What are you doing here?' Slattery demanded. 'You're almost in the front line.'

Stutzmann gave an embarrassed grin. *'Ich bin Sanitäter,* Herr Paddy,' he said. 'I have become a medical orderly. We should have been playing *The Merry Widow* in Torreón for a week. Instead we're playing heroes outside. It was decided to stay and help.'

'Who decided?'

Stutzmann flushed. 'I was persuaded.'

'Who by?'

'Die schöne Magdalena, who else? She suggested it to me. So here we are. Can you imagine her missing the chance to be kind, to be good?'

When Magdalena appeared, the delight in her face at seeing Slattery was obvious. As he grinned back at her, however, her face changed. 'I thought you were in Nogales. I thought you were just an adviser. A staff officer.'

'I earn my keep in a variety of ways.'

She studied him for a moment, her expression grave. 'Why did you come to Mexico, Fitz Slattery?' she asked. 'It's dangerous in Mexico these days. Why don't you go home?'

Slattery shrugged. 'I'm not very much at home at home. Do you *want* me to go away?'

Her expression changed again, and this time it contained unhappiness. There was a long pause then she shook her head. 'No,' she said quietly. 'No, I don't.'

She avoided looking at him by gesturing at the hospital tent with its fluttering flag. 'It's a poor effort,' she said. 'But men are always so anxious to start a fight. They never think who's going to pick up the pieces afterwards.'

Slattery said nothing. To Magdalena – to many Mexicans – the revolution had long since ceased to be an adventure.

He remained with the Stutzmann group for some time while scattered fighting went on ahead and the number of wounded increased, the injured being brought in swathed in bandages made from their own shirts. Then Jesús arrived to say he was wanted forward.

As he left, Slattery was surprised to see Magdalena's eyes sparkling with tears.

'I shall be all right,' he said.

'Always it's someone else who's going to be hurt,' she said. 'The man in front. The man behind. Never you.'

He kissed her gently on the cheek and turned away, aware that she was watching him all the way until he was out of sight.

By next evening the Villistas were in the outskirts of the city and that night Villa flung them forward in a final massive attack - without their huge hats to avoid confusion in the darkness. Within an hour the cheers were going up as the Federals began to abandon their positions and retreat. Trains carrying Federal troops began to pour out of the city to the east and whole groups, trapped in the streets, began to throw down their arms, the officers ripping off their insignia of rank and trying to escape down the back alleys where they might buy or loot a civilian suit to save their lives. As the Villistas entered the city centre through a jungle of hanging wires, Slattery was leading a group of young American mercenaries. There were running figures ahead and as a field gun fired and brought down a wall, the Americans fired back. The running men fell, then, as they turned a corner, a machine-gun opened up. The Americans dived for shelter as the bullets struck the pavement and whined away.

Diving after them, Slattery saw the field-gun fire again and saw the shell strike the corner of a house just in front of him. The flash filled his eyes and he saw bricks arc into the air and felt something strike his arm. As he stumbled away, he was hit on the head by something that felt like a hammer blow. Spinning round, he toppled to safety in a doorway. For a moment he thought he was dead but he could still move, though the pain in his head blinded him and as he struggled to keep his senses he found himself instead sinking rapidly into darkness.

3

Slattery came back to consciousness to find himself staring into Magdalena Graf's face. Her blue eyes were huge with anxiety.

He smiled weakly. 'Am I dead and in Heaven?'

She gestured irritably. Behind her he could see Jesús, spotlessly clean and brushed so that he knew she'd been at him. The first thing she always did when she appeared was to make sure Jesús took a bath and put on clean clothes. Beyond Jesús, Atty was wearing an expression that seemed to indicate that he thought everything that had happened was Slattery's fault and nothing to do with him.

Slattery looked up at Magdalena again. '*Gnädiges Fräulein*, are you going to sing for me?' he asked.

She seemed startled.

'I heard you in Nogales,' he said. 'I thought you were the most wonderful thing I'd ever seen. How did I get here?'

He saw there were tears in her eyes. '*Dummkopf*,' she said gently. 'Oh, you fool, Slattery. I warned you and you still got hurt.'

'Does it bother you?'

'No.' The word was delivered sharply, but then her face crumpled and her manner changed and she gave him a doomed sort of smile. 'Of course it does.'

'Why?'

She seemed confused. 'Because I hate to see people suffer,' she said. 'I hate the sight of blood.'

He could see he wasn't going to get any confessions from her and began to look about him, becoming aware at last that there was a bandage on his head and that his right arm was in a sling.

'What happened? Was it the shell?'

She looked angrily at him, tears still in her eyes, and it was Atty who answered.

'You got a flying brick along the skull, me dear. Mebbe you've got a thick head. 'Tes not as bad as it looks.'

Without thinking, Slattery tried to lift his hand to his head to feel the wound but the pain in his arm flung him back against the pillows. 'And this?' he gasped.

'Another brick.'

'Is it broken?'

'It's cut and badly bruised,' Magdalena said. 'It's black, blue, green and yellow and will get worse.' She seemed to enjoy the thought. 'You'll not be using it for a week or two.'

'Not even for grabbing at you? Where am I?'

'In a bed in the Hospital of the Holy Virgin.'

'It would be more interesting if you were in it with me.'

Atty grinned and she blushed.

'Where *is* the Hospital of the Holy Virgin?'

She responded briskly as though she felt herself on safer ground. 'In Torreón.'

'We picked up guns, grenades, rifles, machine-guns and half a million cartridges,' Atty said.

'How are the boys behaving?'

'Villa threatened to shoot anybody who looted, and he's put a clamp on liquor. He's told all the Spanish they've got to go. He says they're all Huertistas.'

'He's probably right.'

'He's confiscating their property and he's told them if they don't go they'll be put against a wall and shot.'

'Did he pick up rolling stock?'

'Forty railway engines and a lot of freight cars. He can move his men on wheels from now on. He could be running Mexico next year.'

'What about me?'

'*Liebe Himmel*,' Magdalena said, 'you could be out of here tomorrow. Today, in fact, if you don't mind the headache. The scar will show but you can comb your hair over it. There's nothing wrong with you.' She seemed brusque and indifferent again. 'I'm going to Mexico City. Hermann has arranged for us to appear at the Opera House there. The Opera House is a good booking and worth a lot of money.'

'Zapata's playing hell to the south.'

107

'He won't be in the Opera House.'

'You could always stay here and look after me.'

She sniffed. 'You don't need looking after. Jesús can do it. Hermann and the rest of them have already gone. I only waited until you began to show signs of life.'

'Is it that important?'

She flushed pink again. 'I am just the nurse – *Schwester* Magdalena – just a woman trying to help and you happened to be my patient. I'm going to my house in Mexico City and nothing's going to stop me. Villa's laying on a train to Durango. He wants to get the wounded away because he doesn't think he can hold Torreón, and there'll be news-papermen wanting to go south for the election. I'll go to Zacatecas and pick up the train there.'

Slattery was silent for a moment then he smiled. 'This house of yours – is it big?'

'*Dios*, too big!'

'Roomy?'

'If you mean has it got a lot of rooms, yes, it has.'

'Then why not get Atty to take the Studebaker to Durango and meet you? He can take you across country from there. Save time.'

Her manner changed at once. 'Will he?'

'Yes,' Atty said enthusiastically. 'Sure will.'

'Then you can look after me,' Slattery said.

She stared at him, startled. 'Where are you going?'

'With you.'

'You're not fit to go anywhere.'

'You've just told me there's nothing wrong with me, and Atty can put the Studebaker on a flat car in Durango, so that we've got it with us for use in Mexico City.'

Monserrat and Preto appeared. Preto shyly carrying a wilting bunch of flowers, then Jesús bringing the newspapers and full of praise for Magdalena who had bought him a new pair of shoes. Finally, later in the day, Villas himself arrived. He seemed amused.

'*Hola*, inglés,' he said. 'Do all English soldiers behave as stupidly as you? You should remember what I told you. Like

108

a little cat. That's how we move about. It's a good job Preto of the Holy Trinity brought you in. You're going to Mexico City, I hear.'

'I can't do much here for a while.'

'Well, it suits me. Look at the elections for me. They'll be fixed, of course, but I want someone to see them being fixed. You're a good telescope, and far more use to me telling me what the enemy's going to do next than getting yourself knocked about in an attack. We're winning this war, inglés. Now we have Torreón we can go on elsewhere. Especially now. People love me, inglés.' Villa grinned and gestured. 'I borrowed three hundred thousand pesos from the business houses here. They complained a bit but I told them I'd hang them if it didn't appear. I used some of it to buy clothes and food for the poor. I also ordered the bands to play in the square to cheer them up. Oh -' he added as an afterthought '- I shot the prisoners. But only the Oroz-quistas and the Federal officers. Nobody minded.'

'They will when they think about it, Don Pancho. America especially.'

Villa's head went down as it always did when he was angry, and he looked like a bull at bay in the bullring. 'In 1862,' he pointed out harshly, 'when Benito Juárez was fighting with his back to the wall against the usurper, Maximilian of Austria, the Chamber of Deputies – the first democratic assembly in the history of Mexico, compadre, remember that – passed a law decreeing instant execution for any Mexican captured with the enemy forces. There were a few in those days, too. I was only obeying that law. Revolutions aren't made with rose petals and the United States doesn't rule Mexico yet!'

It wasn't hard to get to Mexico City. The fighting was only where the armies were and they were mostly near the rail junctions and the garrison towns, and in the rest of the vast territory that was Northern Mexico there was only emptiness, even areas where the peóns had never seen an army and didn't want to.

The journey was more uncomfortable than Slattery had

anticipated. His head continued to ache, his arm was painful despite the sling he wore, and the jolting of the train didn't help. Atty was waiting at Durango, which still hadn't recovered from Urbina's recent sacking. There were bullet marks on the façades of all the buildings, shop windows were boarded up, and there were still burned-out houses, debris in the streets, and here and there bunches of flowers, a candle, a little home-made shrine, to indicate where someone had died violently.

They spent the night in the open country for safety. Magdalena wore a simple dress and coat with a shawl over her head. It stripped her of all the glamour of the theatre. As it grew dark, despite Slattery's objections she insisted on him having the whole of the back seat of the car to sleep in while she and Atty and Jesús slept on the ground.

''Twill be as cold as Finegan's feet the day he was buried,' Atty grumbled.

Before they reached Zacatecas, on Atty's advice she removed Slattery's sling and helped him into a loose jacket and buttoned it up.

''Tes Federal agents there are, all over the place,' Atty explained. 'Watchin' for fellers with bandages. They know they're not Federal soldiers or they'd be in a Federal hospital.'

The station was full of refugees from the fighting, but Magdalena managed to bribe her way into a first-class compartment. She was beginning to enjoy the adventure. Her hair twisted up into a dark helmet on her head, her face alive with an unexpected happiness, she was revelling in the outburst of domesticity after the unreal world of the stage.

Indians in bright blankets and Chinese with pigtails who had fled from Torreón crowded round the portable tables along the platform where vendors sold food. At midday the train halted at a station which had a restaurant of sorts. A fiesta was being held, with gambling booths and a fair and stalls of cheap liquor lost in a sweltering mass of humanity. Women passed down the train offering tamales, but the passengers from the second-class coaches had noticed that

110

they had halted near an orchard and were busy helping themselves.

There were placards everywhere about Huerta's election as they drove through Mexico City to Magdalena's house. The capital was impressive, though there were still blackened scars from the rising that had toppled Madero, a splintered tree, a grave in a park, an occasional smashed lamp standard. But there were electric lights, streetcars, telephones, a Renaissance-style post office, railways, a marble opera house in the style of the one in Paris, and large prosperous homes like Italian palazzi that were the residences of foreign investors and those who had profited under Díaz and somehow still managed to profit under the new revolution.

But the place was clearly restless because the financial system was chaotic after three years of revolution. The value of the peso had fallen and in the north Carranza was issuing lavishly-designed notes of his own with pictures of volcanos, crossed guns and posturing women representing Mexico. Because of the confusion, Huerta had decreed a succession of bank holidays that kept the banks closed.

The Villa Magdalena was in the Avenida Versailles, a quiet side street off the Paseo de la Reforma. It was a square ugly building but inside there was taste, though it was dusty because it had been left for months to the tender mercies of the Mexican housekeeper who led them through the corridors and up and down stairs, showing them the rooms and uttering loud cries of dismay at the number of people she was expected to look after.

Magdalena was curiously excited and eager, showing them the garden and sending Pilar, the housekeeper, out for food and drink. After dinner, Slattery played the piano one-handed and sang 'Phil The Fluter's Ball'. It delighted Magdalena and she laughed, her eyes sparkling, and got them all to contribute something to the evening. Then she sat at the piano herself and sang items from the shows she'd appeared in. Jesús almost swooned with adoration.

'Why not try *opera* in the Opera House?' Slattery asked.

She studied him half-smiling. 'Adelina Patti said if I

111

trained properly I could have the voice for Puccini roles. I met her once in New York. I've never dared.'

'You could be singing with Caruso instead of that barrel of lard, Stutzmann.'

His comment angered her and the concert came to an abrupt end as she disappeared to bed in a huff. The next morning Fausto appeared and Slattery heard them talking in the salon, their voices raised.

'What did he want?' he asked when she appeared.

'Only to know I had reached Mexico City safely.'

He didn't press the point and, when she had to go to the Opera House, to enable Slattery to go into town if he wished, she bound up his arm and helped him into his jacket. There was no sign of the anger she had shown the previous evening and when his eyes lifted to her face as she bent over him, she gave him a little smile that was warm and maternal.

'You should do this more often, Magdalena,' he said quietly. 'I could grow used to it.'

She flushed and looked hurriedly away, pretending to be busy. Beneath the brittle shell of conversation there were underlying currents that troubled her, as Slattery could tell, and he saw her shiver as though the familiar world had become something new and just a little frightening.

'Men are clever with words.' There was an unexpected gentleness in her voice as she answered and a friendliness that made him feel good. Staring at her, he suspected, as he had on other occasions, that she had an enormous untapped capacity for enjoyment beneath the mercurial temperament of an artiste and the stiff Germanic exterior she never seemed quite able to throw off. There was something else, too, about her – a tremendous wholesomeness that overwhelmed him, and uneasily he came to the conclusion that for the first time since he was sixteen he was in danger of falling in love.

'Have you thought about what I said last night about opera?' he asked. 'In New York you could make a lot of money.'

She smiled. 'I don't need money,' she said. 'I have money. I shall be all right in my old age.'

'You'll never grow old.'

She looked quickly at him and her face grew pink again. It wasn't hard to make her blush. 'That's a nice thing to say.'

She carefully combed his hair over the scar and the narrow bare patch where his head had been shaved, finally plastering it well down with Atty's brilliantine. Then, leaning over, she kissed him lightly on the forehead. It was unexpected and he took her hand.

'What's that for?'

She freed herself gently and smiled at him. 'Because this morning,' she said, 'I am Mexican and, with your hair combed like that, you look like a Mexican, too.'

4

Atty was out shopping with Jesús and Pilar and Slattery was on his own when the doorbell rang.

He opened it warily. Outside, leaning on the wall, was Sholto Horrocks. He was as immaculately dressed as if he were going to a levée at the Presidential Palace.

'What the hell are you doing here?' Slattery demanded.

Horrocks beamed at him. 'Thought you might like a sick visitor.' He seemed to insinuate himself into the hall, almost as though he had slid through the crack in the half-open door. 'Goin' to offer me a drink?' he asked.

'There's some whisky.'

Horrocks accepted the whisky with a nod and looked about him. 'Nice place you've got here.'

'Don't talk bloody silly. What do you want?'

'Thought we might have a little chat. Toss out a few ideas. Spark each other off. That sort of thing.'

'How did you find me?'

Horrocks sipped his whisky. 'Oh, we like to keep an eye on our people.'

'I'm not "your people".'

'Yes, you are, old son. Everybody's "our people" if we once talk to 'em. Just been to see a printer, in fact. English. Name of Turner. His job's making colour plates and printing bank notes for the Mexican Treasury. At the moment he's printing pamphlets backing Villa. Villa don't know it, of course, but he's also printing pamphlets backing Carranza. You've met Carranza. Did you talk to him?'

'You don't talk to Carranza. He talks to you.'

'He'll claim the presidency eventually.'

'I suspect he'll get it.'

'He'd satisfy Washington. But Villa's not out of the running. He's very much admired north of the border as a soldier.'

114

'His past leaves a lot to be desired.'

'His present's not all that hot.'

Slattery studied Horrocks with a considerable amount of hostility. 'Do you people always get involved in everybody else's politics?'

'Oh, always,' Horrocks answered placidly. He sighed. 'Pity London don't. But the Prime Minister isn't even very certain where Mexico is. But that's Asquith all over, ain't it? He don't even know where his left arm is.' He was regarding Slattery with interest. 'Heard you stopped a bullet.'

'Not a bullet; a brick.'

'Don't go and get yourself killed. We could use you.'

'I'm not for sale.'

'You might be eventually. Because it's coming.'

'What is?'

'War.'

'In Mexico?'

Horrocks shrugged. 'Mexico's written on everybody's heart, old son. You'll find it printed on mine after I'm dead. Mexico's important. It don't look important, but it could have earth-shaking influences. So we don't overlook the possibility. It's a difficult situation. The Germans are gettin' very awkward over in Europe.'

'They seem to be getting very awkward over here, too. What are they up to?'

Horrocks sniffed. 'If you want to build a house you first have to put down something sound to stand it on. They're thinkin' ahead to the time when they'll need a solid intelligence service. They're preparing for *Der Tag*.'

'Here?'

'My dear chap, if you were after a woman, you'd put your best suit on to pay court to her, wouldn't you? You'd spend money. Flowers. Chocolates. A good dinner. All to prepare her for what comes afterwards. It's the same with countries. When you're wooing a country, you send your most able servants round with gifts and promises. There are a lot of people backing Huerta, even if the United States ain't. And not just Germany either. Investors, for instance. People like

115

Lord Cowdray. Guggenheim. William Randolph Hearst. Huerta's the sort of leader who makes their investment feel safer.'

'I don't think Huerta gives a damn for Lord Cowdray.'

'The Germans do. They're concerned that his oil shouldn't be available to their enemies if war breaks out.'

'It won't be *our* war.'

'You might be surprised. And if it is, it'll be *your* war as well as mine.'

'We haven't any treaties that affect Germany. If she starts a fight, it'll be against France and Russia.'

Horrocks sighed. 'And do you think, you stupid Irishman, if France goes to war with Germany, that England would allow German warships into the Channel to bombard French ports? A spit and a jump from Dover. Try not to be too half-witted.' He gestured. 'America, of course, will make money out of it. Why not? She'll become the arsenal for the opposing sides, though it would be a bit more difficult for Germany because, while the Americans'll sell arms, they won't ever allow them to be transported in American ships. And there *we'd* have the advantage. Our ships could get the stuff across the Atlantic but the German Navy couldn't guarantee that theirs could, because their warships'll never get out of the North Sea.' Horrocks looked at Slattery in a pained way as if he weren't very bright. 'And the obvious way to counter *that* problem would be to make sure American arms won't be available to *either* side. And they wouldn't, would they, if America went to war with Mexico? They'd use them themselves. Here.'

'It sounds bloody complicated.'

'These things usually are. That's why the Germans are tryin' to stir up trouble, and the more trouble there is, the more nervous the Americans are goin' to be.'

Horrocks held out his glass for a refill. 'Ever met a chap called Fausto Graf?' he asked.

Slattery looked quickly at him. 'Have you met him, too?'

'Not socially. He's a reserve officer of the German army.'

'He's American.'

'Don't make any difference. They can make whom they

116

like a reserve officer. We do. He's also a German agent, very occupied at this moment with stirring things up. After all, fighting's started again, hasn't it?' He gestured at Slattery's arm. 'The start of the final campaign to oust Huerta. When it succeeds, the Mexicans'll start kicking out the Spanish.'

'How do you know?'

Horrocks smiled. 'Walls have mice, and mice have ears. This election Huerta's promised is going to be a farce.' He indicated the newspaper by Slattery's chair. It carried deep headlines. 'Four candidates,' he pointed out. 'But only one winner. And he holds the power already.'

'It's not like England,' Slattery agreed. 'They don't smoke and spit and keep guns in their lockers in the House of Commons.'

'That's the way things happen in Mexico, though, ain't it? The chap with the biggest club's usually the boss. Who are you backing?'

'None of them.'

'Villa seems to be in the news.'

'Villa won't be out of the news until he's six feet under the earth.'

'His success hasn't gone unnoticed. But Berlin don't approve of him. He's too independent. They prefer Huerta. But they'll support Carranza.'

'Why not Huerta?'

'Him, too, old boy. This country's breaking down into small areas run by so-called generals, and the Germans see their job to be to keep the pot boiling by making sure they have guns.' Horrocks blew out smoke and blinked. 'But also,' he added, 'to see that Huerta has guns, too. They want the fighting to go on, to keep America on edge.'

5

Atty was slouched in a chair with Pilar, the Mexican woman, bent over him, administering black coffee.

'*Ebrio*, Señor,' she announced. 'Drunk.'

'I got talking to this feller, Turner, me dear,' Atty said. 'Not the printer. His brother. He works at the telegraph office. He says Huerta's sent reinforcements to retake Torreón, and Villa's decided to let him have it because it's too far from his bases and the supplies from across the American border.'

It didn't take Slattery long to decide that what Atty was telling him was more than likely true. Atty wasn't just a Cornish miner who had found himself stranded in Mexico. He was an intelligent man who had just not had the benefit of a lot of education. His judgements were shrewd and he had a gift for nosing information out of people who didn't think they were in a position to give it. This time there seemed no doubt, and the cartoon in one of the capital's newspapers showing an invalid Huerta huddled under blankets with a nurse saying, 'No change. He can't move yet,' was wildly wrong. The hard-drinking old general had moved enough to make all the right dispositions to stop the rebels, and let his opinion about the American president's hostility to him be clearly known at a press meeting he arranged in a café where he sat at a table with his brandy in a cup and saucer to disguise it as coffee.

'I shall retire,' he said bluntly, 'only when I'm dead and buried.'

His bald skull gleaming, he gestured to the waiter to bring more brandy and tossed coins with the cashier for who should pay. 'Mexico is a snake,' he went on. 'All its life is in its head. And *I* am the head of Mexico.'

That evening, Magdalena came home in a fury. Rehearsals had been cancelled and the preparations for the

118

show called off. Huerta's recruiting officers had taken the stagehands and three members of the chorus for the army. But she seemed almost to welcome the interruption because it allowed her more time at the house in the Avenida Versailles, and two days later she persuaded Atty to drive her with Slattery to Cuernavaca to inspect a small country house she owned there.

Cuernavaca was a place of romantic gardens, crumbling verandahs, statues and fountains overgrown with flowers. Its atmosphere was one of warmth and yearning, as if it had absorbed the emotions of generations of lovers. Slattery was conscious it was working on Magdalena. She was quiet, saying little as she clung to his arm.

Despite its charm, there was a worn look about the place these days because it had been occupied more than once by Zapata's men and the lily ponds were choked with weeds and the tangled groves of oranges and mangoes were in ruins. There was nothing left of Magdalena's house and she sat silently in the car as they drove back to Mexico City.

'Sad?' Slattery asked.

She shrugged. 'No,' she said. 'It was inevitable. One day somebody's going to say to *everybody* here who's a foreigner, "Get out of Mexico." When that happens I want to be able to go without losing too much dignity.'

As Horrocks had suggested, the election was becoming a farce. Posters and placards had been stuck up everywhere but nobody was taking much notice of them. Horrocks' English printer, Turner, had produced most of them, printing both for Huerta and those who wished to oppose him.

'Does a few other little things for us from time to time as well,' Horrocks said. 'Odd government forms we might need.'

On polling day, Atty drove them round the polling stations and, since the Opera House had still not recruited replacements, Magdalena joined them for lunch.

Horrocks gave Slattery an old-fashioned look as she appeared, magnificent in purple with a veil and a flowered

119

hat. 'She's Fausto Graf's sister,' he murmured as they saw her into a taxi afterwards. 'She could supply you with all the information you need. She's no more Mexican than you are.'

'If she were honest, she'd accept that she's American.'

Horrocks was unimpressed. '*No* German-American's American,' he said. 'There are French-Americans, British-Americans, Russian-Americans, Italian-Americans. But not the Germans. They're different. They're German and Fausto Graf's as German as Bismarck. He's been to see her, hasn't he?'

'How do you know?'

'Saw him. What did he want?'

'To see his sister.'

'Fausto Graf never does anything that simple. Are you sleeping with her?'

'No.'

Horrocks smiled. 'Pity. You can learn a lot in bed.'

At most of the polling stations there was a lone official collecting voting slips in a cigar box and occupying his time by completing a few himself. In some places, the ballot boxes consisted of cardboard shoe boxes, chemists' jars, in one place even a cat basket, but none of them had anything in them and, though they toured the city several times, they noticed they remained empty.

Several times Slattery noticed a German face he recognized from Nogales, and once even Sjogren, the Swede, sitting in a car making notes.

'Watching points for the Embassy,' Horrocks observed.

The following evening the streets filled with mobs shouting against Huerta who were clashing with other mobs supporting him, and Atty had to ease the Studebaker in and out of a torchlight procession which was forming from yelling men and boys. Then, near the National Palace, they saw a man appear on horseback, flourishing sheets of paper.

'Huerta's elected!' he yelled.

'The bloody man's not even a candidate!' Horrocks snorted.

A roar of indignation went up and carts and automobiles

120

were overturned. There was a sound of breaking glass as windows were smashed and the two opposing mobs outside the National Palace came together, scuffling and fighting and screaming on the steps of the Cathedral. With difficulty, Atty forced the Studebaker past and they made their escape just as cavalry appeared, swinging sabres and batons, to break up the disturbance. As they headed home, they passed a company of infantry advancing from their barracks at the double, then ambulances and cars full of doctors and nurses heading for the city centre.

The next morning they learned that the candidate in Veracruz had bolted to the American Consulate to claim political asylum. In view of the result and the uproar it had caused, the election had been declared null and void and it had been announced that a new election would be called the following year. Meanwhile, Huerta would continue as president – 'to save the country'. There were noticeably no objections from Congress.

'Of course not,' Horrocks said dryly. 'It's so packed with his bloody officers, they ought to use a bugle instead of a division bell.'

That night Magdalena was in a strange frame of mind, and they decided to celebrate the end of the election with dinner in town. But, because of the lack of currency, growers outside the capital were refusing to bring in their produce, restaurants were closed and kitchen staffs were having to search the markets for something to eat.

'It looks as though we're going to have to eat at home,' Slattery said. 'Can you cook, Magdalena?'

She turned, her eyes bright. 'I open a good tin of corned beef.'

With the Mexican housekeeper's knowledge of the back street shops and Atty's barefaced cheek, they found wine, whisky and a brandy-fed turkey which, although it was on the skinny side, fed all five of them. Magdalena was a terrible cook and her share of the proceedings was a disaster.

'I could learn,' she said. 'When I marry, I'll *have* to learn.'

121

'Who're you marrying?' Slattery asked.

She didn't react. With Atty in the kitchen in shirt-sleeves and with a dishcloth over his arm pretending to be a waiter – squeezing Pilar's waist, pinching her behind or pretending to waltz with her – she sat in a comfortable silence in the salon staring at Slattery over the top of her glass. They could hear Jesús giggling at Atty's antics and the laughter was infectious.

'I've been offered the role of Arline in *The Bohemian Girl* in the United States,' she said suddenly. 'If it's successful they're prepared to try me in *Fra Diavolo*.' Her face lit up with pleasure. 'The music of Auber and Balfe are a step towards opera. With that experience behind me, they think I could make a start on the less powerful roles like Amina in *La Sonnambula* and go on to Puccini.'

'Who's behind it? Our fat Junker friend?'

His arrogant comment annoyed her and her eyes flashed. 'Hermann has my interests at heart. Even before his own. He's encouraging me, even though it means he'd have to find and train a new lead singer. An associate of Charles Frohman's behind it. I suppose you've heard of Frohman. He's *the* leading New York producer.'

She was silent for a moment, then she sat at the piano and began to sing, not with passion or power but, he suspected, because she didn't always know how to behave with him and it was a good way to hide her feelings. At first it was melodies from zarzuela, then tunes by French composers, before finally moving to soft Mexican love songs. Finally, she began to play a phonograph, Lehár and Strauss waltzes, and Slattery took her in his arms and made her dance. At first she tried to free herself but eventually she allowed him to guide her round the furniture.

After a while, he changed the record to ragtime, and they started to do a foxtrot. As they moved backwards and forwards, she clung to him, moulding her body to his, matching her steps to his, her attention concentrated on her dancing.

'Do you do the Turkey Trot as well?' he asked.

Her eyes lifted. 'Badly,' she said.

'The tango?'

'Not much. Too daring. Nice women don't go in for it.'

'Let's try it.'

Putting his arm round her waist, he began to move around the room in quick swoops, deliberately over-emphasizing the drama of the dance as he bent her backwards. She started to giggle at his antics and in the end they had to stop, helpless with laughter, and start again with something simpler. Holding her close, her perfume went to his head a little.

'I like looking at you,' he said and she laughed.

'Don't laugh. I mean it.'

She looked at him, her eyes steady and unwavering.

'The theatre's full of women with better looks than I have,' she murmured, though he could tell she was pleased.

'You're different. It comes from inside. You can't hide what you feel.'

She looked up quickly. 'Oh, but I can,' she said briskly. 'I do. More than you realize.'

She began to hum the tune – to stop him talking, he suspected – then she looked up at him, smiling. 'Did you dance with Amaryllis?'

He looked at her sharply. 'How do you know about Amaryllis?'

'I was told.'

'Who by?'

'Somebody who knows her. He said she was coming to Mexico City.'

'I'll make a point of being somewhere else.'

'That's no way to court a woman.'

'I'm not courting her. I'm dodging her.'

'She must *think* you want her. Or she wouldn't chase you. You should make your peace with her.'

'I didn't know we were at war. Are you taking her side?'

'I'm taking the side of any lonely woman.'

'Then you should look to your own interests.'

Indignation flashed in her eyes and Slattery apologized at once.

123

'I'm sorry,' he said. 'I shouldn't have said that. You don't deserve it.'

The phonograph came to a stop and as their steps slowed he kissed her on the lips. At first it was gentle but when she didn't resist and even lifted her mouth, he became more ardent and she responded just as ardently. Then, slipping from his arms, she abruptly stopped the phonograph, slammed down the piano lid, and began collecting her music.

Pilar was still clearing the dirty crockery with Jesús and Atty and, as Magdalena vanished, she gave Slattery a curious look, her eyes moving to the stairs as if to encourage him.

Going to his room, he undressed slowly, his mind on the moment of happiness they had experienced. Magdalena had touched his hand more than once during dinner, almost as if by accident, as though reassuring herself he was there. But finally she hadn't seemed to want him and, in his anger, he wondered how she would react to a foray by him along the corridor and up the stairs to the third floor where she had installed herself in a room as far away from everybody else as possible.

For a moment longer, he considered trying his luck but, as his anger declined, he changed his mind and, with a shrug, he yanked back the curtains and turned out the light.

Mexico City was nervous. The northern armies were drawing nearer and in Morelos just to the south Zapata was conducting a campaign of blood-curdling cruelty in which hacienda owners and their mayordomos who were unwise enough to allow themselves to be taken prisoner were butchered or tortured.

But Mexico's earth had always been saturated by the blood of its people and Mexican memories were long and the desire for vengeance terrible.

Because of Zapata's reign of terror, farmers were afraid to move their produce and the food situation in the capital was growing worse. The traffic continued to flow, but it was thinner with the absence of petrol, and there were soldiers everywhere. Occasionally you saw groups of men, often manacled, being led away by recruiting officers to the army depots for shipment north.

As the panic died down a little, the Opera House managed to recruit fresh stagehands and new singers were found in Chapultepec and Querétaro and, as the performances restarted, Magdelena became busy and preoccupied. Slattery occasionally found her sitting in a chair wearing spectacles, supposedly studying a score but with a faraway look on her face. He could move his arm now and was able to comb his hair without ending up looking like one of the Mexican pimps whose girls operated round the back of the Cathedral.

From time to time, Horrocks appeared, full of information, not pushing but somehow always with a sense of having Slattery well under control. Usually he appeared alongside him as he sat at some sidewalk café, popping up like a pantomime demon, all smiles and bland sophistication.

'Huerta's in trouble,' he announced. 'Picking up recruits by press-gang methods that would have shamed Nelson's navy. Seven hundred seized at the bullfight on Sunday. Another thousand at a fire in the east end. The American Embassy didn't get its groceries last week because the delivery boy was taken. He's making a mistake, of course. The Indians'll do as they're told. Always do. But he's picking up educated people as well. He'll have desertions.'

Carranza was still playing at being president in the north, appointing 'ministers' to a non-existent administration, ambassadors, consuls, and advisers to foreign capitals for when the time came for them to take up their posts.

'He's picked his son-in-law as ambassador to Washington,' Horrocks said. 'So you'd better warn your friend, Villa, that he's going to have to endure a bit of back-stabbing north of the border.' He paused, smiling. 'How's the diva, by the way? Are you chasing her or is she chasing you? Because if she ain't, Amaryllis is.'

'Do *you* know her?'

'Have done for years. She was in the El Presidente Hotel last night when I returned. Asking at the desk for you. Seemed to think you might be staying there.'

'Was it *you* who told Magdalena about her?'

'My dear chap' – Horrocks was all pained innocence – 'never speak a lady's name in the mess. Never speak a gentleman's in a lady's boudoir.'

'I don't believe you. You're a born bloody liar. Do you know Amaryllis well?'

Horrocks' face was blank and Slattery wondered if he'd ended up in Amaryllis' bed, too. 'Well enough,' he said. 'How well do *you* know her?'

With the success of *The Merry Widow* at the Opera House, suddenly there were Americans making the hazardous journey south to hear Magdalena and Slattery saw less and less of her at the house in the Avenida Versailles. But he was always waiting outside when she appeared after the final curtain surrounded by admirers and members of the cast, all of them eyeing him with slow speculative glances. She was usually tired and in no mood to argue with him, and was content to eat a quiet supper provided by Pilar and drink a glass of wine.

'You know,' he said one night when things had gone wrong and the performance had been particularly trying so that she sat in a cool withdrawn silence, 'you'll suddenly wake up to find you're not who you thought you were. You're not Arline or Rosalinda or Hanna Glawari or any of those people in your operettas. You're Magdalena Graf – here, with me.'

She gave him a narrow look, startled at his shrewdness. With her better voice and superior technique she had always been isolated from the rest of the Stutzmann Company, living in their melodious smiling world without ever being part of it.

'I sometimes grow tired of being someone other than myself,' she admitted. 'To sing *Fra Diavolo* or *The Bohemian Girl* would be good. *Bohème* would be better, but that's beyond me for a while yet. And none of them would be the same as having a permanent home and being myself.' She shifted restlessly. 'I'm tired of living in hotels. I want to stay still, to cultivate a garden, to watch it grow for next year, to build a place that doesn't have to rely on Pilar who doesn't bother to dust when I'm not here to see it. A singer's a woman, too, and I want to live in a house that doesn't just spring to life when I appear in it.'

The taut look in her face had softened to a sad, longing sort of loneliness.

'Sometimes,' she went on, 'I think I'd be happy to give it all up. But it's not easy. After the Opera House, we go north again. Perhaps to El Paso and into Texas. We have a good reputation, and the chance of singing in New York is important. Will you be going back to Villa?'

'Yes.'

Her hand touched his gently, affectionately, as if its proximity meant a great deal to her, as if she longed to keep him beside her. 'He has many enemies,' she said. 'Don't go.'

'I engaged to serve him.'

'You're sick.'

127

'I'm better.'

'Who says?'

'I do. I've decided. It keeps things simple.'

She tried to smile. 'He has many enemies,' she said. 'Others have left him. Some have changed sides.'

'It's not a habit of mine.'

'Killers don't make rulers.'

'Are you advocating Don Venus?'

'He knows how to make laws.'

'You sound like Brother Fausto.'

She turned away, a hurt expression on her face. 'Don't go,' she said quietly. 'Please don't go.'

But he did.

When he returned to Torreón, Villa had emptied the railway yards to mount his troops on wheels for the coming offensive against Huerta. But the looting had been stopped, citizens were not interfered with, and the heavy drinking that had led to the shooting out of windows had been halted.

Almost the first person Slattery saw was Consuela Lidgett. She hadn't found her husband but the newspapermen had been helpful and she had been able to send a few stories north.

'I don't suppose they'll use them, though,' she admitted. 'None of them had much to do with Gordonsboro.'

She looked tired and her clothes were too well-worn, and in an attempt to cheer her up, Slattery bought her lunch. In the square there were flags in every window and the bandstand was a blaze of the national colours of red, white and green, with foliage tied to every upright and sprays of wilting flowers edging the steps.

'It was for General Villa,' Consuela said. 'They had a fiesta with music and bands.'

As they talked, borne on the shoulders of eight staggering cargadores, an enormous bed was making its way down the street. It was vast and wore sheets, blankets, covers, pillows and ribbon decorations. The porters were exchanging winks and bawdy comments with the interested crowd.

'It's for Don Pancho,' one of the cargadores was saying.

It was Atty who provided the details 'He got married again,' he said.

Slattery's eyebrows rose. 'For God's sake, he has two wives already. Where is he now?'

'With his train, me dear. He had the guard's van painted red and fitted it up with a bedroom and a kitchen. All domestic bliss. He's suddenly taken to gettin' shaved and his shirts are washed and have all the buttons on 'em. He even combs his hair now and then.'

'What about the other wives? He's never divorced them.'

Atty grinned. 'He says they're too *corecto* for campaigning.'

'Didn't the priest raise any objections?'

'Panchito showed him his gun and he found it was possible to overlook them.'

When they set off for headquarters, Consuela accompanied them to write an article on Villa. They found the red caboose without difficulty because it stuck out like a sore thumb among the ribbon of hooting engines and freight cars all covered with grey dust. There were curtains at the window and a vase of wilting flowers, and on the walls were pictures of pin-up girls showing acres of bosom and frothy underwear. There was also a picture of Carranza, tucked away in a corner where it could hardly be seen, and a much larger one of Villa himself occupying pride of place. Apart from the table, the only furniture consisted of two wide folding bunks.

Villa was eating a plate of beans and talking to Urbina and a few other men. In the background was a slender dark-haired girl with eyes like pansies. As they appeared, Villa waved Urbina and the other men away and gestured at the girl. 'My wife, Juanita,' he said.

There was no explanation and nobody asked questions. Villa gestured at Consuela. 'Who's this?'

'She's a great admirer of yours, Don Pancho,' Slattery explained. 'She wants to write something about you for her paper.'

Villa eyed her for a moment then glanced at his new 'wife', as though assessing her charms against Consuela's paler attributes. He leaned towards Slattery, his face sly.

'I think Doña Magdalena will have something to say,' he whispered, 'when she finds out about this one.'

'This one's just a reporter, Don Pancho. Nothing else.'

'Then you ought to make her something else. What a pity I have just got married.'

'She wants to write about Mexican women, Don Pancho. How they're helping the revolution. What they're doing.'

'They feed my soldiers,' Villa said. 'They bind their wounds and sleep with them. If their man is killed, they spend the day weeping, then take up with another man.' He slapped Slattery's knee. 'You saw my bed, inglés? It gives me more elbow room, don't you think. Tómas Urbina had the same feeling about a grand piano he heard of. He sent a squad of his men for it, but after they'd wrestled it down the front steps it dawned on them it had only three legs. They'd heard of animals with four legs and humans and birds with two and a few things like snakes with none, but they'd never heard of anything with three. So they ditched it and settled for an upright on four wheels.' He laughed, then his grin died and he leaned forward. 'What about you, inglés? What did you learn for me in the capital?'

'I learned that the Ambassador-Designate for Washington is Carranza's son-in-law, and that he's paying out a lot of money to American newspapers to make out that the bogeyman of the revolution is General Francisco Villa.'

Villa frowned. 'I can deal with him when the time comes. What about now? What else did you learn? What do they think of me in Mexico City?'

'Enough for Huerta to send nothing against Sonora or Coahuila. His troops are all coming up here against you.'

It startled Consuela to hear what Villa had said about her.

'He said that if he hadn't just married,' Slattery smiled, 'he'd have married you.'

She didn't know whether to be flattered or insulted. 'He didn't really mean what he said, did he? About the women going off with another man. Are they married? In front of a minister?'

'Mexicans sometimes dispense with that formality.'

130

She seemed out of her depth and Slattery wondered why she didn't have the sense to go home. He bought her dinner but she sat in silence over it for a long time.

'My husband's here somewhere,' she said eventually. 'I met someone who saw him.'

In Torreón they seemed cut off from the rest of the country. The bare countryside was full of men, swarming everywhere, red-eyed, campaign-worn, dishevelled and riding dust-covered horses. Though their officers held them under some degree of order, they were frayed, weary and bored.

Every train that came north brought a letter from Magdalena. Whatever happened, no matter how often the line was cut, no matter how many bridges were broken, the letters continued to arrive. She was pretending to be simply a woman writing to a man at war but reading between the lines it was clear she was lonely and missing Slattery.

She was hoping eventually to be near the armies again, because the Stutzmann Company was due to make a trip north, performing at Querétaro, León, Guadalajara, Aguascalientes, Zacatecas and Chihuahua. Mexicans loved music and it was usually possible for theatrical companies to move about. Sometimes the fighting drifted across their routes but battles had been stopped before now to let some group of singers through.

As Slattery studied the latest missive, Jesús appeared. He had brushed his clothes and looked clean and respectable.

'*Mi jefe,*' he said. 'Don Pancho wants you at headquarters.'

When Slattery appeared, Villa was just shooing out a group of his officers.

'The little Norteamericana's not with you?' he said.

'No.'

'You're not sleeping with her?' Villa looked disbelieving. 'She's like a little *gattito* – a little kitten. I think she'd like you to. You should try.' He gestured with his head to Slattery to follow and they walked along the track. As they passed, ragged soldiers stood up and grinned and their

131

wives bobbed curtseys. Villa nodded and smiled and patted the heads of their children.

He gestured at the mass of men, women, horses, vehicles, carriages, cars and ammunition limbers. The air was full of the smell of ammonia and horse manure and the stink of unwashed bodies. Above the babble of voices, the barking of dogs and the neighing of horses, they could hear guitars twanging and the sound of singing.

'These are my boys,' Villa said proudly. 'They're going to take Chihuahua and Juárez for me and when we've got them we've got the whole of Chihuahua State. I shall leave a brigade here with orders to retreat if they're threatened. I've got all I need except ammunition.' His big hand slapped his thigh. 'I have only enough for one quick fight, so it's to be hoped there's plenty for the taking in Chihuahua.'

'And me, Don Pancho?' There was obviously a reason for the summons to headquarters.

Villa grinned. 'You stay here, amigo,' he said. 'If Carranza can put out stories about me, I'll put out better ones. You're going to make sure that the Norteamericano newspapermen get the right angles; what a fine fellow I am, how kind I am, how gentle, how I love children, how I made the schools open, how I enforce the liquor laws. They have a powerful anti-alcohol lobby up there. And tell them that when I control the border I intend to stop drug smuggling. That should convince them I value their friendship.' Villa paused. 'No need to mention the shooting of prisoners, of course.'

'And your marriage, mi general? Do I tell them about that?'

Villa looked up and gave a sheepish grin. 'No,' he said. 'They're fussy about these things in the north.'

The great black snake of trains steamed out of Torreón the following morning and headed into the desert towards Chihuahua. Half the town had come to see them off, frock-coated officials surrounded by a mass of dusty people in a sea of sombreros that looked like a field of brown mushrooms. Consuela Lidgett stood with Slattery's group as the trains clanked past.

132

Bouquets were flung to Villa as his headquarters car rolled by. Beyond him in the shadows could be seen the frightened face of his new wife. Behind the red caboose came the hospital train, then the flat cars with his artillery and the box cars with his supplies. Finally came the freight cars carrying the troops and their families. They travelled in three tiers, the lucky ones inside, others with their families on the roofs or clinging to the sides, and a few – mostly boys and young men – riding in hammocks slung between the wheels. Platforms had been built on the buffers and on the fronts of the engines, where families were preparing to camp out, and shelters of blankets, sarapes and umbrellas were being constructed, while fires of twigs to bake tortillas were burning on shovels, pieces of sheet steel or the lids of oil drums. As they crawled past, high-spirited men loosed off their rifles into the air and shot out windows of nearby houses.

As the carriages and freight cars rumbled by one after the other, the wheels clack-clacking over the points, grinning brown faces beamed down at them. A group of men were singing the popular 'Adelita'. Another group were trying to drown them with 'La Perjura', then on top of one of the box cars, Slattery saw Apolinario Gomez García. He had appeared outside Slattery's room the night before, very drunk but full of vague warnings that were difficult to decipher.

'The last coach, your honour,' he had said. 'You will need to watch the last coach.'

What he was trying to get across had not been clear but he seemed sober again now, wedged against a chimney protruding through the roof from a stove somewhere inside. They heard the first faint squeak of 'La Cucaracha' and immediately guitars took up the tune, voices joined in, men's, women's, children's, until the whole string of rolling stock was singing.

> 'La Cucaracha! La Cucaracha!
> Ya no puede caminar – '

Men in sombreros, stetsons and képis taken from dead

133

Federals, peóns, vaqueros, shopworkers, engineers, renegade gachupíns, men with Indian faces, Spanish faces, European and North American faces, field-hardened men, toughened mountaineers, dedicated youngsters of good breeding – they all had their heads back, roaring the rollicking words, filling the air with sound as the iron caravan coiled away in its cloud of dust into the desert.

Then, in the windows of the last coach, just as García had warned, Slattery found himself staring at the faces of four men he had seen before, tall, straight men with stiff collars which made no concessions to the heat. One of them was Fausto Graf and immediately everything that Horrocks had told him rushed into his mind.

Jesus, he thought, I'm behaving like one of his bloody agents! He tried to push the thought from his mind, endeavouring to convince himself it was Horrocks' business, not his.

Atty was watching him. 'Bloody Germans,' he said. 'But they can't do much harm in the middle of the army, can they?'

Slattery gestured. 'Don't you believe it, Atty,' he said. 'When it comes to dirty work, Europe has this side of the Atlantic knocked into a cocked hat. We've been at it longer.' He stared at the tail of the moving train and suddenly, with some force, he remembered more of Horrocks' words in Mexico City. 'If it comes to war, it'll be *your* war as much as mine,' and he realized he *was* involved, despite himself.

'I'm going after them,' he said. 'They'll have Villa attacking Juárez and it only needs a few shells across the border to bring the American army across the Rio Grande.'

7

The hills outside Chihuahua were full of angry, disappointed men.

To Slattery's surprise, he met waggons rolling southwards, lurching and swaying over the ruts of the uneven roads, among them stumbling soldiers, their weapons and equipment in no semblance of order, their faces sullen with all the signs of defeat. With them were their women, plodding after them in their black dresses and blue rebozos, their shoulders hunched under their loads of pots and pans and food, their children clinging to their skirts. Groups of horsemen pushed among them, slouched in the saddle, and here and there was a buggy containing the body of an officer, his sombrero over his face, dripping blood at every step of the horse. Then he passed a gun that had burst; men, horses and fragments of wheel were strewn across the ground and a corpse was caught up in a high saguaro cactus, its entrails showing, its clothes blasted off. In the arroyos were more wounded, and dead men staring with sightless eyes, flies gathering on their moustaches, the vultures wheeling in the empty sky above.

Villa's headquarters were at a ranch to the south of the city and, arriving dusty, thirsty and tired, Slattery found Vegas, of the Holy Trinity, sitting at a table, and no sign of anyone else.

'What's been happening?'

'We've been beaten,' Vegas said sourly. 'We ran out of ammunition.'

'Where is he now ?'

'He gave the rearguard to Herrera and disappeared with eight hundred cavalry and five hundred railwaymen on horses with tools for wrecking the track. It's not like him to abandon his army.'

Slattery gestured. 'You've got it wrong, Vegas,' he said.

135

'He hasn't abandoned the army. He's decided to forget Chihuahua and gone for Juárez instead.'

He found Villa at a small station further up the line. He was stopped two miles to the south of it by a body of horsemen armed to the teeth, who appeared first as a cloud of dust in the desert and drew to a halt in the usual Mexican fashion, in a tremendous flourish that sat the horses back on their haunches.

'Where's your general?'

An arm was flung out. 'Terrazas. Listening in to the Federals' messages on the telegraph. He's going to give those pigs of Federals in Juárez the drubbing we didn't manage at Chihuahua.'

Slattery kicked his horse into a trot. 'Take me to him,' he said.

Terrazas was a small town of colonial houses surrounded by the adobe dwellings of the poor. There was the usual high-towered church facing the mayor's office across a square centred by an ugly purple-and-yellow bandstand of sheet metal and cast iron, and surrounded by clubbed jacarandas in which clouds of magpies chattered. The railway ran along the outskirts and he found Villa in the telegraph office with Rodolfo Fierro, the railway expert Urbina had found, Monserrat, Preto, a few of his telegraphists and the terrified stationmaster. As Slattery appeared, Villa swung round, his face dark.

'What are you doing here, inglés?' he snapped. 'I left you in Torreón to look after my interests.'

'I'm looking after your interests here.'

'I don't need you here. Tómas Urbina picked up two ammunition trains and I'm signalling Herrera now to bring the rest of the army up. We're going to hit Juárez from the west.'

'Whose idea was that?'

Villa's topaz eyes blazed and his erratic temper flared. 'What does it matter to you, inglés?'

'Whose idea, Don Pancho? Was it your idea? Or did it come from the Germans?'

136

Villa's jaw dropped. 'How did you know that? They had a plan.'

'I'll bet they did. If you attack from the west your overs will drop in El Paso.'

Villa shrugged. 'Everybody who attacks Juárez has overs that drop in El Paso. It's well known. Now get out of the way and let me get on with my work.'

'Listen, mi General,' Slattery pleaded. 'Those Germans are hoping for trouble. You want advice. I'm giving you advice.'

'I don't like your advice, inglés.'

Slattery drew a deep breath, aware that he was doing Horrocks' job for him and far from happy at the knowledge. 'Like it or not,' he said, 'an attack on Juárez is just what the Germans want. The border's lined with American soldiers.'

'I can take on the Norteamericanos.'

'Don't delude yourself, Don Pancho. They have more ammunition than you ever dreamed about and, if you start killing people in El Paso, they'll cross the border.'

'Mexico will rise.'

'It might have to, because those Germans will stir it up into an invasion. They want to get the United States involved. Carranza wants it, too, so he can point to you as the villain of the piece. You've become too popular.'

The last point clearly struck home and Villa scowled. 'I don't understand politics.' He was scratching his head as though trying to dig his way to the thoughts inside, frowning heavily like a peasant cheated out of his cow. He looked up at Fierro, his railway expert. 'How long would it take to bring up the army?'

'Five days. Perhaps longer.'

'Very well, we'll do it with the men we have. What have we in the way of rolling stock?'

'There's a train-load of coal from Juárez for Chihuahua.'

Villa whirled round to the frightened stationmaster. 'Wire Juárez that revolutionary forces are threatening the line to the south and ask if you're to risk sending the coal train through?'

A pistol was put at the head of the terrified telegraphist,

137

and a message came back quickly from Juárez that there was no way of guarding the line. Villa's message in reply, apparently originated by the stationmaster, said that two ammunition trains had arrived in Terrazas from Chihuahua but that a cloud of dust was visible to the south and was thought to be the first sight of the rebel army moving north. This time the message that came back ordered the coal train back to Juárez and gave instructions that the ammunition trains were to follow immediately behind it.

There was a whoop of delight from the listening men and Villa grinned. 'The door's wide open,' he said.

'What about the Germans?' Monserrat asked.

Villa gestured indifferently. 'We'll have them shot. But not now. Later. We have things to do.'

Slattery found the Germans in the only hotel in Terrazas. It was constructed round a patio filled with palms, and they were sitting in the shade with outstretched legs, drinking beer. Fausto Graf was with them and as Slattery appeared, he jumped to his feet. Seeing his alarm, the other Germans also rose.

One of them, the tall, good-looking authoritative man Slattery had seen in Nogales, stepped forward. 'I'm Franz von Raschstadt –'

'I know.' Slattery answered in German.

'Who are you?'

'Never mind who I am.' Slattery smiled. 'I've come with a warning. Because I don't want Villa to make a fool of himself and present your country with an incident that might start trouble.'

'What incident's this?'

'In about half an hour's time, he's going to have you all shot. I think that might make an incident, don't you?'

Graf stepped forward. 'This has nothing to do with you, Englander,' he snapped.

'It seems to have a lot to do with you, Fausto, so when your friends leave, it might be as well if you leave, too. That pistol of Villa's has a very fluky trigger.'

Graf stared at Slattery with hot eyes and for once with

no sign of a smile. Then, as the others headed into the hotel to pick up their belongings, he turned on his heel and followed them.

When Slattery returned to the railway siding, the coal train was being emptied in a hanging cloud of black dust, its load dumped at the side of the track by men using shovels, pieces of wood, even their hands, to do the job quickly. Further along, freight cars from the ammunition trains had been shunted into the siding and were also being emptied. Alongside them ramps were hurriedly built of planks and horses led up, then dusty companies of men began to march in. There was no order in their dress or in their drill, and they were led by boys of eighteen in peón cotton or captains of sixty-five in leggings, spats, wing-collars, waiscoats and watch-chains.

'See that the telegraph's cut both ways, Rudolfo,' Villa ordered and Fierro's men began to wrench out the telegraphic equipment and other men on horses were sent along the track with reatas to tear down the wires. Firemen sweated over the furnaces of the locomotives and steam began to hiss.

'How far away is it, inglés?' Villa asked.

'Four hours.'

'We shall arrive just after midnight. Get aboard.'

Grinning excitedly, dark-faced men waited alongside the solitary line that stretched away into flat infinity through a desert purple with evening light. Its open gondolas now filled with men already black from the residue of its cargo, the coal train jerked into movement. As it clunked its way over the points, the other trains followed, the box cars lurching, scared-looking drivers leaning from the cabs, armed Villistas behind them holding cocked revolvers. As they jolted into motion, Slattery pulled himself aboard the last wagon.

Ciudad Juárez appeared earlier than they had expected and the leading train came to a halt on the flat plain just to the south. Men scrambled down to stare at the lights of the city in the distance and the brighter lights of El Paso just across the Rio Grande.

'Is it true, mi Coronel,' someone asked wistfully, 'that Americans eat meat every day?'

Villa called a conference alongside the track, standing in the pale yellow light from the caboose he was using as his headquarters.

'Work back from here,' he told Fierro. 'Tear up the rails and destroy all culverts and bridges, I want no reinforcements coming up until we're ready to meet them.'

As Fierro disappeared, Villa gestured to the distant lights. 'We'll do it quietly,' he said. 'The less damage there is, the more El Paso will like us. You've all been here before. So you know where the barracks are and where the jail is. I want them taken quickly.'

As they rolled into the yards in Juárez there were only the yellow lights in the huts of the track workers to be seen. Here and there an occasional figure moved and an occasional voice called out. As the trains drew to a halt, nobody took the slightest notice of them, then, as the brakes squeaked, doors rumbled open and men in full fighting equipment and covered from neck to waist in ammunition slipped to the track. Quiet orders got them moving. The trains had been signalled and nothing was suspected and, picking up the step, the ragged companies began to push through the town.

Filled with Mexicans and Americans who had come from the other side of the Rio Grande for a night out on the town, the night clubs and casinos were pulsing with the sound of music and the shouts from the gambling tables. A few people were about, mostly Federal soldiers staring at the lights and a few interested gringos moving along the ill-lit streets. Recent rains had formed puddles on the uneven surfaces of the roads and the dim street-lamps cast sinister shadows. Occasionally there was a tinkling burst of piano music, the screech of a fiddle or the twanging of a guitar. The smell of cooking food and stale drink filled the air. Down a side-street someone was singing.

'If to your window should come Huerta
Give him cold tortillas and send him on his way . . .'

From the other side of the street there was an explosion of shouts as a fight broke out. The whole place was alive from the Avenida Septiembre 16 to the American border.

Forming up in dark squares, watched only by beggars and a few late-moving women and children, the dust-blackened invaders kept silent. Then some onlooker, brighter than the rest, realized what was happening and started to run. One of the Villistas saw him and lifted his rifle. The echoes of the shot clattered against the flat walls and sent the crowds scattering for the alleyways as the runner fell on his face, his wide-brimmed hat rolling away like a hoop. A woman screamed and shutters slammed to, then the plank doors that sealed the shops were swung into place and lights were doused.

'No point in waiting any longer,' Slattery said.

Warnings were already being yelled but the Villistas surged through the streets to the brightly-lit centre of the city at such a speed the alarm was swamped even before it got going.

'*Qué viva Villa! Arriba la Revolución!*'

At the shout, saloon doors opened and faces appeared at windows. An outbreak of firing stopped the laughter and the music dead. The hubbub faded and people emerging into the streets to see what was happening promptly turned round and bolted back inside, struggling to break through those still trying to get out to see the fun.

Black-faced Villistas in wide hats and criss-crossed with bandoliers of ammunition appeared in the doorways of clubs, dance halls and casinos, spurs jingling, guns in their fists. Employees and customers were lined up against the walls and invited to make contributions to the revolutionary war chest. No threats were made but most of the civilians and Americans were only too pleased to empty their pockets into the sacks and sombreros held out by the grinning soldiers. The gambling dens were cleaned out to the tune of half a million pesos.

141

The senior officers of the Federal garrison were caught without difficulty. A few nights before they had attended a performance by an American stock theatre company in El Paso where they had been entertained by the cast, and as the Villistas arrived, the American actors were returning the visit and were halfway through an impromptu performance of a scene from *Il Trovatore* with the tenor – almost a replica of Stutzmann – in full stride when the door burst open to reveal a bunch of grinning dusty men, all armed to the teeth. Their bag included the deputy commander and all his staff.

'Norteamericanos over there! No harm will come to you! Federal officers over here! You'll be shot!'

Streaming through the streets, their black faces white-runnelled with sweat, the Villistas were inside the sleeping barracks before anyone knew they had arrived. Sentries, sergeants and officers were swept aside before they could lift a finger. Half-dressed, terrified men began to boil out of doors and windows like ants from a nest, scuttling for their lives down the dark alleyways, throwing aside tunics, caps and weapons as they ran. A leaderless mob of Federal soldiers began to stream from the city towards the ravine of the Rio Bravo and the safety of the desert darkness, or to hide themselves in the throng hurrying for the International Bridge and the shelter of El Paso. Men in fragments of evening dress and uniform hid themselves among the frightened Americans and only here and there a group of Orozquistas, knowing what Villa had in store for them, attempted to resist. They were shot down where they stood.

The attack had been a complete surprise. Within three hours the city was in Villa's hands. In one bold stroke, with eight hundred eager men and five hundred railway track workers, with only a scattering of shots and not a single casualty, the uneducated peón who was sneered at wherever Colegio Militar officers met, had captured the most important city in the north with all its vast stores of ammunition and weapons and its easy access to the cornucopia of supplies on the American border.

Slattery caught up with Villa at the Customs House.

142

'You like the way I did it, inglés?' Villa called out.

'A perfect Trojan horse, Don Pancho.'

Villa's brows wrinkled. 'Who is this Trojan? And what's so special about his horse? See that the Americans put my picture in their papers. Tomorrow, I'll have the bands in the street to show they will come to no harm.'

Persuading Monserrat to drive him to the river, Slattery joined the crowd swarming for the International Bridge, where he hired a car to the trolley-bus terminus and caught a tram into El Paso.

At the offices of the newspaper, he dug out the caretaker and unearthed the address of the editor. At his knocking, the editor's head appeared from a window over the door, red-faced and angry until Slattery told him what had happened. Then, unashamed in pink long johns, he showed the coal-blackened Slattery into his living room while his wife, her hair in curl papers, prepared coffee.

'Captured Juárez!' The editor was bewildered. 'Hell, there's been no fighting!'

As the bodies of the Orozquistas were loaded into carts, outside the Customs House hordes of anxious businessmen, admirers, position-seekers and well-wishers waited to see Villa. News of his victory had been reported by the El Paso paper and the former peón was the man of the hour and newspapermen of every shape and size and representing every possible political angle began to stream into the town.

'Tell them how we won, inglés,' Villa said. 'Tell them *we* did it. Us. On our own, without help.'

While Slattery tried to pass out information to the yelling crowd of men and women demanding facts, the bridges across the border were opened and, to show that all was well and that the Americans had nothing to fear, Villa had the Federal bands mustered and marched through the town to celebrate the victory. Mingling with the crowds of wide-eyed souvenir hunters and government agents were emissaries of foreign powers, soldiers of fortune and women prepared to sell themselves to the highest bidder. Emerging from the murky shadows of Mexican politics, Villa had

143

become the dominant figure overnight, a man whose views were suddenly important, not only on both sides of the border but in Foreign Offices in Europe. Knowing he could well soon be master of Mexico, big businesses which had been backing Huerta started looking round hurriedly for someone who could restore the sort of government that profited them most.

As they celebrated, however, news arrived that the Federal general in Chihuahua was mobilizing another five thousand men to retake the town and a messenger appeared, swamped against the cold in an ankle-length civilian overcoat, with the information that troop trains were being mustered for the counter attack.

Villa shrugged. 'We'll be ready,' he said. 'We'll show Don Venus who cracks the whip in Mexico.'

'You've also shown him that the north's wide open to him,' Slattery pointed out dryly. 'He no longer has to stay in Nogales. And now he can move, he can claim he's the official representative of the whole of Northern Mexico. And since everybody, including you, has officially accepted him as the First Chief of the Constitutionalist Party, that's *exactly* what he's just become.'

Villa looked up under his eyebrows, his hat on the back of his head, his feet shuffling in the dust, his hands thrust deep in his pockets. 'That's not what I wanted to hear, inglés,' he growled. 'You've just spoiled my dinner.'

8

The capture of Juárez had opened the border to the rebels and American arms began to flow across the Rio Grande. They arrived hidden in pianos, under waggonloads of coal, in crates of tinned food, under planks, in trucks labelled whiskey. The prices were extortionate because a lot of people north of the border were making a fortune out of Mexico's tragedy, but the Constitutionalists were happy to pay and Villa was raising the money with rustled steers.

Juárez was just returning to normal when the Stutzmann zarzuela company arrived to put on *Luisa Fernanda*. As the group, lead singers and chorus, all marshalled by Stutzmann in his high shrill tenor, climbed from the train after a round-about journey that had included a motor and lorry detour round Chihuahua by Parral, the soldiers swarming in the station entrance recognized Magdalena and started yelling for her to sing.

It was impossible to refuse so the train was held up as she stood on the steps of her compartment while the orchestra unpacked their fiddles, guitars and cellos and tuned up. She gave them '*La Paloma*'. She sang it first as a love song, low and sweet, then she gave it to them as a battle song, belting it out until the whole crowd, a good two thousand of them, were roaring it with her. As they yelled for more, she raised her hands.

'No, no. That's enough. I'm tired. I need to rest my voice.'

She sang them '*La Golodrina*', the song of farewell, and as she turned away, she found herself face to face with Slattery, tall, strong, red-haired, with his fox's face.

There was always something breath-taking about him that made his appearance like a physical impact, and his bland impudence always made her want to laugh. Finding herself swept away by a mounting wave that was beyond her control, she closed her eyes for a second like a swimmer plunging into the sea.

'Come and see me, Fitz,' she said. 'I'm staying at the hotel near the Church of the Virgin of Guadalupe. Not now – tomorrow. I'm busy now. Hermann's made me a partner and I can't leave everything to him.'

With Atty strutting round the town in a knickerbocker suit, cap and celluloid collar looking for girls, and with Jesús, growing rapidly as he ate proper meals for the first time in his life, in attendance in a store suit as stiff as a plank with a string tie and a straw boater, Slattery was free to head for Magdalena's hotel on his own.

She had risen late after the previous night's performance and was in a loose gown of blue that matched her eyes. She wore little make-up but it seemed to enhance rather than detract from her beauty. She held out her hands to Slattery and they stood for a moment in silence, holding each other, then she pushed him away and held him at arm's length.

'They say you don't love me,' she told him.

'Who say?'

'The company. Hermann. They are most concerned. They know all about you disappearing and they all know I've followed you. Chihuahua to Torreón. Torreón to Mexico City. Mexico City here.'

'You were following *me*?'

She laughed. 'Hadn't you guessed? Of course I was. I persuaded Hermann to find bookings near you. I've a lot of influence with Hermann. He's been in love with me for years.'

Slattery grinned. 'And they say I don't love you?'

Her fingers tightened on his. 'I want to hear it from you. If you have other loves I want to hear it in your own words.'

He looked at her with narrowed eyes. 'You know,' he said, without a smile, 'all this sounds like a line from an operetta.'

She stared at him, blank-eyed and innocent, then she gave a gurgle of laughter. 'It's a song,' she admitted. 'A Mexican song. Mexicans have such a gift for saying things from the heart.'

146

'How much of it is true?'

'If you love me, I shall own a piece of Heaven.'

'Is that a song too?'

She flung herself into his arms, and he swung her round, her feet off the floor. 'It's the same song. But it says everything I want to say. I couldn't say it better if I'd rehearsed it.'

'I bet you did a bit.'

'On, *mein lieber* Slattery, perhaps a little. For when I saw you again. You're not going to vanish this time, are you?'

He shrugged. 'The story is that the Federals at Chihuahua are on their way. There could be fighting. At the slightest sign of trouble, make sure you slip across the border. El Paso will always welcome you.'

'I promise. But come after the show tonight. I'll be on my own and I need you. Promise me that.'

That evening, dressed in his best, Slattery slipped into the theatre at the end of the first act, sent a note to the dressing-rooms, and prepared to wait until the end and fight off all comers for the privilege of driving Magdalena to her hotel. But he had just settled down on a chair thoughtfully provided by an attendant at the back of the pit when Jesús crept in and touched his elbow.

'You're wanted, your honour,' he said. 'General Huerta's sent a large force by rail from Chihuahua. The telegraphist at the station's just picked up the news from Zaragoza. Fierro's moved down the line with locomotives, chains and hooks and started tearing up the tracks. They say he's almost within cannon range of the Federals.'

For a moment, remembering his promise to Magdalena, Slattery considered ignoring the order, but it was urgent and couldn't be thrust aside, and he'd been a soldier too long.

The second act had only just started but it was impossible to wait, so, getting hold of the manager, he wrote a note and left it to be delivered to Magdalena's dressing room. When he reached headquarters, the Mayor of El Paso was with Villa. Apologies had already been made for the single American life lost during the fall of Juárez.

147

'Tell him, inglés,' Villa said '- in good words he can understand – that when the Federals come I'll meet them in the desert far enough south to prevent any bullets flying across the border. Tell him we'll meet them at Tierra Blanca, thirty-five miles away.'

'I don't think he expects you to go that far south, Don Pancho,' Slattery said.

Villa gave him a sly look. 'I haven't chosen Tierra Blanca to please the gringos, compadre,' he murmured. 'When God made Mexico, he forgot the water, and if we occupy the station at Tierra Blanca, we shall have plenty and the Federals, who will be in the plain, will have none.'

The vast shabby horde that lined up on the baked desolation outside Juárez would never have looked like a military host to a European. Supplied from the vast stores captured at Juárez, however, they comprised one of the finest armies Mexico could boast.

It was hot, parching and dry, and the massed columns of the Divisione del Norte began to defile to left and right, lines of soldiers moving from the shade of the few trees into the glare of the sun. Bugles blared their calls and flags flapped, some of them the red, white and green of Mexico with their eagle and serpent symbol, some of them banners bearing private badges, private mottos and private challenges. 'Death to Huerta!' 'The Terror Men.' 'The Golden Boys.'

A few groups were armed only with old Springfield rifles, their cartridges carried in their pockets, and it was only the better-armed, better-dressed, better-mounted units which were close to the spectators. Slattery, busy since the previous evening, had marshalled the correspondents at a good vantage point and a newsreel man was standing in the back of a truck, cranking his camera. As Villa passed, a helper slanted a large round mirror stolen from a hotel dressing-table to throw the sunshine against his face and kill the shadow under his hat.

Among the moving throng rumbled and jolted the field pieces, their iron-shod wheels throwing up dust as they turned. Big-hatted white-bloused pacificos stood among the dark-coated city dwellers and the American tourists from El Paso. An old man driving his goats homeward became entangled at one point and threw the parade into confusion. Out of pure mischief, a group of troopers sent the goats running in different directions while the army shouted with laughter. But when one of the men was foolish enough to show off his prowess with a gun by dropping one of the animals with a shot and a wail of anguish went up from the owner, Villa was on the scene immediately, swinging a heavy revolver. The guilty marksman rolled from his saddle to the ground, holding a bloody head.

'Give him its value!' Villa roared.

'But, mi General!'

As Villa lifted his revolver, the terrified man fished in his pockets and sent a shower of coins flying through the air. The crowd burst out clapping and the ancient goatherd was reduced to stammering gratitude.

'The Mother of God, the Blessed Niño and Our Lady of Guadalupe ride with you, mi General!'

As the parade finished, the army began to move towards the east, as though about to make a wide circling movement back to their encampment, but only troops who were short of weapons and ammunition continued towards the town. As soon as they were out of sight of the spectators the rest wheeled away to where the trains waited. A ten-piece orchestra played them off.

The newspapermen were quicker than the rest to notice that Villa's crack units had not returned and the newsreel man jolted off south on his own with the flat-topped van he used for developing the plates for stills. As Atty drove after them, Slattery sat alongside him in silence. He had written a long letter to Magdalena and left it with Stutzmann, but he knew he would need to do more than that. It had been a cavalier way of treating her and his mind was full of her face, of her half-smiling eyes that suddenly seemed to be inviting, and the way she walked with long supple strides, tall and slender and somehow always summery. He was growing disillusioned with Villa and the war. There had been a time when he had felt war was his whole life, when he couldn't ever imagine being a civilian. Now he wasn't so sure.

As they headed away from Juárez towards a village called San Pedro Solitario where Villa was making his head-quarters, Magdalena was watching from the crowd and saw the big Studebaker go by. She was elegant in purple with a magnificent hat and veil that were completely out of place in the dusty barbarism of the plain. Hermann Stutzmann was with her and, without turning, she spoke over her shoulder to him.

'He's gone, Hermann. I dressed up for him and he didn't even see me.'

'He's a soldier, Magdalena.' Stutzmann was a kind man and was always concerned for the members of his company. He had cared for them through a variety of crises and Magdalena had always been a favourite.

'He sent a letter,' he added.

As the motor car vanished, she stared after it for a while then her eyes misted over and she blew her nose.

'You can't hold a letter in your arms,' she whispered.

During the drive south, Slattery learned that Villa had come up with the Federals at Tierra Blanca as he had planned, just in time to deny them the water tanks, and the following morning news arrived that the battle had started. As the information spread, San Pedro became a hotbed of excite-ment, the newspapermen already on the move, clambering into automobiles and swinging away in a cloud of dust.

By the following day they learned that the Federals, desperate for water, had tried to attack on the opposite end of the front but had been forced back a second time by an army that was well supplied with food and ammunition from Juárez and possessed water in abundance. Already Americans were crossing the international bridge from El Paso with loads of blankets, medicine and money, and private cars were arriving in streams with supplies and volunteer nurses.

There were uneasy rumours, however, that twelve troop

150

trains had been sent up from Chihuahua with reserves for a tremendous final push to take Tierra Blanca. The telegraphist at the station had information that the trains had already left.

A group of Villista officers were crouched over the key in the telegraph office watching the operator's pencil as he demanded news, and at headquarters men arrived on horses and in cars to consult with others bent over maps. Then Villa arrived, dusty from the battle, his clothes splashed with blood. Even as his horse, ridden to the point of collapse, its flanks smeared with froth, was led away in a stumbling walk, he was issuing orders, gathering up reserves and despatching them to the fighting. Seeing Slattery, he made an angry movement with his hand.

'Fierro,' he said. 'He needs help.'

It took only a few minutes to find Atty and raise a troop of reliable men, then the whole lot roared out of town, lashing at their mounts with reins, whips, hats, anything they possessed. Despite the fact that they were supposed to know and respect horse-flesh, the Mexicans always drove their animals to the limit, indifferent if they dropped dead at the end of a heart-straining gallop.

Swinging to the west, they found Fierro's train with its wrecking equipment behind a rise in the ground. Ahead of it, in a long narrow bowl of land surrounded by low hills, the track had been torn up for half a mile and all the telegraph wires pulled down. Fierro's men were waiting, the horses and pack mules they had transported by train behind them as they watched the plain.

Below them, beyond the gap in the track, eleven of the twelve troop trains that had been reported were standing one behind the other, their locomotives dribbling smoke and steam. Alongside them, men had already started to work among the displaced rails and torn-up ties with crow-bars and sledge hammers. The engine of the leading train had been disconnected and was moving backwards and forwards, steam jetting in noisy blasts as it dragged the heavy rails into place.

Fierro was frowning deeply and Atty spoke in that flat,

disinterested way he had. 'Orozco once stopped a trainload of reinforcements with one locomotive,' he said.

Fierro's head jerked round and his eyes glittered as his railwayman's mind understood at once. He was a dangerous brute who took a delight in killing, but he was also a railwayman and knew everything there was to know about locomotives, rolling stock and track.

'Go south, inglés,' he said to Slattery. 'The telegraphist at Tierra Blanca said the last train had been held up with hot axle boxes. Let us know when it appears. We might just have time.'

Circling the stalled trains, from the summit of a small hill to the south Slattery's group saw the smoke of the twelfth train appear over a rise in the contour of the land. Riding back, they found the railwaymen had also by-passed the halted Federals and were swarming across the track at a point where it ran through a narrow gulley in the hills. They were blocking the rails with logs and rocks and, even as Slattery and his men arrived, Fierro gestured and the railwaymen began to withdraw beyond the lips of the gulley.

As the train came in sight, the railwaymen gripped their weapons, their teeth bared in anticipation. It drew nearer, the driver's head visible, then there was a shout and the screech of brakes being applied. As the locomotive halted at the barrier, men jumped to the track to investigate and the crash of Fierro's volley dropped every one of them.

The Federal conscripts immediately began to throw down their weapons and fling up their hands. A few officers tried to organize a defence but the soldiers ignored them and within a quarter of an hour the train was in Fierro's hands and he had the officers, hatless, weaponless, with blood on their clothes, lined up alongside the track.

'Shoot them,' he ordered.

One of them started forward. 'You can't shoot me,' he said. 'I'm German.'

He was only young and Slattery had seen him more than once with Fausto Graf. 'He's German all right,' he agreed.

Fierro was indifferent. 'In that case,' he said, 'he shouldn't be here. Shoot him twice.'

As the protesting man was dragged away, squads of men were already sweating to remove the barricade and shift boxes and sacks from the pack mules to the tender of the big locomotive. The remaining men were split into two parties and sent off in a swirl of dust behind the slopes to east and west. As Fierro climbed into the cab with the driver, the train began to move.

Halting the train again at a point where they could see the trains on the track below, Fierro set his men to unloading the boxes and sacks from the tender and lashing them to the cowcatcher of the locomotive.

'Dynamite,' he grinned.

In a long snake, the eleven trains on the plain were still stationary, engineers and trackworkers swarming across the rails. The troops were keeping out of sight in the coaches to avoid the sun, and the noise of the skirmish beyond the hill had been drowned beneath the shouting, the clang of hammers, the whistling of the locomotives and the roaring of steam.

As Fierro gestured with his pistol, the driver climbed back into his cab with his fireman. Fierro climbed up with him.

'*Vamonos!*'

Steam screeched, wheels spun and the train jerked forward, Fierro's men cantering alongside to the top of the rise. As Fierro shouted for full throttle, the train began to gather speed and the crew jumped from the cab. Fierro was the last to leave. Picking himself up, he mounted a horse led forward by one of his men.

'Now, inglés,' he said. 'Watch. That last coach down there contains explosives.'

The troop trains were still motionless, engine to caboose, engine to caboose, for nearly a mile along the track. The captured train was still moving behind a curve of the land out of sight, gathering speed all the time so that when it finally burst into view, smoke rolling backwards in a coiling grey ribbon, it was rocking wildly in a mad charge down the slope.

As it appeared, figures began to boil out of the coaches

153

in the plain. They heard the clank of couplings and the shriek of steam as the rearmost locomotive jolted forward. But it could go no more than fifty yards before it came up against the rear coach of the train immediately in front. Men began to gesture wildly and the train ahead moved forward in a frantic attempt to make room, only to run into the rear end of the train ahead. The wheels of the caboose lifted from the track and they saw dust and stones flung up as the rails twisted. By now, men were starting to run, scattering into the desert among the cactus and mesquite. As the oncoming engine smashed into the last coach of the last stationary train, locomotive and coach reared up in a thunder of crashing iron and roaring steam, then the whole desert split apart in a sheet of flame. A terrific jolt shook the earth, sending a gale of hot air across the plain, and the running men were felled by the blast as a huge coil of dense black smoke filled with flashes of orange leapt skywards and began to spread outwards in a vast mushroom. The explosions blended into one long howl and flames flew along the wrecked trains like the gush of a blow lamp. Their nostrils caught by the peppery smell of explosives, the watching men round Fierro were caught by a vast hot breath as if they were staring into a furnace.

Huge steel wheels hurtled through the air with fragments of wood and human flesh and showered down among the running men, thudding to the earth in puffs of dust. Planks from the shattered box cars were coming down like leaves, sliding through the air as they fell.

'*María, Madre de Dios,*' someone breathed. 'Holy Mother of God!'

It was a sight Slattery knew he would remember all his life.

For a long time nobody moved, as if the shock of explosion had paralyzed them, then the men who had bolted for the safety of the desert began to turn back to drag their injured comrades from the wreckage.

Fierro laughed. 'It's time to go,' he said.

The whole desert below seemed to be filled with panic-stricken voices as the swarm of armed railwaymen swung down, yelling and whooping. More horsemen appeared in a rush from behind the slopes to right and left, waving rifles, swords and machetes, and the Federals began to tear at the debris in a frantic search for dropped weapons. But the explosion had shattered every scrap of order and the Villistas were among them immediately. As they scattered, another wave of men from Villa's army at Tierra Blanca, alerted by Fierro's messenger, swept out of the hills in that direction.

Unable to advance or retreat, caught on every side, the Federals were flung aside like chaff, only the officers managing to move backwards in an orderly fashion. Within moments, however, they were scattered too and the Villistas were galloping among the running men at full speed as if they had gone raving mad, screaming, shooting, slicing with their weapons at anyone within reach. A young officer, trapped at the side of the wreckage, was caught by Fierro who swung his horse in a cloud of red dust and put his revolver close to the boy's head and pulled the trigger. The headless corpse was flung back against the side of a tilted coach.

Men were charging through the trains now, flinging things out – mattresses, quilts, blankets, clothes, equipment, uniforms, bodies. A group of hysterical women who, confident of the outcome, had been accompanying the officers to watch the battle, were trying to flee and the Villistas were snatching at them, tearing at their clothes and hair as they shrieked for mercy. One of them, no more than a girl, was being heaved towards the scrub by a huge man in a ragged uniform, his face twisted in a great grin.

The only real resistance came from a group in one of the carriages in the centre of the line of trains who fought back bravely until one of the railwaymen, crawling along the track between the wheels, planted a charge and the whole carriage went up in a shower of splinters, shattered planks, torn metal and flying glass.

The slaughter went on until the desert was splashed with blood, the scrub and sand marked with bright red blotches, with pools where men huddled in the grotesque attitudes of death. Scraps of uniform fluttered from the spikes of

155

cactus where they had been flung and the gritty earth was covered with abandoned equipment, weapons and corpses beneath a cloud of vultures which wheeled in the empty sky.

Only slowly did the massacre subside and the shouting and screaming die, to leave a few bewildered prisoners and a few sobbing half-clothed women sitting alongside the twisted iron and splintered wood of the wreckage, their whimpers dulled by the hissing of steam, their shapes blurred by the rolling smoke from the burning carriages.

Slattery hadn't moved from the hill and for a long time he remained where he was, watching the rout. His face was grim and his mind was full of Magdalena, full of a bleak knowledge that he had broken his promise to her in exchange for this horror going on below him in the plain. He had broken promises to her all along the way, too many promises, too many trusts. And uneasily, through his feeling that he had betrayed her, came the feeling that his involvement as a soldier of fortune owing allegiance to Villa and the revolution ran counter to the interests of his own country. In serving Villa, was he failing to serve Britain? Horrocks seemed to think so.

By his side, Atty watched, his face as blank as ever, suffering none of Slattery's doubts. The idea of using the train as a moving bomb was not new, but Mexican vengefulness, Mexican indifference to death, Mexican thoroughness when it came to murder, had carried it far beyond his original conception.

The roadbed had been turned into a blackened smoking hole for fifty yards, scattered with torn rails, scorched sleepers and the twisted wreckage of locomotives and coaches. For fifty yards on either side there were bodies and fragments of bodies, some with their clothing and hair burned away, the few survivors holding their heads and weeping in the middle of a charred wasteland. The few trees had been stripped of their foliage, the brush was scorched, and the track was contorted as if a giant hand had wrenched it up.

For a long time, Slattery stared at the scene. His

156

behaviour, he knew, always gave the impression of enormous self-confidence, but he had often been unsure of
himself in the maelstrom of Mexican politics and their
impact on Europe. Throughout his life he had always acted
on impulse and he suddenly began to suspect that his self-
assertiveness was not sureness but sprang from an uncer-
tainty that made him an easy victim of circumstances.

Desperately aware of his limitations, he shifted restlessly
in the saddle. Atty was studying him now, willing always to
go along with him with a courage and a loyalty he sometimes
felt he couldn't match. Drawing a deep breath, he
straightened his back and kicked his horse to a walk, then
together he and Atty rode slowly towards the plain, moving
in silence through the grinning victors and their wretched
victims.

Part III

1

San Pedro Solitario was full of wounded men, every house crammed with them out of the sweeping dust, the lightly-hurt propped up in doorways away from the wind, the village women forming a procession of black-clad figures to carry water for them from the stream. The Villistas were still celebrating the victory with dancing in the streets when a horseman came tearing into the town in a cloud of dust. As he drew to a stop, his exhausted animal collapsed with a crash, its nostrils blowing out pink froth. Scrambling to his feet, the rider ran in a stumbling gait towards Villa who had driven in to savour his success.

'They've abandoned Chihuahua City!' he yelled.

For a long time Villa was silent, staring at his feet, then, as he looked up at Slattery, he drew a deep breath. His face was expressionless, devoid of triumph. 'They'll not come back,' he said.

While the newspapermen were still fighting in a frantic mob to get their despatches away from Tierra Blanca where the sole telegraphist was wilting under the pressure, Atty Purkiss brought a letter to Slattery.

'Found it on one of the bodies,' he said. 'Fair chap. Not a Mexican.'

It was in German and, addressed to Reserve Lieutenant Erhardt Odebrett, welcomed him to Mexico City.

'I wonder if there was one on every train,' Atty said.

When Villa returned to Juárez, Slattery and Atty travelled with him, the Studebaker lashed to a flat car. There was no sign of Magdalena or the Sutzmann company. Only Stutzmann himself remained, pale and nervous.

'They've crossed the border,' he said. 'We're doing *El Balcon de Palacio* in Houston. It's Magdalena they listen to.

161

Not me. Not the chorus. They become rowdy when the men appear and shout, "Go away, it's the girls we want." '

'Where's Magdalena now?'

'In El Paso.' The fat tenor, older than he looked fished in his pocket and produced an envelope. 'She left you a letter.'

It was a chilly little epistle, offering no solace, no comfort, but also demanding no explanations, simply stating where she was going and no more. It ended with a cold comment 'War seems more to you than civilization'.

'Nothing else?'

'Nothing, my friend.'

Slattery's face was blank as he screwed up the note. He was disillusioned by the butchery he had witnessed. Magdalena had been right. Though Villa was neither the hearty Robin Hood the newspapermen made him out to be nor the evil sadist of the staider journals, there were too many ruthless killers among his lieutenants, too many men noted for their indifference to the sanctity of human life. Civil war, Slattery decided, wasn't for him. The cruelty he'd seen had been appalling, the dishonesty and corruption shocking. His venture into mercenary soldiering had been short and he had reached the conclusion that it wasn't to his taste.

When they reached Chihuahua City the Villistas were already running the telephone exchange, the flour mills and the waterworks. Big-hatted, leather-legginged men hung about with weapons were keeping the slaughterhouses open, and others, equally well armed, were sweeping the streets. The charro cavalry, more used to leaping into one of Villa's *golpes terríficos*, those tremendous mounted charges which had so often swept the enemy from the field, had been sent to the confiscated ranchos in the countryside around, with orders to see the city stockyards were kept supplied with meat.

Political prisoners had been freed, schools were being established and the unemployed were being given free passes for the railway to help them find work. To pay for everything Villa had imposed a tax on foreign industry.

162

Foreign industry didn't like it but foreign industry was always pointedly ignored by the revolutionary leaders.

The fall of the two great northern cities was clearly going to mean the end of Huerta, and the arc light of international affairs was revealing Villa, not Carranza, as the dominant figure south of the Rio Grande. It was Villa who was getting rid of Huerta – the one thing the American government wanted – and they were beginning to treat him with considerable respect and not a little awe. The ballads and the pictures that appeared in the shops were only of him. His round moustached face grinned from every sheet, and photographers and artists were making small fortunes out of the portraits they made.

The Division of the North was already re-equipping for a new drive south. Most of the men were still in rags, but after the capture of Juárez and the supply trains there wasn't a single man now without a blanket and a rifle.

In an attempt to introduce some uniformity, Villa had bought surplus American khaki and stetson hats for his crack regiments, though individual taste continued to add ribbons, flowers, plumes and pictures of the Virgin of Guadalupe. Fast-talking American salesmen, their faces wreathed in smiles at the money they were taking from the ignorant Mexicans, unloaded crates of brightly coloured shirts and red silk bandanas. Villa was not deluded.

'They think they're putting it across me,' he said. 'But their shirts are cheap and a unit in red shirts is easy to pick out from a unit in yellow shirts.'

Despite the changes, however, the army remained basically the same nondescript force, though Villa was already shrewdly weeding out the old men and boys who slowed him down and had formed new and special squadrons of cavalry, carefully picked for their skill as riders and marksmen. They rode the best horses and every man was armed with a rifle and two pistols and was hung about with bandoliers of ammunition. Above all, they were single men unencumbered with wives and children. Because of the polished brass badges they wore, they were known as the Dorados, the Golden Boys.

Surrounded by the euphoria that followed the fall of the city, it was some time before Slattery became aware of carriages piled high with luggage heading out of town.

'The Spanish,' Villa explained. 'I told them that if they're found here after five days they'll be shot. I want no Spanish in Mexico. They cross the border at Ojinaga. I've forbidden them the use of the railway.'

'That means they'll have to make their way on foot across three hundred miles of desert.'

'So?'

Slattery was aware he was doing Horrocks' job for him again. 'The Spanish government will protest,' he said.

Villa shrugged. 'Who cares about the Spanish government?'

'What about the children?'

'They're gachupín children. They grow up into gachupín men and women. Mexico has no room for them.'

'Suppose they were your children?'

Villa gave a snort of rage and, yanking out his pistol, he stuck it under Slattery's nose. 'One of these days, inglés,' he said, 'I shall shoot you for your interference. One day I shall be unable to stand your frozen English face any longer and will put a bullet through you.'

It seemed that the protest had achieved nothing but Villa liked children and something had been stirred in the murky, murderous depths of his mind. For a moment he stared at Slattery, then the pistol dropped and he scowled. 'I think you haven't the stomach any more for war, inglés,' he said. 'Was it the wound you got at Torreón? Wounds trouble a man, apart from the pain.'

'You know it wasn't the wound. I've been hurt before.'

'But suddenly you don't like war?'

'Not Mexican war, Don Pancho.'

'Perhaps the Mexican way of making war's different from the European way.'

'In Europe there are such things as rules.'

Villa scratched his nose, puzzled. 'They have rules? For

164

war?' He paused, silent for a long time then he jerked his head. 'Go after the Spanish,' he growled. 'Do what you can for the little ones. Some of the boys are following to see they don't come back. Make sure they don't murder them for their money.'

In the belief that her husband might be in Ojinaga, Consuela Lidgett insisted on accompanying Slattery. As they passed Villa's orders on to the pursuing cavalry, they saw struggling groups of refugees and the graves of those who had died.

The days were scorching and the nights cold and always there was a harsh dry wind lifting the dust in clouds to roughen the skin and chap the lips, and they had to ride in the noonday heat muffled to the eyes, half-suffocated in their blankets to keep out the flying grit.

They slept alongside their hobbled horses near a fire made of torn-up mesquite. Consuela hadn't realized the hardships she faced, and though she didn't complain her face became grey with exhaustion and before they reached Ojinaga they were having to help her on to her horse and ride one on either side of her in case she reeled from the saddle.

Ojinaga was a group of square grey adobe houses with here and there the oriental cupola of an old Spanish church. It was set in a desolate land without trees where the sun went down with the flare of a dying furnace. It was surrounded by scorched desert and bare savage mountains, and during the day sweltered in a blaze of light. Federal soldiers in their shabby white uniforms were everywhere, their eyes always on the south where they expected Villa and his vengeful hordes to appear, or on the north where they could cross to the safety of the United States, and there were nervous outposts round the town linked by patrols of cavalry, sharp against the dying sun.

The defeated Federals were burning equipment and the dusty streets of the town were piled high with all the rubbish of a shattered army. The town had changed hands five times since the revolution had first started in 1911 and hardly a house had a roof and all the walls had holes in them. They were full of disillusioned soldiers, most of them snatched off the streets in Mexico City by Huerta's draft and totally indifferent to who won.

Sick, exhausted and starving civilians were still straggling in, driven on by the fear that Villa was coming. They had spent days crossing the desert, and as they arrived young Federal soldiers were taking advantage of their helplessness to rob them of everything they possessed.

It wasn't difficult to learn that Consuela's husband wasn't there. Nobody had heard of him or could recognize him from the photograph she held out. Crossing the border into Presidio, they made further enquiries. It was a desolate little cluster of adobe dwellings built in deep sand and cotton-wood scrub along the river. The storekeeper was making a fortune from outfitting the refugees and supplying the Federal army with provisions. In the daytime heat he worked stripped to the waist, a large revolver strapped to his belt.

In the only hotel po-faced agents of both sides were hatching plots in every corner. Among them were arms salesmen, Texas rangers and United States soldiers, Germans, Americans and representatives of foreign businesses struggling to get information on employees lost in the interior of Mexico. Along the river bank United States troops were matched on the opposite side by Mexican cavalry, each group warily watching the other.

There was no sign of Lidgett and at the telegraph office no one had seen any sign of any American who might resemble him, while the sheriff, who looked like the popular image of what a Wild West sheriff should look like, with a shotgun under his arm, a revolver at each hip and a Bowie knife in his boot, had no time to look because he was at his wits' end trying to enforce the law against the carrying of arms.

'He's not here,' Consuela decided eventually.

But the following day she heard that someone resembling Lidgett was in the south.

'I'll have to go,' she said.

'Not on your own,' Slattery said. 'We'll find someone you can trust, to go with you.'

166

She was silent for a moment then she reached on tiptoe to kiss him on the cheek. 'Thank you, Slattery,' she said. 'I don't know what I'd do without you.'

2

'The Germans are back, inglés!'

Villa was sitting at a table in the Governor's office in Chihuahua City with his staff, lawyers, civilian advisers, and Carranza's agents, the Holy Trinity, Monserrat, Preto and Vegas. The table was scattered with documents, law books, a few items of military equipment and weapons, and they were discussing the lack of revenue and the fact that nothing was coming from Constitutional headquarters at a time when enormous sums of money were needed to munition the rebel army.

'They're very persistent, these Germans.' Villa pushed a chair forward with his foot. 'They're offering everything we want. They only ask that we cut off oil supplies to Britain in case of war in Europe. Is there going to be a war in Europe, inglés?'

'There could well be.'

'Very well, compadre, let's cut it off.'

Here we go again, Slattery thought bitterly. Horrocks' unpaid agent doing Horrocks' work; willingly or unwillingly, but still doing it.

'In the event of war,' he said, 'that would make you their ally.'

Villa looked at him shrewdly. 'Is England frightened of the Germans?'

'Yes.'

'So how are *we* involved?'

'If it comes to war, without oil the British navy would be unable to sail its warships. And that would mean that unprotected merchant ships would be sunk and innocent people would drown. Some of them children.'

Villa frowned. The fact that most of the children driven to Ojinaga had been saved had pleased him. The frown vanished to be replaced by a grin. '*Pues*, I suppose we must do as El Inglés wants and ignore the offer.' He scratched his head, digging for ideas. 'But in that case we still need money, because that old goat, Carranza, isn't producing any. We can confiscate the estates of the gachupíns, of course. After all, they confiscated them from such as us in the first place. And the cowboys in the army can round up a few more cattle to send over the border. We'll manage.'

He made his decisions quickly, a statesman without the slightest knowledge of statesmanship making his decrees work in the only way he knew.

Slattery listened silently. Since he had returned to Chihuahua, he had heard nothing of Magdalena. He had been out to her house on the Avenida Pacheco, but Victoria, the housekeeper, had no forwarding address. He wondered what she was doing and where she was. Then the argument round the table started again and dragged his mind back to the present.

'There's one problem, mi General,' Monserrat was saying. 'The food stocks in the city are low.'

'Why?' Villa's question came like the shot of a gun.

'The farmers won't bring in their produce. People are hanging on to their money and they think they'll not get paid.'

Villa turned to Slattery. 'What do they do in Europe, inglés,' he asked, 'when there's no money?'

'Produce more.'

'You mean, print it?'

'Carranza's printing it,' Vegas said. 'Why can't we?'

It was true enough. For some time Horrocks' friend, Turner, in Mexico City had been turning out 'cartones', small notes like tram tickets. They were produced strictly on licence but it didn't stop other less honest printers risking the death penalty to produce them without a licence.

'Arrange it.' Villa was frowning. 'We'll have them covered with official-looking signatures and stamped with the faces of Mexican heroes.'

The Feast of the Dead arrived with bunches of yellow *cinco llagas* – the flower of death – and the children, with their toy death's heads and toy coffins, ate sugar buns shaped like skeletons over the graves of dead forebears. As Christmas approached, the cold winds brought snow off the sierra.

Villa's printed notes, known as 'Dos Caros' from the portraits on them, appeared to everyone's surprise to be a good investment. On Christmas morning, as Slattery made his way to the great brown edifice of the cathedral through crowds of Indians and mestizos, a big black Dodge appeared. Villa was riding in it with Monserrat and Preto, and as the crowd surged round him, he began to fill each raised thin brown hand with bright newly-printed notes. Seeing Slattery, he beamed at him.

'Does your King ever do this, inglés?' he asked. 'Fifteen pesos each. Every one of them.'

The last pocket of resistance in Ojinaga vanished. With the Americans across the border watching from roofs and the tops of railway waggons, the Villistas launched one of their tremendous charges and the dispirited Huertistas bolted across the Rio Grande.

The group of Germans who had been hanging round Villa's headquarters disappeared again, and Slattery learned they had joined Carranza. At any moment he expected Horrocks to appear in one of his pantomine demon acts, as though he came up through a trapdoor in the floor.

Consuela Lidgett was still around, somehow always contriving to bump into Slattery. She was hopelessly out of her depth and struggling to make ends meet, unbelievably poor these days and even looking half-starved.

'The paper backed off,' she admitted. 'They said there wasn't enough Gordonsboro news to warrant me being here, and they stopped my dough. I'll have to go home. But I can't go without seeing Loyce.'

That evening, Slattery was summoned to headquarters. Villa met him with a grin. 'I have a job for a man who doesn't like our Mexican way of waging war,' he said. 'Tómas Urbina's cavalry's down near Torreón, watching the Federals. But Tómas isn't very active these days. Go down there and tell him – personally – to shoot his mother or something but not to get involved in trouble. Those

Germans are interfering again, changing sides so fast they make you dizzy. I've heard they're backing Orozco now, so if you see any of them, shoot them. In the back. It'll be all right.'

Leaving Atty to look after his affairs, Slattery began to pack his belongings. Apolinario Gomez García, the troubadour, had disappeared again in his wandering fashion and he was taking only Jesús with him. As he buckled straps, Consuela Lidgett appeared, her small face unhappy. She had a desperate look about her these days.

'Can I go with you?' she asked. 'I've found him. I really have. He's near Torreón and I've managed to raise a little cash.'

Skirting Camargo and Jiménez, they found Urbina in a house near Jaralito, suffering from one of his bouts of rheumatism and planning a foray towards Yermo after loot.

He listened sullenly to the orders Slattery brought and gestured to the east. 'See Major Ruíz,' he said. 'He's near La Carga.'

They ran into Ruíz's troops on the march. They were on jaded horses, saddled with nothing more than a blanket and for the most part ungroomed and scarred by the brush. For the first time they picked up news of Consuela's husband.

'Near La Escotadura,' Ruíz's men said. 'He handles the machine-gun.'

They followed the column across the plain, a long serpent of ragged men winding through the black mesquite, a red, white and green flag at its head. It was like being in the centre of a vast yellow bowl with the mountains forming ragged lips against a deep blue sky.

Ruíz's men were poorly armed, short of ammunition and lacking discipline. They rode easily but in little order, those with guitars making up boastful ballards as they went. Half of them weren't sure what they were fighting for, though they believed it was easier than working in the mines.

They were disillusioned with the revolution. 'When it's over,' they said, 'it won't be us who get the land of the hacendados. It will be the pacíficos who stayed at home, because they'll be alive to claim it.' Most of them had never

171

heard of Madero, the father of the revolution, and those who had thought he was some sort of saint. They hadn't been paid for months.

At the rear of the column was an old stage-coach which looked as if it had once belonged to Wells Fargo. It was hauled by four mules and was packed with cases of dynamite, which fell off every time it bounced over a rut. The crew didn't seem worried and simply kept stopping and throwing them back aboard.

They stopped the night at a little town near La Carga where someone found a room for Consuela. She looked scared at being surrounded by so many men because, even at their blandest, Mexicans always managed to look like bandits. Slattery found room for his blanket among the soldiers in a stone building filled with stacked rifles and saddles. A guitar softly played a popular song.

Apolinario Gomez García turned up during the night and Slattery wakened the following morning to find him sawing at his favourite, 'O Sole Mio', in the middle of the village street watched by a circle of raisin-eyed children.

'Take care, your honour,' he warned. 'The Orozquistas are close and they have German officers.'

For the next night they stopped at a village wrecked in the earlier fighting and, with García sawing away at a new tune from The Dollar Princess, the Mexicans indulged in their love of dancing. With candles stuck in the walls to cast a flickering light through blackened doorways, the blanketed men started shuffling round together and someone shoved Consuela into Slattery's arms. She seemed startled but then her arms tightened and she clung to him as if she'd fall down without him.

Leaving Jesús to look after their belongings so they could move faster, they covered over fifty miles the following day. There was no water or food to be had and they were choked by the cloud of alkali dust that surrounded them. There wasn't a breath of wind and the heat was terrific. In the afternoon Consuela insisted she would have to rest, so they allowed the column to move on without them and, finding a spot where there were a few low trees, they spent the afternoon moving round beneath them with the shade. As the heat went out of the day, they moved on again to find that the column had halted at a village where the spring was muddied from the number of men and horses which had drunk there. As they arrived a man with a gun shouted a challenge.

'*Quien vive?*'

'I come from General Villa.'

'May he live. Continue, amigo.'

This time Consuela made no attempt to find a room for herself and lay down next to Slattery in what had once been a grain store. She was shy in a way the Mexicans never were, but insisted on holding his hand and the following morning she looked at him in a strange, questioning, speculative manner. She said she was too tired to continue. 'I'll follow,' she said.

Slattery had heard that Loyce Lidgett was somewhere just ahead with one of the outposts and agreed to bring him to her. She gave him a grateful look and waited uncertainly beside him as he saddled his horse.

He rode across a desert of dried creek beds, chaparral, cactus and sword plant, his lips rimmed with an outline of pasty saliva and alkali dust. To the east lay the mountain range, broken only where the pass crossed it. From the top you could see for fifty miles over another arid plain to the distant town where the Orozquistas were supposed to be. It was dark and the moon was up when he arrived and the men of the outpost were nervous. They had heard that the Orozquistas were about to move and were worried because, never allowed mercy themselves, the Orozquistas would never show any to a Villista. Mexican warfare was one in which vengeance played a large part and they would be certain by now to have heard of the butchery near San Pedro Solitario and be eager for revenge.

They were billeted in a huddle of adobe houses, looked forgotten and half-starved, and possessed no more then ten rounds of ammunition apiece. They gave Slattery a meal, nevertheless, and took him to their commanding officer. Major Ruíz was an old man, unshaven, dirty and carrying a huge, dramatic and useless looking revolver strapped to his hip. He wore a khaki tunic and sun helmet, knickerbocker trousers, black and white shoes and yellow spats. He was living in the ruins of an old hacienda attached to the village, a magnificent porticoed palace in the centre of a great square of peóns' houses, corrals and stables, but totally lacking in plumbing. Horses were tethered on the patio and rifles and a few rusty sabres lay haphazardly in corners, while in the middle of the room a fire of corncobs was burning.

When Slattery asked for Lidgett, the old man gestured irritably. 'Over there,' he said. 'With the machine-gun.'

As Slattery moved along the village street, children pointed to the one large house that existed outside the hacienda, a dusty little rancho where men were cleaning a machine-gun of ancient French design that looked like a broomstick surrounded by a spring. When he asked for Lidgett, one of them looked up, his face shadowed under a hanging lantern.

'Who wants him?'

'I'm from General Villa.'

The man waved him into the house. There were more men in the hall who nodded to a closed door, grinning and gesturing with their forearms and fists. It was obvious what they meant and, as Slattery hesitated, the door opened. Lidgett stood in the opening. He looked older and was puffy-faced as if he'd been drinking too much for a long time. He was stark naked and was holding a revolver. Behind him lying on a mattress on the floor, was a Mexican girl, also naked, the yellow light of the lamp picking up the planes and curves of her body.

'Who's asking for me?' Lidgett peered at Slattery then recognition dawned and he grinned. 'The Limey!' he said. 'The Limey on the train! What the hell are you doin' here?'

Slattery explained that he was on Villa's staff and on duty. 'Your wife's here,' he said. 'Waiting for you.'

'My wife?' Lidgett's jaw dropped and, using the muzzle of the gun, he scratched at the mat of black hair on his chest. 'She's here? In Mexico?'

174

'A few miles back.'

Lidgett lowered the gun. 'What in the name of God Almighty is she doin' here?'

'She's looking for you.'

'For Christ's sake, this is no place for a woman! The goddam Orozquistas are only twenty miles away!'

'She's come to find you.'

'Well, hell' – Lidgett gestured at the naked girl – 'I don't want her to find me like this. Would you? Tell her to get the hell out of here.'

'How about telling her yourself? She'll be here soon.'

'Here?' Lidgett's grin died. 'Goddammit, did *you* bring her?'

'No, I didn't,' Slattery snapped. 'She tagged along. She needs to see you and I think she'd be satisfied if she did.'

'For Christ's sake' – Lidgett flung the gun down on the mattress' – I don't want to see her! She'll be beggin' me to go home. All that goddam pleadin' and tears and stuff. I don't want it. I quit. I don't aim to go back.'

They were still arguing as the men in the hallway, who had been watching the scene with great interest, shuffled aside, whispering behind their hands and grinning. Turning, Slattery saw Consuela appear from the darkness between them.

'Loyce,' she said. She was about to move forward when the men in front of Lidgett moved away and she saw he was naked.

'Loyce!' She sounded embarrassed. Then she saw the girl on the mattress. For a long time she stood staring at Lidgett, who made no attempt either to cover himself or to explain, then she managed to speak. 'All these people' – she gestured at the grinning men – 'they knew – I – Oh, my God –!'

Slattery was still wondering what his part in the scene should be when he heard the thunder of hooves and a horse came tearing down the street.

'The Orozquistas!' the rider was yelling through the cloud of dust he had stirred up. 'The Orozquistas are coming!'

175

Ignoring his wife and the fact that he was naked, Lidgett thrust forward. 'How many?'

'Thousands!'

The girl on the mattress had been smiling at Consuela, certain of her hold on Lidgett, but now she hurriedly began to search for her clothes. Consuela tried to grab at her husband as he reached for his shirt, and he whirled on her, his face red with fury.

'You got no sense?' he roared. 'Leave me be! The goddam Orozquistas are coming! At night, too! For Christ's sake, get the hell out of it!'

3

The houses were vomiting men. In one corner of the great square of the hacienda a mob of women with torches were struggling to gather their belongings. In another a bunch of frightened horses swung together, their heads up, their ears back, the whites of their eyes showing, and galloped to another corner where they gathered again, milling around furiously in a cloud of dust.

Men were running out into the moonlight clutching rifles, trying to catch horses or throwing saddles over the backs of animals that had been trapped. More were rummaging among the badly-stacked weapons for their ammunition. Nobody seemed to know where to go and, despite the hour, a cockerel was crowing as if its heart would burst.

His shirt flapping over his trousers, a peón's straw hat on his head, Lidgett was yelling to his men who were bringing up the solitary machine-gun on a cart.

'Where are they?'

'About four kilometres away.'

'What happened to the outposts?'

'They were overrun.'

'Jesus,' he said. 'At night! They must be crazy!' A man holding a horse called to him and, totally ignoring Consuela who stood looking lost, bewildered and frightened, he ran awkwardly to it, impeded by the big spurs he was wearing. Dragging himself into the saddle, he swung the animal round and galloped off.

Consuela gave a little moan. 'He'll come back,' she said to Slattery. 'It'll be different when he does.'

The moon hung like an icy ball over the mountains, flooding the plain with light, and over a dark line of trees the heavens were full of stars that seemed to grow brighter with every minute. But there was no sign of the advancing Orozquistas and Slattery began to wonder if the panic was

177

for nothing. Behind him the uproar was beginning to subside a little and, now that the frightened horses had gone, the dust was settling and a huddle of sheep, stirred from their sleep, moved into the street.

There were still a lot of men near the wrecked hacienda and the old major appeared, complete with yellow spats. Carefully adjusting a pair of motoring goggles over his eyes, he climbed on to a horse that looked as ancient as he was and, followed by a small group of men, plodded off down the road towards the hills, looking like Don Quixote about to tilt at windmills. It was possible in the moonlight to watch them all the way, appearing and disappearing in and out of the rolling terrain, trailing a plume of white dust as they moved.

Then Slattery noticed puffs of dust like shell bursts silvered by the moon moving against the base of the mountains, and realized they were the Orozquistas. They were moving in and out of the folds of the land now, advancing slowly towards him, and he saw they were heading east to come up on the flank of the defenders.

Leaving Consuela with the women, he saddled his horse and rode forward a little to see what was happening. The puffs of dust were drawing nearer and moving further and further to one side. Then they seemed to disappear and Slattery heard the faint crackle of rifle fire and then short bursts – brrp, brrp – which he recognized as a machine-gun.

A man came galloping back, his eyes wild. 'We need ammunition!' he yelled. '*Madre de Dios*, we can't keep them back with ten rounds each!'

The driver of the old stage-coach was trying to harness the mules. The dynamite was still aboard with the boxes of ammunition but, because the ammunition was underneath, he was intending to drive the whole lot to the defenders. Another rider thundered towards them. He had been hit on the side of the head and blood was streaming in long trickles down his face, black in the moonlight.

'For the love of God,' he yelled. 'Ammunition!'

When Slattery looked again at the distant puffs of dust,

178

they were nearer and men were tearing back at full speed. One of them pointed to the other side of the hacienda. 'They're on that side, too,' he yelled.

The puffs were bigger now, and Slattery saw the women begin to collect children, pots and pans and the uncooked meal, and start wrapping things in rags and handkerchieves. One of them started to drive off the sheep, another started throwing stones at the roosting chickens to scatter them. A pig squealed and bolted, followed by its young.

Consuela was looking scared. A last group of riders heading from the hacienda towards the fighting had halted, uncertain what to do.

'It's over!' one of them yelled, and, turning, Slattery saw dozens of men streaming back. Immediately, the waiting riders swung their horses round and fled.

The firing had grown closer and the man trying to push the mules into the coach was beginning to panic. There were now dozens of figures moving through the chaparral. It was impossible to tell which side they belonged to, but occasionally they heard bursts of firing and one of them dropped. Heaving on his reins, Slattery cantered back to where Consuela was waiting.

'They've stolen my horse,' she wailed.

A bullet whacked against the wall of the hacienda, gouging out a lump of plaster, and the women began to scream, scattering in all directions. A man galloped past, his face black with powder, and the driver of the coach, fumbling the last adjustments of the harness straps, began to make the animals nervous. As they backed away, he lost his temper and punched one on the nose. It started kicking wildly, the waggon tongue snapped and the animals bolted into the desert, trailing the remains of the tongue and the loose leather straps. The driver stared after them for a second and started to run. Then, unexpectedly, the coach exploded with a roar and a flare of flame that lit up the whole village, sending glass, planks, wheels and fragments of wood in every direction.

Reaching down without a word, Slattery heaved Consuela up behind him; she was slight and light as a feather. As

179

they left the hacienda, they were almost caught by a posse of men coming out of the shadows, covered with sweat and blood and powder burns, their horses staggering after a mad gallop. Bullets started to peck at the walls and, with a moan of terror, Consuela buried her face in Slattery's back. As the horsemen went past, one of them began shooting backward, then they disappeared, crouched low, their sarapes flapping, the wide brims of their sombreros bouncing up and down.

There were men everywhere now, moving in and out of the shadows, shooting from the saddle at anything that moved, and behind them came more, line after line of them. The horse moved with difficulty over the uneven ground with its double load. About a mile from the hacienda was a huddle of adobe houses with crude plank doors and shutters. Already, women were barricading themselves inside. Then, suddenly, the horse stopped dead and nothing Slattery could do would make it move. Dismounting, he saw it had been hit and blood was streaming from its mouth and nostrils. He had just dragged Consuela from its back when it dropped with a crash.

The shooting was still going on behind them as they started to run and they saw men on their left bolting in a group, with another group on horses galloping to cut them off. By the grace of God, they were moving in a different direction and they saw them vanish among the chaparral. By this time Consuela was whimpering. 'I can't go on,' she kept saying. 'I can't go on!'

Slattery was beginning to wish he'd never seen her. 'Just a little further,' he panted. 'Then we'll find somewhere to hide.'

A man ran across their front with the horsemen after him. They were shooting at him and eventually he fell. Then they saw another group, in front of them the ancient major in his knickerbockers and yellow spats, his motoring goggles round his neck. His chest heaving, unable to run any more, he stopped to face his pursuers as they came at a gallop over a rise in the ground. They all fired together and the shock of the heavy bullets lifted him off his feet to

180

drop him on his back, half-propped up by a mesquite bush, his face white in the moonlight.

Coming to a narrow cleft in the ground, they dropped into it and burrowed into the shadows among the thorny brush that grew along it. As they crouched down, there were shots and yells and the thudding of hooves. Bullets cracked through the brushwood and, lifting his head, Slattery saw Orozquistas in their red shirts led by a man with a moustache shooting at a cart dragged by a frantic foaming horse. Lashing at the horse he recognized Loyce Lidgett.

His shirt was torn almost from his back and there was blood on his face. Clinging to the cart, trying to hold the gun down was a boy aged about thirteen, but, as they watched, he cried out and fell to the ground. Then one of the shafts broke and the horse, its legs tangled with the trailing wood, came to a stop, whinnying nervously. Lidgett jumped down, reaching for the revolver strapped to his waist. As he fired, one of the approaching riders fell from the saddle, but others turned towards him and began to close in on him.

Turning aside again, he tried to flee, running away from the spot where his wife was crouching with Slattery, but the riders swung after him. He seemed to bear a charmed life for a while then the leading horse caught him with its shoulder. In the light of the moon the rider's face was plain. It was Fausto Graf. What he was doing with the Orozquistas Slattery could only guess. Only that tortured diplomacy that infuriated Villa and allowed the Germans to run with the hare and hunt with the hounds could explain it. As Lidgett staggered, he tried to fire but the shot went wild and he fell, and Slattery saw Graf and the Orozquistas riding backwards and forwards over him, firing downwards as they did so.

Feeling Consuela move, he grabbed her quickly.

'I must go to him.'

He didn't argue but thrust her down and sprawled on top of her, holding her still by his weight.

In the moonlight they could see the Orozquistas riding up and down the village street, shooting at anything that moved. A child trying to run to safety was knocked flying by a horse and ended in a dusty bundle of rags against the wall. Squealing pigs were shot as they ran, and men, struggling to escape, were killed without hestitation. By one of the houses, lit by the moon, a girl was weeping. She was only young and one of the Orozquistas had backed her against the wall and was standing in front of her, one hand carelessly holding a revolver, the other wrenching open the front of her dress. She made no attempt to move but stood quite still, petrified with terror as he pulled the material aside, his hand moving slowly as if the girl's fear added savour to what he was doing. Then, unbuckling his belt, he grinned at her plump young breasts and pushed his hand forward to force her against the wall. Little by little the two of them slid down out of sight. As the girl started to sob, Consuela began a strangled protest and Slattery clapped a hand over her mouth.

The Orozquistas had begun now to kick the doors down to get at the screaming women. The girl they had seen with Lidgett appeared, shrieking, and a hand came out of the lamplit doorway after her, grabbing at her dress. The material tore away, leaving her a thin, brown naked figure and a horseman snatched her up as she ran. But another man with a rifle emerged from inside the house and, as he fired, the rider fell from the saddle one way, the girl the other, landing on her back in the dust. As she staggered to her feet, blank-eyed and half-stunned, the man with the rifle snatched at her hand and dragged her back into the house.

As the harsh screaming started, Consuela began to moan and Slattery pushed her down into the dusty earth. Half-hysterical, she began to struggle and he brought his hand up to slap her hard across her face so that she collapsed against him. Then, putting his arm around her, he pulled her closer to him and held her tight.

By the time the darkness faded the Orozquistas had disappeared and the shooting had stopped. The village street was full of flattened figures sprawled in the dust, half-hidden by their huge sombreros. Two or three dazed women and girls stumbled past, weeping, then an old woman carrying the corpse of a child.

After a while, with the light increasing, Slattery pulled Consuela to her feet and they moved cautiously along the narrow arroyo, keeping low, praying that no one would see them. The sun was hot and the chaparral, cactus and the long interlaced spikes of the espada slashed at their clothing.

Eventually, they decided it was safe to leave the arroyo and the first thing they saw was a man sprawled on his back, half covered with a red sarape. His trousers and shoes had been taken but his shirt had been left because it was saturated with blood. A little further on lay the carcass of a horse beginning to swell in the increasing heat, its legs sticking up like the branches of a tree. Underneath it lay another man.

Slattery's leg was hurting and they were growing desperate for water because the dust in the river bed had parched their throats. In the distance they could see a solitary horseman moving slowly in the same direction and they realized they were approaching another village.

Consuela was staggering, and Slattery put an arm round her. Then a man appeared driving a few goats he had managed to hide from the Orozquistas. He helped to support the wilting girl and around noon they stumbled with stiff legs into the village. There were a few of the old major's soldiers there, some of them wounded, and, despite their own poverty, the villagers were digging into their stores of food.

After a meal of eggs and cheese Consuela began to recover and someone indicated a stream hidden by willows where they could wash the dust away. They stripped off their clothes and scrubbed away the grime and the stink of fear. Other men and women joined them, all standing together naked in the stream. Consuela was embarrassed but, occupied with what they were doing, no one bothered to look at her and she gave Slattery a quick nervous smile.

By the time they returned to the village, more soldiers were beginning to straggle in. They looked exhausted, their lips split and dry, their legs slashed by the espadas. Some wore bandages, and their ammunition and rifles were gone, their bodies foul with dirt. There were only a few of them now but their women were still with them, and, slipping from swaying horses, they exchanged news of their comrades as the animals sucked greedily at the water. One had lost a friend, another his brother, a third his wife and child. The village women, shadowy in their black clothes, moved about with ollas of water, their eyes large, and only late in the afternoon did the weary procession come to an end.

With a sick feeling of futility, Slattery helped carry wounded into the little house. In one an old man was dying, but no one suggested the injured soldiers should not be allowed shelter there. The unwounded were already recovering their spirits and with good Mexican bombast were telling of the numbers of Orozquistas they had killed before they had been obliged to turn tail. Always they had fought until their ammunition was gone and always their horses were down before they had run. Slattery listened quietly, knowing many of them had bolted long before the Orozquistas had even come within range.

In the sky above the plain vultures floated over dead men and horses but a few of the soldiers began playing a form of pelota against a wall and others pretended with a ragged cloak to be bullfighters. Nobody suggested going out to search for wounded until Slattery insisted.

As the light faded, the sky became a flaming crimson that touched the dark faces as it was reflected from the walls. The street was falling into shadow but the sun, lighting up the distant mountains, still left the tops of the trees in a brilliant orange glow. One of the villagers offered Slattery a bed in his house. It was nothing but an old-fashioned iron frame on which the springs had been replaced with wooden boards and a horsehair mattress. There was a single tattered blanket but already a woman was running in with a sheet and a girl was busy with a broom, sprinkling water to lay the dust. A little prie-dieu made from a picture postcard of the Virgin Mary was set up on an old wash-stand, one end of which was propped up with a stone, and rush candles were lit on either side. From the frilled pink paper decoration hanging over the door it was obvious that this was the room kept for visiting notables, and the owner stepped back and gestured to Consuela.

'May you be blessed with sleep,' he said.

A small crowd of children and wounded men watched with interest. Consuela looked startled but the owner nodded in encouragement and gave a little bow.

As the door closed, Slattery sat on the edge of the bed. Consuela remained standing, her eyes shadowed.

'He didn't love me,' she said softly. 'I guess he never did.'

'What will you do?'

'Go home. There's nothing to stay for. Can I stay here tonight?'

'Of course.'

'With you? Please.' She stared at him for a moment, embarrassed. 'I guess I'm not as brave as I thought. I've never been involved in anything like this before.'

She was silent for a while. 'Things change, don't they?' she whispered. 'I was shocked at the way Mexican women simply took up with another man when their own man died. But that old man was right. This is where I want to be.'

There was no coquetry, no smiles, and as Slattery stretched out on the bed, she lay down beside him without embarrassment. Her hand touched his then he felt her fingers tighten as she clutched it. He put his arm round her and, as she crouched against him, he felt her shuddering and heard her crying weakly. Outside a guitar twanged softly, then another. Then he heard García's voice and a fiddle scraped.

'They've got the village orchestra to serenade us,' he said quietly. 'They feel it's romantic. But they won't waste it. They'll have a dance in the house next door.'

He heard her laugh, then she began to shake with mirth. There was hysteria in it but comfort, too, and a lessening of fear. Then she gave a shudder and he held her to him until the shaking stopped. For a while she was silent, then

185

he felt the sudden quivering tension of her body. As the music changed outside, slowly, deliberately, she began to kiss him with an eagerness born of despair and, taking his hand, opened her shirt and placed it on her breast.

'Oh, Slattery,' she whispered. 'I never thought I'd want to do this with anyone but my own man. But I do, I do, I do.'

4

'Why?' Magdalena's face was twisted with anger as she swung round, flourishing the pistol in her fist. Slattery had been back from La Escotadura for no more than a week when she had appeared in his hotel like an avenging angel.

What had happened at La Escotadura, the attack by the Orozquistas and the rout of Urbina's men, was common knowledge now. Enjoying her moment in the limelight, Consuela had not hestitated to recount her adventure to anyone who would listen, and everyone knew what had occurred, how Loyce Lidgett had died, how Consuela had spent the night with a man in a Mexican bed. She had mentioned no names but it hadn't taken people long to put two and two together. Villa had winked at Slattery and the Holy Trinity had eyed him with something akin to envy because Consuela, petite and fair, was the sort of woman Mexican men liked. Since she at last had something to pass on to Gordonsboro that concerned a Gordonsboro man, she had even sent home a romanticized version of the event, in which Lidgett had died fighting off the Orozquistas to save his wife, and when the paper had syndicated it, it had so caught the American fancy it was in half the journals that crossed the border. For the first time in her life, Consuela was important.

'Why?' Magdalena demanded, no longer Mexican or German but pure outraged American in her anger.

Her fury was spectacular enough to turn heads and for a long time they stood staring at each other, Magdalena's face pink, her eyes like a blue explosion.

Slattery suspected she was instinctively extracting the full histrionic value from the occasion and, watched with interest by the desk clerk, without a word he took her arm and began to lead her to his room. Her eyes raging, she tried to snatch her arm away, but he refused to let go and she found herself almost running alongside him, still clutching the pistol.

'*Madre de Dios*, where's your whip?' The words were bitten off short by fury.

He ignored her and, pushing open the door, almost threw her into a chair. In her rage, she looked younger than she was, with a loveliness that made his heart thump. For a while, as she watched him light a cigarette, her face angry and wretched, he said nothing.

'Why?' she demanded yet again. '*Du liebe Gott*, why?'

But already the fury was fading from her face and, seeing the glisten of tears on her eyelashes, he decided the best explanation was the simplest one. What had happened between him and Consuela had seemed as natural as breathing. She had put her arms round him, calling his name with a weak desperation that was a mixture of horror, fear and a total rejection of Loyce Lidgett.

'Because,' he said, 'she'd just discovered her husband was a shit. But she'd also just seen him and a lot of other men and boys butchered and a dozen women raped, and she was exhausted and terrified. The Orozquistas did it. Orozquistas led by Germans. If she'd been a man she'd have wanted to cut out somebody's tripes. As it was, the only thing she knew to do was what she did.'

She was silent for a long time, digesting what he had said. When she spoke again, she seemed shaken.

'Where is she now?'

'God knows. She disappeared. Probably gone home to weep on someone's chest. Mine just happened to be handy at the time.'

'She doesn't belong in Mexico!'

'She never did.'

She gestured with the pistol then managed a twisted smile that was wretched in its lack of happiness. 'She's not for you, Slattery.'

'I know that as well as you.'

Because he refused to lose his temper, her own anger faded. It was always a transient thing, exploding and dying just as quickly. And, delivered with all of Magdalena's

188

splendid vocal powers and gesture, it was nothing else but stage technique. Beautiful, statuesque, commanding, her brilliant eyes dramatically enraged. He had a suspicion that once again she had been playing a part she had felt needed playing.

But indignation had vanished from her eyes now and an infinite pity and distress flooded into them. 'Poor soul,' she said, her voice full of compassion.

'What are you doing here?' he asked. 'Why did you come?'

She answered wearily. 'I was in El Paso. I'm going to sing in New York.' She stared at him, still on the edge of nervous tears that forced her to gulp and swallow to control herself. 'I came to tell you. I felt forgiving. I thought we might celebrate. It should have been so wonderful.' The flush had gone from her cheeks now and her face was pale. 'I heard that you were going home. That you had finished with Villa.' Her expression set and she went on a little desperately. 'I made a fool of myself. Are you going back to Villa?'

'Yes. When the fighting stops, I'll go home. I think I've finished with Mexico and everything in it.'

She gave him a hurt look, as though he had included her in his condemnation. 'I thought you loved me,' she said quietly. 'It was in Mexico City I began to think so. In my house. But I was wrong. I was just a camp follower – Madam Butterfly, waiting for her man to turn up.' She sighed. 'There was too much imagination, too much romance, too much zarzuela.'

Slattery studied her. Was he in love with her, he wondered. It had begun to dawn on him that, in the atmosphere of Mexico's troubles, with death cheap and love affairs so easily destroyed by a bullet, it had become time to stop running away from responsibility. Coming to Mexico had been running away. He had a feeling he hadn't always been fair to her.

She sighed again, subdued now and weary. 'This awful war,' she said. 'Will it never end?'

'Revolutions are easy to start but they have a tendency to go on longer than expected.'

189

'Why can't they get round a table and work things out?'

'Because that's not how revolutions behave.'

As they talked Jesús appeared with clean clothing from the laundry women and smiled at her. But she didn't notice him, as if she were in a daze, as if all she had hoped for had gone wrong, as if her mind kept sliding off at a tangent into a haze of disbelief.

Slattery laid his hand on hers, and she took it gratefully and squeezed it, fighting to hold back the tears that threatened to overflow down her cheeks.

'I'd better go,' she said abruptly, collecting her belongings. She stuffed the pistol into her bag and gave him a sad, sheepish look. 'I would never have used it,' she said. 'Perhaps it's best. I'll go to New York. I thought I might not. But I will now. I'll play out my contracts first – Mexico City, then Córdoba. After that –' she shrugged. 'There are no definite dates. They say it will lead to Italy and London. I've never been to Europe and I'd like to go.'

'Why not come with me?'

She shook her head. 'Our backgrounds, our professions are too far apart. I realize now. It would be a kind of warfare. Theatrical people are notoriously bad companions. Perhaps I should cry a little. Quiet ladylike tears –'

'Magdalena, stop acting!'

She responded angrily, her eyes hot. 'It wouldn't work! You're English!'

'Irish.'

'Irish then. I'm German.'

'American.'

'Oh, *Dios*! American then!'

He looked at her with a faint smile on his face. In ten minutes she had run the whole gamut of outraged American, stiff German and tempestuous Mexican.

'It's a pity you can't make up your mind,' he said. 'It's 1914 and people are pretty broadminded these days. People even manage to marry foreigners these days without being struck by a thunderbolt. Even Germans. Your father did. For God's sake, does Germany mean that much to you any more?'

190

She drew a deep breath and pushed back a lock of hair that had fallen over her nose. At the door she turned and as she spoke there was a wealth of sadness in her voice. 'To Germans, it does,' she said. 'Especially these days. Especially to me. There are thousands of years of Germany in my blood, and only twenty of America.'

5

Villa was in a bad temper. By his own will, his own strength, his own skill, his own murderous intelligence, he had pushed himself upward and he had suddenly found that where he had arrived wasn't what he had expected. He talked with the mighty these days, no longer a peón, a bandit, a guerrilla leader of dusty armies of unskilled men, and he had managed to recruit for the Division of the North one of the finest artillerists in Mexico, a cosmopolitan educated in Paris, Berlin and the Chapultepec Military College, a man of self-discipline bound by a code of honour less punctilious men couldn't understand, and he was finding it hard to live up to.

The new man brought colleagues in uniforms of blue and gold, ceremonial and even a medal for Villa that was presented at an enormous public meeting. Villa didn't think much of it.

'This is a hell of a little thing,' he said as it was handed to him, 'to give to a man for all that heroism you talk about.'

Even the music changed. 'No "Pancho Villas' Wedding",' he insisted. 'No "Killing of Resa". No "Pancho Villa Rides". Especially no "Pancho Villa Rides".'

There was talk of a push south to recapture Torreón but by now Villa was paying court to another girl and didn't want to move. Then, one morning as Slattery left his hotel, he heard rumours of a rail disaster in the north-west where two trains had collided with great loss of life and, as he reached headquarters, he discovered the disaster had not been an accident as he had imagined, but had been deliberately engineered by some desperado after loot who claimed to be one of Villa's lieutenants.

With the anarchy that was spreading across Mexico, whole areas of countryside were these days in the hands of leaders running small bands of desperate men who relied on ambush, treachery and the sacking of small towns. Haciendas and ranchos, whether owned by Mexicans, American, British, Germans, or the ubiquitous Mormons were all fair game to them, and they left them blazing, their owners dead, the cattle run off, the women snatched, the land ruined.

Villa was stamping up and down in a spectacular bout of fury offering to shoot everyone in sight, while headquarters staff, sentries, and even senior colonels tried to keep out of the way.

'There are too many chiefs in this revolution!' he was yelling. 'Too many hats about! A few need removing! That damned bandido's spoiled everything! Just when I had the Norteamericanos eating out of my hand, too! Get up there, inglés. Go to El Paso and persuade them he's nothing to do with me. Tell them if they catch him to give him to me so I can give him a fair trial and have him shot!'

The disaster had not only lost him the admiration of the Americans but had also deprived him of coal for his trains, and he was livid with Carranza who, he felt, was keeping it from him.

'That old billy goat's as two-faced as a church clock,' he snapped. 'He's afraid I'll get to Mexico City before he does.'

Slattery's interview with the mayor of El Paso was difficult. The mayor didn't like Mexicans *or* Britons, but when he saw the gold Slattery had brought his tune changed. Gold meant business and the coal was moved swiftly across the border to be reloaded into Mexican gondolas.

The Stutzmann company had been performing in El Paso before moving back to Mexico and Slattery was outside their hotel as they gathered in motor cars to be transported across the International Bridge to the station at Juárez where they could catch the train south. They were like a lot of bright butterflies, pretty women and handsome men, all in fashionable clothes they often couldn't afford, their voices higher and stronger than those of the passers-by, the girls eyeing Slattery with interest as they always did. Stutzmann was talking with Magdalena and as he saw Slattery he smiled, touched her arm and quietly disappeared.

193

'Slattery,' she said softly.

There was no enmity, just a deep sadness. He had found he couldn't get her out of his mind and he had a feeling that neither of them could ever entirely reject the other for long.

'I'm sorry for the things I said,' Magdalena pointed out. 'I can't change things but I shouldn't have been so angry. I know about Escotadura now. Fausto was there and he told me of the dreadful things the Orozquistas did.'

He was tempted to tell her of her brother's part in the affair but he rejected the idea. 'Have you seen him?' he asked, always at the back of his mind Horrocks' suggestion that Fausto Graf used her to pick up information.

'Yes.' She sighed and shrugged. 'He wanted money. Money and "*Deutschland über Alles*". He's too involved with the German-American Bund and leaves his hacienda to his mayordomo. He doesn't even pick mayordomos well. Vegas was nothing but a bully.'

'Who?'

'Florentino Vegas. He beat the peóns. He's with the army now.' She was merely making conversation, distant, lacking the enthusiasm there had always been before. 'There's another one now, just as bad. Did you see Fausto at Escotadura? I told him you were there.'

'I saw him,' Slattery said shortly.

His manner was enough to dissuade her from any show of warmth. 'We're going to Córdoba and Veracruz,' she said. 'To clear up contracts.'

'It's Zapata's territory down there.'

'Mexicans always let music through.'

'I don't think Zapata's very concerned with music.'

Stutzmann began to push his cast towards the motor cars. Magdalena gazed at Slattery for a long moment, her eyes on his face as though she were nailing it to her memory.

'Goodbye, Slattery.'

He watched the vehicles as they moved away, a forest of waving arms and handkerchieves, the high twittering voices of the company rising above the sound of the engines. Then Stutzmann started a song from *The Gypsy Baron*, and the

194

vehicles rolled towards the river, the sound growing fainter until they finally disappeared.

The twenty-four hours Slattery remained in El Paso had a strange quality to them. For some reason he had a feeling he was being watched and on one occasion he was very nearly knocked down by a motor car which didn't stop.

'Goddam drivers,' Atty snorted as he hauled Slattery upright. 'They buy an automobile, spend ten minutes finding out what the levers and switches are for, then 'tes out on the road, large as life and twice as nasty, trying to kill everybody in sight.'

Heading south again to Chihuahua, near Gallego they were stopped by a troop of horsemen, stationed across the road in a wide half-circle.

'*Alto!*' one of them shouted. 'Stop the engine!'

Atty refused and the man who had spoken rode forward. He had a revolver in his hand, and Slattery was just about to rise in his seat when the weapon came up. With a sweep of his arm, Atty slammed him down again and opened the throttle just as the bullet starred the windscreen.

As the Studebaker leapt forward, they could hear shots thudding into the tonneau of the vehicle. Slattery's hat was whipped from his head then, with horses rearing and flashing hooves hanging over their heads, they were through. Only two men waited ahead but, as Atty drove straight at them, they swung aside and one of the horses went down with a crash, the rider sprawled alongside it. Bullets were still whacking into the rear of the car and Atty was crossing himself furiously.

'Holy Jesus,' he was saying. 'Don't let 'em hit a tyre!'

Eventually the horsemen dropped out of sight and Atty eased his foot off the accelerator and looked at Slattery.

'You been bad-mouthin' somebody, me dear?' he asked. 'Or have 'ee been upsetting Magdalena so she wants your head on a pole? A lot of fellers seem to want 'ee dead all of a sudden.'

When they returned to Chihuahua, Villa was still raging

195

about the orders he had received to move south. From Juárez on the American border down to Mexico City the railway divided the country into two halves, crossing desert and mountain for two thousand miles, and along it had sprung up a series of important military posts with Torréon the key to them all. Though Obregón was driving down from Sonora and another army was still trying to move down the east coast, it was Villa who had the key route and outside Juárez ten enormous trains waited in the desert, the horses tied to the mesquite among the hanging sarapes and the strips of drying meat.

'We're not ready,' Villa insisted furiously. 'We're short of ammunition! We're short of artillery! Herrera hasn't arrived! Urbina's got rheumatism again! Besides' – he looked sheepish and Slattery knew he was thinking of the girl he was courting – 'I'm busy just now.'

The camps began to spring up, everybody disappointed that there was to be no move. But Villa was adamant. 'I need to gather guns. I need Urbina. It's all right for that old fool, Don Venus, to push for an advance, but he doesn't have to make the arrangements. I stay here! Until I'm ready. Nothing anybody says will move me!'

There seemed to be no argument and Slattery was just arranging with Atty to have the Studebaker removed from the flat car where it had been lashed for the move south when Jesús appeared at the run.

'Mi Coronel,' he yelled. 'The General wants you!'

The faces at headquarters showed that another crisis had blown up. An English rancher had been shot dead, and Villa's face was dark with rage. 'What do I do, inglés?' he demanded. 'What would your king do? He pulled a gun on me.'

Clanking across the room, he turned on his heel, his face flushed. 'The Norteamericanos are demanding action,' he stormed. 'They're talking of invasion.'

That eternal bogey of the Mexicans, invasion from the north, was before them again. No matter how much they boasted of their ability to handle it, they were terrified of the possibility.

'They're asking for details of the trial.' Villa gestured angrily. 'He didn't have a trial, damn it! He came in here saying we'd stolen his cattle. Perhaps we had – I don't know – so I ordered Fierro to get rid of him. I told them he was shot, but now that fool, Fierro, tells me he didn't shoot him. He took him outside and hit him on the head.' He scowled. 'Well, I've had him dug up, shot and buried again, so they can't argue with that.' The heavy head went down. 'There's too much going on around here, inglés.' He gestured at the men about him. 'Let's get the boys aboard and start the trains moving. It's time we were heading for Torreón.'

6

In the middle of the desert a battered water tank, a half-demolished station and a siding comprised the town. Around it men were camped in the chaparral, among the carts and guns and piles of equipment, watching cavalry mounts being unloaded. Covered with sweat, a ragged soldier plunged into the centre of a crowded cattle car and, dodging the flying hooves, swung himself on to a horse's back. As he jammed in his spurs and yelled, the boxcar's side seemed to bulge under the drumming of hooves as the frightened animals surged about inside. A horse fell backwards out of the door on to the sand at the side of the track, rolled over and picked itself up, terrified. After it came more horses and mules in ones and twos and groups, jumping or falling, then scrambling to their feet to flee in terror, their nostrils flaring their eyes bulging. The watching men were swinging their reatas and running through the choking cloud of dust, and the nervous animals began to circle in panic as officers, orderlies and soldiers searching for their steeds swung to their backs and tried to gallop out of the confusion.

As the horses were ridden clear, kicking mules were backed up to the shafts of artillery caissons, watched by foot soldiers looking for their units. From the top of the boxcars where they were camped under their little tents of sarapes and umbrellas, the wives, the soldaderas and the children watched as the stragglers trudged past, shouting down for news of husbands and sons and friends. Occasionally, as a man complained that he hadn't eaten in days, one of the women tossed him down a stale tortilla in return for a cigarette. Round the engines, more women were demanding water, ignoring the curses of the driver who was threatening to shoot them if they came any nearer.

Villa had begun his move against Torreón. Without a

198

word of warning, he had closed telephone and telegraph lines and stopped all mail and railroad traffic, then his vast serpent of troop trains had slowly begun to head south. The little towns that lay astride the route – Camargo, Rellano, Jiménez – were all already written into the Villa legend from the days of Madero's rebellion.

In addition to agents and diplomats, Jiménez was full of newspapermen, all wanting to know when the fighting was going to start. Among them, to Slattery's surprise, was Horrocks. He was wearing an alpaca jacket, white duck trousers, spats and a solar topee.

'What the hell are you doing here?' Slattery demanded.

'Come to see you.'

'I'm not interested.'

'You'd better be. Graf's here and he doesn't like you.'

'I don't like him very much.'

'He's watching you. Did you know?'

'I had an idea he might be.'

'He'd like to remove you.'

'I had an idea about that, too.'

Horrocks shrugged. 'Amaryllis is in Mexico City, by the way. I think she's picked up your trail.'

'Did you help her?'

Horrocks looked shocked. 'I'm not interested in what you do after dark,' he said.

'What are you interested in?'

'Keeping the old eyes and ears open. Things have changed in London, y'know. There's a new professionalism there. About time, too, because the Germans have widened the Kiel Canal. Now what could that be for, except to get their dreadnoughts into the North Sea against our fleet?' He lit a cigarette but didn't bother to offer one to Slattery. 'We've just withdrawn recognition of Huerta, incidentally.'

'American pressure?'

'We try to oblige. That means he's in trouble. And that pleases Washington. But the Germans are still behind him. They've offered him aid and we know they're loading arms in Hamburg for Veracruz. We even know the ships: *Ypiranga. Bavaria* and *Kronprinzessin Cecilie.*'

'Do the Americans know?'

Horrocks looked absorbed. 'We're wondering whether to pass on the information,' he said.

Horrocks disappeared as suddenly as he'd appeared, but for once Slattery wasn't certain he was glad to see the back of him. There were too many questions to ask. Jiménez was a wartime centre and a third-rate company performing at the theatre only brought nostalgia. Old Stutzmann posters announcing Magdalena Graf were all over the town, shabby and dog-eared now that the company had moved on, and often obscured by the posters of the new company. Slattery found himself stopping in front of them to read the names.

He was certain now that he had backed the wrong side, yet was unable to see an alternative. Villa's reputation would always exclude him from real power in Mexico. But, while Carranza offered legality, he also offered a reputation for corruption and a totally indefensible personality. If Villa could never become the ruler of Mexico because of his past, it seemed that Carranza could never become the ruler because he was totally unloveable.

The dilapidated main street was full of soldiers, and a single streetcar pulled by a staggering mule came past crammed with drunken Villistas. Carriages full of officers and girls sheered out of its way as it went by. The Divisione del Norte was making up for lost time or for the time that might never be, and every window contained a girl talking in low tones to a sarape-wrapped man. The night was cold and through the darkness came the sound of guitars, snatches of song, laughter and low voices. In the dark back streets there were shouts and even an occasional shot fired by some light-hearted soldier. A regimental band was playing in the square near a statue of the deposed dictator, Porfirio Díaz, which nobody had bothered to push off its pedestal.

Hundreds of little electric bulbs had been switched on about the plaza for the paseo, and a column of young men was going one way, another of girls going the other. Occasionally they threw handfuls of confetti at each other or slipped a note across, but no words were exchanged and the paseo never stopped and no one let their interest be too obvious, because if you picked someone else's girl by mistake it could be a killing matter. At one side of the plaza lay the ruins of a store looted when the army had arrived and at the other the ancient pink cathedral among the fountains and trees. By the entrance men were buying drinks from a stall.

Troops of horsemen, faces shadowed by the brims of their conical hats, jingled past. One of the riders was Florentino Vegas, of Villa's Holy Trinity, Graf's old mayordomo, huddled in the saddle, his hat down over his eyes, his sarape up over his chin.

'Looks as if he's plotting a murder,' Atty said.

The following morning, arriving at the headquarters caboose, they found Villa in a bad temper; the Holy Trinity, Carranza's group of young envoys, was no longer complete.

'Somebody shot Preto,' Villa said. 'They found him on the corner of the street with three bullets in him. You know Preto, inglés. He liked to dress like you. Why should anyone want to shoot him? Perhaps someone mistook him for *you.*' He grinned and gestured indifferently. 'There's one of Carranza's chocolateros in the hotel near the station. Let him know what happened.'

Vegas was riding towards headquarters as Slattery headed for town. As he saw Slattery, he reined in sharply to stare at him, then swung his horse away and set his spurs savagely into it.

The old American woman who ran the hotel was in the habit of refusing entry to anyone she disapproved of. She had the Stars and Stripes over the door and didn't like Mexicans. She studied Slattery with suspicion, but it turned out she had an Irish grandfather and she spotted his accent at once.

'In there,' she said, indicating the salon.

Two men were sitting inside, smoking long Mexican cigarillos, cups of chocolate on the table before them. One of them was Sjogren, the Swede, dressed in a lavender suit with spats, a red carnation in his buttonhole. The other was Fausto Graf. With them was a woman and, though she had her back to him, Slattery could see she had peroxided hair and that her face was painted. There was something familiar about her.

'Look who's here,' Sjogren said sharply as Slattery appeared. It seemed almost like a warning.

Graf rose to his feet quickly, looking curiously uncertain for once. As the woman turned her head, Slattery saw it was Consuela Lidgett.

The silence became embarrassing, and she spoke nervously. 'I didn't go home,' she said, giving Slattery a defiant look. 'There's nothin' to go home for, now.'

Graf was watching Slattery closely. He seemed surprised to see him and for once appeared to be stuck for something to say. Then his brows came down and he gestured to Consuela who rose and disappeared without a word.

'Affairs of state?' Sjogren asked, leaning forward.

'Not *your* state,' Slattery snapped and Sjogren's face grew pink.

'Not even *your* state, Fausto,' Slattery said. 'Unless you're here as Carranza's representative. You'd better inform him that one of his observers with Villa's army's just been shot dead.'

As Slattery left, Consuela was sitting in the hall. As he appeared she rose, clearly uncomfortable in front of him. She was wearing new clothes but she looked sulky, the expression odd against the harsh newly-blonde hair and painted lips.

'I came here after Escotadura,' she said. 'It seemed okay, so I stayed.'

'Newspaper started helping again?' he asked.

'No.' She shook her head. 'They gave up. But I'm livin'. Kinda livin', anyway. I ran out of dough.'

'I could let you have money.'

Tears started to her eyes. 'I don't want your dough,' she said. 'I'll manage. I earn it. It was easier than I expected. The first time was with someone I knew.'

202

'Fausto Graf?'

She didn't answer. It had come as something of a shock to her to find that sex could be different from the rough and ready tumblings with Loyce Lidgett. She had often been warned of the sins of adultery but felt that Lidgett's unfaithfulness excused her. 'I picked the wrong guy is all,' she said stubbornly. 'I guess I'll stay here. Fausto's offered to look after me. I was a fool, believing in that Loyce. I'm never going back to Gordonsboro! That's for sure. Relatives leaning over your shoulder, telling you what to do. "Good boy, Loyce," they said. "Just the sort to give a girl a good time." Sure he could. Any girl. All girls. But not often me. I'm okay, Slattery. The Mexicans don't worry so much about morals and Fausto says he'll marry me.'

Slattery drew a deep breath. 'He's married already, Consuela,' he said quietly.

It wasn't hard to arrange for a pass that would enable Consuela to ride the trains to the border. The information that battles were pending and that Graf had lied to her had finally convinced her she should leave.

'I guess I'll go,' she said. 'But not back to Gordonsboro.'

Because the line north of Jiménez was jammed with Villa's rolling stock, Slattery arranged for Atty to drive her to Camargo to pick up a train and gave him instructions to stay with her until she climbed aboard.

Preto was buried with all due honours. Because there were no gun carriages to spare, the coffin was placed in the back of a cart which had carried vegetables the day before and had been scrubbed out for the occasion. A flag covered the body and the driver wore a long drape of black crêpe round his sombrero. Villa and his staff stumped along with the priests and acolytes and the soldiers carrying the wreaths. Behind them shuffled a crowd of officers and soldiers, and behind them again the ordinary townspeople, none of whom had known Preto but all of them true Mexicans with no intention of missing any ceremonial occasion which might brighten their lives. The arrival and departure of trains was regarded in the same spirit. Their mourning was blacker than any other mourning in the world and made their dark faces look green. Afterwards, there was a sombre meal to eat before returning to headquarters. Atty was waiting with the Studebaker.

'She didn't turn up, me dear,' he said. 'The old touch at the hotel said she'd caught a train to Mexico City instead.'

'Why? Did she say?'

Atty shrugged. 'What she's at these days, me dear, is more profitable in Mexico City than along the border.'

There was nothing they could do about it. Consuela had made her own decision. Instead, they found a bar and sat drinking for a while and speculating on who had shot Preto.

''Twasn't a quarrelsome feller he was,' Atty pointed out. 'Not the sort to pull a gun on anybody.'

'You don't have to be quarrelsome these days,' Slattery said. 'It's too easy to get shot without.'

They were late returning to the hotel and, going to his room, Slattery was surprised to find Jesús stretched on his bed, clutching one of his shoes and sobbing as if his heart would break. As he entered, the boy sat bolt upright, stared at him wide-eyed, then, flinging the shoe aside, rushed to him, clutched his hand and kissed it fervently.

'What in the name of God's all this about?'

'I thought you were dead, your honour. There was another shooting. An hour ago. I went to the street to wait for you because you were late, and I heard shots and saw a man lying under the street light. I saw them lift him up. It was you, mi Coronel. It was you.'

Villa was furious. 'Another of my aides,' he stormed. 'Who keeps killing them?'

There had been no witnesses, but the dying man had managed to gasp out that he had been fired on from a two-wheeled carriage as it had driven past him, and enquiries showed that a two-wheeled spider had also been seen driving furiously near the spot where Preto had been found a few nights before. Questions at livery stables revealed nothing, however. Nobody had hired a spider and it seemed that no private owner had been on the streets.

When Slattery returned to headquarters he learned that Vegas had disappeared and Villa was in a foul temper, obsessed with the idea of treachery around him and the usual need to remove a few hats.

The dead man was buried with the same show of grief as Preto. With Vegas still missing, Villa's face was dark with fury and Slattery's suspicions, which had started while he had been hunting coal in El Paso, resolved themselves into a hard core of certainty. When Atty appeared, he took him aside. 'How good are you with a gun, Atty?' he asked.

Arranging for a squad of soldiers under Monserrat to be placed at his disposal, that night, as he left the headquarters train, he noticed occasional spiders still on the streets. It was midnight by the time he had stabled his horse and begun to walk to his hotel. Almost at once, he heard the crack of a whip and the sound of a horse's hooves.

Gripping his revolver, he strode towards where Atty waited in the shadows. The sound of galloping came again and he saw a spider driven by a man in a wide-brimmed hat approaching. As it neared him, he stepped quickly from the light of the street lamps into the doorway where Atty waited. The driver of the spider held a gun but before he could pull the trigger Atty fired.

A whip cracked and the horse picked up speed, but further down the street Monserrat's men were waiting and a volley of shots whined past. The spider turned back on its tracks at once but, as it approached the street light again, it swung into one of the cross streets. There was another volley from more of Monserrat's hidden soldiers and it was forced to whirl back towards the light.

'Shoot the horse!'

As Slattery gave the order, a slight figure leapt from a doorway into the path of the galloping animal. Just as it seemed it would be knocked flying, there was a flash and the roar of a gun. As the horse went down, the recoil of the ancient weapon bowled its owner over backwards. Running to him, Slattery dragged him to his feet. It was Jesús and he was beaming all over his face.

'I stopped him, mi Coronel,' he grinned. 'I stopped him.'

205

As the horse had fallen, one of the shafts of the spider had broken and it had slewed round, flinging out the driver who was sprawled on his back in the road. There were two bullets in his chest and he was dying. He turned out to be the owner of one of the livery stables, and as the priest was sent for to give absolution he started talking.

'Vegas?' Villa was puzzled. 'Why should Vegas pay him to murder you, inglés?'

It didn't take them long to learn at the station that Vegas had been seen catching the train to the Tex-Mex border and, carrying a rifle, Slattery turned silently and headed for the hotel next door. As he entered, the old American woman was at her desk and she jumped to her feet as she saw his expression.

The bar was still open and at the far end, in front of a large mirror decorated with curlicues of frosted glass, Graf was sitting at a table. A gun lay near his hand. Sjogren sat with him. They both looked nervous.

As Slattery stopped in front of them, hefting the rifle to the crook of his arm, the bar became silent. His eyes glued to the muzzle, Graf rose slowly to his feet, the colour draining from his cheeks, his eyes flickering one way then the other. Almost as if pulled by the same strings, Sjogren rose also. Atty poked him with his gun.

'Sit down,' he said.

The owner of the hotel appeared with a policeman in a képi and white spats, who tried to put a hand on Slattery's arm. As he shook it off, Graf reached for the gun.

The rifle roared and Sjogren gave a yelp of fright as the mirror shattered. Graf had stopped dead, his body rigid, his face pale, the hole where the bullet had smashed the mirror only a few inches from his head. Chairs scraped and a sliver of glass slipped slowly from the mirror and tinkled at his feet.

As the policeman moved forward, Slattery gestured to him to stay where he was.

'I'm the law at the moment,' he said. 'If you're in any doubt, see General Villa.'

206

He spoke slowly, staring at Graf. 'Vegas got the wrong man, Fausto,' he pointed out. 'Twice. You weren't clever enough. Neither here nor in El Paso. If I laid the facts before Villa he'd have you shot at once. But that would make it too easy and it's something I hope eventually to do myself. Get out of Jiménez, Fausto.' He gestured at Sjogren. 'And take your lapdog with you. If you don't, I'll kill you where you sit.'

The army moved on again, construction trains driving ahead to rebuild burned bridges and repair torn-up track. Behind them came the artillery, the hospital train, and the gypsy procession of troop trains, so crammed with horses and men that at a distance they appeared to be covered with foliage. Every box-car had its guitar-twanging, joking, singing complement, banging out 'Adelita' and 'La Cucaracha'. Every yard of roof had its sarape spread against the wind, its corn-husk fire smouldering on a sheet of tin, its patient, inscrutable Indian woman grinding corn and slapping out tortillas for her man. As they waited at Yermo, sorting themselves into regiments and brigades, one of Fierro's telegraphists tapped the wire and the listening men grinned as they realized they were picking up Federal reports of alarm.

With darkness the wind rose, lifting the sand and shifting the scraps of vegetation. As it grew stronger a vast cloud of driving sand swept across the landscape to raise an opaque curtain to the south.

'Nobody can see us now,' Jesús said. 'Even God's on the side of General Villa.'

From the fires alongside the track and on the roofs of the box-cars, sparks, whipped by the wind, streamed away. All around were pinpoints of light where the soldiers smoked their cornhusk cigarettes and chanted their ballads. Apolinario Gomez García had arrived, limping and ragged and scraping his fiddle. He had been in Torreón and had information on numbers and guns.

'Today, your honour,' he told Slattery, 'we meet the enemy.'

Atty touched the instrument under his chin. 'You keep your head down, Old Man,' he said. 'You can't fight the Federals with a fiddle.'

The flying sand bit into faces, dried lips and parched throats, but, above the low susurration of its movement, through the darkness there was the constant murmur of the huge army, the occasional nervous cry of '*Quien vive?*' – 'Who goes there?' – and the high yells of engines calling to each other like worried monsters.

Jesús had been put on sentry duty and had even been prevailed upon to clean his ancient carbine for the occasion.

'Now keep guard,' Atty said. 'And stay awake.'

Within ten minutes, Jesús was fast asleep.

When they woke, peering squint-eyed into the driving dust, the cavalry was already moving off, spreading out like the spokes of a wheel, bits jingling, equipment clattering. Each column had its standard bearer with his red, white and green banner slapping harshly in the wind, the great brim of his sombrero bouncing under the gusts. An occasional pale shaft of sunlight picked out a gleaming rifle barrel as the horsemen streamed away into the mesquite, the devoted plodding women behind them.

Villa was leaning in the doorway of his red caboose, collarless, his hands in the pockets of his store suit, watching his army come to boiling life with the yelling of commands, the blare of the bugles and the shuffling of trudging feet. Gnawing at an orange and spitting out pips and pith, the juice running down his chin, he gave his orders as officer after officer appeared. Torreón was protected by a mesh of irrigation ditches and a tumbled area of low hills and deep ravines. It was also covered by the stoutly-built little towns of Gómez Palacio and Lerdo and further protected by the Cerro de la Pila, a barren cone of land commanding the railway that had to be stormed before any advance could be made.

The first moves came to nothing. Every attempt to move forward was blasted to ruins by a strategically placed battery of Federal quick-firers and by next day the road through the hills had become known as the Calzada de la Muerta, the Highway of Death.

The dead and wounded had been removed during the night and the waiting troops kept to the shelter of the rocks

209

and folds of ground on either side, camping along a nearby stream-bed, a confusion of half-disciplined soldiery, unruly animals, women, children and flea-bitten dogs. A few shifted restlessly, like maggots on a carcass, hacking hunks of meat from slain steers, tossing fodder to weary horses, buckling on weapons. While their women slapped clothes in polluted water, others deloused themselves or crouched over a game of cards. Swarms of flies hovered over the sore backs of animals, the food and the eyes of the babies.

Occasionally, someone wanting to join a *compañero* at the other side of the road jumped up and ran across, bent double, to yell and dance with glee when he reached safety, but the slightest movement of any number brought immediate retaliation from the Federal guns. To keep up the spirits of the waiting men, Villa had sent forward one of the regimental bands and it was playing a selection from Bizet's *Carmen*.

Waiting for the move forward, Slattery brooded on his future. He had agreed to stay on at Villa's headquarters until the campaign was ended one way or another, but after that he could see little that could continue to attract him. After the fighting would come the politics and the manoeuvring for power and, with German help, the anti-Huerta armies were already beginning to disagree among themselves. Afterwards, every 'general' who had taken part would demand some say in what happened.

He wondered where Magdalena was and whether *her* plans were working out. She always seemed to be in his mind, returning when he least expected it, her image always bringing with it, like the ache of an old bruise, a feeling of futility.

Suddenly he became aware of laughter and looked up to see Jesús hurtling towards him. As he arrived, he tripped over the guy rope of a tent and fell flat on his face. He leapt up as if on a spring.

'Mi Coronel,' he yelled. 'Don Apolinario is bullfighting with the enemy! He's been at the *aguardiente*!'

Scrambling after the boy, Slattery saw the tattered figure of the old troubadour strutting up the middle of the road,

210

his worn red cloak over one shoulder, one hand on his hip like a torero advancing in the grand parade in a bullring. The murmur of voices around them died as he halted and stood erect, waiting. As Slattery moved, Atty grabbed his arm and held him back.

'No,' he snapped. 'No, me dear!'

They became aware that the music had changed to the blood-curdling *'Deguello'*, the traditional Spanish march of no quarter, the hymn of hate that spurred soldiers in their final assault. There was an immense silence as the old man swept off his hat, which he had twisted into a vague resemblance of the black-knobbed montera worn by a torero, and bowed with a flourish towards the enemy guns. His straggly hair had been screwed up into a bullfighter's stumpy pigtail.

Flinging the hat over his shoulder, he slowly unfolded the worn sarape. Immediately, they heard a distant shot, and a round from the quick-firers whirred past to explode among the rocks. It was close enough to stir the tattered cape as García swung it defiantly in a posture, as if playing the missile like a charging bull. Pirouetting, stiffening, swerving into graceful veronicas, half-veronicas, mariposas and naturals, he swept the cloak close to the earth as if dragging a bull's head down for the kill. Once again the distant gun fired and a second shell whirred past to explode behind the scarecrow figure.

'Y'old fool!' Atty yelled. 'Come away in!'

García paused and, seeing Slattery, his faded smile appeared. 'The Germans are in Torreón,' he said. 'Did you know?'

'Never mind the Germans. Get under cover.'

'El Señor Horrocks will want to know.'

Slattery's jaw dropped. García was still posturing and weaving in the roadway.

'Who the hell *are* you?' Slattery demanded.

The old man smiled again, then he gestured at the smoke still hanging over the road where the shell had burst. *'Mucho teatro,'* he said. 'They have a big bull in Torreón today. It has long horns and moves very fast.'

211

He was in full view of the enemy, posturing wildly, and some officer somewhere in the town had restrained the musketry which would have brought him down. Everybody, both the Villistas and the Federals, was watching every shot, and the artillery were timing their fuses so that the shells exploded well beyond the old lunatic. The band was still pounding out its music and the watching men began to cheer every pass, every twirl of the cape. Again and again the old man turned and acknowledged the onlookers, gesturing to the band to play harder.

'Jesus,' Atty said. 'Belmonte never fought a bigger bull than this one. And he never fought it better.'

Another shell whirred past, and sombreros were flung upwards in delight as the ragged figure curvetted and turned to the wild dianas of the band.

There was only one way it could end and finally, as if the battery commander, who had been enjoying the show by the gentle old idiot, had been instructed by a senior officer to end the charade, there was a charge of shrapnel. As the red-hot balls whipped down, the old man stiffened then sagged slowly to the ground to lie in a dusty huddle in the middle of the road. The band slowed in the middle of its music and one by one the instrumentalists stopped, until only a solitary trumpeter, occupied with his task, played on. Then he, too, stopped. The firing ceased and there was a strange silence over the battlefield.

Atty crossed himself quickly. 'They're getting a good fiddler in Heaven,' he said.

They brought the body in after dark and buried it at the side of the road, wrapped in the sarape that had one duty as a cape. As the priest said the final words over the small dusty mound, they stood bleak-faced in the lamplight, Jesús weeping openly.

Slattery was deep in thought. Who the hell *was* Apolinario Gomez García? The fact that he was a troudabour of sorts was by the way. There were a dozen questions that needed asking. Was he one of Horrocks' agents? Otherwise, how would he know of Horrocks? Horrocks had said he'd been building up a team. Was the mad old fiddler one of them? Come to that, who the hell else were his agents? Was Atty one? He had attached himself happily to Slattery as soon as he'd appeared in Chihuahua. Was he there to watch him?

As he struggled with his thoughts, his arm was touched. It was Monserrat. '*Vengase pronto*,' he said quietly. *El jefe le llama*. The Chief wants you at headquarters.'

Villa was worried. Sitting at a table outside a little cantina picking food from a tin with his knife, he looked up angrily. Things weren't going as well as he'd expected and Slattery suddenly wondered if he were as good at war as everybody thought he was. Or had he just been lucky? Had the newspapermen persuaded him he was better than he really was?

The massive head was down and Villa was frowning. 'I've got a job for you, inglés,' he said. 'A nice easy job for somebody who doesn't like fighting.'

Slattery let the insult pass and Villa went on. 'We're short of coal for our trains again. That old billy-goat Carranza's keeping it from me because he's afraid of me. As of now, you're an Englishman again and a civilian. A tourist. A spectator. Go down to Mexico City. Find coal for me. Let the Federals think it's for them if you like, but find it. If there's none to be had there, try Veracruz. And, while you're down there, go see Zapata. All he does is sit in his hills and pull faces at Mexico City. Tell him, for God's sake, to make some sort of move so Huerta can't send reinforcements against me. Blow up the railway. Knock down a bridge or two. Ambush a few Federals. Tell the bastard to move!'

As the first assaults began against the Cerro de la Pila, Slattery drove south with Aty and Jesús, the Studebaker's huge wheels making light of the desert road. The capital was in a ferment. The newspapers carried stories of Villa, black with powder, rallying beaten troops, of men armed with cigars and sticks of dynamite crawling up to the muzzles of machine-guns. It was clear that everybody thought Huerta was almost finished.

The last news of Magdalena had come from Chihuahua and the house in the Avenida Versailles was empty, so they found a hotel and, at Atty's suggestion, threw themselves on the mercy of Pilar, the housekeeper, for a meal. She greeted them with delight.

'*La casa de Ustedes*,' she said. 'The house is yours. The diva would have it so, and I would like it. The brother was here.'

'What did he want?'

'To talk with the diva.'

Did Magdalena supply him with information, Slattery wondered.

There was no coal in Mexico City. It had all been bought up by German agents.

'Why?' Slattery demanded. 'Why do Germans want Mexican coal?'

'Because they prepare for war, señor?' the coal factor asked, shrugging.

Since there was no coal available, Slattery decided to head next day for Zapatista territory in Morelos. Zapata had attacked a number of towns recently but Huerta's generals had retaliated by burning villages and dragooning farmers and field hands into uniform and shipping them to the northern front. But the plan had back-fired because now, whenever Federal troops approached, the villagers fled to the hills, to filter back after the troops had left, so that it was the planters who suffered, losing their field hands to the army while their haciendas remained subject to raids. Morelos had lapsed into a stalemate, with Huerta's soldiers little more than policemen, and the Zapatistas moved through the hills at will, robbing a train here, collecting a ransom there, never trying anything more ambitious than a raid against a small garrisoned town.

With Atty heavily engaged with Pilar in the kitchen of the house in Avenida Versailles, Slattery ate alone in town and, not entirely unexpectedly, Horrocks appeared alongside the table, smiling. He was dressed this time in an immaculate suit with a walking stick, spats and a homburg that made him look vaguely German and every inch a diplomat.

'I thought it might be you,' Slattery said.

Horrocks eyed him coldly. 'Anyone would think I wasn't welcome,' he said.

'On balance, you're not.'

'Good.' Horrocks was undisturbed. 'I'll sit down and join you.'

He ordered a brandy and sat opposite Slattery, sipping it.

'Are you having me watched?' Slattery demanded.

Horrocks stared at him blankly.

'Who was Gomez García?'

'Who?'

'Old boy who played the fiddle.'

'Oh, that chap!'

'Who was he? One of your bloody agents?'

'Oh, yes, he was one of my chaps. Much more to him than met the eye and he could get around a lot with that fiddle. Very useful. Like many others. When you add all the little bits together it makes a very interesting whole.'

'Well, he won't be supplying you with any more.'

'Why not?'

'He's dead. He was killed at Torreón. Acting the bloody fool, pretending to be a torero.'

'It was a habit of his.' Horrocks lit a cigarette languidly. 'Pity.'

Slattery stared at him. 'You're a cold-blooded sod,' he said bitterly.

Horrocks shrugged. 'Certainly not an emotional Irish romantic.'

'Was he watching me?'

'He kept an eye on things.'

'Is Atty one of your bloody spies, too?'

Horrocks smiled placidly. 'Perhaps he ought to be. He's got a lot of sense and he doesn't get into a state like you.' He sipped his brandy, completely unmoved by Slattery's anger. 'The American president's in trouble,' he pointed out unexpectedly.

'You sound delighted.'

'Not really. But when Woodrow Wilson's in trouble, Britain's in trouble, too.'

'There speaks the patriot.'

Horrocks sniffed. 'I'm not a bloody patriot!' He made it

sound like an insult. 'I leave that sort of thing to the boys just out of school. They're the ones who'll rush to the colours with cries of "Honour" and "Duty", and posture in front of the flag with their heads bandaged and their eyes ablaze when the war comes.'

'Oh, Christ!' Slattery sighed. 'That bloody war!'

Horrocks looked offended. 'It's nearer now than it was a week ago,' he said. 'There's trouble in the Balkans and now the Americans have become involved with the Mexicans in Veracruz. Their navy was short of petrol for its picket boats or whatever they're called and they sent a whaler ashore to organize supplies. It was arrested by one of Huerta's officers.'

'Oh, splendid. Just the thing to delight the Americans.'

Horrocks lifted an eyebrow. 'It's since been released,' he said, sounding almost as if someone were being careless and letting slip something that could make a splendid incident. Then he smiled. 'However, the American admiral's one of these General Custer types and he's demanding an apology and a twenty-one-gun salute to the Stars and Stripes.'

'How can a country demand a salute to its bloody flag from a government it refuses to acknowledge? Is it serious?'

'Of course,' Horrocks was lighthearted. 'There's talk of war.'

'And you're stirring it up?'

'Oh, dear me, no! We don't want war between the States and Mexico. You know we don't. I've explained often enough why not. Looks very nasty, though. Especially as we've had reports that the German arms ships I told you about are on their way. The first of them, the *Ypiranga*, is due within a week or so.'

8

Eventually Horrocks took his leave and Slattery sat brooding over the remains of his meal. What Horrocks had told him bore out what he had always thought – that Mexico was nothing more than a pawn in the manoeuvrings of the Great Powers, and that the civil war that was destroying her was a boon to their ambitions. Wondering how much of what was going on in Mexico and had been going on now for three years was the result of foreign machinations, suddenly he found he was beginning to think Horrocks' way. He often had in the past but now it seemed to be forming into a strong core of certainty.

When he returned to the house in the Avenida Versailles, Atty was just leaving. His had a smug look on his face, like a cat that had been at the cream. Jesús had gone out.

'He's growin' up, that kid,' Atty observed. 'He's noticin' the girls.'

Pilar was worried, because she had had a long telegram the day before to say that Magdalena was due in Mexico City in two or three days time. Her last performances before going to the States were due to take place at Iguala, and the Zapatistas had just taken the town of Chilpancingo close by, and were running riot and burning everything in sight.

Deciding he might as well return to his hotel, Slattery had barely reached the set of rooms he'd taken when the bell rang. Opening it, he found himself face to face with a hotel porter and behind him, smiling, Amaryllis. Her arms were full of maps and guide books and she was wearing the sort of clothes only a wealthy woman could afford. She looked cool, blonde and expertly sure of herself.

She gestured at the porter. 'Give him a tip, old Paddy,' she said. She beamed at the man with the suitcases and gestured at Slattery. *'Mio marido,'* she said, her voice rising in the manner of all English people with an indifferent

217

command of any language other than their own. 'My husband. Found him at last!'

The porter beamed back at her, obviously as much under her spell as everybody else who met her, and backed out. As the door closed, she tossed down the maps and her handbag. 'Try not to look as if you've been hit on the head with a coal hammer,' she said. 'I've just been to Chapultepec. Doesn't compare with Versailles or Fontainebleau. Even seemed a bit on the grubby side.' She smiled. 'Kind of you to invite me in.'

He grinned. 'I hadn't noticed that I did.'

She gave him the smile that had got her into his bed in London. 'I think I arrived just in time,' she observed. 'I heard you were going to disappear into the blue again.'

'Who told you that?'

'Old friend of mine. Sholto Horrocks. He said you've got a woman here. I went to her house looking for you. The door was opened by a man with a West Country accent so thick you could cut it with a knife. Who's he? Her husband?'

Slattery grinned. 'My aide de camp, I suppose you'd call him. Atty Purkiss. He's smitten by the housekeeper. They seem to spend a lot of time getting into dark corners.'

'This woman of yours? Do you share her with Sholto? He's a great one for sharing.' She smiled at him cheerfully. 'Who is she, some little nut-brown Indian thing, all Mexican meekness and humility?'

Slattery grinned. 'As a matter of fact, she's five-foot-eight, German-American and a famous singer, and she has no humility whatsoever.'

Amaryllis was staring round her. 'Come to think of it I found the place a bit Gothic,' she commented. 'Germanic, I expect. Always a bit stodgy, the Huns.' She gestured. 'They're growing very strident in Europe these days. It's becoming very difficult over there.' Here it was again, the war, cropping up like Horrocks every time anybody opened their mouth. 'It's not exactly easy over here, of course. Are you going to marry her?'

Slattery shrugged. 'She decided not. Says there's too much difference between the Germans and the English.'

218

Amaryllis pulled a face. 'She's probably very wise. It could be pretty awkward if there *were* a war. Do you love her?'

Slattery smiled. 'Wouldn't make much difference if I did. She doesn't love me.'

'Told you so, has she?'

'Not in so many words, but it seemed clear enough.'

'Hard luck. Well, if she's turned you down she can hardly object to me grabbing you, can she? It's months since I saw you. One grows lonely and' – she smiled archly – 'I'm very warm-hearted. Where's the bedroom?'

Slattery laughed. 'You don't waste time, Amaryllis.'

'If there's going to be a war, perhaps there isn't a lot of it left. Lead the way.'

She beamed at him and began to chirrup a jingle she knew.

> 'Never jeer, never mock
> The little girl who's on the knock.
> Many a lowly curate's wife
> Has found it adds a spice to life.'

She was quite shameless and was throwing her clothes across the room even before he managed to close the door. For a second, nagged by a feeling of guilt, he thought of Magdalena, then he rejected it at once. She didn't want him and she wasn't the sort to change her views in a hurry.

Amaryllis's figure was as rich as ever and in the warmth of a Mexico City evening she was far from unwilling to provide him with a view of it. As she approached him, she was reaching with her lips for his mouth and in the same movement with long cool fingers for his shirt.

'It's been a long time, Paddy boy,' she said softly. 'One gets out of practice.' As she put her arms around him, she began to nuzzle at his ear. 'I haven't enjoyed you being so far away. It's very boring. It gets you down.' She gave a little giggle. 'Perhaps that's not quite the *mot juste*, because you certainly haven't been getting me down a lot lately.'

Clinging to him, she backed to the bed and they fell across it. She gave a little squeal of laughter as Slattery banged his head on the bed post, then she flung the pillows aside and squirmed underneath him.

'Oh, Paddy,' she whispered. 'It's almost like old times!'

As they resurfaced, she studied the room then looked at him across the pillow.

'Is she married?'

'Who?'

'This singer of yours.'

'She's not my singer. Not any more.'

'Perhaps she should be. No hope?'

'Looks like it.'

'Pity.' She tapped him on the chest then traced a line between her breasts. 'Does she go in for the same sort of thing we go in for?'

'No.'

'I bet you've tried.'

'No.'

'What a waste of a splendid piece of man!' Her fingers were tracing a light path across his stomach. 'There's such a lot of you and I do enjoy you.'

She sighed. 'You ought to come home, Paddy. I'm not staying here. The hotels are all right, though the food's awful and I think there aren't going to be any grandees in Mexico to write about before long. They're all bolting to the States. I think I'll go to New York instead. That's where the money is and American millionaires would love to see themselves written about in the same terms as European aristocrats. They'd buy thousands of copies.' She gave him a warm smile. 'Why not come with me? Forget General Villa. I hear he's nothing but a common murderer, anyway. Tear up your contract.'

'There is no contract.'

'Then just forget it. Come home.'

'I suspect Horrocks doesn't want me to.'

'Oh!' She looked startled. 'Why not?'

'He has a job for me, he says.'

'Well, everyone has to have a hobby.'

'It wouldn't be a hobby.'

She sighed again. 'I don't really mind you persisting in this silly habit of yours of wanting to fight everybody in sight, of course.'

'I've stopped fighting. These days I just talk.'

She was silent for a long time. 'Well, you know,' she said eventually. 'I have a lot of time for Sholto Horrocks, but there are plenty of things you could do in England. If this war they're all talking about comes, surely the War Office could use you.'

'It's trying to use me already. Here. That's what Horrocks is after.'

'Why?' she demanded. 'A revolution among a lot of little brown men has nothing to do with you.'

'I've found it has a lot to do with me. And for your information, with Sholto Horrocks, too. He's even managed to convince me it also has a lot to do with England.'

'Curiously, Lord Reah said the same thing to me. I've been seeing a lot of him lately. He's big and strong like you and makes a good substitute for my old Fitzpaddy boy.'

Slattery smiled. 'Let's get down to brass tacks, Amaryllis. Do you love me or something?'

There was a momentary hesitation before she replied. 'No,' she said. 'But I could marry you.'

He grinned. 'Shotgun weddings never work out.'

She climbed from the bed, reaching for her clothes. 'Perhaps I'd better push off,' she said. 'Sholto Horrocks said I could stay with him.'

Slattery laughed. 'I bet he did.'

'*And* James Reah. He's in Zocatlán.'

'Look out for him. He might try to get into your bed.'

She grinned at him, the old shameless grin that gave her so much character. 'He's been,' she said cheerfully. She made a final appeal. 'Wouldn't consider joining me in London, would you? You'd be a knock-out with the literary set.'

He gave her a quiet smile. 'They wouldn't touch me with a barge-pole.'

She touched his cheek. 'You've changed, old Paddy. You know that? You're quieter than you used to be.'

He *had* changed. He knew he had. 'Perhaps I've grown up, Amaryllis,' he said. 'It was about time.'

She eyed him shrewdly. 'Well, I used to enjoy you stamping round the bedroom but, you know, in a way, I think I like you better this way. Is it this girl?'

He shrugged. 'Perhaps it's Mexico. Perhaps it's the knowledge that a lot of what's happened here is *our* making. Ours and the Germans' and the Americans'. We all want something out of it and it pays us to keep it going. So take care in Zocatlán, Amaryllis. It's Zapata country and international agreements don't mean much in Mexico these days.' He kissed her on the cheek. 'But perhaps you'll be better off than going with me.'

'Why?' her eyes widened. 'Where are *you* going?'

He smiled. 'Same direction,' he said. 'But I'm going to see Zapata.'

9

Chilpancingo lay in a valley on the slopes of the Sierra Madre del Sur. Though it had little to recommend it, it was an ideal base for Zapata because it was close to the mountain regions into which he liked to retreat.

The train ran to Cuernavaca, the capital of Morelos, which was as far as Huerta's control ran. It had a shabby look these days and Slattery was reminded sadly of the day he had spent there with Magdalena. Somehow, something seemed to have gone out of the world without her.

Leaving the train there, he reached Yautapec by horse to find it full of Zapatistas. Nobody questioned him but when he started making enquiries, he found himself being followed. Stopping, he explained to his pursuers what he wanted. At once, hats came off and there were promises to contact him, and the following day, a man in cotton trousers and cowhide sandals was waiting for him in the street.

'Your honour.'

Round the next corner, three men were standing in the doorway. They were dressed in charro costume and armed with revolvers and rifles.

'We shoot traitors and spies here,' one said.

'I'm not a spy. I come from General Villa.'

They conferred for a moment then jerked their heads. 'Follow, señor.'

A motor car was standing down the road and they drove in it to the outskirts of the town where horses were waiting. The road soon became rough and they seemed to travel interminably. At one point they transferred to a light railway and rode for an hour in a battered carriage with the windows shot out. Then, at a wayside station surrounded by heavy foliage, they transferred to an American Dodge and clattered along a dusty road, at the end of which more horses waited.

223

Chilpancingo was full of armed men. They were smaller than the men of the north and lacked the northerners' brashness, as if their oppression had lasted longer. They wasted nothing on uniforms and wore huge straw hats with white cotton trousers with purple, pink or green socks pulled up over them as if they were about to go cycling. Their rifles were of every shape and size and behind their smiles was a hint of the cruelty for which the south was notorious. Among them were battalions of young boys, even of women. Clad in looted finery, they looked more terrifying than the men.

They eyed Slattery curiously, impressed by his size and the colour of his hair. More soldiers waited in the doorways, clutching their palm-leaf hats in their hands, and in one of the great audience rooms of the governor's palace a crowd of them were grouped round a table. Most of them had a bottle or a glass in their hands, the air was foul with smoke and the heavy smell of sweat, and some of them were clearly drunk.

Zapata was organizing the removal of the booty he and his men had captured when the city fell. Unlike Villa, who always looked badly dressed and dusty in his store suit, he was neat and clean in a charro costume of black, edged with decorative lace, the short jacket showing a spotless shirt. On his head he wore the huge sombrero that was the symbol of his loyalties. Unlike Villa, who was willing to adapt to American ways and use American know-how, he had set his face against change. Morelos and the south were his and he preferred them to remain as they always had been.

As Slattery was ushered in, the guerrilla chief gave him a long stare from jet-black eyes under heavy brows.

Slattery gave his name. 'General Villa sent me to you,' he said. 'He's heading for Mexico City and the overthrow of Huerta.'

Zapata said nothing, studying Slattery with a silence that was strongly menacing. He had never been a peón like Villa but was still a man of no learning, simple, vigorous and convinced that it was his duty to return to his people the

224

land stolen from them by the hacendados. His brooding eyes seemed to burn with fervour. 'Mexico will be a slave to no man,' he growled. 'It is better to die on your feet than live on your knees.'

Slattery had heard the phrase before and decided that, having discovered he had made a profound statement, Zapata liked to repeat it whenever he could.

'General Villa is dedicated to Mexico,' he said. 'Like you, Don Emiliano, he believes in democracy and the freedom to own land. He has sworn to get rid of Huerta.'

'Huerta deserves to die,' Zapata said in a flat voice. 'What does General Villa want?'

'He needs help. He wants you to make a move.'

Zapata thought for a moment silently, then he said, 'Unlike General Villa, we're short of arms. But I'll put a ring of men round Cuernavaca. They'll never dare let that go.'

When Slattery returned to Mexico City the place was in an uproar.

'Villa captured Torreón,' Atty said.

The vaunted Cerro de la Pilla had finally fallen, and Villa had battered his way into the city yard by bloody yard, dynamiting his way through houses as his artillery had pounded away at the place at point-blank range. In Mexico City, the exodus had already started, with all those people who had reason to fear Huerta's fall heading for the coast in cars packed with their belongings.

'Spanish, most of 'em, me dear,' Atty explained. 'They've got no hope here because Carranza's told the Americans that expelling 'em's part of *his* policy, too.'

It was obvious that all Americans didn't think like President Wilson, and an El Paso newspaper Atty produced had exultant stories of American women in Juárez celebrating the victory at Torreón by dancing in the streets with Mexican soldiers.

The exodus of the Spanish from the capital went on all day. It was clear it wouldn't be very long before the Constitutionalists arrived, because General Obregón was

225

also now beginning to make swift progress in the west, while the army in the east, unable to make Monterrey and Saltillo, had simply swept past them to Tampico. Oil had made it a boom town and the eastern army was now within ten miles of its outskirts.

Zapata kept his promise and had started attacking trains, and there were stories of passengers stripped mother-naked, even of having oil poured over them and set on fire. Though they were largely Huerta propaganda, they were more than enough to throw the foreigners into a panic.

Even Stutzmann was packing up scripts, playbills and costumes. He smiled nervously at Slattery. 'She isn't here,' he said. 'She's heading for Córdoba. It's her last engagement before she goes to New York. It's her farewell performance. Artistes give farewell performances as they give presents. Sarah Bernhardt has one every other year. She said she might go to Veracruz. She has property there.' He gestured. 'The South is no place to have investments these days, though, Herr Paddy. Veracruz is awful. Flies cover everything, and dysentery kills all the children.'

Stutzmann sighed. 'There was one whose father worked for her. He couldn't afford a priest and he carried the coffin on his head. A grave had been dug but the coffin, the flowers and the shroud had to be returned to the shop where they'd been rented and, because they couldn't pay the rent for the grave, the pobrecito was due to be dug up and tossed into a mass ditch at the end of the month and the plot re-rented. She bought it for them and put up a headstone.' He shrugged. 'They probably thought she was mad.'

'I'm going to Veracruz. I might run into her, Hermann.'

'Try her agent – a man called Agosto Parra. He'll know where she is. I think she'd like it if you did.'

'Why should she?'

Stutzmann's shoulders moved again. 'She didn't explain. She just said "Because I'm Magdalena Graf and he's Fitz Slattery."' Stutzmann looked up shrewdly. 'I think that is sufficient explanation, don't you, Herr Paddy?'

Taking only Jesús and leaving Atty in the capital searching

for coal, Slattery headed for the station. The forecourt was crammed with Spanish, Americans and other foreigners, with their children, servants and luggage, their voices querulous under the arched roof as they demanded the times of trains to the coast. They were all worried because the rebels were close to the railway line and if they cut it there would be no more trains south.

The journey was hot as the train dropped down from the highlands into the tropical zone. It was crowded and uncomfortable, and the bullet holes in the windows didn't add to anybody's confidence. In addition, there was depressing news that the incident in Tampico involving the Americans had blown up into a major crisis.

With the rebels approaching, bandits had proliferated and wealthy rancheros in the area were sitting up all night with guns in their laps. Because of rebel activity near Veracruz, the train went via Jalapa and turned south to the coast.

At Cordel they learned that the train just ahead of them had been dynamited, and the stationmaster informed them that it would probably mean delays. Then they were told that they had to get out and walk past the wrecked train to another which had been sent to meet them from Veracruz. Their clothes damp, their faces streaming with sweat, they began to struggle with heavy suitcases, children, even pets, and after a while both Slattery and Jesús were carrying exhausted infants.

The dynamited train was slewed across the rails. It had carried a brigade of Huerta's conscripts, some of whom were lying by the track with dreadful injuries. A French priest was kneeling on the floor of a carriage that was slippery with blood, to administer the Last Sacrament to a dying boy, and stretcher parties were carrying blanket-covered figures that moaned and twisted as they passed. The engine, which was lying on its side, had taken three coaches with it and men were working with axes to free people trapped in the wreckage. Near them a woman was kneeling in the shadow of an up-ended coach, rocking backwards and forwards, the body of a child in front of her on the dusty grass.

227

The huge driving wheels had gouged deep ruts in the ballast and the smashed coaches were telescoped into the tender and locked in a tangle of splintered wood and twisted metal. Indians had appeared from the trees and were dragging boxes of beer, sardines and conserves from the wreck. Nobody seemed to take any notice.

Passengers from Veracruz going north passed them in exactly the same condition as they were in themselves, struggling under luggage, children and pets. The waiting train was another battered wreck with the stuffing oozing from the seats and bullet holes in the windows and woodwork. There were more rebels across the line further along, but this time there was no attempt to stop them and the train moved slowly past, the passengers crowded at windows for a glimpse of the terrifying men who were bringing down a government. They looked small and dirty but they were all well-armed, and they waved and grinned as the train edged past their positions.

Veracruz came up at last, a squalid town that was still an artist's delight with its blue sea and sky and the whitewashed walls of the Fortress of San Juan de Ulua where vultures, seagulls and lugubrious pelicans perched. But, as they entered the city, Slattery could see dozens of men-o'-war in the bay. At first he thought they were there to take off refugees but then he learned that the rattling of sabres between the United States and Mexico had increased and that the murmuring over the incident of the flag had grown to a shout.

10

They seemed to have run straight into preparations for war and there were soldiers everywhere.

With difficulty, Slattery obtained a place in a hotel, but because of the crisis visitors had not been expected, and when he went to his room he found the maids had simply whisked the sheets off the bed after the last visitor and were ironing them unwashed on the floor.

Almost the first person he met as he went downstairs was Sjogren, the Swede, advancing across the hall. As he swept past, swinging his cane, Slattery stared after him. If Sjogren was there it meant the Germans were there, too.

The commercial and government buildings, the hotels, markets and churches were close to the waterfront, mostly old structures of Spanish design with flaking plaster and peeling paint. The plazas and gardens had once been enjoyed by Spanish Viceroys but the streets were narrow and still mostly cobbled, and there was a brooding stillness everywhere.

Magdalena's agent, Parra, had an office in an old building surrounded by arcades where dogs fought with the vultures for rubbish tossed from a nearby restaurant. To Slattery's surprise, Horrocks was sitting in the most comfortable chair. He didn't seem at all startled at Slattery's appearance and gestured languidly at Parra. 'Friend of ours,' he explained. 'Has been for years. You've arrived at the wrong moment, old son. The Americans are about to invade.'

'What in God's name for?'

'Well, *they're* calling it an occupation but it looks uncommonly like an invasion to me.'

'The incident was magnified, señor,' Parra insisted. 'The arrest of the American sailors was nothing. An apology was made at once and everybody thought it had been accepted,

229

but it just goes on and on. The Americans are looking for an excuse.'

'They can't invade over a misunderstanding, surely to God?'

'Oh, yes they can!' Horrocks was in no doubt. 'The *Ypiranga*'s expected at any moment with the German arms for Huerta and there are trains waiting at the station for its cargo. Washington thinks the arms could help Huerta win the war and that's something they don't want, so they've sent their fleet down from Tampico to stop it.'

So it had finally arrived, the crisis everybody had feared. They'd been expecting for months that the disputes American and Mexican interests had been shouting about for years would come to this, and now it had. Without doubt, the Germans had had a hand in it.

'The Mexicans are going to resist,' Horrocks said. 'But it'll be a token resistance because they've only a thousand men. They've had to recruit prisoners from San Juan de Ulua to make up their numbers. They daren't surrender, of course, because there's been a law providing death for any Mexican who helps an invader ever since Maximilian.'

At Parra's invitation, they joined him on the roof of his office, borrowed binoculars in their hands. The day was dark, with no sun and massed clouds. The waters of the bay were grey with whitecaps. Beyond the breakwater they could see the warships. Between the wharves floated the refuse from the city, coconut husks and palm fronds, watched by hundreds of vultures on the seawall – scaly, hunched, wings akimbo, hopping on their skinny legs, privileged creatures because they cleaned up the city's garbage and couldn't be harmed. Behind the city were the houses of the wealthy, of brick, granite, concrete, even white coral, with painted balconies and thick doors of carved wood and studded metal. Cheek by jowl with them were the slums of the poor, overhung by a blue haze of smoke from cooking fires.

Judging by the sky, it was building up to one of the northerly gales that blew away everything not staked to the ground, stripping the palms of old fronds and bringing down any tree with its roots in shallow soil. The waves were higher than before and the grey light seemed ominous. Then, as Slattery watched, the clouds parted and the hot sun filled the plaza beneath them. Labourers on the pier were preparing for the departure of a liner carrying refugees to make way for the German arms ship.

Parra reappeared from a visit to his office. 'The German ship's arrived,' he announced. 'I've just heard from the Customs House. It's outside the breakwater, waiting to come in.'

With the binoculars, Slattery swept the hotels, the lighthouse, the market area, the plaza with the statue of Juárez and the nearby naval cadet school. There seemed no sign of danger, however, and in the market area, people were still haggling over chickens, fish and fruit, while naked children played among the stalls. Under the arcades of the hotels he could see both Mexicans and Americans enjoying a late breakfast, and women were selling candles outside the cathedral. Newsvendors shouted on corners. Children pestered drinkers to buy lottery tickets. Shoeshine boys yelled under their metal stands. Tortilla makers squatted over their primitive braziers. Deformed beggars wailed over outstretched palms. Donkeys jogged from door to door, tin jugs of milk in their leather panniers. Servant girls in rebozos gossiped on corners. There was even a merry-go-round working under the trees.

Then Horrocks touched Slattery's arm and gestured seawards. Suddenly there seemed to be a great deal of activity around the American ships, with flashing signal lamps and strings of flags, and the water came alive with launches for the shore. Horrocks watched calmly, Parra quivering alongside him, twisting his hands and tugging at his lower lip.

American sailors and Marines were scrambling up the granite steps of the piers now. Crowds of curious civilians had gathered to watch. The Americans among them, who'd long been hoping for intervention in the civil war that so inconvenienced them, were in a gala mood and a woman was waving a flag. Not a shot had been fired.

Then the Mexicans suddenly seemed to realize what was happening and the atmosphere changed at once. Soldiers waiting in the Calle Independencia suddenly began to move with purpose and as the crowds fell back under the arcades, iron shutters clattered down, and children started pouring out of a nearby school and bolting for the suburbs. The market vendors were folding their awnings and gathering up the heaps of fruit and vegetables. Even the vultures seemed to sense danger and were leaving the area to roost on buildings and trees, half a dozen of them on the arms of the cross above the cupola of a church.

'I ought to get out of this bloody place,' Slattery observed.

Horrocks shrugged. 'Save your breath,' he said. 'The railway terminal's come to a standstill because they're expecting the Americans to seize it to get control of the trains.'

'They'll be too late,' Parra said. 'The trains have all been sent to Tejeria.'

'How do you know?'

'Because I am a Mexican and I telephoned the terminal that they were on their way. The Norteamericanos will find nothing but a few old coaches and two or three disabled locomotives.'

From the roof, they saw a sailor on the railway terminal flagwagging the ships. Khaki-clad marines were advancing in silence across the Plaza and down the street towards the cable station. There was still no sign of resistance and the only sound came from the barked orders and the rhythmic tramp of heavy boots. But along the Puente Independencia and under the arcades Mexican soldiers were waiting, and on the corner a group of prisoners from San Juan de Ulua lay on the rough cobbles. Others had taken up positions on the roofs of hotels and offices.

Sweeping the streets with the binoculars, Slattery suddenly saw a familiar figure standing behind a pillar in one of the arcades. It was Fausto Graf and he immediately understood the presence of Sjogren in Veracruz. Enamoured of German strength, he was lickspittling round

232

the Germans in his attempt to feel he was part of the Potsdam Empire.

Swinging his binoculars again, Slattery wondered what Graf was up to, then, as the German raised his arm, he realized he was holding a pistol and was staring out of the arcade towards the advancing Americans. At first Slattery thought he was going to fire at them, then it dawned on him that in the hair-trigger atmosphere that existed, he didn't need to.

As the head of the American column came into the line of fire of the Mexicans, he saw Graf pull the trigger. He wasn't aiming at the Americans but the shot shattered all hopes of a peaceful occupation. Immediately, men nervous under the tension fired from every direction and the signalman on the roof of the Terminal fell out of sight. Bunched together, the advancing Americans made an excellent target. Men dropped, but the rest continued to advance, moving in close order, shooting at rooftops and church steeples and into the arcades – wherever they suspected there was resistance.

There were already more casualties among the bystanders than among the combatants, and as firing swept the roof where he was watching, Slattery went down to the street where by slipping through offices and out of back doors it was still possible to move about. Some of the Americans had smashed down the door of an export house and were dragging out sacks of rice and coffee to make a barricade, stuffing their pockets with cigars and cigarettes as they emerged. Machine-guns had been set up at street corners, there was a field-gun in front of the US Consulate and cannon shots driving snipers away from the Juárez statue had smashed off one of the decorative eagles.

In the naval school there were a few teenage cadets, and as the Americans advanced across the open ground of Juárez Park, an affronted boy, taking a pot-shot at them, started a scattered volley. As the soldiers dispersed, a signal went out for artillery support, and warships lying broadside-on at close range, poured a barrage of shells into the building.

When Slattery returned to his hotel, Jesús was missing.

In a rage, Slattery set off to find him. All manner of people were in the back streets now, attending to the injured. Jesús was among the helpers and, as he watched him, Slattery realized that he was no longer a child but a strong, tall and eager youth.

They began leading moaning men and hysterical bloodsplashed women to shelter. Foreigners, even a few Americans, were working with the Mexicans as doctors, nurses, orderlies and stretcher-bearers. Parra was there and Slattery was surprised to see Horrocks also, his jacket discarded, his white duck trousers splashed with blood.

'Well, the Germans have got their incident,' he snapped at Slattery.

By afternoon the worst of the fighting seemed to have died. By this time the Americans were trying to arrange an armistice but, knowing the inexorability of Juárez's law, the Mexicans were not offering themselves as go-betweens; while convinced there was going to be a drive on Mexico City, their troops were moving inland, tearing up the railway track behind them.

By the time darkness came there was only sporadic firing. The Mexican regulars had all left the city but the ex-prisoners and other civilians were still roaming the streets, their pockets full of ammunition, looting shops and shooting at anything that moved.

Slattery and Jesús spent the night on the floor of Parra's office. Outside, an American Marine, squatting with his friends under the arches, was singing hoarsely.

> 'I didn't raise my boy to be a soldier,
> I brought him up to be my pride and joy.
> Who dares to place a musket on his shoulder
> To shoot some other mother's darling boy?'

The following morning Parra brought the information that no Mexican official had still yet dared to offer himself as a go-between.

Apart from occasional shots, by midday the city was totally occupied by the Americans and the streets were reasonably safe, though there was an embarrassing number of dead

234

civilians sprawled in doorways. Dogs and vultures clustered round the bodies and it was the Americans who had to drag them away.

Still not a single Mexican official had come forward to help and in every small plaza crowds were listening to impassioned speeches of hatred. Bricks were thrown through windows and the newspapers were full of fury, claiming the landing was an invasion rather than, as the Americans insisted, only a temporary occupation of Veracruz.

'Official reaction seems to be varied,' Horrocks observed blandly. 'Carranza says Wilson *doesn't* know what's best for Mexicans. Obregón says he'll fight but he's not making any move. Villa seems to be the most realistic. He says anything that helps get rid of Huerta is a good thing. I don't think there's going to be war after all.'

'I suppose you're bloody glad,' Slattery snapped.

'Well, at least, the bloody Germans haven't stirred up what they hoped. Of course, Huerta still has to go, but at least it looks as if it's not going to be Woodrow Wilson who kicks him out.'

The shooting had died away completely when Horrocks appeared again. He was accompanied by a man in the uniform of a British naval officer.

'Chap here wants some assistance,' he pointed out. 'Thought you might be interested.'

'You Slattery?' The naval man spoke with that cheerful arrogance every man in the Royal Navy seemed to possess, from the smallest pink-cheeked midshipman to the most senior admiral. 'They said you'd served in uniform.'

'That's correct.'

'Navy?'

'Flattering of you to suggest it, but no. Army.'

'Never mind,' the other man said condescendingly. 'Doesn't matter. We need a little help. We've got warships going up to Tampico. It's a mess up there. The oil tanks have been hit and the place is covered with thick smoke. We're sending a chap inland to bring out the refugees. Fancy going with him?'

11

Tampico was not a pretty place and possessed few good buildings, and the river water was mixed with spillage from the oilfields which ran down in pale fluorescent streams with debris, foliage, trees and branches to make the movement of small boats difficult. On the opposite side of the river as far as the eye could see there were swamps, trees and heavy undergrowth.

The British admiral didn't seem to have grasped that Mexicans were different from Europeans. He had protested about women being in the firing-line with the soldiers, only to be told by the Mexican officers that if they didn't allow the women in the men wouldn't go either. He was full of news from inland, most of it wrong, and Villa's was obviously the only name he'd heard. 'We've got an officer ashore,' he said. 'But our chaps aren't very good at these frog lingos. I gather you are.' He made it sound as if being able to speak a foreign language was like contracting an unpleasant disease.

Slattery was introduced to a naval commander called Tweedie, a tall, good-looking man surrounded in abundance by naval mystique, then, full of naval gin and with a Union Jack and a white flag, three of them, Tweedie, Slattery and a Spanish-American called Franco, found the refugees at a wayside station. They were dirty, hungry and tired and meekly did as they were told. As they brought them in, Tweedie and the others assumed the job was finished, but an American officer arrived in a hurry to tell them there were more refugees further along the line and they were taken back to the railhead by American Marines. As they set off walking through the intense heat once more, Mexicans were tearing up the track and burning the sleepers.

Eventually they ran into a Mexican patrol which agreed

236

to let them pass, but a mile further on, sweat making damp patches in their clothes and Slattery starting to limp, they ran into an armed mob in ragged clothes.

'Bandits,' Franco said.

It didn't seem to worry Tweedie in the slightest, wrapped as he was in the supreme confidence that everything fell away before the Royal Navy. There were dozens of armed men in the bushes, and rifles were being directed towards them when someone shouted an order and all the Mexicans rose to their feet. There were ten times as many as they had expected, but the officer who had given the order turned out to be a man who knew Franco and he was delighted that no one had fired.

'Not half as delighted as I am,' Tweedie observed.

They were passed on to Tejeria, where there were no bandits, just an off-duty officer who provided a locomotive and a truck to take them on to Soledad.

'Where's Soledad?' Tweedie asked.

'About a hundred miles along the track.'

'Good God! We might as well go to Mexico City!'

'I have a feeling we will.'

They were met at Soledad by an officer who turned out be the commanding general for the area. He had been warned of their arrival by telegraph and he admitted that the position in Mexico City was critical, with rioting outside the United States Embassy. 'There are seven hundred people wanting transport to the coast,' he said.

Salvoconductos were provided and the little train continued. Slattery had telegraphed ahead and Atty was waiting at the station in the capital, the Studebaker adorned with a large Union Jack.

'At the moment, me dear,' he said, ''tes a better insurance than the Stars and Stripes.'

He gave them what information he had. 'The doors of the Consulate have been broken down and they've smashed the windows of American businesses and hotels.'

'Where's Huerta?'

'Probably drinking brandy in some café, but with the way things are, I reckon he's in the National Palace. 'Tes safer.'

237

He drove them to see the British Minister who was worried about the refugees. 'I can't get an interview with Huerta,' he admitted. 'But they've agreed to run trains to Puerto Mexico with English guards.'

Tweedie wasn't satisfied and asked for volunteers to take a train direct to Tampico. The embassy was crowded with businessmen anxious about their affairs, and six of the younger ones offered to help at once; they spent the day stuffing the train with provisions – among them, Slattery noticed, a case of whisky and a case of gin.

Collecting passes at the National Palace, Slattery was given a bundle of despatches from the legations and from Huerta himself, who handed them over personally. When he returned to the station, the train was waiting with steam up, filled with men, women and children clutching everything they possessed, all of them tired, hungry and frightened. At the last moment, he noticed Atty was still with him.

'Hadn't you better be taking the motor back to its garage?' he asked.

'I have done.' Atty said. ''Tes locked up safe. I'm coming with 'ee. This train's for American people scared to stay in Mexico City in case they get their throats cut. Somebody might think *I'm* an American people.'

They left late at night and reached Soledad again at noon the next day. It was a sad-looking place with no building higher than one storey. A few limp trees provided the only shade in a street which was shared by pigs, donkeys and chickens. As the train drew to a stop a Federal Officer appeared and said that in their absence in the capital a hundred refugees had been brought to the town – all, he thought, United States citizens.

Instructions were given to hold the train but the driver was nervous and Slattery despatched Atty to his cabin. He noticed he had a revolver as big as a howitzer in his belt.

'There's a hotel across there,' Atty said, pointing to a flat-topped building down the street that seemed to sag under the weight of the dust stuck to it. 'I'll take him for a drink. 'Twill stop him leaving without us, and it's kinder than giving him a bonk on the conk.'

The Americans were housed in a prison, all dirty, miserable, crowded and unhappy. The women had originally been locked in one building and the men in another but nobody had been harmed and they had been imprisoned for their own safety because the mob wanted to lynch them for what was happening in Veracruz. They were in a pitiful state because they had been unable to wash, and when they had asked for food and drink, the Mexican guard had told them not to worry about food because they were going to be shot. They were all scared and almost all of them had had to walk long distances. They had come from places near Orizaba and the Córdoba area.

'Córdoba?' Slattery said, alarmed immediately as he remembered Magdalena had been heading there. Then, among the crowding people, he recognized faces from Stutzmann's company. Their finery was bedraggled and their splendid voices were being used only to wail complaints. Stutzmann himself pushed his way through the mob, his jacket torn, his collar dirty.

'Where's Magdalena?' Slattery asked at once.

Stutzmann looked puzzled. 'She was with us when we arrived.'

'Is she all right?'

'*Mein liebe Freund,* of course. But it was terrible. The mob set everything on fire. They stopped the show while we were on stage and tried to burn the theatre down. They said they were going to shoot us.'

Worms of worry beginning to crawl in his mind, Slattery watched Tweedie struggling to convince the officer in charge that it was his duty to let the civilians go.

'Tell him to contact the general,' he suggested. 'He let us through to Mexico City. Surely he'll let us back.'

Another long argument followed. It was largely Tweedie's autocratic air rather than Slattery's Spanish that won the day and in the end the officer agreed to send the message. While Tweedie remained with him to make sure he did as he promised, Slattery pushed through the yelling crowd

239

into the street. He was surprised to see the train driver advancing towards him at a run, his hands in the air, Atty just behind him flourishing his revolver. Seeing Slattery, the driver promptly dodged behind him.

'I wanted to see 'ee, me dear,' Atty explained. 'So I had to bring him, too, in case he tried to bolt. He thinks I'm going to have him shot.'

Between them, they calmed the driver down then Atty blurted out his news.

'*She's* here,' he said.

'Who's here?'

'Her. Magdalena.'

'You sure, Atty? She's not in the prison.'

'Did 'ee expect she would be? She's got the other one with her, too.'

'The other what?'

'The other bit of fluff. The one I met when she came to the house in the Avenida Versailles that night. There are a few more as well.'

'For God's sake, Atty, where are they?'

Atty indicated the hotel and Slattery started to run.

As he approached the door, it burst open and Magdalena appeared. Her expression was a mixture of delight and relief as she flung herself at him. Her face was dirty and devoid of make-up but her head was high and her eyes were bright, and she made a splendid figure in what appeared to be one of her stage costumes, a pale blue dress ruched, gathered and pleated so that it showed every inch and curve of her figure. As he put his arms round her, her expression was one of sheer joy.

'Fitz! Fitz! Fitz!' She seemed unable to stop speaking his name. He gestured at the building behind her. 'Everybody else is in prison. How did you manage a hotel?'

'I am Magdalena Graf.' She spoke without pride, simply making a statement which she clearly considered should be obvious. 'I threatened and bribed. I sang to them. I pretended to be a helpless woman and you know how important Mexicans are when they think they've got a woman to protect.'

240

'How did you explain Amaryllis? She's there too, Atty said.'

Her face split in a smile. 'I told them she was my sister. She acted the part very well.'

'I can believe that, too.'

'Have you come to take us away?'

'There's a train at the station. This is the driver.'

As she turned to him, the driver swept off his cap and bowed.

'I think we'd better get you to the train, in case the officer at the prison changes his mind. He didn't seem very certain.'

She nodded soberly, her effervescent spirit dying quickly. 'Are you in love with Amaryllis, Slattery?'

'No.'

'She said not but I didn't believe her. She's very beautiful.'

He laughed and kissed her cheek. She stared at him for a moment then she turned back towards the hotel. After a couple of steps, she stopped, swung back abruptly and kissed him on the mouth. As she vanished through the door, they heard a woman's plaintive whine through the window.

'Where are we going?'

'To safety.' Magdalena's voice came briskly.

'The chap on the white horse is here.' This time the voice belonged to Amaryllis. 'He's got the reprieve in his gauntlet.'

'I don't want to go. It's dangerous.'

'Do you want to be put in prison?' Magdalena's voice was sharp, high and splendid, and Slattery guessed that as usual she was acting a little.

'They wouldn't dare. Not with a British subject.'

There was the sound of a slap and Amaryllis's voice again. 'Don't you believe it. Get on your feet or I'll tell them you run a whorehouse and you're looking for customers. They'll be after you like rats up a drain.'

Slattery was still wondering by what chemistry these two imperious beings had managed to become friends when the women began to appear. They looked tired and bedraggled and one of them, plump and overweight, was being pushed ahead by Amaryllis, who was stumbling a little because the heel of one of her shoes was missing.

She beamed at Atty and the engine driver and then at Slattery. 'Good morning, old Paddy,' she said gaily. 'We managed to quell the mutiny.'

12

As the reply they had been waiting for arrived, the rest of the prisoners moved down the dusty street towards the train in a stumbling, weary column. The driver was only too eager to start and they moved off at dusk, rattling through the night, Slattery with Magdalena asleep against his shoulder, her face sudenly drawn with tiredness.

As they approached Tampico there was another hold-up. The officer in command at Tejeria had the train backed into a siding, but Atty saved the situation with a few bottles of beer. The next stop was for the gap where the rails had been torn up by the dynamiting and they all had to climb down and walk past the wreckage of the train. There were wails of protest.

'Think they'll shoot at us?' Amaryllis asked cheerfully.

Stumbling along the torn-up track, they passed bodies lying among the foliage, but it was impossible to tell whether they were Federals or rebels. The heat was appalling and a woman collapsed and had to be carried in a blanket by four struggling men. Then, with the end of the ruined track in sight, shooting started again and Slattery, who was carrying a child, grabbed Magdalena's arm and dragged her to the safe side of the raised roadbed where they crouched together among the huddle of frightened people, their arms round the screaming infant.

After a while the firing stopped and Tweedie began to wave his white flag. Nobody shot at it so they could only assume that the riflemen had been driven off and slowly, warily, they climbed to their feet and set off again, keeping to the sheltered side of the roadbed. Eventually they came to undamaged rails and finally, rounding a bend, saw a small engine with what looked like a coffee pot on the funnel waiting with a string of battered coaches. One after the other, the weary people began to hurry, finally breaking into a run, until they were nothing but a mob. A Federal officer waiting with a squad of soldiers jerked his hand at the carriages and they began to push the old and the young and the women aboard. Half an hour later, they were passing American-held positions, and a newsreel man standing on a flat car began taking pictures of them as they walked along the station platform.

Horrocks was there, too, waiting with Jesús. He had news of an impending attack and that the *Ypiranga*, the German arms ship, forbidden to enter Veracruz, had arrived in Puerto Mexico, further south, and was unloading there.

'Seems a lot of people have been killed in Veracruz for nothing,' he remarked dryly.

The tide was running strongly against Huerta now. Monterrey had fallen and Saltillo was on the point of capture. 'If Huerta don't go soon,' Horrocks said, 'there'll be nowhere for him to go to. At the moment, the only place available's Puerto Mexico. The German cruiser *Dresden*'s down there waitin' for him to make up his mind.'

Despite their successes, however, the Constitutionalists were already falling out among themselves. In a fury at the lack of supplies Villa had resigned command of the Divisione del Norte and, eager to eliminate his most dangerous rival, Carranza had been quick to accept it, only to find that Villa had had second thoughts and, to show what he was capable of, had captured Zacatecas. But the break had come. Villa's troops were immobilized for lack of coal and Carranza had directed all reinforcements and supplies to Obregón.

The attack on Tampico came two nights later when shells started to fall in the town. Another oil tank was hit and a great column of black smoke lifted into the darkening sky. American ships were evacuating their nationals and the British were sending up a steamer to remove everybody who was left. The refugees were gathered in a single hotel, British and American together, listening to the crashes as the Federal gunboats pumped shells into the rebel positions on the eastern bank of the river. It was obvious the govern-

244

ment troops were pulling out and four trains full of soldiers disappeared southwards. Watching from the window, Slattery saw files of men tramping past suddenly fling down their rifles and scatter. Then a group of mounted Rurales galloped up, picked up as many as they could and rode off with them pillion-fashion.

Eventually British sailors, wearing wide straw hats and sweating under gaiters, equipment, rifles and ammunition, appeared; and an officer went down the street waving a white flag to stop the shooting. As it died, they all picked up their belongings and climbed to their feet, sailors carrying the younger children. The steamer they'd been expecting was waiting at the wharf, bullet-proof plates screwed to its sides. As everybody began to file on board the First Mate appeared and told them to go below.

'In this heat?' It was the same fat woman who had done all the complaining in Soledad.

It was then for the first time that Slattery became aware of the weight of the air. It seemed clamped to the earth by the heavy clouds that had built up.

As the last refugee filed aboard, the wind started – hot and humid and breathtaking. Mexican dock workers dropped the mooring ropes into the water and, as the clanking winches hauled them aboard, the ship edged into the river. As they began to move, it was possible to see the last of the Federal gunboats slipping away ahead of them.

By this time the wind was whipping the tops of the trees, and suddenly a tremendous squall slammed against the ship and the palm trees began to bend like bows. A flash of purple lightning split the sky, to be followed at once by a violent clap of thunder. A second followed and, as the thunder roared once more, the rain came. It was like being inside a big drum with the water falling in torrents.

All the voices aboard the ship, the complaints, the exhortations, the calls of the sailors asking people to hurry, the appeals, the cheers at being safe, the whole solid murmur of sound, changed to a howl of misery. Then, spitting the rain from his lips as he stood with the sailors trying to push everybody below, Slattery became aware that above the

245

crash of the thunder he could hear the sound of firing and realized the rebels had taken advantage of the storm to creep to the river's edge, and the Huertistas were firing back at them across the ship.

Hurrying along the deck, he found a line of people rushing children to safety. Magdalena was there among the sailors, passing them to Jesús; Amaryllis, in charge as usual, was pushing their mothers after them. Magdalena still wore the blue stage costume. It was stained now and dirty but somehow Slattery couldn't imagine her in anything else.

He could hear bullets cracking against the upperworks of the ship and, as he reached out to push her to safety, he heard her cry out. She staggered and almost fell but, because of the child she was carrying, she struggled upright again, one hand against the bulkhead to support herself. As he took her arm, she turned to him and he saw she was making an attempt to smile.

The child was wailing with fright and he snatched it from her and handed it to Amaryllis, then as Magdalena sagged to the deck, he swept her up and began to carry her below, her cheek against his, her wet hair across her face.

The saloon was full of people. They seemed to occupy every inch of space and filled all the banquettes.

'Move over,' Slattery said.

The fat woman's angry face lifted to him. 'I was here first!'

Amaryllis gave her a shove so that she landed on the deck with a thump. As Slattery laid Magdalena down her eyes opened. 'What's all the noise?' she asked.

'A little shooting, that's all.'

'Have I been hit?'

'Yes.'

'Oh, *du liebe Gott*! There are too many bullets in Mexico these days.' Her voice was slow and tired.

As he searched for a doctor Slattery saw they were passing the Federal gunboats, which were pumping shells into the river bank as fast as they could load. It was impossible to see more than a few yards and all he could make out were bulky shapes and the flashes of the guns.

246

There was no doctor on board but the First Mate had some skill at first aid. The refugees, diverted from their fear by this new event, had made a circle round Magdalena and Atty was pushing them away angrily.

'Move back,' he was saying. 'Let the dog see the rabbit.'

Cutting Magdalena's dress away, they saw the bullet had entered her side. There was surprisingly little blood, just a small bruised hole in the white flesh. For a moment, Slattery thought she was dead but then the Mate looked up. 'It hit a rib and ran along her back. It's still there. It must have been near the end of its trajectory or it would have done more damage. We'll plug it and keep her quiet until we reach the Navy. *Hermione*'s just down the river. Is she your wife?'

Slattery shook his head, wondering why not.

Veracruz was quiet when they arrived and the Americans were in complete control. They had half expected to march on Mexico City, but President Wilson was not prepared to go that far and they had settled down to make themselves comfortable.

The city looked battered, the cornices chipped, the electric street globes smashed, the pink-painted façades spotted with white where shell splinters had removed plaster.

Magdalena was in considerable pain. The naval surgeon removed the bullet from where it lay just beneath the skin in her back and held it out to Slattery.

'Mauser,' he said. 'I took quite a few of these out of our chaps in the South African War. The Boers had 'em. The Germans supplied 'em.'

He was quite unmoved. To him Magdalena was just another casualty among the hundreds of innocent people who were being injured in Mexico. To Slattery it was different. When he himself had been hurt at Torréon it had not seemed to matter much and he had felt no resentment, but that Magdalena had been wounded seemed an outrage.

Her agent, Parra, had prepared her house for her and, with Jesús to run errands, his wife offered to act as nurse.

'I'm going to be all right now,' Magdalena said faintly. 'After all, it was only a tiny bullet.'

'A German bullet, Magdalena,' Slattery pointed out quietly.

She gave him a quick look and turned her head away in silence.

It didn't take the press long to discover what had happened and Atty arrived with the newspapers. *Diva Shot*, they announced. *Many Months Before She Can Sing Again*.

They were fulsome in their praise, paying tribute to her courage and, since they knew little of what had happened, laying stress on her ability as a singer.

'It's the best press I've ever had,' she murmured.

Stutzmann came, in a panic that his leading lady was hurt. 'But it will be all right,' he said. 'We will abandon the farewell performance to get you well enough to go to New York. You can always say farewell later.'

Other members of the cast also appeared, dressed in new finery, all of them overacting and filling the house with the cadenzas of their splendid voices. Outside the house, the situation remained the same. Every day it was expected that Huerta would finally disappear, and the railway was being opened to Mexico City. But the split in the Constitutionalists' ranks widened. Villa still needed coal and Carranza was blaming all his diplomatic troubles on him.

At the end of the month, Horrocks appeared. He had been recalled to Mexico City and was in a curious mood.

'The heir to the Austro-Hungarian Empire's been assassinated in Serbia,' he said. 'The Austrians have sent an ultimatum backed by the Kaiser, and all the German agents in Mexico are heading like iron filings to a magnet in the direction of Mexico City. It looks very tricky.'

Amaryllis arrived to say goodbye. They had seen little of her. She had called once or twice but had never remained long, as if she suspected she was in the way. Slattery guessed she had been staying somewhere in the city with Horrocks.

Soon afterwards they learned that Huerta's régime of drunkenness, terror and disgrace had come to an end and he had left Mexico in the German cruiser for Spain. The

248

efforts to keep him in power had come to nothing, but Slattery had a feeling the trouble hadn't even started yet. Although Villa's plans to arrive first in Mexico City had been thwarted by the lack of coal for his trains, Zapata in his turn had thwarted Carranza's aims and, having opposed Díaz and Madero and Huerta, the sphinx-like southern leader was now preparing to oppose the First Chief.

By this time, Magdalena was moving about, slow, pale-faced but cheerful, with Jesús, splendid in new clothes, openly adoring her. 'He's worried my career has been ruined,' Magdalena smiled.

'He thinks the world of you,' Slattery reminded her gently. 'And he deserves more than just following the armies. He needs you. Perhaps you need him.'

Her fingers closed round his. 'I'll look after Jesús,' she said.

With Europe exploding into war and armies finally on the march, Slattery was occupied for a few days trying to find out what his own position would be. Though he was no longer a British soldier, he was surely likely to be needed and he was involved with trying to get in touch with the Embassy in Mexico City. When he appeared at Magdalena's house again, he found her surrounded by newspapers cadged for her by Atty from the American Marines. She was in a curious mood and had lost all her gaiety.

She gestured at the newspapers. 'The whole world's at war,' she said.

He nodded and she looked at him steadily. 'What will happen to you?' she asked.

He felt sure she was demanding that he lay his cards on the table. But fresh news had come from Europe, and Horrocks' assessment of the situation was proving an under-estimation.

'The only treaty Britain had,' he explained quietly, 'was one that everybody had forgotten. The Germans have gone into Belgium and we had guaranteed Belgian territory. We're in, too.'

She said nothing for a long time then she sighed. 'Fausto will be pleased,' she said.

'Magdalena, did he try to get information from you?'

She gave a nervous little laugh. 'What would I be able to tell him? How Hermann missed a high C and the audience jeered. How Rosemary de Bosio likes to sleep with Arthur Miranda and Evangelina Oropesa likes to sleep with everybody. How two of the children from the chorus are going to get married. How Jorge de Barrio eats garlic when he's going to sing with Oropesa because she hates it and he hates her.'

'I'm serious, Magdalena. Has he ever asked what you've seen along the border when you've crossed it?'

She stared at him. 'You *are* a British agent,' she said slowly.

He shook his head. 'No, Magdalena, I'm not. And I shall be leaving now, anyway.'

'Where for?'

'England for a start.'

'And then?'

'Wherever the fighting is, I suppose.'

She turned her head away, so that he shouldn't see her unhappiness.

'I'll come back when it's over, Magdalena.'

She sighed. 'Perhaps it will be pointless,' she said.

'What do you mean?'

She pushed forward one of the newspapers Atty had brought. It was a New York daily and it covered the first moves of the war in Europe at some length. The headlines were unequivocal.

'*German Atrocities in Belgium. Liège under Hun Fire.*'

'I'm a Hun,' she said.

250

Part IV

1

'You're a bit bloody naïve, old son,' Horrocks observed, 'if you think we're going to let you disappear to England.'

'I'm a soldier,' Slattery said.

'With that leg of yours?'

'I go to war sitting down. I'm a cavalryman.'

'You have the brains of a cavalryman too.'

'What the hell were *you*?'

'Something cleverer than a horse soldier.' Horrocks sighed. 'Anyway, it's turned out to be an infantry war and the cavalry's dismounted. What's more, they're killing 'em off like flies. Fifteen thousand of our lot so far, not counting wounded. French run to a million or more. Goin' to be a long job and tossin' in everybody who can pull a trigger or ride a horse ain't the way to do it. We can use people like you here. Mexico's suddenly important because she supplies almost every drop of oil used by the navy.'

Slattery was silent and Horrocks went on cheerfully. 'Germany's delighted with the way things have turned out, of course,' he said. 'And they're bound to try to stir things up further, because there'll be no hurrahs for Woodrow Wilson for Veracruz and he'll be glad to hand it back as soon as the time's ripe, you'll see.'

He offered Slattery a drink and went on, happily speculating. 'Fortunately for us, the old Hun's not in a position to take too much advantage of the situation because he's suddenly rather heavily involved in Europe. Getting to Paris turned out to be a bit more difficult than they'd anticipated and they started getting nasty-tempered and committing atrocities. So bloody stupid. Never seem to think.'

'At least Huerta's gone.'

Horrock gestured. 'Oh, he'll be back. When it suits the Germans. He'll be like Napoleon on Elba. Germany's bound to try to get the States sucked into a war against

253

Latin America. There've already been rumours that the Japs have landed in Mexico. Came from the German cruiser *Geier* in Pearl Harbour. Sending 'em out over her wireless with her band playing at full blast on the quarterdeck to drown the noise. All adds to the old confusion.'

'On which you thrive.'

Horrocks shrugged, unperturbed. 'How's the Diva?' he asked.

'She's on her feet.'

'I bet Amaryllis ain't.' Horrocks gave a sly little snigger. 'She's back in London, did you know? Lord Reah's also back and you know what he's like. Goes at it like a ferret. Now the war here's finished, I suppose you'll be out of a job. Unless, of course, another starts at any moment. And it might, because Villa can't stomach Carranza and threatened to shoot Obregón as a traitor; Obregón won't wear Villa; and Orozco's gone over to Zapata; while Zapata as usual's against everybody. They're going to hold a conference at Aguascalientes to talk things over, did you know? Everybody who opposed Huerta. It'll be hell. What are your plans?'

The only plans Slattery had were to get Magdalena home, and he said so firmly.

'Under the circumstances then,' Horrocks said. 'You might just as well join up with us.'

'Suppose I don't want to?'

Horrocks looked surprised. 'Surely you don't think we're going to let someone go with all the training in treachery you've had? After all, everything that's been happening here in the last year was only the preliminary to what's going to happen now. I once told you Mexico was written on everybody's heart, in letters of blood, letters of gold, letters of fire in the sky if you like. Hundreds of feet high, old son. Mexico might not look it but she's one of the main keys to the struggle in Europe and everybody with any sense knows it – British, Germans, Americans. Perhaps even the Mexicans have noticed it. If the Germans get America involved in Mexico we can say goodbye to Europe, and with your country in peril, the Germans likely to invade, and the

Sinn Feiners knocking at the back door, you can hardly go back to being military adviser to an ex-bandit who's going to end up defeated.'

'Is he?'

'Of course. The States are going to come down on Carranza's side.' Horrocks smiled. 'A wire to the ambassador would make you official. Or at least official in my department. You'd be a sort of attaché. Attached to me. An attaché's attaché, you might say. After all, security covers a lot of ground – mostly what it shouldn't.'

As Slattery still hesitated, Horrocks' eyes widened. 'What's the matter?' he demanded sharply.'Don't you fancy being part of the great civil service? Not many people get in by the back door, you know, and you might even find yourself running the whole shooting match yourself one day. I'm due for promotion. It would put a bit of money in your bum pocket and that would be useful now you've chucked Villa.'

Slattery was still wary, and he went on cheerfully. 'With your experience you'd be out in the field a lot. Sort of field hand, you might say. Keeping an eye on British interests in Mexico. Because, believe me, there are plenty to keep us active.'

'I haven't the temperament to be a diplomat.'

'You won't *be* a diplomat.' Horrocks managed to make it sound insulting. 'We have more important things to do than stand around saying the right things and looking pretty. Our job's Intelligence, even if it's unofficial, and that means being where things happen and watching what the Germans are up to. We do what we like and go where we like and at the moment we're working with the Americans because they're as aware of what the Germans are up to as we are. Officially your job will be to rescue the perishing and those half-wits who haven't the sense to know what day it is in a foreign country, but when you aren't out in the field you'll have the office next to mine in Mexico City to keep an eye on things when I'm not there.'

'What about Atty Purkiss?'

'Is that his real name?'

'I think, in fact, it's Arthur.'

'Well, he's good. Knows a lot of people. Comes up with a lot of information. Let's have him on the payroll as a field hand's mate.'

Atty regarded his translation to the Diplomatic Corps with his usual aplomb. The following day he turned up in a new suit with a celluloid collar, spats and a cream homburg. They didn't go with the cynical expression he invariably wore, but they were clearly what he considered a Foreign Office official ought to sport, and that, he also considered, was what he had become.

For Slattery it wasn't so easy. He had fought all along to avoid becoming involved with Horrocks. But Horrocks had never really left him alone, hinting, nudging, persuading, and he had constantly pushed him off, feeling vaguely that Horrocks followed a shabby profession. But now he was committed, part of Horrocks' organization, available to betray, to cheat, to listen at keyholes, to be as dishonest as Horrocks for the dissemination of falsehoods and the repudiation of other people's falsehoods. He managed to persuade himself that the fact that his country was at war made it acceptable.

When he moved Magdalena back to the house in the Avenida Marseilles, Pilar immediately threw up her hands and started wailing with dismay at her wound, until Atty fetched her a clout at the side of the head and told her yelling was no help.

It took only twenty-four hours for the newspapers to become aware of her arrival and they became ecstatic about their wounded heroine. Discreetly ignoring her German father and her American naturalization papers, they chose to consider her Mexican, and there were paeans of praise about her courage, and artists' pictures in the coloured magazines the Mexicans enjoyed at weekends – alongside drawings of girls being snatched from their families by bandits, and monks being eaten by coyotes – of her running from shellfire along the deck of a ship, her arms full of children. They made Magdalena laugh, even though laughing was still painful.

With Huerta gone, the Federal troops had moved out of the capital and the city uneasily awaited the arrival of the Constitutionalists. Tired of playing politics, Zapata had retired once more to the hills of Morelos and, because Villa was stalled by lack of coal for his locomotives, Obregón was the first to arrive. He was followed shortly afterwards by Carranza who headed towards the National Palace in a typically splendid procession that was marred only by the squabbling of his generals about which side of the First Chief they should ride. Attempts to include Zapata were rejected at once. Zapata didn't like Carranza any more than he had liked Díaz or Madero or Huerta.

With the police disarmed and no one to prevent thieving and killing, the northern generals began to move into the homes of wealthy families, while their soldiers contented themselves with confiscating horses and cars and settling private scores. For safety, Slattery moved into the house in the Avenida Versailles, with Atty and Jesús in the servants' quarters with Pilar – and an attempt to loot the place was stopped on the front steps by Atty's pistol.

The would-be looters were four Zapatista stragglers, small dark-eyed and swarthy, swathed to the eyebrows in bandoliers of ammunition. They started by begging but were on the point of drawing their guns when Slattery arrived, with Jesús just behind with an ancient muzzle-loader.

'You must be quiet,' Slattery begged. 'Because of the wounded Diva lying upstairs at death's door.'

His words silenced the argument, and when he produced the newspaper with pictures of Magdalena, the Zapatistas were immediately full of apologies and one of them shyly asked for a postcard of her which, to show his admiration, he stuck in his hatband with the picture of the Virgin of Guadalupe.

Aguascalientes, where the Constitutionalists' planned convention was to take place, was a quiet spa town crowded with Mexicans of all shapes and sizes, all armed to the teeth.

They sat in the Morelos Theatre clutching their weapons and signifying their approval of what was being said by crashing rifle butts to the floor, and their disapproval by shooting holes in the ceiling.

It was obvious the convention could only end in disarray. In the circus atmosphere that existed, nothing could come of its deliberations, but as a show it was a great success, moving constantly from tragedy to farce and back again. Everybody appeared to be praying for Mexico but nobody could agree on the form of prayer. Solemnly the delegates signed the national flag and exchanged embraces, and that night, as a newsreel of the revolution was shown, unable to find seats in the crowded hall, Slattery and Horrocks took their places among the diplomatic attachés, intelligence men newspaper correspondents who had appropriated chairs and were watching from behind the screen.

As the heroes of the revolution appeared on film there were cheers and vivas from the audience. Only Carranza's face produced a chorus of boos and, as he was shown making his triumphal entry into Mexico City, the uproar culminated in some over-excited delegate firing two shots at the screen. They penetrated it at the First Chief's chest to strike plaster from the wall just above the heads of the men in the chairs.

'If he'd entered on foot they'd have hit us,' Slattery said through the shout of laughter.

'If he'd entered on foot,' Horrocks observed dryly, dusting plaster from his clothes, 'he wouldn't have been Carranza.'

Carranza had refused to attend the conference, while Zapata had sworn to have nothing to do with it until there was a promise to give back the land stolen from his followers by the hacendados. The possibility of trouble between the Constitutionalist generals was increased with every word that was spoken and, as the two opposing forces began to take shape, the rebel leaders who had defeated Huerta had to decide to which side of the fence they belonged. Most of them stayed exactly where they were, but Villa was shocked to learn that several of his best men had refused to back him.

It was noticeable that Sjogren, the chargé d'affaires from the Swedish Embassy, was keeping a sharp eye on the voting from one of the boxes of the theatre where he was making extensive notes. Doubtless Graf was also somewhere around, Slattery decided.

The convention bogged down into stale arguments but the unexpected arrival of delegates from Zapata brought it to violent life, with shaking fists, threats and pistol shots, and the confusion was completed with a letter from Carranza demanding the immediate disappearance from the field of his old enemies, Zapata and Villa. Zapata's men greeted it coldly. Villa insisted that Carranza should retire before he would, and the farce ended in a complete split.

'*Madre de Dios*,' Villa growled. 'It's going to start all over again. I shall need you, inglés.'

'Not any more, Don Pancho.'

Villa scowled and for a moment, remembering the fluky pistol, Slattery thought he was going to kill him on the spot. But Villa stepped up to him and, with an enormous abrazo, half-lifted him from the ground in his arms. 'Why, inglés?'

'My own country's at war now, Don Pancho. Things have changed.'

'I know. I understand. Don't talk about it. What are you going to do?'

'I'm going to Mexico City.'

The amber eyes glittered, and the burly figure tensed. 'You're not going to join the Huertista lot, are you? Everybody's trying to cut everybody else's throat these days – especially their friends' throats.' Villa put his arm round Slattery's shoulders and, knowing his ability to change moods at lightning speed, Slattery wondered again if it were the preliminary to a bullet in the back.

He explained about the war in Europe and how it affected him, and they talked for an hour, Villa still angry that he had been betrayed by the men who had gone over to Carranza. 'Why didn't you desert me too, inglés? Maclovio Herrera did. Guzmán gave me a Judas kiss. Why not you?'

'Perhaps because I can beat you at cards, Don Pancho.'

Villa laughed and gave him another abrazo.

'I knew Benavides might betray me,' he said. 'And, of course, Roblés. I never trusted *him* and should have had him shot long since. Never you, though, inglés. I never understood you, but I always trusted you.'

He accompanied Slattery to the station and watched him board the Pullman coach. On the platform he spoke to the conductor.

'This is one of my men,' he pointed out. 'Take good care of him. Remember how well I shoot.'

There was a last abrazo.

'Look after yourself, inglés. I have no complaints. You served me well. Do the same for your own country. You're free now.'

As the train began to speed into the darkness, Slattery looked back. Villa was still standing on the station platform, his hands on his gun belt.

'So much for your little playmate.' It was Horrocks, popping up as usual from nowhere and appearing in the compartment. 'You'll have to watch your step, old boy. He's a difficult man to cross.'

2

Mexico City was worried. Though Huerta had gone, nobody felt they had seen the last of him.

As Horrocks had predicted, there were no hurrahs for President Wilson. The Mexicans weren't interested in moralizing from north of the border. The only thing they wanted from the Americans was guns, and with the country on the point of becoming a battleground again, hordes of pistol-happy horsemen began to move.

As the opposing sides began to line up, it was clear that Obregón at least had not forgotten the idea that lay behind the revolution and the talk swung away from fighting for loot to hammering at the foundations of a better life. Some of the land stolen by the hacendados was returned, self-government was given back to the municipalities and trades union were allowed. In return, the unions raised battalions for Obregón; and Turner, Horrocks' English printer, found himself installed with a printing press in a box-car in the railway sidings, with an editorial office to produce propaganda, the one essential for winning wars that Villa lacked but which Obregón understood perfectly.

Turner was also producing news-sheets explaining the Allied cause in the war in Europe, but it was Slattery's belief that in their spare time the Mexican workmen he employed were producing others for the Germans which said exactly the opposite. With the capital short of ready money, Turner was also being paid to turn out Carranza currency. But, as he watched the sheets running from the old flatbed machine he used, he was nervous and unhappy. 'I wish I was my brother,' he told Slattery. 'He works for the telegraph office. If Villa comes he'll probably shoot me.'

By this time Slattery had moved into Horrocks' office in the Avenida Juárez, close to the Embassy. From there he was involved with Washington, New York and England, certain suddenly that he was doing the right thing. And when London newspapers turned up, the horrifying lists of the British army's dead in France made him realize that Horrocks had probably done him a good turn.

Mexico city grew more and more dilapidated. Trams stopped running, cabs vanished as horses were stolen, and bandits of one side or the other entered houses as they pleased, making the girls they found there strip naked, not to rape them but because they wanted their clothes for their girl-friends. It was nothing to find a dead man lying in the porch after hearing shots during the night.

Magdalena was moving about almost normally now, and occasionally they dined in the city, drove to Chapultepec or walked in the Alameda Gardens. Other strollers watched them with interest because they were an eye-catching pair, Slattery tall, well-built and red-haired, Magdalena beautiful and well-known about the capital. Sometimes they even provoked a ripple of clapping.

'You and I,' Slattery observed, 'could walk down Picca-dilly, the Champs Elysées or the Unter den Linden, and makes eyes click in their sockets every time.'

She laughed and hugged his arm. She had completely forgotten their quarrel in the security given by her rescue at Tampico, and she was warm, affectionate and happy. She had started a daily régime of practising so that the house was filled with throat clearings, trills and arpeggios. She seemed constantly to be singing – something from one of the operettas, traditional Mexican tunes, an aria.

'Opera is a more serious taskmaster than operetta,' she said. 'But I can reach the high notes, and there is no longer any pain when I breathe.'

She was planning to go to Chihuahua until she felt it time to cross to El Paso for the train to New York. 'If I'm in Chihuahua and fighting breaks out, I shall be close to the border and the International Bridge. I hope the New Yorkers will like me.'

'They'll love you,' Slattery insisted.

She gave him a radiant smile. Then her expression became unexpectedly sad at the thought of parting. 'I wish –'

262

she began. Then she stopped, drew a deep breath and went on briskly. She was taking Jesús with her, she said. He had grown very attached to her and had refused to stay behind, and she was happy to have him.

'There'll be plenty for him to do,' she said. 'Hermann will be coming as soon as his present show finishes. He will act as manager for me and arrange percentages, matinées and the number of seats. Jesús can be under-manager.' She frowned. 'There's only one snag. What is his name? The Americans will want to know and he has no birth certificate and doesn't know his parents or where he was born,'

'Use *your* name,' Slattery suggested. 'Call him Graf. Atty will fix the documents. Atty can fix anything.'

With Atty taking to walking out with Pilar and Jesús discovering the joys of adolescent love with a girl from Hermann Stutzmann's office, the house on the Avenida Versailles was often empty except for Magdalena and Slattery. The absence of other people seemed to worry Magdalena occasionally and certainly began to put ideas into Slattery's head. But he wasn't sure how to play his hand. He had never worried much about such things before but somehow Magdalena was different. Then, with the troops of Carranza and Zapata facing each other uneasily on the southern outskirts of the capital, in Europe the fighting flared up and Stutzmann turned up at Magdalena's house in tears, his weak, handsome face gloomy, his plump cheeks trembling.

'I have been told to report to the German Consul,' he said, stroking Magdalena's hand distractedly. 'With the war, all Germans have to report. Not you, of course. You'll still be able to go to New York without me. The contract is still good. Moore's Theatre will be booked as soon as you're fit. I received a letter from your brother, by the way. He now considers himself a German officer. He says he's coming to see you.'

'I don't wish to see him.'

Graf turned up, nevertheless.

'She is still my sister,' he said furiously as he was halted

263

at the door. 'She is German. I insist on seeing her. You can't stop me.'

Slattery didn't move. 'I could always shoot you,' he said. 'I once promised to and, given the state of the city at the moment, nobody would notice.'

The house was empty as usual, as Graf turned away angrily, Slattery ran upstairs to Magdalena's room. It was a large salon next to her bedroom, decorated in blue with wispy drapes at the windows. On the piano was a photograph of Slattery and one of Hermann Stutzmann addressed to '*Die schönste Magdalena*.'

She was wearing a flimsy summer gown and looked up as he appeared. Putting down the score she was reading, she gave him a welcoming smile. He didn't return it.

'Fausto was here,' he said.

Her eyes filled with a lost look. 'Oh, Mother of God,' she said. 'Will it ever go away?'

'He's always around.'

She managed a twisted smile. 'So are you.'

'What does he want?'

'To see me. He's my brother.'

Fausto was more than that, Slattery thought. He was no longer just someone he disliked and distrusted, a foreigner stirring up trouble. He had become an enemy, and was dangerous and ruthless.

'He likes to know what you're doing,' she went on.

'And you tell him?'

'No.'

'Why not?'

'It's none of his business.'

'It always was before.'

She was angered by his unexpected aggressiveness and turned away from him, back to her desk.

'He's a German agent, Magdalena,' he said.

'I know.'

'Working to get Mexico involved in the war in Europe.'

'I know that too. But I don't think he means *you* any harm.'

Slattery gave a harsh laugh. '*He tried to have me murdered,* Magdalena!'

Her head swung round, startled. 'I don't believe it!'

'It's true.'

'Why didn't you tell me?'

Slattery's voice rose. 'For the same reason you don't tell *me* things! Because he's your damn brother!'

She put down her glasses and headed towards the bedroom. In the doorway, she turned, her eyes as angry as his now. 'Why should he want to see you dead? Why?'

'Because I saw him in Escotadura.'

'I know. I told him.'

'I saw him kill the Lidgett woman's husband. That's why he wanted me out of the way. He was with the Orozquistas. He'd been living with her and was worried she'd find out what he'd done. When he learned I'd seen him – when you told him – he tried to have me removed. Twice. *Twice*, Magdalena! But they were clumsy and two other men died in my place.'

She turned by the bed, her face shocked, her voice shaking. 'God forgive me! I didn't realize!' She was contrite but he failed to notice in his anger.

'Do you pass *everything* on to him?'

Suddenly she lost her temper, too. 'Yes,' she snapped. 'Yes, yes!' There was anguish and despair in the way she swung round to face him. 'I always told him what he asked!'

'*You were a German agent?*' Despite everything, Slattery found it hard to believe. 'Do all Germans ask their sisters to do their dirty work? Their mothers? Their grand-mothers?' So he had been right all along when he had wondered about her, he thought bitterly. Horrocks had been right. 'Is that why he was always turning up? Is that why he came today?'

'He liked to ask questions. I didn't understand at first why. I do now. And it wasn't hard to give him answers. Because I was Magdalena Graf. I met everybody and they talked.'

'Why are you telling me all this now?'

265

Her eyes sparkled with moisture. 'Because people like Fausto and Kloss and Von Raschstadt are tearing Mexico apart.' Her face was full of misery. 'There were always questions! About Díaz. About Madero. About Huerta and Carranza and Villa. About Americans I met. About you. He's still trying to get answers from me. He threatens to tell the Americans I work for Germany. So I shan't be able to go to New York. He talks all the time about *Kameradschaft* and German solidarity.'

He accepted that pressures had been put on her. He'd been subjected to the same pressures from Horrocks and been forced to submit to them.

'So why give up now?'

'Because of you. Because I love you.'

He stopped dead, and she faced him, her face pale with unhappiness. 'Oh, Fitz,' she whispered, 'Why do we always quarrel? Why do we hate each other so much?'

The misery in her face knocked all the stuffing out of him. Aghast through his outrage at the unhappiness he had brought her, it was beyond his power to resist. Calling himself a big soft-hearted, sentimental Irishman, he put his arms round her and held her close. 'There,' he said stupidly. 'Steady on.'

He felt her body relax and slump against him, shaken with terrible paroxysms of sobs. Her arms went round him, clinging desperately as if to the last refuge in a gaping sea. 'If you go on like this you'll break your heart,' he said.

He sat on the bed, still holding her, and she put one hand behind his shoulder and gave a little moan. Because she had been angry with him, her capitulation was more complete and, as he held her, his lips against her forehead, she was clutching his hand, kissing it with a desperate ardour, using Mexican and German endearments she had heard her mother use to her as a child because she had never learned any others. It was as if she had suddenly realized she needed that love she had always denied herself in her concentration on her career and, as they sank back, she offered no resistance, throwing away caution, pride, everything.

266

'Oh, Fitz,' she whispered.
It sounded almost like a cry of despair.

3

A warm breeze was coming through the open windows, stirring the curtains, the shutters making great slashes of shadow and butter-yellow sunshine. Outside they could see the palms and the gum trees in the garden and smell woodsmoke from a fire somewhere.

Slattery felt dazzled and humbled. He'd planned and plotted for this moment, he realized, from the day he'd first met Magdalena on the train to Chihuahua, but when it had arrived it had come unexpectedly when they were staring at each other with fury in their eyes. Because of their anger, their passion had been all the more powerful.

As he turned his head, he saw her studying him. She didn't return his smile. All her life she'd been supported by the religious and moral instruction she'd undergone as a child. Her family had been good practising Catholics and in their teachings she had always been able to find the answer. Now she felt she no longer could.

'I'm confused,' she said. 'I've lived all my life with Fausto's lies and now I'm uncertain and guilty. I don't know who to believe. And I need to believe. I need to be able to trust. Don't ever let me down, Fitz.'

He took her in his arms. Outside the swallows were high in the air, crying thinly. He knew his hold on her was still tenuous but he was determined not to let her slip through his fingers again.

When he saw Pilar in the hall that evening, she gave him an odd look and he realized she knew exactly what had happened between them – and even approved. Magdalena remained curiously reserved, trying to behave as if nothing were different when she knew very well it was.

He saw her off for the north on the evening train a week later. The new war in Mexico hadn't yet progressed from manoeuvring to shooting and it was still possible to travel the length of the country. He was waiting at the station when she arrived, a tall woman in blue velvet over a pink blouse with a whalebone neck and a veil, and a magnificent flowered and feathered hat. As she swept across the dusty platform to the train, Jesús was trailing behind with her dresser and a porter pushing a trolley with her luggage. He was changing fast, broadening and growing handsome, and Slattery noticed several girls turn to eye him. For the journey Magdalena had bought him a fine blue suit and a soft felt hat.

'Look after her, Jesús,' Slattery adjured him. 'If there's trouble, telegraph me at once.'

'Of course, sir.'

As they stood by the steps to the carriage, Magdalena nervous and unable to stop talking, Fausto Graf appeared. Consuela Lidgett was with him, together with a blond young man with a turned-up moustache and a high stiff collar, who had Potsdam written all over him.

'Fausto's wife doesn't seem to enter his plans much these days,' Magdalena commented. 'Is he living with her?'

Graf spotted her. 'My little sister,' he said, approaching. 'We'll be travelling together.'

'I'm travelling with my dresser,' Magdalena announced coldly. 'You can travel with whom you like.'

Graf looked at Slattery, full of smiles. 'Though we are on opposite sides of the fence, Herr Slattery,' he said, 'it doesn't mean that in a neutral country we cannot be friends.'

'Don't be bloody silly,' Slattery snapped and Graf's smile widened.

'Well,' he conceded, 'perhaps not *friends*. But we can treat each other with politeness when there are ladies present. No?'

That night Slattery dined at Silvain's. It had once been a favourite haunt of Huerta's but with his departure the clientèle had changed and Slattery bumped into Hermann Stutzmann with Consuela and the young German he'd seen on the station platform. The German was polite and chilly, what the Germans called 'correct'. Consuela looked prosperous. She gave him a distant smile and, as she disappeared with the young German, Stutzmann remained behind, fumbling with his hat and cloak until they were out of sight. He was as eager as ever to be friendly.

'Splendid show tonight, Herr Paddy,' he said. 'I had to promote Evangelina Oropesa to Magdalena's rôles and in the second act, she was almost as good as Magdalena. But not quite. Nobody can be La Graf. Unfortunately, I foresee difficulties.'

'What sort of difficulties?'

'Fausto is paying too much attention to Oropesa.'

'Is he chasing Oropesa?'

'Everybody chases Oropesa. She doesn't have a faithful heart.'

'What about Consuela?'

Stutzmann's gentle face sagged. 'It is very sad because she thinks Fausto is faithful. She came with him once to ask for a part. She said she could sing.' Stutzmann gave a huge shrug. 'She couldn't, of course. She sounded like the honk of a motor horn. It was then that Fausto met Oropesa. She has a nice shape, of course, but she has a brain like a plate of sauerkraut and in a few years she'll be nothing but a top C and a double chin.' He paused to draw breath. 'He'll have to be careful now La Lidgett's back, of course. He has enough troubles already.'

'What sort of troubles, Hermann?'

Slattery was hoping for something important but it turned out to be only another of Fausto Graf's sexual adventures.

'Elizabeth von Boenigk.'

'Who's she?'

'Wife of Baron von Boenigk.'

'Come on, Hermann. Who's he then?'

'One of General Kloss's aides. You'll know of General Kloss. He was Huerta's director of munitions and ordnance. Von Boenigk is a handsome good-natured willing boy and he has a handsome good-natured willing wife.'

'Is Fausto chasing her, too?'

'Where Von Boenigk is these days, my friend, Unser Fausto is, too. He keeps Oropesa just for Mexico City – when Consuela isn't around. He's a free-ranging man.'

270

The food at Sylvain's was indifferent. It always was these days, because Zapata was preventing supplies from entering the city and, knowing that the Carranza currency in use would be declared worthless as soon as Obregón left the capital, stores were hoarding their stocks. Two days later the water also disappeared as Zapatistas blew up the pumping station and the stench became appalling.

Filth and pestilence had become normal and the streets were dangerous. And, with the Church reaping the consequences of consistently backing the wrong horse, sacred buildings were also being sacked and drunken soldiers wandered about with their heads through magnificent religious paintings. Encouraged by Obregón, who was an agnostic, they rode their horses up to the altars and smashed the plaster saints with a sweep of their swords.

Despite the show of power, however, it was always Zapata sitting in the hills of Morelos just to the south, who controlled the city. Obregón was finding he could no longer hold the place and Carranza was talking of shifting the seat of his government to Veracruz on the coast. The Americans had never been in the slightest danger of being thrown back into the sea, and had spent their time there trying to clean the place up. The Mexicans, who had always accepted flies and smells as part of life, thought they were mad, and showed no surprise when Woodrow Wilson announced they were due to leave on Mexico's Independence Day.

'Neat sense of timing,' Slattery observed.

The disappearance of the Americans was a stroke of luck for the hard-pressed Carranza and he stripped the capital of everything he could carry and began to move to the coast. From near Horrocks' office, Slattery watched as the Carrancistas headed east along the Paseo do la Reforma. Some were aiming for the station, some were for chancing it on the road. Carts, cars and waggons were all moving steadily in the same direction, followed by men on horses and squads of troops on foot. As the last of them vanished, Slattery turned towards the Avenida Versailles, only to see men on horses approaching from the direction of Chapultepec. At their head, his face shadowed by his huge sombrero, was a slim figure in black.

'Zapata,' Slattery said. 'Back again! This bloody place's becoming a no man's land. Nobody wants it, but nobody can afford to ignore it.'

Immediately horses began to disappear again and brides were left weeping in their wedding carriages, the horses ridden away by Zapatista soldiers. Stable owners took to sitting up all night with guns on their knees and Atty was careful to hide the Studebaker under bales of hay in the stables behind the house.

Unused to cities, the Zapatistas eyed everything with suspicion, especially the street cars, and several firemen were picked off as they hurried to a fire by sharpshooters who thought the fire engine a new form of weapon and the brass helmets they wore the uniform of a new invading army.

Despite the distance, the war in Europe had started to affect life. The assassination in Sarajevo had scarcely caused a ripple, but the sinking of three British cruisers in the English Channel by a submarine brought a shout of triumph from the German residents, and Atty returned home with a furious face after being jeered at in one of the neighbouring bars.

'The bastards are saying they've found a new weapon that'll win the war,' he snarled.

With Carranza gone, news came from Horrocks at Tacuba further north that Villa was on his way to join up with Zapata, and the arrival of the northern armies brought a new saturnalia of debauchery, looting and murder as the Villistas exacted revenge on anybody who had spoken against their chief. Then Turner appeared on the doorstep, complaining that Carranza's paper money had been declared worthless.

'What am I supposed to do?' he demanded.

'Change your plates,' Atty said bluntly. 'And start printing Villa's "Dos Caros" notes.'

By this time, in a military situation which was rapidly becoming chaotic, the leaders of armed groups were

272

wavering in an agony of indecision about which side to support, knowing perfectly well that in the roulette game of rebellion swift promotion had to be staked against a dishonourable death.

Growing nervous of his involvement, Zapata withdrew once more to the Morelos hills and, as the armies began to line up for battle, railways, always the prime military objectives, were blown up, patched together and blown up again, until mountains of scrap began to rise in the railway yards. Walls gaped roofless and were pocked with bullet holes, and hanged men withered in the sun on trees and telegraph poles.

You could always tell which side the soldiers were on from the songs they sang. Villistas tended to favour *'Adelita'*, Carrancistas preferred *'La Cucaracha'*, while Zapata's hordes sang to the melting *'Valentina'*. Some were ranchero units, some were led by priests who had unfrocked themselves to join their rebel congregations. The Zapatistas were a peasant army clad in white cotton. The northerners wore scraps of uniform bought from the United States in job lots, with colourful additions of their own, and travelled on trains, using the locomotive as a machine for towing, an armoured fighting vehicle, or a bomb on wheels. The age span for soldiers stretched from seven to seventy. Below twelve, a boy became a bugler, a drummer or a courier; over twelve he was a fully-fledged soldier, and even the women pitched in when occasion offered.

As fighting began to flare up along the border, on the American side, every window facing Mexico was filled with steel plates, bales of hay or sandbags and blocks of wood, but it still didn't stop American citizens being killed, and finally the American troops along the border had to withdraw their positions a humiliating mile into their own territory to avoid casualties.

Although Magdalena had been intending to rest before crossing into the States to fulfill her contract, Slattery picked up news of her singing in small theatres in northern Mexico and eventually a packet of theatre bills and programmes arrived with the explanation that she was using these

273

performances to bring her voice back to pitch and to make sure she was capable of carrying out the terms of her contract.

'Soon I shall be leaving for the States,' she wrote. 'I send you a kiss.'

It wasn't much but it was unexpectedly warm.

With the war in Europe glued to a line of trenches that ran from the Channel to the Swiss border and the struggle in Mexico still nothing more than skirmishing, he wondered if the situation was stable enough to see her before she crossed the border, and he was actually on the point of closing the office and booking his ticket when Horrocks did one of his pantomime demon acts and arrived on his doorstep without warning.

He was dressed in a haphazard fashion that was far from his usual immaculate style and he was livid. He had arrived from Veracruz that morning and been stopped in the Alameda Gardens by drunken soldiers.

'Nine times they pretended to shoot me!' he spluttered furiously. 'And each time they stole another piece of clothing, until I was as naked as the day I was born. I had the greatest difficulty persuading a cab driver I wasn't drunk and getting the damn man to drive me to my hotel. I then had to get him to call the manager and borrow some clothes before I could cross the lobby.'

Slattery grinned. Only the Mexicans, with their gift for humiliating the paler-skinned northerners, could have managed to infuriate the imperturbable Horrocks. 'Next to shooting a man to death,' he pointed out, 'they like most of all to scare him to death.'

Horrocks glared. 'They put me up against a bloody wall,' he snarled. 'And told me to show my profile! Then the other profile! Then full face! They could barely stand up for the drink they'd taken.'

'Or doubtless,' Slattery grinned, 'for laughing.'

'It's not funny!'

Slattery's smile died. 'No,' he agreed. 'Mexico is never funny. but it still raises a sad laugh occasionally.'

Horrocks snorted. 'We're not in the business of laughter,

274

sad or otherwise. We've lost Kloss! You know Kloss – he was Huerta's director of munitions and ordnance. He's also a German agent, and we've lost contact with him. He's important and we need to know who's getting his advice. Because, whoever it is, he's going to win this new war. We want him. Find him.'

4

There were various ways of finding Kloss but Slattery decided Stutzmann would provide the best lead. He found him in the wings of the Opera House stage, his plump face made up into a mask of ferocity for his role in *Dolores Ruíz*. Onstage, Evangelina Oropesa was hitting the high notes in a solo.

'*Mein lieber Freund*,' Stutzmann said. 'You and I shouldn't be talking together. We are on opposite sides of the fence.'

'You and I, Hermann, will never manage to be enemies.'

Stutzmann gave him a grateful smile. 'I'm sure you want something,' he said.

'I'm looking for Fausto Graf. Where is he?'

'*Mein lieber Kamerad*, I am told it's my duty not to talk to you, because you are British and I am a Hun. Otherwise it is *Rassenverrat* – race treason. That is what they impressed on me when I reported at the Consulate where it was considered I could do a better job here for Germany than reporting as a reservist. You must ask the Frau Lidgett. She ought to know.'

That evening, Slattery dined at Sylvain's again. As he'd half-expected, Consuela was there with the young German who'd been seeing Graf off at the station. Her clothes were good and she wore pearls but he noticed a growing tightness about her mouth.

As the German clicked his heels and left, she gestured to Slattery to join her. Her eyes hungrily took in the big rangy frame, the red hair and the amber fox's eyes, and almost immediately she began to talk.

'I tried going back to Gordonsboro,' she said. 'But Gordonsboro's not for me any more.'

'And Fausto?'

'He says he's getting a divorce.'

276

'I saw him heading north. What happens to you when he's not here?'

Her face grew taut. 'I look after myself. It's not hard and he pretends not to know. I don't mind about Loyce now. He didn't love me. He wasn't trying to save my life, like I said in the article I wrote. He didn't even know I was there.'

They chatted for a while then she tapped his arm with the fan she carried.

'Will you see me home?' she asked quietly. 'My friend had to leave and the streets these days are no place for a single woman.'

They finished their wine and he sent a waiter to call a cab. In the darkness inside, watching the crowds and the occasional drunken soldier, she said nothing and made no attempt to touch his hand. Her apartment was on the second floor of a block just on the right side of the district where the bourgeois quarter touched on the slums. As she unlocked the door, an Indian maid, dressed in what looked like old finery of Consuela's, greeted them and produced a brandy bottle. Consuela eyed Slattery speculatively and pushed the bottle towards him.

'You can stay the night if you wish,' she said.

'I think not, Consuela.'

She touched his arm. 'I mean it. I want you to stay. I get lonely.'

He gently prised her fingers from his wrist. 'I think I'd better go.'

Her face showed a little spasm of unhappiness and her voice became quieter.

'You know what I am these days, Slattery?' she asked suddenly. 'I'm a tart. A whore. I sleep with people and they give me presents. I've got no pride any more.' She was silent for a while. 'You know why I went to Gordonsboro? Because I was having a baby. I told them it was Loyce's. But it was Fausto's, and I have to have money to pay for him. He's up there now, being looked after.' She drew a deep breath like a sigh. 'If Fausto doesn't keep his promise to me I don't know what I'll do. I've got no money.'

'Where is Fausto now?'

'Querétaro. On business. German business, I guess.'

'Querétaro?' Horrocks said. 'Kloss is at Querétaro? How do you know?'

Slattery explained and Horrocks frowned. 'Well, I suppose it makes sense, because Obregón's at Querétaro and he's got a group of German officers with him who've just come from the fighting in France. Villa's at Irapuato and Carranza's determined to make an end of him. But it's in Britain's interest to have him around a little longer, so you'd better get up there. You've got influence with him. See he doesn't make a fool of himself.'

On his journey north, Slattery passed Villa's artillery struggling up from El Ebano in a welter of dust and sweat to bring the guns he needed to his aid. 'Tell him to wait,' the artillery commander begged. 'We're coming as fast as we can.'

Also near El Ebano Villa's old compadre, Tomás Urbina, was loitering with his brigade. 'I need more time,' he insisted, but to Slattery he had the look of a man who was in no hurry.

Slattery arrived far too late. Obregón was well dug in at a place called Celaya and Slattery found Villa already about to launch his attack and not prepared to listen to reason. He had a tremendous gift for inspiring his men but he was a headlong fighter and against Obregón's cool ability he could bring nothing but impulsiveness. And the hatred he bore for Obregón was making him reckless so that he was approaching the battle as if it were a personal gunfight.

'Sure,' he agreed. 'We shall get hurt a bit. Battles were never won with kisses.'

'Wait, Don Pancho,' Slattery urged.

The heavy head moved. 'I can't wait.'

'Obregón has German officers who know how to use machine-guns and barbed wire and artillery.'

'I know how to use artillery.'

'Don Pancho, you haven't got any. It's three days away.'

'Tómas Urbina will bring guns.'

278

'Urbina will never arrive on time. For the love of God, wait!'

Villa's amber eyes blazed and his gun came out. 'I always swore I'd shoot you for your interfering, inglés. Now would be a good time.'

'Put it away, Panchito,' Slattery said calmly. 'You won't shoot me because you know my advice is good and because you know I'm one of the few people in Mexico who's never tried to betray you.'

Villa glared, his eyes glowing yellow and angry, but the gun was lowered. 'The battle goes on,' he said slowly.

A curious fatality seemed to brood over him. It wasn't the old Villa speaking, full of vitality and ideas. He seemed tired and disillusioned. 'This is the last campaign,' he said. 'I want peace to farm my land and educate my children. After I've beaten Obregón. I shall retire.'

'Panchito,' Slattery said earnestly, 'you won't beat Obregón. Not with the methods you're using. The British army's been throwing men against German barbed wire and machine-guns in Europe ever since the war started. They never succeed in breaking through. Neither will you.'

'It's too late,' Villa said heavily. 'I've given the signal.'

That evening as the first shell burst in the outer defences of Celaya, there was nothing else to do but leave Atty to watch and drive back to Querétaro to telegraph Horrocks of his failure. Under the sinking sun, clouds of smoke were already rolling across the battlefield.

Atty had found them a hotel but the Germans had found it, too, and as Slattery arrived there was a shout of triumph from the dining-room. One of the American correspondents appeared, frowning.

'The Krauts,' he said. 'Just heard that their Zeppelins have bombed London.'

Atty brought news of the battle. 'Villa's beaten,' he growled. 'He was stopped by the barbed wire and machine-guns just like in France. He's done. Kaput. Finito.'

The Germans were beaming when they entered the dining-room that evening and were shouting for bottles of

279

German Sekt. Fausto Graf was among them, in a uniform that owed more to Prussia than to Mexico.

'Halloa, Englander,' he said when he saw Slattery. 'So your friend Villa is finished. As England will be before long. Our Zeppelins are reducing London to ashes, and our submarines are making a scrap-heap of the British merchant fleet. Meanwhile, the British army, like Villa's, destroys itself by hurling itself against our lines.'

'You, Fausto,' Slattery said, 'are beginning to believe your own propaganda.'

But there was little to cheer them. Waiting outside Querétaro, they saw sullen-faced men, dusty and blood-splashed, struggling away from the battlefield. A few rode on horses or in buggies but most were on foot, with here and there a desperately wounded officer in a carriage. A son carried his dying father on his back, another man his dead son. Among them was Monserrat, the only member of the Holy Trinity still with Villa. He had been searching for Urbina.

'He betrayed us,' he said bitterly. 'He never intended coming. He took a million-dollar payroll and bolted.'

His eyes red with weariness, his clothes stained with the blood of his men, Villa bumped into Slattery at San Luis la Paz as he struggled to get his trains away. There were tears in his eyes.

'Damn them!' He choked on his words. 'They've whipped me, inglés. And I would rather have been beaten by a Chinaman than by Obregón!'

5

With captured Villistas being despatched by machine-guns in the bullring at Celaya, Slattery received a message to proceed to New York.

'Somethin's up,' Atty said in a doom-laden voice.

All had not gone Obregón's way at Celaya. He had been struck by a shell splinter which had torn off his right arm, but he was recovering rapidly, and news had arrived that Villa had now lost Guadalajara and looked very much as if he were about to lose more of his strongholds.

With his defeat, his army had broken up and, as Slattery crossed the border to El Paso, the country was beginning to descend once more into anarchy, with soldiers-turned-bandits terrorizing lonely farmers, crops and cattle stolen, and smallpox and typhus everywhere. As he climbed aboard the train north he saw Fausto Graf on the station. With America neutral in the war in Europe, it was possible for sympathizers of the warring factions to enter her territory without question and at Kansas City he saw him leave the train and disappear down the platform carrying a suitcase.

New York hadn't changed much. If anything, it had a greater air of bustle and prosperity than ever, as though the conflict in Europe was putting money into the pockets of Americans of all classes. There seemed to be more motor cars on the streets, more goods in the shops, more lights in the theatres, and there was an atmosphere of excitement, as though everybody in the place had become aware of its importance.

Horrocks was waiting with a taxi. 'You've been brought up here for a week or two,' he said as they were driven from the station to the hotel where a suite had been booked for Slattery, 'for good diplomatic reasons. The Germans are becoming too bloody aggressive and, on instructions from London to slow 'em down, we're working with an

American state agent called Midwinter who's overseeing everything they get up to. The President might believe in peace and goodwill to all men but, fortunately for us, there are a few who trust the Germans less than he does; and Midwinter's got the job of watchin' 'em. You're here because you know a few of those involved.'

'What about Graf?' Slattery asked. 'He's north of the border. He was on the same train as I was. He left it at Kansas City.'

Horrocks frowned. 'Interesting,' he observed. 'What's he up to? He only has to take a train to St Louis from Kansas City and he can go either to Washington or come here to New York.'

'Is Kloss running the show here?'

Horrocks shook his head. 'No. It's not Kloss. It's a new chap called Franz von Rintelen and German sympathizers are crawling out of the woodwork in dozens. Among them our old friend, Huerta.'

'*He's* back! Already?'

'With his eye firmly fixed on Mexico.' Horrocks began to feel for his cigarette case, talking as he fished inside his jacket. 'The Germans are behind him, of course. A comeback for Huerta would be like a red rag to a bull to President Wilson. He'd charge head-down into a worse mess than Veracruz. Who do you reckon would support him?'

'Villa wouldn't.'

Horrocks waved a dismissive hand. 'Villa's finished.'

'Don't you believe it. Panchito will always have a few surprises up his sleeve. But he'd never back Huerta.'

'Carranza?'

'If he thought he could use him to gain power and then ditch him afterwards. Huerta might agree for the same reasons – if he could ditch Carranza.'

'Zapata?'

'He supports nobody.'

'Obregón?'

'He says all Mexican presidents are thieves, but that now he's got only one hand he couldn't steal as much as the others. People think he's just being funny but it's significant.

282

He *might* back Huerta to put himself in power. If anybody's ready to support him, it's Orozco. He's anxious to get back among the payrolls.'

Horrocks was silent for a moment. 'Like a lot of honest men,' he went on eventually, 'President Wilson expects everyone else to be honest, too, and with Villa, Zapata, Obregón et al, he's as lost as a parson in a knocking-shop. Because every damn faction down there has its own set of supporters up here, all trying to put on pressure, and the place's packed with people with German relations.'

Horrocks paused to wave away smoke. 'With Huerta shoved back into the mess, the Americans would be so fully occupied at home they'd not be much help to us in Britain. Wilson, of course, would like both sides in Europe to kiss and make up, but that's no good because it would leave Northern France still occupied and there'd be nothing to satisfy the French but Wilson's prayers.'

He drew on his cigarette for a time in silence, staring into the distance as the taxi manoeuvred in and out of the traffic. 'We know everything the Huns are doing, of course.'

'How, for Christ's sake? We're not mind readers.'

'Nearly,' Horrocks said blandly. 'Somebody had the bright idea the minute the war began of cutting the German transatlantic cables so that all their messages now have to be sent by the only way open to 'em – wireless. And to wireless, of course, anybody can listen. So we set up listening stations and when intercepts started pouring in we roped in people to decode 'em because we've come into possession of their three main code books.'

'Do the Americans know all this?'

Horrocks looked shocked. 'Hardly likely to tell *them*, are we?'

'Don't they tell us things?'

'Oh, yes. They're very trusting.'

'Seems a bit one-sided.'

'That's the way departments like ours work.'

Horrocks arrived early the following morning to pick up Slattery. He was using the same cab, Slattery noticed, and instead of taking a direct route, it seemed to thread its way back and forth among the busy streets, moving past the Flatiron, Woolworth and Singer buildings as if trying to throw off a pursuer.

'Are we trying to dodge someone?' Slattery asked.

Horrocks lit a cigarette without bothering to offer his case. 'We're *always* trying to dodge someone,' he admitted. 'This is one of *our* taxis. We have a few.'

They stopped outside a small block of offices near the docks. In a third-floor room Horrocks introduced Slattery to a lean, fair-haired, lantern-jawed man chewing the stub of a dead cigar.

'Gus Midwinter,' he said. 'Here from Washington.'

Midwinter's grip was hard and he stared at Slattery with eyes that were as blue as cornflowers. He was keeping a sharp eye on the official German attachés in New York, he said. It wasn't difficult because they all used the German Club and held their conferences in the Manhattan Hotel.

'With their German-American Bund,' Horrocks explained, 'they think they're winning the war here. But we have Czecho-Slovaks and Austro-Hungarians who had to flee from Austria who're now naturalized Americans and speak German. One of 'em's maid to the German ambassador's wife, and there are four in the Austrian Consulate. Some are waiters, some work in German clubs and firms. They supplied the names of every German reservist trying to reach Europe and we picked the lot up as soon as the ships they were in entered waters under our control.'

'This country's too goddam divided,' Midwinter growled.

Horrocks lit another of his expensive cigarettes and placed it carefully in the amber holder. 'Eastern seaboard sympathetic to us,' he explained to Slattery. 'Western seaboard completely indifferent. Midwest solidly behind Germany. They have German breweries there, German restaurants, German traditions, German songs.'

Midwinter scowled and tossed a sheet of paper to the table. It was a report on the German agent, Von Rintelen. He was known to have entered the country on a Swiss

284

passport and was presenting himself as the director of an import-export firm.

'Speaks excellent English,' Horrocks said. 'Lived here for years as representative of one of Germany's biggest banking organizations.'

'He's known to have half a million dollars available,' Midwinter added darkly. 'To organize strikes and slow-downs among longshoremen and munitions workers. And he's a clever bastard, too. He even persuaded some damnfool Russian into letting him provide supplies for the Russian army. But they never arrive. The ships catch fire. The lighters capsize. Have the Germans found some weapon that can penetrate a ship's hull without making a hole?' He tossed a report down. 'Take a look at that. *Phoebus*. Tramp carrying arms for Russia. Cargo suddenly bursts into flames. Captain can't explain it. No explosion. Nothing to cause spontaneous combustion. It wasn't a submarine.'

He bit the end off a cigar with a savage gesture and stuck it in the corner of his mouth. 'At lest we scared off one of Rintelen's contacts. Guy called Bunze. Sent freighters to sea loaded with coal. But somewhere *en route* they happened to meet up with German raiders who helped themselves to the coal'.

He pushed a photograph across the table. 'That's Rintelen. Taken with one of these new snap cameras outside their Consulate.'

The picture was blown up, grainy and blurred, and showed a group of men talking on the steps. Slattery grinned.

'I know him,' he said. 'I met him in Mexico. He was calling himself Von Raschstadt in those days. I know the other chap, too. The little one in the boater. His name's Scheele.'

Midwinter nodded. 'Runs a drugstore in Brooklyn. He's a chemist.'

'More than that, I think.' Slattery explained how he had met Scheele in Nogales and Midwinter was alert at once.

'What kind of secret weapon?' he demanded.

'Lead tube. Size of a cigar. Hot enough to ignite wood or coal.'

'Or explosives!' Midwinter slapped his hand down on the desk. 'Jesus, just the thing to introduce into a cargo of ammunition! And half the sonsabitches working the waterfront here are German or Irish.' He grinned at Horrocks. 'You Brits certainly made a lot of enemies.'

'Burden of Empire,' Horrocks murmured.

'One of those things set to go off in four or five days, and you've got a ship on fire in the middle of the ocean with nobody guilty. Suppose they've put one in the *Lusitania*.'

The words produced a silence because the 32,000-ton Cunarder was the largest transatlantic liner still in service and was still regularly carrying Americans to Europe.

'Where is she now?' Slattery asked.

'She must be approaching the west coast of Ireland.'

'The Admiralty regard the west coast of Ireland as of no strategic importance,' Horrocks pointed out.

'It is,' Midwinter snapped, 'if they sink ships there! Have you seen her supplementary manifests?'

'Have you?'

Midwinter grinned. 'I'm not supposed to, but I have. They include cases of shrapnel and cartridges from Remington Small Arms. Enough to be an excuse to have a go at her. You can bet Rintelen knows about 'em.' He glanced at Slattery. 'You know friend Huerta. What about the guys who supported him? You know them, too?'

'The whole boiling of 'em.'

Midwinter lit a large black cigar that made Horrocks move to the other side of the room. 'The shooting south of the Rio Grande makes a lot more noise in New York than the shooting in Europe,' Midwinter went on. 'And, if one of the factions down there sold out to Huerta, there are plenty willing to rally round.' Suddenly he broke into a smile which was youthful and cherubic and entirely altered his face. 'Unfortunately, there's one thing they ain't got – neither Rintelen nor Huerta or any of their supporters – and that's security. They're bein' watched night and day. By me. By Sholto here. And now by you. Also by Department of

Justice agents, Carrancista agents, Villa agents, Obregón agents. There are so many of the bastards, they're fallin' over each other.'

They dined together at Lüchows on 14th Street.

'German,' Midwinter observed, gesturing about him. 'I reckon, if you could investigate 'em all, you'd find the goddam place was full of German spies every night of the week.' He glared about him savagely. 'What's wrong with 'em?' he said. 'They're naturalized Americans. Isn't that good enough for 'em? Jesus, *I'm* German! Born Gustav Midwinder in Hamburg. But I'm American now and getting all the benefits there are from being American. So why do all these bastards claim to be German? All I ever wanted to be was a Yankee Doodle Dandy.'

Midwinter had an appointment at the British Consulate and Horrocks was due to call at Cunard's, the owners of the *Lusitania*. As they separated. Slattery walked down Broadway and studied the posters outside Moore's Theatre.

'Charles Frohman,' the posters announced, 'presents Magdalena Graf in *Der Zigeunerbaron*.' They had Strauss's name in large letters and had retained the German title instead of the English one, *The Gypsy Baron*. Below were the names of the most important members of the supporting cast. Below them still had been pasted strips announcing that officials of the German-American Bund would attend the opening night and that German anthems would be sung.

On an impulse, Slattery went into the theatre and, in exchange for a dollar bill, found Magdalena's address. A house had been rented for her on Fifth Avenue and Jesús showed him in with a wide grin, only for him to be shooed away immediately by a horde of women, all of whom seemed to be holding dresses or bolts of cloth and have their mouths full of pins.

Then Magdalena saw him from the other side of the salon and pushed everybody aside to reach him. She was swathed in blue silk that trailed along the floor as she moved, followed on her knees by a woman with a tape measure and a pin cushion.

'Fitz!'

As he put his arms round her it was like clutching a hedgehog and she gave a gurgle of laughter.

'You've come at a bad time,' she said. 'I'm in the middle of fittings, and I'm too nervous to be normal. Frohman's put everything he's got into the show. It's absolutely splendid.'

'Have dinner with me.'

'When we know whether it'll be a success or not. I'm too much on edge at the moment. What are you doing here? Jesús has taken care of everything. He's a very clever boy and so proud of his name's now the same as mine. I've made it official. After this show there'll be another. Frohman told me so in his suite at the Knickerbocker Hotel. He's gone to London to see what's being put on, but when he comes back he's going to start thinking about it straightaway.'

She pushed a book of newspaper cuttings at him. 'Look what they're saying about me,' she said.

Stutzmann hadn't hesitated to tell the press of the wound she had received at Veracruz and the newspapermen had made the most of it: 'Singer's Heroism', 'Yankee Diva's Courage.' Like the Mexicans, they had twisted her background to suit themselves and were making it appear she was American born and bred.

'Things become more hysterical with every hour that passes,' she was saying now. 'You never think you're going to be ready in time. But we open on May the twentieth even if I have to appear in my underwear. Hermann will be here two days from now to attend to everything. Frohman's a wonderful man to work for. It's a pity he's gone to Europe but he had to see the latest Barrie show with music by a new man, Jerome Kern.' She was chattering wildly, in a state of near-hysteria with excitement and tiredness. 'We'll go to see *Daddy Long Legs* together. It's the longest-running show in town. Or *The Celebrated Case*. That's a Frohman show, too.'

She gave him a quick kiss and pushed him to the door. 'Now you must go, or I shall be in trouble and so will you.'

He paused in the hall and looked back at her. 'Have you ever thought of giving up the stage, Magdalena?' he asked.

Her reply was immediate, and in the same near-hysterical tone. 'A singer can't rest on her laurels. And I enjoy the smell of powder and paint, and the roses that appear in the dressing room, and all the –' She stopped dead and looked steadily at him, all the enthusiasm suddenly gone. 'I could give it up tomorrow,' she said.

'Never, Madame!' The dresser, who was chasing her round the room on her knees, shook her head. 'The great rôles will come soon and you'll remember them all your life.'

Magdalena nodded and smiled, then she looked at Slattery as he stood by the door. 'Be there on the twentieth. I shall look for you in the front row of the stalls. Put on your evening dress. Look beautiful for me. Come and wish me luck.'

When Slattery returned to his hotel, he had a drink sent to his room and lay on the bed sipping it, his thoughts on Magdalena. It was long after midnight when he fell asleep, and at some point towards morning he began to dream that guns were firing. Abruptly, he sat up. The hammering came from his door, and outside he could hear Horrocks' voice.

Stumbling across the room, still half-asleep in the early daylight, he found Horrocks fuming in the corridor. He had cut himself shaving and there was a piece of tissue paper stuck to his cheek. Without a word, he placed a hand on Slattery's chest and shoved him back into the room.

'Give me a cigarette,' he said. 'I've run out.'

Slattery tossed a pack across and Horrocks lit one. He drew the smoke down in an enormous gulp so that Slattery half expected it to come out of the bottoms of his trousers. His hand was shaking.

'What in Christ's name happened?' Slattery asked. 'Have the Germans won the war?'

'They might have,' Horrocks snapped. 'They've sunk the *Lusitania*.'

6

Midwinter was already in his office when they arrived. Horrocks tossed a signal to the desk. 'From the Embassy,' he said. 'Picked up by the Royal Navy in Ireland. It's from the *Lusitania*. "Come at once. Big list. Ten miles south of Old Head Kinsale." Originated 2.14. p.m.'

'Scheele?'

'Even Scheele couldn't sink something as big as the *Lusitania*.'

'A submarine?'

'There aren't any submerged rocks round there.' Horrocks tossed more signal forms to the desk. 'That one's from the wireless station at Valentia. "*Lusitania* in distress off Kinsale." '

Midwinter scowled. 'Well, the bastards warned everybody. They put an ad in the papers telling people not to travel in her.' He tossed a newspaper across his desk. Beneath the advertisement for the *Lusitania*'s sailing there was a small black-edged inset notice. 'Travellers intending to embark on the Atlantic voyage are reminded that a state of war exists between Germany and her allies and Great Britain and her allies.' It was signed 'Imperial German Embassy, Washington, DC, 22 April 1915.'

'The British Consul-General says the Cunard offices here are full of German spies,' Horrocks pointed out.

Midwinter frowned. 'He may be goddam right.'

Slattery spent the morning trying to find out more details at the Cunard office. Cunard were insisting that everybody had been saved but by afternoon they had learned that an estimated thousand dead were expected.

'Jesus,' Midwinter breathed.

No official announcement had still been made and the chief story from Europe was of the struggle against the Turks in the Dardanelles. When the specials finally

290

appeared on the streets New York went into a frenzy of horror. As they saw the words flashed on the bulletin boards above the newspaper offices, numbed men and women began talking in the streets to total strangers, unable to believe it. The *Lusitania* was familiar to all New Yorkers and they had seen her come and go so many times it seemed impossible she could simply have vanished.

Queues formed at the Cunard offices, anxious relatives and friends storming the counters where harassed clerks were working overtime to answer hundreds of long-distance calls. By evening they had more details. A hundred and twenty-four Americans were among the dead and they included internationally-known names such as Alfred Gwynne Vanderbilt, the multi-millionaire sportsman. The casualty list seemed endless.

In Manhattan's smart German club, German officers in the city on their country's business were hailing the sinking as a master-stroke and toasting *Der Tag*, and when they went to Lüchows' to eat they found it crowded with German-Americans singing *'Die Wacht am Rhein'*. A large noisy party had draped a red, white and black German naval ensign with its Iron Cross insignia alongside a blue flag with a yellow cross, over a palm near their table.

'Swedes,' Midwinter growled. 'If I uncover any of 'em who had anything to do with this, I'll have the bastards sent home.'

He had his men on the streets immediately, watching the German Consulate, the German clubs, German firms, the homes of German officials and German sympathizers. There was a great deal of activity to be seen, with cabs coming and going all the time, their occupants hurrying in swift strides across the pavements, clutching canes, gloves and homburgs, their faces wearing expressions of grim determination mixed with a sort of unholy glee.

The news began to come in thick and fast. The *Lusitania* had sunk within sight of the Irish coast and already the illustrated magazines were appearing with dramatic drawings of men in the sea trying desperately to support drowning women and children. Information arrived that the

Germans were talking of striking medals, of the sinking being applauded in Sweden, and of children in Germany being granted a holiday from school. With a thousand dead civilians, many of them women and children, it all seemed in incredibly bad taste, and the German ambassador, who had arrived in New York from Washington, had become a virtual prisoner in his suite and had deemed it wiser to stay away from a special performance of *Die Fledermaus* at the Opera House on behalf of the German Red Cross. Fearing trouble, the management had detectives in the theatre and the German flags, which had been decorating the boxes, had disappeared abruptly with the announcements about the singing of *'Deutschland Über Alles'*.

The headlines were unanimous about the disaster:

> *World Aghast At Germany's Atrocity.*
> *Huns' Most Cowardly Crime.*

The British were lying low, doing their best to appear as innocent as possible, and as the fury came to the surface, German sympathizers were being insulted and attacked, and the German attaché, who had taken the place of the German ambassador at the Opera House, was jostled and pushed in the foyer. One other unexpected result appeared as Slattery was driving down Broadway in a cab. As usual, he glanced at Moore's Theatre for the progress of *Der Zigeunerbaron* and immediately spotted the red-lettered strips pasted over the new posters – CANCELLED.

Pushing his way into the theatre, he found the cast and orchestra sitting in the stalls in groups. They looked stunned and Magdalena's expression was shocked.

'It's been withdrawn because it was written by Strauss,' she said.

'Strauss was a Viennese.'

'In New York that's the same as a Berliner.' She gave Slattery an agonized look. 'It's really because Charles Frohman's one of the dead from the *Lusitania*. Nobody knows what to do.'

'It'll be all right, Magdalena,' he said. 'Something will be sorted out.'

'Will it?' Enormous eyes stared at him. 'On my door last night when I got home there was a notice. It said "Hun". That's all. "Hun".'

'Then it's up to you to issue a statement to say you're American. If I send a bunch of newspapermen round, will you do that?'

'I couldn't face them.'

'Magdalena – ' He gestured at the singers and musicians and the group of frightened chorus girls. 'Think of these people. If you say firmly you're American, somebody might think again about the show. And take the train to Philadelphia on Sunday. There's to be a meeting there, of newly-naturalized Americans. The President's going to address it. Let yourself be seen there – being American.'

'Will you come with me?'

'I have to stay in New York.'

The flash of anger was abrupt but it soon died. 'I'll get Hermann to take me,' she said. 'He's due in New York. He'll be glad to.' She sniffed. 'He'd like to marry me, you know. He once asked me.'

Despite her doubts, she did as she was told and the story appeared the following day: *Graf Denies German Sympathy. Grieves For Bereaved. I'm an American and Nothing Else, She Says.*

It was a timely appearance because, with the revulsion that was being shown, after their first gleeful celebrations the Germans were now keeping very quiet and everybody was wondering what America would do. Even German-Americans had come round to the thought that the disaster might precipitate America's entry into the war, and suddenly Horrocks began to cheer up.

'Wilson hasn't uttered a word,' Slattery reminded him sharply.

Midwinter snorted. 'There won't be one,' he growled. 'They want the German Mid-West vote for 1916.'

Two days later, Hermann Stutzmann turned up at Slattery's hotel. He was understandably nervous.

'What are you up to?' Slattery demanded at once.

'*Nichts. Nichts.*' The tenor put his hands to his face, his

293

splayed fingers pushing the flesh out between them in folds. 'I come to look after Magdalena and I discover there is nothing to look after.'

'Where's Fausto Graf, Hermann?'

'*Himmelherrgott*, I don't know.'

'You've seen him often enough.'

Stutzmann sighed. 'He says I don't do enough for Germany and I must work with him. Herr Paddy, I am scared of him.'

'Stay that way, Hermann,' Slattery advised. 'It's safer. What's going to happen to Magdalena?'

'I came to ask *you* that, Herr Paddy. It's expensive in New York and she can't afford to stay here without work.'

By this time, the figures for the *Lusitania*'s casualties were being accepted as complete. One thousand one hundred and fifty passengers had had to be assumed dead and British soldiers were digging huge graves at Queenstown in Ireland. President Wilson had been expected to express the outrage of the United States by declaring war at the meeting of the newly-naturalized Americans but it had proved a damp squib.

'He talked of *peace*!' Midwinter looked shocked. 'Said there was such a thing as being too proud to fight. When I was at school that meant the guy was scared.'

Wilson's stance had started a new round of infuriated charges in New York, with the British, American and German port officials each accusing the others. In a shaded corner of Cunard's main office a table had been spread with photographs of the bodies that had been recovered, in the hope that they might be identified. It was a grisly business, because they included children, a mother clasping her dead baby in her arms. Groups of people stared endlessly at them.

A huge reward had been offered for the recovery of the body of the millionaire, Alfred Vanderbilt, and last tributes were paid to Frohman at crowded ceremonies in different cities. The cast of *Der Zigeunerbaron* had been told nothing and, with no apparent future, were on the point of splitting

294

up. The statement in the paper insisting Magdalena was American seemed to have done little good, while nobody seemed to have noticed her at the meeting in Philadelphia. They ate a gloomy supper at the house she had rented. She was angry with Slattery for not going with her to Philadelphia but he suspected her anger wasn't genuine, and the conversation was one-sided, with Slattery doing all the talking and Magdalena's mind far away.

Then the telephone rang and Jesús appeared in the doorway. As Magdalena headed for the hall where the instrument was situated, there was a long silence then Slattery heard a shriek.

'*What!* María, *Madre de Dios!*' There was a shout of amazement and delight, a few babbled words in German he couldn't catch, then she reappeared and flung her arms round him.

'Fitz! Fitz!' Her happiness swept him along. 'That was Hermann! It's happened! Telegrams have been sent to everybody in the show! It's on again.'

He was on his feet, as delighted and excited as she was.

'No, no! Not *The Gypsy Baron*. Another one. Auber's *Bohemian Girl*. Charles Frohman's brother's forming a company to manage his brother's stars, but they feel Strauss isn't the thing just now. They feel it's best to have someone who isn't German. Auber was Irish, so that should please everybody. It's going to be nothing but rehearsals from now on. I shall get corns on my vocal cords. How marvellous it is!'

As she flung herself at Slattery again, he whirled her round, her feet off the floor.

'We've all got to be at the theatre tomorrow! Hermann will be there. So will Daniel Frohman. He's going to explain everything. He wants his brother's name to be remembered, and he says this is to show the world what he would have done. And they want *me*! They saw that statement in the paper, and someone saw me in Philadelphia.'

She kissed him enthusiastically and waltzed away, calling for Jesús, for her dresser, for everybody in the house to come and help. For a long time, Slattery stood near the abandoned meal, watched by the housemaid who had appeared to clear the dishes, then he shrugged, picked up his hat and headed for the door.

7

With the excitement over the sinking of the *Lusitania*, they had almost forgotten Huerta. But he was still in New York, closely attended by German agents and just as closely watched by allied undercover men.

'Rintelen's called a meeting about him,' Midwinter reported. 'Manhattan Hotel. We've got the number of the suite and we've hired the one next door. We'll install bugs.'

The following day they found clear proof of Scheele's activities. 'Tramp steamer, *Kirk Oswald*,' Horrocks said. 'On her way to Europe with arms for the Russians. Diverted to Marseilles, which is a shorter trip, and when they unloaded they found one of Scheele's cigars in her hold waiting to go off. A docker who must have been brighter than most took it to his boss.'

Slattery, who had had dealings with Scheele and knew him better than anybody else, was given the job of following him round New York. Always he seemed to be with a girl. At a builders' merchants in the Bronx he found he was buying thin lead conduit and water pipe. At a chemical refinery that supplied an electroplating plant in Connecticut, he discovered he had brought sulphuric and picric acid. It was a question now of finding where his devices were being manufactured.

There were plenty of premises in and around New York that could be used for their production, but surveillance provided nothing. Then Slattery realized that in New York harbour there were dozens of German ships caught by the unexpected beginning of the war and interned there, and with them were their officers and crews. Noticing that one of the interned captains had been treated for severe burns to the hands and hip by a doctor with a German name at Mount Vernon, he made further enquiries and discovered that the burns had been of a chemical as well as of a pyrotechnic nature and the next day he started to prowl round the docks, moving quietly among the crews, warehouses, yards and landing piers. It was misty and for a long time he listened to the eerie cries of the gulls and the foghorns booming through the coal smoke hanging over the grey water, and watched the rats slipping among the crates along the waterfront. At the allied docks they were piled high, but the German quays were empty and in a dockside bar he listened to the bitter arguments of the interned German sailors.

Returning to Midwinter's office, he found Horrocks poring over a map of New York's working-class districts.

'There are plenty of German-owned workshops,' he was saying.

'There are plenty of German ships, too,' Slattery interrupted. He explained the way he was thinking. 'I suspect that German captain had one of Scheele's cigars in his pocket,' he continued. 'And it went off unexpectedly.'

'Are they accurate?'

'Surely not *that* accurate.'

Midwinter was pleased with their discovery. He studied the papers on his desk for a moment before looking up, his eyes hard. 'Well, we know Rintelen subscribes to the *Shipping News*. He even has a lawyer who knows the ins and outs of international maritime law. Name of Boniface. Smells of whiskey and looks like a mangy hyena. Works out of his hotel room, knows all the loopholes and has friends in the Police Department who feed him information. I'll have him followed.'

The meeting at the Manhattan Hotel produced nothing but two days later they picked up a lead on Boniface.

'Seen aboard the interned steamship. *Friedrich der Grosse*,' Midwinter said. 'Going to the engine room. Why? He's a lawyer, not a marine engineer.'

'It's just the ship they'd use,' Horrocks agreed. 'Same name as the flagship of the German High Seas Fleet. Nice and symbolic.'

'She's in Hoboken, right in the heart of the docks,' Slattery pointed out. 'And there are dozens of stranded

German seamen round there. And, as a ship's part of its motherland, if they manufacture them aboard the *Friedrich der Grosse*, technically they're on German soil and not breaking American law.'

Midwinter took his suspicions to his superiors but when he appeared the following day he was sour-faced with disappointment. 'They say there must be no breach of neutrality,' he announced. 'Goddamn it, isn't setting fire to ships a breach of neutrality?' He slapped the desk. 'Hell, there must be some way of stopping that sonofabitch Scheele! He must have some weakness we can play on.'

'He likes pretty girls,' Slattery pointed out with a grin.

Midwinter glared. 'You can't run a guy in for canoodling with a dame,' he said.

As the *Lusitania* slipped from the mind, other events crowded in.

'Rintelen's working a deal with Huerta,' Midwinter said. 'They've asked Berlin for arms and support and U-boats to land weapons along the Mexican coast. Huerta's promised that when he regains power, he'll declare war on the good old US.' He grinned. 'Plotters are always pretty free with their promises when they want something.'

'Not what we were taught at school, all this, is it?' Horrocks observed to Slattery as they left. 'Stand up and fight, face to face, man to man. Straight left and all that, they used to say. Lost us a lot of battles. Much better to shoot a chap in the back when he's not looking. What Huerta gets up to is of the greatest importance to Britain. So where's Graf? He's Rintelen's man for Mexico, but we've seen nothing of him since he crossed the border. Ask your German lady friend what he's up to.'

'She doesn't know,' Slattery snapped.

Horrocks gave him a cold accusing look. 'You haven't asked her,' he said. 'Suppose you try.'

8

Magdalena was virtually unreachable. The producer of *The Bohemian Girl* had clamped a ban on visitors to the theatre and whenever Slattery called at her house, she seemed to be asleep, with Jesús guarding the front door.

'When Doña Magdalena is awake she's rehearsing, your honour,' he said. 'When she is not rehearsing, then she is asleep.'

She managed to telephone him at his hotel imploring him to support her on opening night. 'I shall be good if you're there,' she said.

'You'll have the critics eating out of your hand and New Yorkers fighting to get in for the next six months.'

'Just be there. Don't let me down. You left me in Juárez and Mexico City and Chihuahua. Please, Fitz, not again! I've sent you two tickets for the front row of the stalls. Right in the middle where I can see you. Bring a girl with you. Enjoy it. But only have eyes for me. Sometimes I'm terrified, especially when I miss the high notes. The theatre's so silly. You sing like an angel for weeks but one cracked note can ruin everything. It's like a bull fight. You're not allowed a single mistake. I think I'm going to have a cold. I'll lose my voice. And I'm still not sure of my entrances.'

'Magdalena!'

There was an abrupt silence over the line and then a meek, 'Yes. Fitz?'

'You're not going to have a cold. You're as strong as an ox. You won't lose your voice. Your entrances will be exactly right.'

'I'll forget the first words.'

'They'll come when you want them. You'll not dry up.'

'Only if you're in the front row, looking at me. If you do that, everything will be all right.'

'Who else will be there?'

300

'Hermann, of course.'

'What about your brother? Won't he? He's in New York, too, isn't he?'

There was a moment's silence. 'He's not interested in *my* career. He's interested only in Germany and the war. And he's not here any longer, anyway. He's gone back to Mexico. His ranch was burned down and his wife murdered.'

As the opening night of *The Bohemian Girl* drew near they learned more of the preparations for Huerta's rising in Mexico, the arrangements to be followed as he crossed the border, the deals with the various factions in Mexico who were prepared to back him – the cientificos, the foreign investors, the tycoons, the hopeful politicians, the ambitious soldiers, and above all, Orozco, who had been such a bright light in Madero's revolution in 1911 but had somehow since been left behind and wanted the limelight again. Agents of the Hamburg-Amerika Line and a German banker were involved with them in New York and Midwinter had discovered that eight million rounds of ammunition had been purchased in St Louis and a preliminary sum of eight hundred thousand dollars deposited in a German bank in Havana. In addition, Huerta's family had arrived from Barcelona, while Atty sent information that there was to be a rising in the south of Mexico to draw off troops as soon as Huerta crossed the border.

From Stutzmann, Slattery learned that Graf had wasted little time mourning his wife. He had gone to look over new properties at Hidalgo de Parral and San Geronimo but had since left the area and been seen north of the border again.

'He was sent there,' Stutzmann explained.

'Why?'

'To study the terrain, I heard.' Stutzmann looked uncertain and unhappy.

'He knows the terrain,' Slattery snapped. 'What's he up to, Hermann?'

Stutzmann gave him a desperate look and his hands went to his face to press in his cheeks in that gesture of despair he had. 'I cannot tell you, Herr Paddy. I am told I must keep silent.'

'Hermann, you're not a very good agent. You can't hold your tongue and your face shows what you're up to. You look as guilty as hell even now. I could pass it on to the Americans and you could be deported. You could even be put in prison.'

'Oh, *mein Gott*, Herr Paddy, no! I wish to be American. And if I am deported to Germany they would make me fight. I do not know how to fight. I should also be frightened.'

'Then tell me, Hermann. Why was Fausto Graf sent to study the terrain along the border?'

'Oh, *mein lieber Kamerad*! In case of military action.'

'By whom?'

Stutzmann's eyebrows worked wildly, then he threw up his hands. 'Huerta,' he said. 'He is to arrange a route for German reservists interned in America to enter Mexico.'

'Just let 'em try,' Midwinter snorted. 'The bastards'll find themselves being accused of running up debts, on charges of assault, of fraud, larceny, any goddam thing. There are a lot of legal ways of detaining a guy who's trying to cross the border, and nobody's going to stir up a revolution in Mexico if I have anything to do with it.'

The opening night of *The Bohemian Girl* had been fixed for Saturday, 26 June, to allow the reviews to appear in all the Sunday newspapers. Then, with Midwinter fully occupied with blocking the German reservists through the law courts, one of their Czecho-Slovak contacts brought the information to Slattery that Huerta had bought tickets for a policeman's ball. He passed the news on at once. For the rest of the day, Horrocks disappeared. The following morning Midwinter vanished too, then in the evening Horrocks called Slattery at his hotel.

'We're going to take a train ride,' he announced.

'Where are we going?'

'I'll tell you on the way. It's all a bit unexpected. Midwinter's handling everything. As soon as he's fixed the tickets, we'll be off.'

302

'Now?'

'No reason why not, is there?'

It took Slattery a feverish five minutes to get through to Moore's Theatre and it was the stage doorkeeper who answered. 'They're busy,' he said.

'Well, get Miss Graf to the telephone.'

'I can't do that.'

'We'll, get somebody. Somebody who can pass on a message.'

The doorkeeper wasn't very enthusiastic. 'They've just broken off for coffee.'

'Get Miss Graf,' Slattery grated.

'I think she's in the office with Mr Daniel Frohman and Mr Stutzmann.'

'Then put me through to the office.'

But the office was as slow as everybody else. 'She's just gone.'

'Where to?'

'God knows. Probably back onstage. The rehearsals are at a very delicate stage just now.'

Slattery hung on to his temper. 'Put me on the stage extension,' he said.

'Sorry, buddy, we've all been told nothing's to interrupt them.'

'Listen –'

'*You listen!* Do you know how much this show's costing? It's got to be a winner but it won't be with guys like you wanting to interrupt all the time!'

They caught the train by the skin of their teeth and Horrocks sat back, bland and indifferent, blinking at the late sunshine. As they clattered out of the suburbs of the city, they appeared to be heading into the sunset. Slattery looked up sharply.

'Where are we going?'

'West at the moment.'

'Why?'

Horrocks smiled. 'Huerta bought those tickets for the policeman's ball to put people off thinking he was going

303

anywhere. But, as a matter of fact, he's aboard this train at this moment. He said he was going to visit the exposition at San Francisco. But he isn't, of course. He's heading for the border and a meeting with Orozco.'

'What about us?' Slattery asked in alarm. 'Where are *we* going?'

Horrocks smiled. 'Same place,' he said.

Slattery was barely speaking to Horrocks. His mind was full of savage thoughts of pushing him off the train, even *under* the train. Only with the greatest of good luck could he be back in New York by the following evening.

Through his bitter thoughts, too, rose considerable moral doubts. He'd had them when he'd been acting as Villa's envoy and manipulator of dirty work, and he was having them again now as Horrocks' maid of all work. His only consolation was that his country was in danger and dirty work had to be done by someone.

But, as Horrocks prattled on about the scenery, he sat scowling, hoping and praying that his absence wouldn't put Magdalena off. To a performer little things like omens, good luck charms, supporters, lovers, friends, were crucial.

'Why the hell are *we* going to the border, anyway?' he demanded, the words exploding through his anger and concern. 'It's not our affair.'

'Huerta,' Horrocks said slowly, 'is always our affair. What he's about to do could damage our war effort. And we're going because Gus Midwinter's asked us to. Officially I'm a British diplomatic representative going to see fair play. You're going because Midwinter's demanded you – because you can identify Graf. Even Huerta, because you're the only one of us who's met him and they may try to disguise him.'

'I also know Orozco,' Slattery said bitterly.

Horrocks was unmoved. 'Good. It all helps.'

As the train drew into Kansas City, Midwinter stepped down to the platform and waited behind a trolley full of luggage.

'There goes Huerta,' he said quietly. 'Know the guy meeting him, Paddy?'

304

'It's Graf.'

The taxi they followed led them to the Topeka Hotel and they waited outside to allow Huerta and Graf time to register. The desk clerk, who was one of Midwinter's men, knew everything that was going on.

'They've arranged to put him on the same train tomorrow,' he said. 'He gets off twenty miles short of El Paso at Newman. Orozco's waiting with a car.'

It was a touchy moment. If Huerta crossed the border, Washington could find itself facing another situation like Veracruz.

It required telephone calls ahead of them to El Paso and to the station yard, and there was a long argument with the traffic controller who was loath to do anything to help. But in the end they were provided with a locomotive and a single coach and they clattered out of Kansas City at full speed.

Slattery remained awake throughout the night, his thoughts bitter as he saw time slipping away. The first night of *The Bohemian Girl* was now only a few hours away and he couldn't possibly get back to New York in time.

As the sun lifted to the horizon, the dusty desert turned pink, then yellow, then bronze, then golden white. As the train halted at Newman and they climbed down, stiff after sleeping sitting upright, a thickset man in a store suit and wearing a gun approached them.

'What's this train?' he demanded. 'It isn't scheduled.'

'Who're you?' Midwinter asked.

'I'm Cobb. State Department agent here.'

Midwinter grinned. 'Well, State Agent Cobb, I'm your boss.'

Cobb gestured at men waiting behind baggage trolleys, and at an army colonel in uniform with a group of soldiers. 'I got your reinforcements,' he said. 'I got two marshals as well. I told 'em not to look interested. I guess you might need 'em.' He jerked his head. 'If you take a look along the track, you'll see motors. That's the Mex welcoming committee.'

Midwinter nodded, his eyes narrow. 'Well, I aim to arrest those guys. Orozco and Huerta both, State Agent Cobb.'

305

He gestured to Slattery to move nearer to him. 'Step up close, Paddy. I'll be needin' you.'

They had just cleared the track, with the made-up train hissing steam on a loop line by the water tower, when the train from Kansas City appeared. It came to a halt near where Midwinter was smoking one of his cigars. As it stopped the motor cars waiting by the track moved forward. Nobody else moved. Nobody seemed interested. The soldiers seemed to be occupied with loading a truck and the two marshals were deep in conversation.

The yellow sun was slanting along the platform as Huerta stepped down.

'That him, Paddy?' Midwinter asked.

'That's him.'

'Do you formally identify him? No mistake?'

'No mistake.'

A tall moustached man wearing a stetson had climbed out of one of the cars and was walking towards the train.

'And that?'

'Orozco.'

'You formally identify him?'

'I do.'

'No mistake?'

'No mistake.'

'Right. Let's go. Got your gun handy?'

'I don't carry a gun.'

Midwinter glared. 'That's goddam silly,' he said. 'These guys might put up a fight.'

Huerta was peering shortsightedly about him as Orozco approached him. No one seemed to be aware of them but, as soon as they shook hands and turned away, Orozco's arm about Huerta's shoulders, the whole platform came to life. As Cobb stepped forward, behind him were the two marshals, with the colonel and the group of soldiers bringing up the rear.

'Not so goddam silly,' Slattery commented dryly. 'The welcoming committee's decided they've picked the wrong place.'

306

The drivers of the cars down the track were hurriedly cranking their engines to life and, one by one, the vehicles began to move. Orozco's heard jerked round and he was about to step towards them, on the point of breaking into a run, when Midwinter appeared in front of him, solid as a rock, backed by the two marshals, their hands on the butts of their guns.

'General Pascual Orozco,' Midwinter said loudly. 'General Victoriano Huerta. I'm a US State Department agent and, as you have been formally identified, I have orders from Washington to arrest you.'

9

The arrest brought a surprise reaction. El Paso was doing well enough as an assembly point for horses and mules from Texas and New Mexico before they were shipped to the allied armies in France for nobody to want to upset business. The Mayor agreed to be Huerta's attorney and Orozco was reported to have ten thousand men waiting to rally to him and, in the end, with the affair apparently about to end in shooting, Midwinter had to release his prisoners on bail.

When the Sunday newspapers from New York arrived, Slattery snatched them up as soon as they were released. Wrenching at the sheets, he found the theatre page.

'*New Star*,' read the headline. '*Charles Frohman Reaches from the Grave to Launch* Bohemian Girl. *Bookings like Forest Fire.*'

'Magdalena Graf,' the report continued, 'was overwhelmed by her success after the first night of Auber's *Bohemian Girl* at Moore's Theatre last night. She had to take fifteen curtain calls and the audience stood to applaud her.'

There was more in the same vein, every paper carrying the same message. The German-owned journals were rapturous and openly called her 'the German-born diva'.

As they waited, messages began to flood in from Atty. Mexico City, he said, was in turmoil again and could be occupied by anybody who was ready, including Huerta. Zapata was never reliable enough to be a direct threat and Obregón was too far away. Villa had been thrashed again at León and, convinced he was surrounded by treachery, was occupied in executing any of his officers he felt were betraying him. His men were melting away into the hills and, enraged by Urbina's defection and the theft of his war chest, he and Fierro had appeared outside his hacienda and shot his old comrade-in-arms dead.

308

El Paso, meanwhile, was bubbling with fresh news. An urgent message had been received from Washington ordering Orozco and Huerta to be lodged in the county jail. Rather than face arrest, Orozco had jumped bail and vanished into Texas but Midwinter had happily turned the key on the former President.

'Thank Christ that's over,' he said. 'As long as he was free it could have meant war.'

Rintelen had vanished by the time they arrived back in New York and Midwinter had to turn his attention to picking up those of his accomplices against whom he had proof. It took them all day to plan their swoop, and men gathered in the little office by the docks as Midwinter began to draw plans on a blackboard. There seemed to be enough agents to arrest half New York and as it grew dark Slattery left them to it.

Heading for Moore's Theatre, as he approached he could see Magdalena's name in lights over the entrance a hundred yards away - GRAF. Nothing more. A large denomination bill persuaded the doorman to let him in. Magdalena was onstage, her voice stealing through the auditorium like a spirit. She looked very beautiful and a mounting ache went through him as hc watched her, then, after a last brilliant cadenza, like a vast breaking wave thundering on a shore, like a waterfall solid and sustained, came the salute. People rose, waving programmes and throwing flowers, while Magdalena stood in the centre of the stage, curtseying. There was no doubt about her success and Slattery found his heart beating a little faster.

Making his way to the dressing-room, he noticed that everyone backstage seemed to be in a high state of excitement. Success was obvious and it had affected them all. No one noticed him as they threaded their way about the cluttered wings.

Tapping on the door of the star's dressing-room, he pushed his way in. The room seemed to be full of people, chiefly theatrical agents and newsmen, with Magdalena at the dressing-table oblivious to them all. The air was heavy with the scent of roses, and he quietly placed the bouquet he had brought on a *chaise-longue* that was already covered with blooms. Behind a screen, the dresser was hanging up costumes and Magdalena was in a wrapper touching up her make-up. She didn't even look in Slattery's direction as he stood in the background away from the lights that edged her mirror. Then, as she moved things about in the spilled powder on the dressing-table, she became aware of the figure in the shadows.

'Who's that?' she asked, without turning her head.

'It's me, Magdalena. Slattery.'

Immediately, she swung round, scattering powder in a cloud, and rose to her feet, her eyes blazing. 'You weren't there!' she snapped.

It came in a high rich tone that stopped the chatter at once. Every head swung round to stare and Magdalena turned to her dresser. 'Get everybody out,' she said, gesturing with a long fine-skinned hand.

As the door slammed, she stared furiously at Slattery. 'You weren't there,' she said again. 'I begged you to come.'

'Tomorrow, Magdalena.'

'It was on the first night that I needed you. You let me down again.'

'You didn't need me. I've heard what happened. It's all over town.'

'That was because we'd changed the show. Because I was hit by a bullet in Veracruz. Everybody knew about it – the press agent made sure they did – and they knew how little time we had.'

'It wasn't that. It was you, your voice, your looks, your personality.'

'Why didn't you come?'

'It was impossible.'

'Where were you?'

'Near El Paso.'

'What were you doing there?'

'I can't tell you.'

'I very nearly couldn't go on. The show was a disaster.'

She was acting again. 'Dammit, Magdalena, it was a triumph!'

'The critics hated it.'

'The critics said it was wonderful. I read the reviews. Goddammit, Magdalena, how much more of a success do you want? I was out there just now and I know you've been offered another show to follow this one and a chance in opera.'

The anger died and she looked scared, a little girl suddenly. 'I'm not good enough for opera. I can't sing Mimi.

'You can do anything you want to. Mimi's only the start. The big rôles will follow.'

'I don't want –' she began, her eyes suddenly anxious, then she stopped, and the anger returned. 'Go away! I'm due on for the last act in a few minutes. There's a lot to do. María, bring my costume.'

Slattery edged towards the door, loath to go but anxious not to disturb her at a critical point in the performance.

'I'm having supper at Lüchow's with Hermann,' she said. Lüchow's serve good German food and good German wine. Loyal German's eat there.'

'For God's sake,' Slattery snapped. 'You're not German, Magdalena!'

She seemed awed for a moment by his anger but she recovered quickly. 'My sympathies are with Germany.'

'I don't believe it. You're just angry with me. Frohman drowned because of a German U-boat.'

Her eyes filled with tears. 'No, I –'

He could see she was confused and moved forward, but she picked up a heavy silver hand mirror. 'If you come any closer, I shall hit you with this,' she said. 'I know what you are. You're a spy. That's why you're interested in me. You're spying on my brother and wanting to know where he is. That's all you ever wanted from me.'

She faced him with blazing eyes, clutching her wrapper over her bosom with one hand, holding the silver mirror with the other. 'María,' she said, 'show this gentleman – this man – out. If he stays any longer I shall break down. I

311

shall let down the whole cast and the management of the show. Make him go away. I don't want to see him again – ever!'

Slattery was silent for a moment. 'All right, Magdalena,' he said at last. 'I'll go. I'll not trouble you any more.'

As he began to close the door, she stepped forward. 'Fitz–!'

But he was already outside and didn't hear her and as the door clicked she stopped dead. Turning, she tossed the hand mirror angrily to the dressing table where it knocked the powder bowl flying in a little pink cloud. Tears sparkled in her eyes, then she stiffened and forced them back. '*Pronto*, María,' she said. '*Schnell*! Let's get on with it. We'll be late for the curtain.'

Heading through the whispering people in the corridor and out into Broadway, Slattery decided the safest thing to do was get drunk. When he returned to his hotel, however, he was stone-cold sober.

He continued to half-hope to hear from Magdalena, convinced that the exchange had been the result of tiredness and nerves. But there was no message and two nights later he dined late at Lüchow's, knowing she would arrive after the show. She was with Hermann Stutzmann and Slattery caught his eye and gestured with his head. Stutzmann looked nervous, as he always did when he was involved in plotting, however innocuous. As he vanished to the vestibule, Slattery crossed to Magdalena. She didn't respond to his smile.

'I'm with friends,' she said coldly.

'Hermann's a friend of mine, too. Hermann's everybody's friend. He's incapable of being an enemy.'

'He's *your* enemy. He's a Hun. Lüchow's is notorious for being full of Huns.'

Her hostility irritated him. 'For Christ's sake, Magdalena, how can you support a country that's guilty of so many atrocities?'

'British lies,' she snapped. 'The first victim in any war is truth.'

When Stutzmann returned, she rose. 'I think we'd better go, Hermann,' she said. 'I don't like the custom at Lüchow's tonight.'

Horrocks remained in New York, determined like Midwinter to contain the German agents there. Few of the newspapers were neutral and there were many definitely pro-German, the most virulently anti-British the Hearst press. In addition, there were Sinn Feiners eager to see Britain defeated, whose leaders were known to be in touch with German agents. German propaganda was winning hands down against the ham-fisted British productions.

But then the British Admiralty produced a set of papers taken from an American courier for the Germans when he was picked up as his ship entered British waters. They contained reports of German-planned strikes among munitions workers in the States, proof of payments to saboteurs and plenty of German contempt for the 'naïve' Americans. Once again the spy mania flared up and the newspapers began to see agents everywhere. Then, as Slattery was about to take the Sixth Avenue Elevated Midwinter popped up alongside him, a glint in his frosty eyes. He indicated two men nearby.

'Guy with the briefcase,' he said quietly. 'Spymaster for Rintelen. Let's see where they go.'

At 23rd Street the German's companion left the train and, as they passed through the following stations, the German, his brief-case at his side, began to nod in the warmth of the compartment. As the doors opened for 50th Street, he came to life with a start and headed for the door, his briefcase forgotten. Immediately Midwinter rose and, picking up the case, slipped out of the far end of the car.

'Hey, Mister!' A girl yelled a warning. 'He's got your case!'

As the German realized what had happened and turned back, he found his way barred by a stout angry woman trying to leave the car. As he pushed her out of the way, he found himself face to face with Slattery, and they danced

313

from side to side, the German trying to pass, Slattery always in the way.

'I'll do it just once more,' Slattery said cheerfully, 'then I'll have to go.'

He was flung savagely aside, but the German was too late and, as he dived for the stairs, Midwinter jumped on the rear platform of a passing trolley car.

The brief-case contained plans to obtain the whole American supply of liquid chlorine for use in gas shells, to ferment strikes, to acquire the Wright Airplane Company to deny its facilities to the allies, to obtain control of the Bethlehem munitions plant, and finally to gain control of the cotton exports of the entire South.

Midwinter scowled. 'The goddam crooks,' he said. 'Let's get this stuff along to Washington pronto.'

Slattery continued to hope but no word came. Bitterly, he began to wonder if what had happened between himself and Magdalena in Mexico City had been part of some devious plan arranged by Fausto Graf to obtain information. He couldn't really believe it, but stranger and more ominous things had happened. In the end he dismissed the idea, but he found it hard to put everything out of his mind. Finally he thought of Helen Frankfurter, the New York girl with whom he had virtually shared a cabin on the now vanished *Lusitania* on his way over to America from England. He knew her address and tried to telephone her.

'Who?' she sounded puzzled, as if she couldn't remember him, then the bewilderment changed to alarm.

'Oh, shit,' she said. 'Fitz Slattery! Jesus, go away, Fitz! I'm married now. To a guy called Hackhofer, would you believe it? I changed Frankfurter for Hackhofer! And he and my mother are banging on the drum as hard as they can go for the Kaiser. They'd murder me if they knew about you.' Her voice changed and she gave a little laugh. 'Not me! *I* don't think that way. We had fun, you and me, Fitz. But you see how it is.'

Slattery saw, and replaced the telephone gently. As he

did so, one of the bellhops appeared with a letter for him. 'Just arrived,' he said.

Thinking it might at last be a note from Magdalena, he wrenched it open. It was from Amaryllis.

'Dear old Paddy,' she wrote. 'In New York. Reah had to go to Canada. Come and have a drink some time.'

He didn't bother to read any more but found a cab and drove to the Manhattan Hotel to seek the comfort of Amaryllis's ample bosom. Finding her room number, he went up in the elevator and tapped on the door. She had taken a suite as big as the Crystal Palace and on the table was an ice bucket with champagne.

She grinned as she handed him a glass. 'I'm here to do a book on the American top two hundred,' she announced. 'There's a guaranteed advance and the certainty of good sales.'

'You're brave,' Slattery said. 'Crossing the Atlantic with submarines active off the American coast.'

She shrugged. 'Money was involved and I'm a good swimmer.' She looked at the clock. 'What are you doing here?' she asked. 'Shouldn't you be at Moore's Theatre?'

'I've been thrown out of Moore's,' Slattery said savagely. 'By Magdalena.'

She was silent for a moment. 'She'll expect you to go back. Women who kick men out always expect them to go back.'

He shook his head. 'Not again, Amaryllis. It's happend once too often.'

'There's no such thing as "once too often." '

'This time there is. You know why I've come.'

Amaryllis frowned and shook her head. 'No, Paddy,' she said. 'Not this time. I'm not here to seduce you. I watched you in Veracruz and I watched her. You don't belong to me any more. You're looking at a touch of nobility, old Paddy. It's frightening when you see it in somebody like me. But she's probably weeping over you like sleet in a south-easter and she's not going to accuse me of taking you away from her.'

He gestured angrily. 'When Reah starts worrying about me, you can start worrying about Magdalena.'

She studied him, a sad look in her eyes, and kissed him on the cheek. 'If you're determined to go on thinking of her –'

'I'm not.'

'Then try not to look as if you are.'

Slattery left the hotel frowning heavily. Amaryllis knew every sexual trick in the book and she made no bones about enjoying them, but she'd turned him down. Even as he hated himself for what he'd contemplated, he had to admire her for refusing him. She had her own code of morals, odd as they might seem.

He was in low spirits when he appeared in the office the following morning and he expected Midwinter to be the same. He had been depressed at the lack of support he'd had from his superiors about Scheele but suddenly his mood had changed.

'Scheele,' he said immediately. 'I've discovered that here in New York State we have a law that exacts high penalties for anyone trying to seduce a dame. It's been exploited before now. You don't like a guy down the street, you get your girl to say he's been making advances and he gets fined or goes to jail. Suppose Scheele was accused?'

It seemed worth trying and when one of Midwinter's men was set to watch the German chemist, it was noticed that he regularly frequented the Hudson ferry, chiefly, it seemed, to pick up girls.

'All we want now,' Midwinter said, 'is a dame.'

'I think,' Slattery said, 'that I can find you one,'

'Have you ever fancied,' Slattery asked, 'being a British agent?'

Amaryllis looked startled. 'What's the matter? Have you run out of candidates?'

'For this we need a female with looks, confidence, a bit of acting ability and a lot of cool cheek.' He explained what was wanted and she grinned, not only delighted to join the conspiracy, but flattered to have been recruited.

316

'Does he have to seduce me?' she asked.

Slattery laughed. 'Not this time. All you have to do is accuse him of it.'

Two days later, Scheele appeared on the deck of the Hudson ferry, looking prosperous and wearing a lavender-grey suit and the usual boater with its pink ribbon.

Amaryllis was standing near the rails, staring across the river, and as Scheele passed, she dropped her umbrella. Scheele was quick to jump forward and pick it up. As he handed it back with a click of the heels and a little bow, she fluttered her eyelashes at him.

As they fell into conversation, Slattery, watching from the upper deck, rejoined Midwinter in the saloon. 'I think,' he said, 'that we can now leave it to the expert.'

Two days later, Amaryllis reported that Scheele had made a date with her. 'What a pity he's such a little toad,' she said. 'However, it's all most exciting and when I write my memoirs it will have pride of place. *Amaryllis Eade, British Agent*. I can see the title now.'

Within a week, she was able to report that Scheele had dined her out and was asking her to take a trip with him. 'He suggested a weekend in the country,' she said. 'I can imagine what he has in mind. He says he knows a good hotel in Pleasantville, where they don't ask questions.'

'Get him to take you through Irving,' Midwinter suggested. 'Tell him you've heard there's a good view. We'll have a man on the road just outside the town. He'll know what to do.'

They were standing among the trees outside Irving as Scheele's motor appeared. Amaryllis was wearing a pink outfit and an enormous confection of pink flowers, feathers, fruit and ribbons on her head. Scheele's vehicle was a Model T Ford and it was vibrating heavily.

'Poor Amaryllis,' Slattery grinned. 'What she's done for England!'

Parked by the roadside was a big Dodge and, beside it, smoking a cigarette, was a man with a large moustache, a

317

cream homburg, a red tie and a carnation. As the Ford approached, they saw Amaryllis lean forward to study him then, as she sailed past, she turned suddenly and slammed her umbrella down over Scheele's head. His boater was crushed and, as the car swerved and came to a stop in the middle of the road, she started screaming and waving her arms. Scheele, the pink ribbon of his hat round his neck, was screaming back at her.

'*Liebchen! Meine liebe Freund!* What is the matter?'

Amaryllis was shrieking wildly. 'I'm going to report it! I'm going to report it to the police!'

The man by the parked Dodge stepped forward. 'I *am* the police, Miss,' he said. 'Can I help?'

Amaryllis jabbed a handkerchief to her eyes and set up a wail. 'This man is trying to seduce me,' she howled.

The man in the homburg was alongside the Ford now. 'That sort of thing's against the law, Miss,' he said. 'I'd better run him in.' He turned to the bewildered Scheele. 'I'm going to arrest you, bud, on the grounds this young lady's just reported.'

'But this iss ridiculous,' Scheele yelled. 'This lady iss my friend!'

The man in the homburg produced a notebook. 'You got anything to say, bud?'

'Iss a misunderstandink. A dreadful mistake.'

As they were arguing, another car appeared, driven by a man in a brown derby, who announced that he was also a policeman.

'Right,' the man in the homburg said. 'Just keep an eye on this guy. I'm going to take him in for assaulting this young lady. Park your flivver and ride shotgun.'

A week later Midwinter announced that Scheele had disappeared.

'Atty says he's turned up in Mexico City,' Slattery reported. 'He's waiting for the first conflagration.'

For her services to the war effort, Slattery dined Amaryllis in the best restaurant in New York. 'We'll also buy you a new umbrella,' he promised.

'Don't bother,' she smiled. 'I shall have it photographed and use it when I write my memoirs.'

He studied her affectionately. There was something about her. Courage. Intelligence. A brazen style of humour. She would always attract him by her common sense and her love of life. Was it always going to be like this? Suddenly he realized he was growing too old for promiscuity. He needed to settle down.

'Marry me, Amaryllis.'

She looked up startled, then she laughed. 'The answer's no, of course, old Paddy, because you'd never have asked me if Magdalena hadn't chucked you. Besides, there's another thing. Reah's promoted to Washington. So I'm going to marry *him*. I decided it was time to settle down, too, before what I get up to begins to show in my face, as it's bound to eventually. I've been wondering for a long time how to break it to you.'

Slattery stared at her in amazement. 'Good God, Amaryllis,' he said, 'I'm startled! But pleased for you. Reah's not a bad chap.'

She shrugged. 'He's got a lot of money and I need a lot of money. But I'll try to be faithful, because Reah's rather a nice man and he talks of children. Of course, if I have sons and someone tells them their mother was a whore, that's something they'll have to put up with, because I've certainly been no prude. But if anyone dares to call them little bastards, even if only in fun, they'll have to answer to me because that's one thing they won't be. Lady Reah, though! Can you imagine it, old Paddy? It ought to sell a lot of books.'

Slattery laughed out loud. Conscienceless and brisk, she was telling him it was over between them for good. She had finished with the old life and put on the new in her usual breezy fashion, and he had a suspicion that Lord Reah was getting better than he deserved. It would be God help him if he strayed, because if Amaryllis gave her mind to it, she would be the most strait-laced woman in Europe.

She was watching him intently. 'You should go back to

319

Magdalena,' she said quietly. 'She's what you need and she's going to need you eventually.'

He made no comment and she went on earnestly. 'I went to see her the other night. She was good.'

'Better than that, I think.'

'The audience was certainly with her. It's a gift she has. I went backstage. I told her I hoped the show would continue to be a success. On the other hand -'

'On the other hand, what?'

She kissed his cheek. 'Do you see a lot of musicals, Paddy?'

'Not as many as you, I imagine.'

'Exactly. Well, she's good, Paddy. But she's not good *enough*. I've seen many shows and I've met many singers. Patti. Melba. Caruso. I've talked to them, written about them. She's not got what they've got. She's beautiful and talented and captures the audience. But something's missing, old Paddy. That lot are selfish and self-centred and as tough as Old Nick's nag nails. She isn't, and she'll break her heart first.'

Part V

1

Slattery had still continued to half-hope to hear from Magdalena, but she had made no move, and two days later he bumped into Jesús on Broadway. He had grown tall and handsome and was feeling pleased with himself.

'I am now part of Doña Magdalena's family,' he said. 'I have her name. It's all official. I think eventually I shall go into the theatre, too. I don't fancy the stage, but in California they are making moving pictures and want young men -'

'Jesús' - Slattery stopped him dead - 'how is it with Doña Magdalena?'

Jesús pulled a face. 'I have tried to talk to her about you, sir. I think something dreadful has happened. There was a time when I thought - when I hoped -'

Slattery put a hand on the boy's shoulder. 'There was a time when I hoped, too, Jesús.'

The following morning New Yorkers woke to a new scandal as they learned the contents of the briefcase Midwinter had picked up on the Elevated. The government had rejected the papers on the grounds that the plots were little more than fantasy, but the *New York World* had seized on them with glee. It was only a small victory, but it made the Germans look ridiculous and was something to chalk up against Berlin, and Horrocks was just wondering how they might celebrate when Midwinter arrived.

'The goddam government's gone crazy,' he exploded as he threw down his hat. 'It's switched its policy! I've just heard! They've decided to recognize Carranza as President of Mexico!'

They stared at him, shocked. The White House had been saying for weeks that it was impossible to deal with the vain, obstreperous and hostile Carranza. Now they were throwing all their weight behind him and, with Carranza secure and known to be under the influence of the Germans, there were unlimited opportunities for trouble.

'For God's sake,' Horrocks snapped at Slattery in a fury of frustration. 'Get down to Mexico City! I don't know what the hell you're doing up here, anyway! You should be looking after the shop!'

Arriving in Mexico City in a rush, Slattery found Atty running the office remarkably efficiently and well established with Pilar, the housekeeper, in the servants' quarters of Magdalena's house. He disturbed him more than a little with the information that when Magdalena took up residence once more he would probably be considered *persona non grata*.

'You mean, you blew it?' Atty said.

He had news. One more of their enemies had vanished from the scene. Orozco had been shot dead by a sheriff's posse in Texas. But Turner, the printer, was in an agitated state again. Since Villa had pitched headlong to defeat and Wilson had reversed his policy to back Don Venus, he was expecting Carranza to return to the capital and declare all the money he had printed as valueless and refuse to pay for it.

'This is no way to earn a living,' he complained. 'Villa was only a blown-up bandit, anyway.'

Blown-up or not, there was still plenty of spite left in him and Slattery heard he'd been seen heading north for a final show-down. He had trapped a Carrancista general at Agua Prieta on the border and was reported to be crossing the Sierra Madre towards him. Because of snow, most of his army couldn't keep up, but reports indicated that he was still powerful enough with a little luck to win an unexpected victory and re-establish himself in the north.

'I've heard different,' Atty said. 'He's lost Fierro. Got hisself drowned in the Laguna de Guzmán. He was wearing a money-belt loaded with gold and his horse fell. But Villa's still dancing up and down the border like a terrier looking for someone to bite. Fausto Graf's behind him, telling him his only hope now is to force an American invasion that would rally the Mexes behind him again.'

'Where did you get all this?'

'A cousin of Pilar's. Villa still wants to sweep old Don Venus under the carpet and this is the way he thinks he'll do it. And that suits Unser Fausto fine. I heard he was up near Agua Prieta, too. I reckon we ought to go and see what's happening.'

By the time they reached Nogales, Villa had emerged from the mountains. His march had been brutal and he had only a scarecrow band to push across the desert, but refugees were already arriving in the town which still contained remnants of the Spanish families he had driven north in 1913, all praying for his defeat and final descent into hell.

They had put the Studebaker on a flat car at El Paso but it had refused to start and they were still trying to acquire horses when the news came in of Villa's final defeat. He had done all he could to avoid annoying the Americans and had even lined up his artillery so that the 'overs' wouldn't fall across the border; but, throwing everything behind his new friend, President Wilson had permitted Carranza's reinforcements to be transported by train across American soil north of the Rio Grande, and in a desperate night attack, the Villistas had found themselves suddenly illuminated by searchlights which had showed them up starkly against electrified barbed wire entanglements for the massed machine-guns and artillery to slaughter. The retreat had become a rout and eventually a ghastly ghost march through the clouds back over the mountains.

There were no slopes in the world more naked than the Sonora sierras. Even in summer they were foodless, waterless and often without a blade of grass and, with the snow covering every pass, the retreat was a nightmare for the ill-clad, blinded, exhausted men. Toiling horses had sunk exhausted and starving men had stripped their bones for food and used their hides as a bloody covering for their shivering bodies. The only discipline left in the ragged army was among the Dorados.

Slattery saw them emerge, men with the staring fish eyes of the exhausted, stubbly faces blackened with frostbite, eye sockets rimmed with gun grease against snow blindness, their feet, encased in rags, shuffling in mechanical rhythm. He was standing by the trail as they passed and Villa rode past him, unseeing, his face blank, his features bleak and hard as iron.

Villa was finished and he had now vanished again with the few survivors, his force annihilated, the garrisons of his once powerful strongholds crumbling, his generals seeking surrender terms, Villa himself swearing revenge on the gringos who had caused his defeat.

The reporters, hard-faced men who had seen every kind of villainy in Mexico, were stunned less by the finality of the defeat than by their own country's treachery.

'They say American soldiers were working those search-lights,' they told Slattery.

The situation in Mexico remained chaotic, with armies moving like mass migrations. Their leaders had failed to see Carranza with his long white beard as the guardian of their heaven, and his rallying calls were being ignored. Though Villa's defeat had left him safe, his power was already draining away.

The German-owned newspapers that came down from New York were still full of Magdalena, and there were pictures of her visiting interned German sailors in hospitals, talking to reporters, sitting on the Hudson ferry showing far more leg than Slattery imagined she would like. In all of them she was not referred to as Mexican or American but always as German. Fausto Graf's friends had been very busy.

Christmas came and went and the signs once again seemed to be that America was edging towards war with Germany. Then, just after the New Year, news came in that a band of Villistas had waylaid a train at Santa Ysabel in the State of Chihuahua and, lining up seventeen American mining engineers who happened to be aboard, had stripped and shot them.

The roar of fury that went up across the border could be heard even in Mexico City and once more Mexicans looked nervously at each other as the bogey of invasion reappeared. Inevitably a telegram arrived from Horrocks for Slattery.

'Meet me El Paso. Canadian among dead. British businesses along border demand representation.'

2

The citizens of El Paso were looking for Mexicans with guns in their fists and hatred in their eyes. There had already been lynchings and the Mexican residents were cowering in their homes. The family of the murdered Canadian had arrived to collect his body and were furiously demanding revenge.

Horrocks, who had arrived from New York, was in a towering rage. 'The bloody town's been put under martial law,' he snapped, 'and there's a volunteer posse a thousand strong threatening to rush the border and take it out in Ciudad Juárez. You know what the Texans are like. They're going on about murder and pillage and American women being outraged, about fates worse than death and the sacred honour of the State. Their congressmen and senators are all blowing the "Charge". German agents are behind it, of course.'

'And Wilson?'

'Still saying he won't go to war with Mexico. Let's hope he continues, because that's just what Germany wants.'

As Horrocks vanished north again, Slattery stared at Atty. 'Where's Villa?' he asked.

'He was at Parral.'

'How do you know?'

'Pilar has a brother there. He says Santa Ysabel was nothing to do with him, but he's spoiling for a fight after that business with the searchlights. There are Germans with him and Pilar's brother says he has his eye on an American border station.'

'He must be mad.'

'Not if he catches 'em when they're looking the other way. Pilar's brother said he left two days ago and headed up the main railway line towards El Paso.'

'He'd never attack El Paso.'

Nobody was talking but it was obvious something was in the wind. That evening Atty reappeared, a little drunk, to confirm what he'd said. 'Pilar's brother says I'm right,' he pointed out. 'A feller he knows called Favela and several others bumped into a gang of Villistas and the Villistas hanged one of 'em and shot two. Favela got away and managed to follow 'em and he saw 'em heading towards Columbus.'

Columbus was a small straggling place seared by the sun and in danger of being buried by drifting sand. It had neither electricity nor telephone and was entirely dependent on the telegraph and the railroad. They arrived at midnight, just as a train pulled in filled with half-drunken soldiers returning from leave among the delights of El Paso.

'Some guys have got the German bogey on the brain,' a burly top sergeant told them. 'This is a quiet stretch and has been for the last five years.'

Nobody had ever heard of Fausto Graf and, tired and dispirited, for a while they sat in the hired car, smoking.

'Fancy a beer?' Atty said.

He fished among the luggage and produced two bottles. 'Cold,' he said. 'I bought 'em in El Paso and shoved some ice in with 'em.'

They sat on the board walk, dusty and exhausted, with thirsts like camels. Not far away, in the dim light of the guardroom of the American base, they could see the officer of the day inspecting the guard.

'I think we'd better knock up the hotel and find a room,' Slattery said. 'There's no sign of Villa here.'

They had just lifted the bottles to their mouths when they heard the sound of horses' hooves. They came abruptly out of the silence as though the animals had approached at a walk and been kicked from a standstill to a full gallop. As the thunder increased Atty carefully placed his bottle on the boardwalk and fished under his jacket to produce a vast revolver.

'Boss,' he said quietly, 'I reckon *this* is Villa.'

*

329

As they started running, they heard high-pitched yells of *'Qué viva Villa!'* and *'Mueran los gringos!'*, then round the corner and down the street from the western end of the town poured a river of horsemen in vast sombreros. A soldier shouted and there was a shot and the soldier staggered backwards.

The officer of the day appeared with a pistol in his hand. As he did so, a Mexican emerged from the shadows and fired at him. The officer's hat flew off but he shot the Mexican and began to sprint across the parade ground to the guardhouse. Already a heavy fire was coming from the darkness, but the horsemen seemed to have vanished as quickly as they had appeared, filtering between the buildings.

Atty had found a place outside a store where barrels were stacked on the sidewalk. As they crouched down, he passed Slattery his revolver and fished out another from under his arm.

'Where the hell do you hide them?' Slattery asked.

'Never without 'em. One each side. Keep me evenly balanced.'

Bullets were whacking into the woodwork of the store and they heard women screaming inside as the windows fell in. The Mexicans appeared to be everywhere and there seemed remarkably little retaliation. Somewhere in the darkness they could hear a soldier swearing and never repeating himself, as he complained that the rifles were locked up and that the officer with the key wasn't available.

'Shoot the lock off, you dumb bastard,' someone yelled at him.

A blaze shot up nearby as the Mexicans set fire to the timber dwellings, and the old houses, dried by the sun, went up like a bonfire. The scene was lit by the flames and there was a confusion of shots, screams and the crackle of burning buildings.

The Mexicans seemed to be spreading through the town now but a few weapons had begun to appear in the hands of the defenders. A Mexican running towards them with a flaming torch stopped dead as Atty rose from behind his barrel. As the Mexican reached for his gun, Atty and Slattery fired together and the heavy bullets lifted him off his feet to drop him on his back in a puff of dust. As Atty picked up his rifle, a horseman in a big hat thundered out of the shadows and he reversed the weapon and swung it with all his strength. The butt caught the Mexican full in the face and he went over the tail of his horse as if he were shot.

'Two,' Atty said, tossing the fallen man's rifle to Slattery.

The Mexicans' main targets appeared to be the bank, the hotel and the store, and within minutes petrol stacked in drums caught fire, blazing fluid flying in all directions. In the light of the flames, the defenders began to do better as the Villistas – previously enjoying the cover of the shadows – were lit up. Atty was using his rifle with great skill and as two Mexicans dragged away an American from the blazing hotel, he picked them off one after another, so that the American was able to bolt for the darkness.

Together, they moved along the street. There seemed to be bodies everywhere now, most of them Mexican. Eventually, they came to a house standing on its own and, as a group of men appeared round a corner, they both dived automatically for the stoop. Putting their shoulders to the door, they burst in. By the light of a single lamp, a woman in a nightgown threw herself at their feet. 'Leave the children,' she screamed. 'Take *me*!'

Atty hoisted her to her feet. 'Get under the bed, lady,' he said. 'Look after the kids.'

As the group of horsemen thundered past, Slattery brought one of them down with a crash. The shot emptied his magazine and he slipped out to retrieve the Mexican's weapon. The Mexican stank like a polecat with sweat, dirt and cheap wine, as if the raiders had been nursing their resentment in some cantina on the other side of the border until the right word had sent them off in a drunken charge against the hated Yanquis.

The shooting in their particular area seemed to have died down a little now but there was obviously fierce fighting further along. 'Stay here,' Slattery said to the woman. 'Hide yourself and the children.'

A few panic-stricken inhabitants had locked themselves in an adobe building nearby and, though Slattery hammered on the door and demanded to be let in, they were refused, so they ran along the street, keeping to the shadows behind carts and boxes and the terrified horses hitched to the ramadas outside the store, which were rearing and tossing their heads and neighing with terror.

The American soldiers had recovered from their surprise now and were appearing with weapons in their hands. One man with a baseball bat was pounding at a kneeling Mexican. Across the street, several more Mexicans were trying to break down a door when suddenly it was snatched open and a woman flung the contents of a steaming pan over them. Screaming with pain, they staggered away, clawing at their eyes.

The woman managed a shaky grin at Slattery. 'My Ma once stopped Indians with a pan of scalding water,' she said.

With the hotel in flames, it was as light as day now and the Americans were fighting back fiercely. Frontier instincts they'd imbibed with their mother's milk had taken over and the raiders were beginning to get the worst of it.

Slattery, Atty and three more men took shelter in a saddlery and every time the raiders tried to get near the bank, their shots stopped them dead in their tracks. Eventually the noise began to die.

Stepping out into the street holding Atty's revolver, Slattery peered about him warily. The sound of hooves warned him that it wasn't quite over and he heard the screeching of Mexican bugles, higher and thinner than American bugles, beginning to sound the retreat. Mexicans appeared from the shadows, running for the west, followed by riders blazing away haphazardly behind them. The last raiders tumbled down the front steps of the burning hotel, their arms full of loot, to grab their horses and, sped on their way by a last few shots, thundered out of town. The fight seemed to be over.

As the dust settled and the first light appeared, people began to arrive in the litle plaza. Several bodies were stretched out like broken dolls in the grotesquerie of sudden death, the high-crowned sombreros giving the final touch of macabre inconsequentiality to the scene. A few Mexicans, badly wounded but still alive, were being dragged off to jail. The hotel entrance was jammed with a dead horse and two dead men. Their rifles trailing butt down in the dust, the townspeople began to collect, half-dressed, grimy and dazed. A few were struggling to save the store and a few more fought to put out the flames at the hotel. A man wearing a dark suit and a black bowler appeared, driving a flat boxboard buggy with his name on it in white letters and the word 'Mortician' beneath. He was collecting the bodies one after the other, his face expressionless.

'Our boys first,' he kept saying. 'Our boys first.'

There was a lot of activity round the army camp and they could hear orders being shouted. Then there was the rumble of hoofs and a squadron of cavalrymen swung out and began to head for the border, their faces devoid of mercy.

Atty stared after them, his face as expressionless as always.

'That's it,' he said in a flat voice. 'The Germans have finally got their invasion.'

Just when everything appeared to have quietened down and the flames killed, a fresh fire broke out in the livery stable. It was a fierce conflagration, the sparks whirling upwards on the breeze and, though bucket chains were formed from the pumps and the horse trough, it was impossible to put it out and they could hear trapped horses screaming.

'God damn it,' the owner yelled furiously. 'The goddam Mexes never came near *us*!'

They were all staring hopelessly at the flames when Atty appeared alongside Slattery. In his hand he held a straw boater. It had been trodden on and round it was a pink ribbon.

'Scheele,' he said.

3

'What in Christ's name were they up to, to allow it?'
Midwinter snarled. 'Eight American soldiers and ten
civilians dead, and eight more wounded.'

He had arrived with Horrocks in a hurry from El Paso
just as the avenging cavalrymen had returned. Behind them
were the civilian volunteers who had formed a posse. Some
of them were dragging at the end of lariats the bodies of
Mexicans they had caught. Others, who had brought their
victims home strung across the saddles of their own horses,
were just unlashing them and pushing them over to thud
into the dust.

Slattery watched with Atty. A woman washing the blood
off the steps of the hotel stopped to look. Slattery peered
more closely at one of the bodies and, snatching up her
bucket tossed the water across it.

'Hey,' she yelled. 'No need for that!'

He took the cloth from her hands and wiped away the
dried blood and dust.

'It's Vegas,' he said.

Horrocks had been talking to the army men. 'They claim
they killed a hundred,' he said.

'Somebody sure killed somebody,' Midwinter agreed.
'Who was it? Villa?'

'They were yelling for Villa,' Slattery agreed.

'Wilson'll *have* to act this time,' Horrocks observed.

'Any sign that Germany was behind it?' Midwinter
demanded.

'Just Graf,' Slattery said.

'You saw?'

'I know.'

'That's no goddam good!'

Slattery indicated the body at his feet. 'There's him,' he

said. 'He was Graf's man. And there's this.' He held out the crushed boater with its pink ribbon.

'Scheele,' Midwinter said at once. 'Did you see him?'

'No. But it looks very much as if he was here.'

'Would you be prepared to stand up in court and swear that Graf was here?'

'No.'

'Why not?'

'I didn't see him.'

'*I* wouldn't mind saying I saw him,' Atty said.

'Did you?'

'No. But I'd be prepared to say I did, to nail the bugger.'

Not only Columbus but the whole border seemed stunned by the raid and there were reports that the American ambassador in Berlin had telegraphed that it had been organized there. Certainly, there seemed no reason for it beyond the fact that Villa was desperate for horses, weapons and revenge.

'*Delirio de grandeza*,' one of the Mexicans in El Paso told Slattery. 'He's gone off his head.'

Atty's view was different. 'German money,' he said. 'Berlin's going to love it.'

Allied to Villa's new anti-Americanism, it seemed a sound enough explanation and an isolated American town near the border was an obvious target. More evidence of German complicity was coming in and there was news of German officers in Tampico, German plots along the border and more in Chihuahua, Sonora and Durango. In addition, it was clear the arms Rintelen had bought for Huerta were now going to Villa, transported over the border in coffins or chartered oil tankers.

The activity along the Rio Grande was tremendous. Within days, troops, equipment and supplies began to pour into Columbus.

Midwinter brought the news. 'They're sending a force into Mexico,' he said. 'To capture Villa. Wilson had to give way.' He frowned. 'It'll be another Veracruz. The Mexes will lose nothing - up here there's nothing to lose except sand – and *we'll* lose our dignity.'

*

335

Columbus began to fill up with men, horses and waggons. For the second time the Germans had worked on the passions of the Americans and this time in no way could Washington claim that what they were proposing was a temporary occupation. This time it was an out-and-out invasion of Mexican territory. One column of four thousand men was to head due south, while a second column two thousand strong was to move along the border area.

But the Americans weren't finding it easy to build up the force they had proposed because American hustle had moved too fast for what America possessed. They didn't have a single military unit ready for service in Mexico and a week passed before what had become known as Wilson's Punitive Expedition was ready.

Frantic officers contacted other units, struggling to complete their equipment, exchanging sick, lame or useless horses for healthy ones, and damaged wagons for sound ones. Weapons were checked and sabres sharpened, and ammunition, tents and rations collected.

Slattery and Atty were to ride with the larger column.

'Midwinter,' Horrocks explained, 'thinks you know Villa better than anyone and will know what he intends.'

The whole area was filling up with men, horses, waggons, radio vans and field hospitals, even a tractor in case of emergencies. A new element was introduced with the arrival of a couple of aeroplanes, Curtiss JN two-seaters with wide wing-spans, which seemed in greater danger from the curiosity of their own side than from the hostility of the Mexicans.

'You guys keep back there,' the pilots yelled furiously at the interested soldiers. 'You touch that fabric and it'll tear!'

A third aeroplane landed soon afterwards, sending the civilian onlookers running as its whirling propeller stirred up clouds of red dust which blew over the picnics they had brought.

As the time for departure drew near, regimental musicians began to lick the mouthpieces of their instruments and a man with a camera on a three-legged stand manoeuvred blindly under his black cloth to set everything

336

on record. There was a scream of command and the whole mass of men stiffened. One of the regiments was Custer's old command, the Seventh Cavalry, and as the column began to move off in a cloud of dust with flapping guidons, Midwinter stared after it with cynical eyes.

'Let's hope they don't run into another Little Big Horn,' he said.

With all the activity moved from New York to the border, Midwinter and Horrocks settled down in El Paso.

Sent to Juárez, Atty came back with the information that the fleeing Villistas had ransacked stores in Chihuahua City. 'Except,' he pointed out dryly, 'them with German names. They say the German consul's smilin' all over his face. He knows the Punitive Expedition won't get near Villa because he's had a week to hide himself, and, whether they support Carranza or Villa or who the hell they support, the Mexicans sure as hell won't support the Americans.'

Atty was dead right and it was Midwinter as usual who brought the news. 'That goddam Carranza!' he snarled. 'He's forbidden us the use of his railroads!'

'He's a Mexican,' Slattery pointed out. 'He's behaving like a Mexican.'

Midwinter wasn't to be consoled. 'It means we have to supply our force by motor transport,' he said. 'And we don't have any goddam motor transport!'

4

Weeks later, three hundred miles inside Mexico, the Americans were no nearer to catching Villa, but were growing nearer every day to a full-scale clash with the Mexican army. Twenty times or more Villa was reported by the newspapers as captured, dead, run to earth, murdered by his own men or hanged by Carranza, until the colossal military fumble became a farce.

Despite their vast financial resources, the Americans had neglected their army so much after the Cuban War they were having to advertize for trucks, and civilian drivers and mechanics to run them.

'What a goddam army,' Midwinter grated. 'We couldn't fight a monkey in a dustbin.'

There had already been several skirmishes, hardly to be classed as battles, and the wind was blowing strongly, rolling vast clouds of red dust across the plain, as Slattery joined the flying column. It was already in a wretched state, supply vehicles travelling for miles without ever moving from first gear. The troops, dirty, dusty, thirsty and flea-bitten, were shedding useless equipment as they went and lorry-loads of discarded sabres had made their way back to Columbus. Saddles were defective, rifle scabbards were not the right shape, stirrup leathers were wrong, and in the scorching days and freezing nights, the gale was the final straw.

Heads down and buffeted by snowstorms, they wound along the mountain trails until the supply waggons were outstripped and they were living on nothing but beans and dried corn. Thirty-six miles from Guerrero they learned that Villa had just taken the place and, riding ahead of the army, Slattery found himself on a twisting dusty trail having to make way for a battered carriage pulled by a bony horse. To his surprise, it was occupied by the bulky shape of Villa, one leg bandaged and raised on to the seat in front. He stared at Slattery with the blank suspicious expression of a fox surprised with its prey. His face was running with sweat and grey and drawn with pain.

'Why are you here, inglés?' he snapped at once. 'Are you seeking me for the Norteamericanos?'

Slattery's heart thumped as he saw Villa's hand fall on the butt of that fluky pistol of his.

'No, Don Pancho,' he said. 'I'm nothing to do with the Americans. I'm a British diplomatic official now.'

It wasn't entirely true but he didn't fancy a bullet in the back.

Villa stared angrily at him then, as Slattery shifted in the saddle, he relaxed.

'I've been wounded, inglés,' he growled. 'I'd been watching the American column for days. They blunder about like blind mules. You can see them coming a day away with the dust they make. But they know how to keep order with their gente, how to transport ammunition and water and food, and I wanted to learn how they did it. We took Guerrero and I was sitting in the square when a boy discharged his pistol as he was cleaning it. The bullet hit me above the knee. The first wound I ever had – and, Dios, by an accident! They wanted to hang him but I said no. He was only a child.'

Villa shifted in his seat, the solid muscled body twisting with an attempt not to show the agony he was enduring. 'The bullet's still there,' he went on 'It's a .45. That's a big bullet and there's an infection. I've got to find a doctor or I'll lose my leg.'

'Be careful, Don Pancho,' Slattery said. 'The Americans mean business.'

'They'll never find me. I know these hills like my own backyard.' Villa's hand fell to his gun again. 'But I have a problem, inglés. You. What do I do about you? You could tell them where I'm heading.'

'If you believe that, Panchito, you'll believe anything.'

Villa nodded and the gun was pushed back into its holster. There was a last wave then the carriage rolled on.

Slattery's thoughts churned. Where in God's name in this

339

chaos that was Mexico did his loyalty lie? Mexico needed an end to Villa, the most troublesome of all the leaders it had produced. Slattery's own country needed an end to him, too, because for as long as he was alive he was a potential ally of the Germans and, after the disaster at Agua Prieta, his one declared desire was vengeance on the Americans.

But Villa was Villa and, against all sense, Slattery knew his loyalty remained with him. He had known him too long, shared too many hardships. Villa was a dangerous man but he had done Slattery many favours and had never shown enmity towards him. Many times they had disagreed but never for long and this pursuit of him by the Americans, Slattery decided, was Washington's business, not his.

As he returned to the American column, the exhausted horses were being pressed into a forced march through the night.

'We've heard Villa's at Guerrero,' he was told. 'We're going in.'

Slattery said nothing and, as daylight came, the American cavalry went in with a rush. The first thing they discovered was that, as Slattery was aware, Villa had escaped the previous night.

There were more skirmishes in a dozen places but Villa's guerillas were never rounded up and, with Horrocks watching the border, Slattery was finally ordered back to Mexico City. When he arrived, Atty, who had gone ahead, was camped out on the doorstep of his apartment with all his luggage.

'*She's* back!' he said furiously. 'She's in the house. I had to move out. And Turner the printer's been arrested.'

Slattery's head jerked round. 'What for?'

'What he always expected to be arrested for. Printing dough. He went to his shop on Saturday afternoon when the Mex workmen were having a day off and saw plates and blocks on the bench he didn't recognize. They were for forged currency. There was also a stack of forged notes.'

'What happened?'

'Carranza's decree gives the death penalty for forgers and Turner was scared.' Atty grinned. 'I would be, too. If there's

one thing the Mexes are good at it's executions. He grabbed
the plates and the forged notes, locked them in the safe and
headed for his brother's as fast as he could for advice. While
he was there, the feller who'd made the forgeries returned
and found everything gone. *He* was terrified, too. Only
mebbe *he* kept his head better. He went to the police and
denounced Turner before Turner could denounce him.
Turner's going to be shot on Monday. His brother's scared
because he thinks he'll get shot, too. I reckon you'd better
see the British Minister.'

The British Minister wasn't very happy about the situation but promised to do what he could and, although the
day was Sunday, he eventually emerged from the prison
governor's office to tell Slattery he had obtained a reprieve.

'But Turner's not released,' he pointed out. 'It's up to
you now to find out who *is* guilty, because he won't be
released until you do.'

'Atty,' Slattery said. 'You've got a job.'

It took two days of leaning heavily on a number of jobbing
printers employed about the city to discover exactly who
had been responsible, and Slattery and Atty were waiting
at the prison as Turner was released. Beside himself with
relief, his brother swept them all to Sylvain's to celebrate.

'We shall never forget you,' he said. 'And we have something for you in return. I work for the Mexican Telegraph
Service and I have noticed that Mr Sjogren, the assistant
to the Swedish chargé d'affaires, has been visiting the telegraph office far more often lately than the relationship of
Sweden with Mexico would seem to warrant. Does it mean
something?'

It didn't take long to find out that the flurry of telegrams
was because the Swedish chargé d'affaires was fishing for
a German decoration and that Eckhardt, the German
Minister, was actually requesting one for him.

'Well, we know the Germans like to hang things all over
themselves until they look like Christmas trees,' Slattery
mused. 'But why one for a Swede?'

Atty went to work at once and came up with the answer

341

within days. 'The German Minister's handin' messages for Berlin to the Swedish chargé d'affaires,' he said. 'And Sjogren's havin' them transmitted to their Foreign Office in Stockholm. From there, they're being sent to Berlin.'

Knowing was another small advantage, but the mood in the office in Mexico City remained gloomy. The Germans never let up. There was a new group down in Cuba who were worrying them. Who were they, and why were they there? They were like lice crawling out of the woodwork. What were they up to and were this latest lot officers or agents? And what the hell was Berlin expecting to get from them?

When he appeared, Horrocks expressed himself pleased with what they had achieved, nevertheless. He seemed to spend a lot of time these days north of the border chiefly in Washington, leaving Mexico to Slattery. He tossed a sheet of paper on to Slattery's desk. 'Passed on from London,' he said. 'It's an intercept. From the German Minister in Mexico to Berlin. Via Sjogren's Roundabout.'

'Something must be done to move the Mexicans,' the message read. 'We are constantly thwarted by British and American officials. We need something of great moment to make the Mexicans know we mean business.'

'You appear to have been more successful than you imagined,' Horrocks said dryly. 'We don't seem to achieve much and the old Hun keeps givin' us a bloody nose but, despite all that, we seem to be harassing him more than we thought. They've even started sending their messages from Washington to Berlin on the American cable.'

Slattery's jaw dropped. 'I don't believe it!'

'Fact,' Horrocks said. 'As you know, up to now they've been using the wireless station on Long Island but that's under American censorship, and Sjogren's Roundabout is probably too slow, so the German Ambassador complained that, though Berlin's eager to support Wilson's proposals for peace, they're unwilling to submit confidential terms through Long Island because there are too many leaks. On the advice of some half-baked ass, Wilson agreed to them using the State Department cable.' Horrocks smiled.

342

'London's reading everything they send. And they're not all about peace. Sooner or later they're going to put their foot in it. All we have to do is wait.'

5

The fact that Magdalena was in the city and not far away was unsettling. Try as he might, Slattery couldn't put her out of his mind.

For a long time, he considered what to do and in the end he went to the house in the Avenida Versailles. Jesús opened the door. His months in New York had made him a man. He was well-dressed, smart and clean and was speaking good English.

'Hello, Jesús,' Slattery said. 'Can I come in?'

Jesús looked nervous. 'My instructions, sir,' he pointed out, 'are that you mustn't.'

'From Doña Magdalena?'

'Yes, sir.'

'How is she, Jesús?'

'She is very well, sir. The show was a success. It is still running but she has left the cast because a new show is being lined up for her next year and she felt she needed a rest.'

'And you?'

Jesús smiled. 'I am a sort of agent, sir. I attend to small things. Eventually I shall do bigger and more important things.'

'I'm very pleased for you, Jesús. What does she feel about me?'

Jesús's face fell. 'She never mentions you, sir.'

'Never?'

'Once, sir. Her brother, Don Fausto, came to see her. There was a lot of anger. I didn't hear what happened but I caught some of it. She told him she was finished with you.'

'What did he want, Jesús?'

'It was about me, sir. He was telling her she had no right to allow me to take her name.' The boy's face was troubled.

344

'He said no dirty Mexican was going to be part of *his* family. Sir, I am not dirty –'

'Go on, Jesús.'

'He kept saying, "We are Germans, and Indians have no part in our affairs." '

'Where is he now?'

'I believe he's here, sir. In Mexico City.'

'And Doña Magdalena?'

'Lunching with El Señor Stutzmann. He's given up everything to act as her business manager. He says his voice is going and he is growing too fat to play leading parts. He says she should go back to New York.'

'Why?'

'He thinks she is no longer popular in Mexico.'

There was no response to the message Slattery left for Magdalena. It was difficult to follow what she was up to because the Mexican newspapers were suddenly ignoring her, and Slattery sought out Stutzmann, who had set himself up in a new office near the Cathedral.

He looked nervous but he was far from unwilling to talk. 'She can be launched on a great career,' he said.

'Does she want a great career, Hermann?' Slattery asked.

'All performers want a career.' Stutzmann sighed. 'She is very much loved in New York.'

'But not here any more?'

Stutzman shrugged. 'Mexico loved her because she was a Mexican. But when she went to New York, they felt she sold herself to the Yanquis.'

'Can't you tell them the truth?'

'With the country invaded by American soldiers?' Stutzmann's hands went to his face and the splayed fingers made valleys in his plump cheeks. 'Perhaps success is not what she wants.'

'What else could she want, Hermann?'

Stutzmann's shoulders moved again. 'If I knew, I might be able to make her happy. It certainly isn't me.'

Carranza was now lording it over the Mexican capital with

a government that grew increasingly corrupt, and it wasn't difficult to see his closeness to Eckhardt, the German Minister, because they were meeting quite openly in his office in the National Palace.

'That feller Sjogren's the contact,' Atty said.

'What's he after?' Slattery asked.

'Somebody's after *something*, me dear,' Atty agreed. 'The Union of German Citizens ain't paying out six hundred dollars a month for nothing.'

'How do you know they're paying out six hundred dollars a month?'

Atty touched his nose and Slattery didn't argue. There were times these days when he felt Atty knew more about the job than he did himself.

'One of the bank clerks told me,' Atty explained. ''Tes related to a relation of Pilar's he is.'

'Is everybody related to Pilar?'

Atty's face was blank. 'Mexicans have big families,' he said.

'What's the money for? Arms?'

'Not when 'tes paid to the Minister of Telegraphs.'

Across the Atlantic little changed. In Britain Lloyd George had become Minister of Munitions and in Germany a man called Arthur Zimmerman had become Foreign Minister. In America both were considered good choices – Lloyd George because his appointment meant more shells for the allies, and more shells for the allies meant more business for America; Zimmermann because he was a self-made man and because he was considered a good friend of the United States.

But German agents were still busy and a report from the border indicated that the German consul was financing a group of Germans meeting in Juárez. Sinister rumours seemed to be coming from all sides at once and now they began to pick up word of something called the Plan of San Diego.

'What is it?' Slattery asked. 'Another political manifesto?'

Word of the plan, whatever it was, was enough for Atty to disappear on one of his unexplained jaunts into the back

346

streets and eventually a message was brought by a small boy to say he would turn up at Slattery's flat late that night.

It was in the early hours of the morning when he appeared, to usher in a Mexican whom he introduced as Manuel Orriosca. The Mexican was a minor clerk in the office of the German Minister but his daughter had married an American and now lived in San Diego, California, where he hoped eventually to join her.

He was dressed for the occasion in stiff collar, spats and slicked-down hair, and he was nervous, but he produced a crumpled carbon covered with typing in Spanish. It contained references to the German consul in Monterrey and was addressed to the German Minister in Mexico City. He had found it in the waste-paper basket and had noticed it because of the name on it.

'He's trying to learn all he can about San Diego for when he joins his daughter,' Atty explained.

Slattery's eyes widened immediately because the carbon contained the details of the Plan of San Diego they were seeking. It outlined a scheme for a revolution to be started in Texas with German arms and support, which was to spread across New Mexico, Arizona, California, Nevada, Colorado and Oklahoma. It would establish the former Mexican territory as an independent republic populated by Mexicans, negroes and indians, which would eventually affiliate with Mexico itself and finally assist the negroes of six more southern United States to revolt and set up a purely negro country.

'This is political dynamite,' Slattery said. 'Who wrote it? Graf?'

'There's been no sign nor sound of Graf for a long time now, me dear,' Atty pointed out. 'He probably got shot at Columbus.'

'He wasn't among the bodies we found.'

Atty shrugged. '*Somebody* got Scheele there.'

The following day's newspapers brought news of a vast new battle taking place in France where thousands of men were dying for a mile or two of shell-torn ground along the River Somme.

347

'Only one way we can win this war now,' Atty decided gloomily. 'And that's with American troops. Which is why the bloody Germans are trying to get them into a war with the Mexicans.'

'After five years of revolution,' Slattery growled, 'if there's one thing Mexico doesn't need it's a war.'

The discovery of the Plan of San Diego came to little. It stank of the century-old hatred of the Mexicans for the gringo, but there was little doubt it was German-inspired, and despite the efforts of Midwinter and Horrocks, Washington refused to move because it had not come from any official German source.

As the Plan of San Diego vanished into limbo a new danger appeared. With the war become a stalemate, the only chance for the Germans was to unleash their submarines in an unrestricted campaign against world shipping. Then, as the threat began to increase, information arrived that all German residents remaining in the United States who were reserve officers or NCOs in the German army were to register at their consulates.

'To make up the losses on the Somme?' Slattery asked.

'More'n'at,' Atty commented. 'they've been ordered to register here. *In Mexico*. It concerns *us*, not them in France.'

The signs were growing ominous when a telegram arrived in code from Naval Intelligence in London. It quoted a Berlin message directed to Mexico City via Germany's Washington Embassy. 'Regret failure San Diego Plan. Appreciate British activity. Major plans afoot Mexico.' London was wanting an explanation.

'What major plans?' Slattery asked. 'And how did Berlin learn about San Diego? Their transatlantic cable was cut in 1914 and there isn't a wireless transmitter in Mexico powerful enough to send across the Atlantic.'

Atty grinned. 'Mebbe that's what the Union of German Citizens are paying the Minister of Telegraphs for, me dear,' he said.

Finally, a darker note appeared. Atty heard that Carrancista troops were taking up strategic positions along the lines of communication of the Punitive Expedition in Mexico, with orders to fire on any units moving in any direction but back to the border.

'Where did you hear this?' Slattery asked.

Atty touched his nose. 'Feller I know in the Mex army,' he said mysteriously. 'It's supposed to be a move to finish Villa off, but you can believe that if you want to.'

Slattery didn't argue. Atty's information was invariably reliable and, whether he obtained it by bribery, blackmail, drink or threats, it was rarely wrong.

'There are ten thousand of 'em near Juárez,' Atty pointed out. 'At a place called Villa Ahumada. We have British nationals with land up there so we've got a good enough excuse to stick our nose in. If I was you I'd arrange to nip up to El Paso and see 'Orrocks.'

'I've got a better idea,' Slattery said. 'We'll both go.'

6

As they waited at the Northern Station they bumped into Consuela Lidgett. She looked thin, shabby and suddenly no longer very prosperous. Her face was pale and there were dark circles under her eyes. She carried a battered suitcase and there was a taut sense of anger about her.

'I'm looking for Fausto,' she said immediately. 'His wife was killed, you know. The hacienda was raided and she got shot. I reckon *he* shot her. He was tired of her. Either way she's dead.'

'Does that mean he's free to marry you, Consuela?'

She gave Slattery a bitter look. 'Not me. That damn German baroness. Her husband was killed at Celaya, so she's free. He said he was going to marry *me*. He said it would be the first thing he'd do.'

She opened her handbag for him to see inside. It contained a revolver.

'What's that for?'

'It's for Fausto.'

'For his use?'

'Yes. To kill him.'

Slattery was silent for a moment. She was obviously in a state of high tension. 'Is he still around?' he asked.

'You bet he is. He kicked me out. You know that? They made him a vice-consul and he said I didn't match up to the job. He told me I was a whore. How about that? Who made me a whore?'

She accepted several banknotes with tears in her eyes and, as her voice trailed miserably away, she lit a cigarette and dragged the smoke down hungrily. 'He went north, in case you're interested,' she went on. 'His sister went north, too. But not with him. I hear she's doin' okay. I'm glad for you, Paddy. There's no harm in her, but if I thought he'd

350

suffer I'd wish her dead. She's gone up to Chihuahua to put flowers on the grave of his wife. Because *he* never has.'

Horrocks and Midwinter were in Chihuahua when Slattery arrived.

The whole of north Mexico was nervous. Far from destroying Villa, Wilson's Punitive Expedition had made him a country-wide hero. The Americans had badly misjudged his influence. He wasn't just the bloodthirsty savage the Carranza propagandists liked to portray. He was a born leader of considerable native intelligence with a compassion for the poor, and the groundswell of support that followed his victories, minor as they were these days, made him even stronger. All Wilson's Punitive Expedition had achieved was to make more powerful the hatred of the Mexicans for the Americans who were harrying Villa, and the American military leaders were now urging caution on their local commanders rather than the aggressiveness with which they had entered Mexico.

Chihuahua City was edgy and it occured to Slattery that Magdalena might find herself faced with hostility. For some time he debated warning her with himself but when he finally went to the house in the Avenida Pacheco, Victoria, the housekeeper, informed him she had taken a car to Villa Ahumada and beyond to Carrizal.

'For the flowers, your honour,' she said. 'On the grave of the little sister-in-law. It is much neglected.'

'Where is she staying?'

'When she go to Carrizal, she always stay at the Rancho Santo Domingo. The owner get her to sing. He say it is all the payment he want.'

As they picked up the train to El Sueco, Atty eyed Slattery suspiciously. 'Why are we goin' to El Sueco?' he asked. 'It don't sound like 'Orrocks's business to me.'

Slattery's reply was abrupt. 'It isn't Horrocks's business,' he said.

At El Sueco an American engineer warned there were a lot of Carrancista troops across the road to Villa Ahumada.

'You should hit Carrizal from the west,' he said. 'Then you'll be okay. There are Yankee troops round there.'

They hired horses and set off. The road was little more than a track and they found the Santo Domingo Ranch without difficulty. The owner was worried because he was expecting trouble.

'You can smell it,' he said. 'The Mexican people have had enough of the American army trampling all over their territory.'

'What about Doña Magdalena?'

'My foreman took her to Carrizal in the buggy yesterday. He dropped her at the hotel. But soon after they left the cavalry arrived here from Casas Grandes. They said they were going to ride through Carrizal.'

The foreman had been questioned by the American officer about Carrancista concentrations. 'There are a lot of Mexican soldiers there, your honour,' he told Slattery. 'It looked to me like a trap. But he had a guide with him who said Mexicans were cowards and would always run away.'

'Who was this guide? Do you know?'

The foreman shrugged. 'He wasn't a Norteamericano. But he also wasn't a Mexican.'

The sun was well up by now and the air was hot. As they jogged eastwards towards Carrizal, Atty reined in and pointed. A small cloud of dust on the horizon was resolving itself into a group of horsemen riding hard. They drew to one side and the horsemen, black soldiers of the United States cavalry pulled up their lathered horses. They looked exhausted and panic-stricken and some had no weapons.

'They've massacred the Tenth Cavalry!' one of them yelled through the cloud of dust they had stirred up. 'The captain and the lieutenant are down. We're headin' for Galeana for reinforcements.'

Without further explanation, they set spurs to their jaded horses and headed westwards again. Shortly afterwards three more men appeared with the same news, then several

352

small fast-riding parties, all obviously bolting but all claiming to be going for help.

The Mexicans in Carrizal were deployed along an irrigation ditch. There were signs of recent fighting in scattered and broken equipment, a dead horse, and scraps of abandoned clothing. A group of Mexicans were carrying away the body of an American soldier. At first they assumed Slattery was another American but when they learned his nationality they welcomed him as a witness to what had happened. They were flushed with triumph but had deliberately not pushed their advantage and insisted they had warned the Americans.

'We have twenty-three prisoners,' they said. 'It will mean war.'

Since there were no American consular officials available, it was obviously Slattery's duty to do what he could for the captives and they were led to a shed to the north of the town. The black soldiers, wounded and unwounded, had been stripped of their weapons and clothing and were scared, hungry and expecting to be shot.

'Why did you do it?' Slattery asked one of them.

'Because the captain said so. The guide said there was an American woman held prisoner in Carrizal. The captain thought we ought to save her.'

Leaving Atty with the prisoners, Slattery headed for the centre of the little town. The hotel was a large dusty building and was full of soldiers. Magdalena was sitting in the lounge on an upright chair, pale and dry-eyed. She was dressed in black with a wide black hat with a veil, and she was clutching a wreath. Jesús was with her, his face filled with determination.

As Slattery appeared, Magdalena's head lifted and her eyes met his, but nothing came from within her to meet him, and her face remained secret and enigmatic.

'Why in God's name did you come here?' Slattery demanded sharply.

'To put flowers on a grave,' she snapped back. 'I was told it was safe.'

'Who by?'

She didn't answer and he made his own guess. 'Are they holding you a prisoner?'

'Nobody was interested in me until the fighting started.'

Slattery indicated the door. 'I'm taking you away,' he said. He was aware of an inward tribunal summing him up. 'They won't let you,' she said quietly. 'Even if I wasn't a prisoner at first, I am now.'

'I can fix it.' He spoke with confidence. 'I'm taking you to Villa Ahumada to put you on the train to Chihuahua. Wait for me there. Get your things together. I'll be back.'

The Mexicans were still being co-operative but the burial of their dead had stirred tempers and a mob had gathered near the shed where the American captives were held and were hurling stones.

'I want them on the train to Chihuahua,' Slattery insisted.

'They'll be murdered on the way,' the Mexican officer said.

'Not if you provide a strong escort. It's up to you. The fate of Mexico could be in your hands.'

The Mexican agreed at last and Slattery hurried to the telegraph office to contact Horrocks.

It was already dark but the telegraph was still working. Outside the office there was a group of shadowy figures standing at the end of a nearby alley. Leaving after sending his message, Slattery paused to light a cigarette. As he threw the match away, he was aware of one of the men from the alley alongside him.

'Come with me, your honour,' he murmured.

Slattery looked around him warily.

'It's all right, your honour. I promise.'

The man took Slattery's arm and, against his better judgement, Slattery allowed himself to be pulled along. As he reached the alley end, the dark shapes, their faces obscured by the wide sombreros they wore, seemed to envelop him. He was just wondering if he hadn't been a fool and walked into a trap when his arms were seized and a pistol was stuck up to his nose. He could smell the burnt powder and gun oil. A familiar voice came out of the darkness.

'Holá, inglés.'

Slattery's head jerked up. 'Don Pancho! What in the name of God are you doing here?'

It was impossible to see Villa's face but there was no mistaking the voice. 'This is Mexico, inglés,' it said coldly. 'Nobody has forbidden me my own country. This is *my* land. Chihuahua. Villa land. Nobody tells me what to do here.'

'What do you want, Don Pancho?'

'I've come for you, inglés. You betrayed me to the Americans. You told them. After they took the bullet out, I had to hide in a cave in the hills and they were searching for me. They were just below us. I watched them. They knew I was there somewhere.'

His heart thumping, Slattery managed to keep his head in spite of that murderous pistol just below his nose. 'I didn't tell them, Don Pancho. When I met you, you were many leagues from Guerrero and they thought you were still there when they attacked it. What you saw was a patrol, I expect, who had no idea you were there.'

'You didn't tell them?'

'No.'

There was a long silence as Villa churned over what he had heard. 'I expect that's right, inglés. You wouldn't betray me. I brooded on it. But I was in great pain and it made things go hazy in my mind.' There was a pause. 'You aren't frightened of my gun, inglés. You're never frightened of it, yet it frightens most people.'

Slattery almost laughed. Anybody facing Villa's pistol had a good reason for being frightened. He tried to speak calmly.

'I'm not frightened, Don Pancho, because I'm not guilty.'

'*Dios*, you English! You're so smug. Still, now I have you, I can use you.'

'I don't betray my country, Panchito, any more than I betray you.'

Villa nodded. 'You'll be free to go. You're too thin-skinned to be of value to me, anyway, and this is a world where cold-bloodedness counts most. I won't hold you.'

'What do you want of me?'

'I need my mouthpiece.'

355

Slattery drew a deep breath, determined not to be drawn into the intricacies of Mexican politics again. 'I'm not your man any longer, Don Pancho,' he said. 'I'm working for my own country.'

'It is of no matter. I just need to tell someone the truth. This affair in Carrizal is nothing to do with me.'

'I never thought it was, Don Pancho. Is that all you wanted of me?'

'Not all of it. I was not responsible for Columbus either, inglés. That was the Germans. It was German money. Carranza money. They used some of my gente. I was in Sabinas in Coahuila at the time. I had given up the fight against Carranza. I even made a farewell speech to my gente. There was an American there who tried to tell them, but they chose not to believe him. When those engineers were shot at Santa Ysabel I was in Parral. That was also nothing to do with me. It was arranged by a German working with Carrancista agents. But I am a convenient scapegoat. For the Germans. For the Americans. For Don Venus. Tell people all this, inglés.'

It was a long speech and Slattery didn't know how much of it to believe.

'What now, Don Pancho? Shall you cross the border?'

'Into America?' Villa sounded startled. 'They'd hang me.'

'I thought the other border. Into Guatemala.'

Slattery caught the flash of teeth as Villa grinned. 'I am all right, inglés. I have no need to worry. Not after Carrizal. After Carrizal the Germans are just waiting for the Yanquis to make their intervention a full-scale invasion. The foreign businessmen would like that, German propaganda has pushed the rumours that America is intending to annexe everything as far south as the Panama Canal not only into Mexican heads, but into Norteamericano heads as well.'

As always, Slattery was surprised at Villa's shrewdness. 'What then, Don Pancho?'

Villa grinned again. 'It's only three months since they wanted to hang me for Columbus, but now both Carranza and the Norteamericanos are so busy with each other they've forgotten me.'

*

356

The following morning, the American prisoners, chained together and still only half-clothed, were packed into open lorries. As soon as the population of Carrizal learned what was happening, they began to gather, spitting, shouting, throwing stones and ordure.

'For God's sake,' Slattery snapped at the Mexican officer. 'Couldn't you have found covered lorries?'

'They won't be denied their revenge,' the Mexican said stiffly. 'And who am I to cheat them? If they want to throw filth, let them.'

Atty had hired a Model T Ford and they clattered up to the hotel while the yelling and the insults were still going on. Magdalena was waiting for them, pale and nervous. As she left the hotel, a woman spat at her. 'Americana,' she said.

As they drove off, the lorries were just leaving under a shower of stones, filth and dead rats and cats, but as they left the town the crowd thinned out and finally vanished. The sun was hot and the strong wind was lifting clouds of grit and dust and rattling them against the isinglass side-curtains of the car.

Somehow, information had reached Villa Ahumada ahead of them and there was another crowd there. Persuaded by Slattery, the Mexican officer kept the lorries on the edge of the town until the last moment, waiting until they saw the smoke of the locomotive appearing from the north, then they roared in, dumped their prisoners on the wrong side of the track as the train drew to a stop and bundled them aboard a box-car before the waiting crowd realized what had happened. Cheated, their showers of filth and stones bounced ineffectually off the sides of the closed car.

Throughout the journey, Magdalena said nothing, staring out of the window at the scorched brown landscape, lost in her own thoughts. As the train drew into Chihuahua, it seemed they had thrown off the vengeful crowds. Nobody was aware of their arrival beyond the soldiery who had turned up to meet them with three covered vans. The prisoners and the wounded were pushed inside and the vans clattered away towards the jail.

357

Magdalena was waiting quietly with Jesús in the shadow of the station buildings. As the cab dropped them all at her house, she turned on the doorstep.

'Fitz –' she began.

He gestured to the waiting taxi. 'I'll be back,' he said shortly. 'I have things to attend to. It may take a while.'

The cab dropped him at the hotel Horrocks and Midwinter always used. He wasn't surprised to see them in the foyer.

'What in the name of God happened?' Midwinter demanded. 'Was it a defeat?'

'If you call forty-four casualties a defeat, yes, it was.'

'Forty-four? Jesus, the Germans are going to love this!' Midwinter's eyes blazed. 'What the hell were they doing at Carrizal? They were miles from where they should have been. Who was behind it?'

'Graf.'

'How do you know?'

'I always know. He said the Mexicans would run.'

Midwinter glared. 'From now on, if that guy lifts a finger to flick the snot off his nose, I'll want to know why. The general in Columbus is throwin' a fit. Washington was on the point of withdrawin' our boys from Mexico. Now they can't. It'd look like we'd been kicked out. Hell' – his eyes were like ice – 'and if they stay it'll be out-and-out war.'

Magdalena's house was in darkness when Slattery arrived outside. There was no sound and no sign of life, just the silver-white of the moon.

As the iron gate slammed behind him, a light appeared and, as he tapped on the door, he heard Jesús's voice.

'It's me, Slattery!'

The door opened a fraction and, in the light of a candle on a table, he saw Jesús, a kitchen knife in his hand, barely awake.

Magdalena was at the top of the stairs by the door of her room. She had been in bed and her hair was loosely tied in a knot so that it hung to her shoulder. She was wearing a dressing-gown over a white night-dress.

Slattery gestured. 'Beat it, Jesús,' he said. 'Go back to bed.'

Magdalena seemed about to protest but changed her mind, and as the boy vanished Slattery moved slowly up the stairs. She met him at the top, standing in the doorway of her room, facing him, her eyes fixed on his.

'Why?' she whispered at last. 'Why did you come to me at Carrizal?'

He was about to say brusquely that it was because he had been on duty, but he changed his mind even as the words formed on his tongue.

'Because I had to,' he said. 'You once explained it yourself. Because you're Magdalena Graf and I'm Fitz Slattery.'

As he moved forward, almost as if she were unaware of what she was doing, she retreated in front of him until he was inside the room, too. As he faced her, they gazed at each other in silence, her eyes entreating understanding. For a while, he was expecting her to push him away, but suddenly she moved into his arms, clutching him like a frightened child, as if she'd been terrified but had been holding her terror at bay with every fibre of her body. As his arms closed round her a whimpering sigh escaped her. Struggling with the last of her conscience, her only protest was a weak appeal to propriety.

'Suppose someone comes?'

Slattery pushed the door to with his heel. 'They won't,' he said.

7

The mistake Horrocks had predicted the Germans would make came earlier than anyone expected.

When, on the seventeenth day of the new year, 1917, the duty officer at British Naval Intelligence in London opened the first message of the morning, he realized it was in non-naval code, and directed it to the political section, where it was immediately noticed that it was of an unusual length. A closer inspection showed that it was in German code and the decoders examining it began to search the code books to decipher the name of the sender.

'Zimmermann?' The man crouched over the message looked up. 'The German Foreign Secretary? What's he want?'

A little more work showed the words 'Most Secret' and 'For Your Excellency's personal information.'

The decoders looked at each other. 'It's directed to Washington,' one of them said. 'It must be for the German ambassador.'

Within a short time the word 'Mexico' appeared and then 'Japan' and there was mention of an 'alliance'. The decoders stared at each other again. Alliance? Japan was on the allies' side. Surely she wasn't considering switching to the Germans? The pages of the code book flipped back and forth with the rustle of paper as word after word was tried and discarded. After two hours' work, they had no more than an incomplete version of the message, but its significance was already such that they couldn't believe their eyes.

The situation in Europe was growing worse daily and the U-boats were making a cemetery of the waters round the British Isles, while, with American ships' captains unwilling to sail because of the threat, urgently needed cargoes were piling up in American ports.

In Horrock's hotel room, littered with papers, telegrams and cigarette ends, they worked out what they knew. There were reports that the Union of German Citizens in Mexico now had twenty-nine district committees spreading German *Kultur*; the Iron Cross Society had reported seventy-five branches, and its members were all engaged in promoting Germany, some from positions in the Mexican army; German money was subsidizing Mexican newspapers; agents were fomenting strikes in Tampico and among Mexican labourers in Arizona and California; while more German money was buying up mines vacated by Americans who had fled north from the chaos across the border.

'What nobody seems to have noticed, though,' Slattery said, 'is that Carrizal might be to our advantage.'

Heads came up and he gestured. 'Villa's relishing what's happened. It's only a few weeks since Columbus and already everybody's forgotten him. He can start to rally his gente again. And a resurgence of Villa would mean the one thing we all want – Wilson too – the withdrawal of the Punitive Expedition – has become possible. The Mexicans will be too occupied with getting at each other's throats to be interested.'

'Mebbe you've got something,' Midwinter conceded slowly, his brow twisted in bewilderment. 'Nothin' turns out as you expect, does it, and nothin' means what it ought to mean. This is a hell of a profession to be in.'

Slattery was right. The internecine strife in Mexico had made the withdrawal of the Punitive Expedition possible at last, and the movement back across the border began. Whatever Wilson might make of it, the invasion had turned out to be another of his blunders over Mexican pride.

'Even his peace in Europe doesn't seem to be catching anybody's interest,' Horrocks commented. 'Chaps in the trenches aren't very impressed.'

With Horrocks heading back to Washington, Slattery escorted Magdalena to Mexico City and established himself with her in the house in the Avenida Versailles. Atty wasn't slow to make sure of a place in the servants' quarters.

361

A lull at the end of the year enabled them to celebrate Thanksgiving and Christmas together. Magdalena spent most days now in Stutzmann's office arranging the details of a new trip to the States. Her presence in Carrizal had been kept quiet and American producers were eager to promote her, but they had decided that before offering her to New York in opera, she should do a small tour across Texas in *The Bohemian Girl*. Slattery had never seen her more carefree as she went every day to the Conservatory for singing lessons and instruction in the technique of the new medium.

Occasionally she gave little private concerts for him, singing her high Cs disdainfully, as if she could waltz round the room as she uttered them, so that Pilar, watching from the door, heaved a sigh. 'Like a bird,' she whispered. 'A bird full of the joy of living.'

She was still nervous about her debut, however. 'I'm afraid,' she said.

'What of?' Slattery asked.

'Of you being here and me being a thousand miles away. Of ruining your life. I don't know how to be married. All I have ever been is a singer. We shall quarrel. I shall throw things. You will beat me.'

He laughed and put his arms round her. Her concept of conjugal bliss seemed more suited to a dogfight than a marriage. Slattery had the feeling that while they would certainly hurt each other, they would also caress each other, supporting, devouring, sinking and rising, and would still be doing it a lifetime ahead.

'Magdalena, you can't shut out love any more than you can shut out pain. It'll work out without too much anguish.'

She let him kiss her then lifted her eyes, frowning and uncertain.

'Hermann has a new singer,' she went on. 'Dolores Mendoza. She's pretty and has a good voice. With help she'll be very good.'

'And that's worrying you? Because something is.'

She sighed. 'No,' she admitted. 'It isn't that. He went to Chihuahua to make arrangements for her to appear at the

362

Theatre of Heroes and he learned Fausto had been there. At my house. Will anything happen to him?'

'After Carrizal, if he's caught on American soil, yes.'

She was silent and he went on forcefully. 'We're not in operetta, Magdalena. Things don't always come right in the end. Keep away from him. He could be the cause of you being banned from the United States for ever.'

She was silent for a long time. When she spoke again it was slowly as if she were deep in thought.

'What I want,' she said, 'is peace. And children, not opera. I've lived out of a suitcase so long I've forgotten until now that I've got all the instincts a woman usually has. I need to worry about someone, protect them, offer up prayers for their happiness and safety.'

As she climbed aboard the train for the north two days later, she seemed suddenly impatient.

'I'll be back in Mexico City within a month,' she said. 'I have only to stop off in Chihuahua to collect costumes before going on to the border. Jesús will look after me and Hermann will be there, too. He's decided to make an appearance in *The Bohemian Girl*. Props are going up from Mexico City and we're meeting in El Paso for the final run-through.'

As she vanished towards her compartment Slattery turned to Jesús. In the boy's eyes Magdalena, who had clothed him, fed him and given him a pride in himself, could do no wrong.

'Take care of her,' Slattery told him.

'Of course, sir.' The boy put down the bags he was carrying and opened his jacket. It was long and fashionable and hid the fact that he wore a gun at his hip.

'How long have you had that?'

'Some time, sir.'

Slattery smiled. 'Better keep it out of sight,' he advised. 'They're not so keen on guns on that side of the border.'

8

When Slattery appeared at the office the following morning, Atty jerked a thumb.

'He's back from Washington,' he said. 'And you're wanted.'

Slattery didn't hurry. It was a small matter of pride that he couldn't be summoned willy-nilly. Instead, he went to his own office and glanced through the papers on his desk. Things hadn't altered very much. Germans were still being greeted by the Mexicans with cheers and Americans with boos or brickbats. And Carranza was preparing himself to be formally inaugurated as president. For once, there appeared to be no rival candidates, though Zapata was still in the Morelos hills and Villa still had the ability to pop up anywhere at any time.

Six years of bloodshed had long since broken the country down into small autonomous states under the leadership of bandits-turned-generals or generals-turned-bandits, and the graft in Mexico City was clear. Carranza's officials speculated in everything, selling offices and concessions, organizing thefts from the National Treasury, trafficking even in pensions. Though there was peace of a sort it was a disturbed peace of small uprisings and rebellions, and life remained cheap and easily forfeited.

When Slattery finally appeared in front of him, Horrocks was looking particularly blank-faced and enigmatic, something which had been growing more marked with every visit to Washington. He glanced pointedly at his watch.

'You're late,' he said.

Slattery waited. Horrocks always liked to develop his tactics with a maximum of dramatic effect amid the aura of mystery with which he wrapped himself.

For a moment he said nothing, then he gestured.'Shut the door,' he said. 'And lean on it.'

Again there was a silence then Horrocks announced that he had been sworn to secrecy.

'So why tell *me*?'

Horrocks frowned. 'It goes no further than you,' he said.

He went on to explain that a telegram from the German Foreign Minister, Zimmermann, had been intercepted in London. 'It's to the German ambassador in the States.'

'He was ordered home.' Slattery said.

'The telegram was sent before he left. London's been holding it.'

'Why?'

'You'll see in a moment. It begins with a passage about them commencing unrestricted submarine warfare on February 1st –'

'Old news. It's already started.'

Horrocks gave him a cold look. 'The Irish never make good agents,' he snapped. 'They can't hold their tongues. We know that, of course, damn it! What we didn't know but what the telegram makes clear is that if American hopes of remaining neutral in spite of submarine warfare are to prove false and they join the allies, then the German ambassador is instructed to propose to Mexico an alliance in which Germany and Mexico will make war on the States together.'

'War!' Slattery's jaw dropped.

'Not intervention. Not an incident. *War.*'

'Is this true?'

'I'm not in the habit of disseminating gossip.'

Slattery was silent for a moment. 'Why am *I* being told?' he asked. 'It's not usual to inform the galley slaves about this sort of thing?'

'It's not usual to inform *me*,' Horrocks pointed out coldly. 'But, as you'll see in a minute if you'll just, for God's sake, hold your tongue, it's important for us to know. In return for war against the US, Mexico is to be offered Texas, New Mexico, Arizona and all former Mexican territories. It's the Plan of San Diego without the frills.'

'Do the Americans know?'

'They will. In time.' Horrocks smiled. 'There's more.

Japan's to be invited to join the fun. The idea behind it all, of course, is the old chestnut that if the Americans should come in on our side in Europe over the submarine campaign, this will nullify their efforts by keeping them busy on their own side of the Atlantic. As they found out when they set up the Punitive Expedition, they haven't the where-withal to fight two wars at once. Not for a long time. And, if it came to a choice, they'd inevitably choose the one on their own side of the ocean.'

Horrocks' glance at Slattery was smooth in its smugness. 'This old son, is that mistake I always felt we'd eventually force them into. Thanks to a little luck and a bit of smart footwork on our part, Berlin's finally been forced to offer an out-and-out alliance in return for an out-and-out invasion.'

'There can't be any mistake, I suppose?'

'My dear chap, you haven't heard the whole of it yet. To make the offer, they used the facilities Wilson granted them. They actually used the US State Department cable to offer a chunk of continental United States to Mexico.'

'It's enough to bring the Americans in without hesitation.'

'If we can prove it, it will set the Americans roaring for guns, and ships to take them across the Atlantic.'

'Has Washington been told?'

'Not yet.'

'Why not?'

'London's afraid the reaction would be that it's a fake.'

'We've surely got proof of its arrival.'

Horrocks gave him a pitying look. 'Of course we have.' he said. 'But – if we offer it as it stands, Berlin will know at once that we've broken their codes and immediately change them. So it has to be done another way.' He lit a cigarette and placed it in the amber holder. He seemed totally in charge of the situation. 'Because of its importance, the telegram was sent in code by three different routes. By wireless from Berlin to Long Island; by Sjogren's Swedish Roundabout; and over the US State Department Cable by courtesy of President Wilson.'

Slattery waited in silence. There was more to come, he

knew, and Horrocks was dealing with it in his own languid way.

'The telegram which conveyed the final decision about U-boats,' he went on, 'was numbered 157. But there was a second one, number 158, which contained instructions to be passed on to the German Minister in Mexico City on what to offer Carranza. It will have significant small differences from the original. Dateline. Address. Signature. And so on. If we produce that one for Washington's delectation, the Germans will assume it was stolen in Mexico City and blame it on bribed secretaries or agents inside their embassy here. We have to find it.'

Slattery grinned. 'Turner,' he said at once. 'The printer we rescued from a firing squad. His brother works at the telegraph office.'

Horrocks vanished again as suddenly as he had appeared, leaving Slattery puzzled by what he had been told. It seemed an extraordinary development and all the proof they could find would be needed. But he had no doubt that Atty would produce the telegram they wanted and suddenly his attention was diverted by trouble near Torreón.

The Mexicans hadn't forgotten the Punitive Expedition and there were a few Americans there anxious to go north of the border to safety. With the American Consul still occupied with flung stones, broken windows and the far from remote possibility of lynching, the British Vice-Consul was handling things on his behalf. But he was a very young and inexperienced man who had slipped into the job largely by accident and was appealing for help from someone with more knowledge. Knowing it could do Britain a power of good in the White House, Slattery packed a Gladstone bag for the journey, tossing in a bottle of brandy and two tins of meat for safety. Trains often stopped running at night and were even occasionally blown up and the passengers stranded.

'It's only a day's ride further on to Chihuahua City,' he explained to Atty.

Atty grinned. 'And *she's* there,' he agreed.

The journey north was slow, with a variety of alarms and excursions but he reached Torreón by evening. It was bitterly cold and he was glad of the heavy ulster he wore. The Vice-Consul met him.

'The officer in command here's General Murguía,' he explained. 'He's supposed to be the terror of his own officers and hates rebels. Any he catches he hangs at once. He's known as Pancho the Rope. What's the best way to approach him?'

Slattery smiled. 'If he's no diplomat, he'll probably not welcome diplomatic talk. But as a soldier he might be interested to have your request in short sharp sentences and then have you shut up.'

'You think so?'

'At least you'll get your answer more quickly.'

Murguía's private railway coach lay on the line on the outskirts of the town, and as they approached it, one of his aides catapulted down the steps to the track, to pick himself up, dust himself down and disappear with as much dignity as he could manage.

'Not an auspicious moment to arrive, it seems,' Slattery murmured.

The Vice-Consul drew a deep breath and climbed the steps with Slattery on his heels. 'Better now than never,' he said.

Murguía was dressed in the uniform of the old Porfirian army, with a visored képi that gave a sinister expression to the shaded eyes and emphasized the hard lines of the mouth. He was a grim-visaged, dark-skinned man with a scarred face; and he was obviously on the point of leaving.

'Well?' he barked. 'Who're you?'

The Vice-Consul explained.

'I'm busy. I've just been informed Villa is heading this way and I want to be ready. What do you want?'

The Vice-Consul drew a deep breath and loosed his words in a flood. As he finished, Murguía stared at them for a moment, making no comment, asking for no credentials and showing no emotion. He simply barked a request

368

for the number of American men, women and children who wished to leave. Then he clapped his hands and an officer appeared at the double. The rasping voice continued, dictating an order for safe conduct.

'To cover all Norteamericanos and their families,' he said. 'They will be put in passenger coaches which will be hauled by military trains to Piedras Negras.' As the officer turned away, Murguía stopped him with another bark. 'The death penalty for anyone molesting them,' he snapped. 'Let it be made clear.'

The Vice-Consul seemed startled at the suddenness and completeness of his agreement and was standing with his mouth open when Slattery touched his arm.

'I think you'd better make sure everybody's ready,' he murmured. 'The General doesn't seem to be the sort of chap who'll take kindly to delay.'

Such was the anarchy in the area the Vice-Consul had to leave at once for Esterito to the south, where a British farmer had been attacked by a group of bandits, and could only offer Slattery the local hotel.

'I can't even give you a meal,' he said. 'My cookhouse has been burned down. I'd advise you to eat at the station. It's better than the hotel.'

The hotel was shabby and, heading there through the dark streets, Slattery noticed the marks of the numerous sieges the town had suffered in charred shop fronts and shattered houses. With its naked lights and buggies and the saddle horses tied to hitching posts, it had the look of a frontier town rather than a railway centre.

Slattery was tired and his leg painful. A policeman eyed him as he limped past. Outside the hotel, he came face-to-face with Fausto Graf. He had stopped dead, his face pale and strained. Above the upturned moustache his blue eyes were fierce as he stared at Slattery, startled and hostile at the same time.

'The Englishman with the crippled leg.'

'Honestly earned, Fausto,' Slattery said. 'In a better war

369

than yours. What are you stirring up here? What new misery are you plotting for Mexico?'

Graf's face broke into a wide smile, handsome, intelligent, defiant and treacherous. 'Something you will not know, Englander, until it hits you.'

They stared at each other, like old opponents in a game that had been going on far too long. Then Graf's mouth twisted.

'Why are *you* here? You are in my way. You are always in my way. You have been in my way from the first day you arrived. I should have removed you. I still should remove you. Your removal would concentrate my sister's mind. Without you, she might give her affection where it should belong, to someone of her own race and creed and culture.'

'What do you know of culture, Fausto?' Slattery's voice was stiff with dislike. 'What do you even know about Germany? You're a Mexican.'

As he had guessed, he could have offered no greater insult and Graf's face darkened with hatred.

'You have their gift for treachery, Fausto,' he went on. 'Their love of mindless vendettas. You're not a German. You're just another of those little brown men you despise so much.'

As he had been speaking, Graf's hand had been moving towards the pocket of his coat. Slattery guessed he had a gun there and he shook his head and smiled.

'I should leave it there, Fausto,' he advised. 'You might be tempted to use it and there are too many witnesses.' He indicated the men standing outside a nearby bar and the policeman with his slung rifle. 'Even in Mexico murder's still considered a crime. What a pity you couldn't have met me a few minutes ago further down the street at the end of a dark alley. That's the proper place for an assassin.'

Graf stared at him, bitter fury in his eyes, then he brushed past and vanished. For the first time since he had met him, Slattery felt a trace of sympathy for his blank fanatic patriotism. Nothing would ever change him. Come the end of the world, Graf would still be preaching German superiority to anyone who would listen.

*

The station meal was indifferent and the place was empty except for one other man, who sat slumped over his plate.

'George Wiley, of the *Post*,' he introduced himself. 'I met you in Nogales in 1913 when we were all interviewing Carranza.'

He was also staying at the hotel and when Slattery had finished eating they persuaded the woman who ran the restaurant to send for a taxi to take them there. When it arrived, they piled inside but Wiley had been drinking whisky and was slow moving and slurred of speech and had difficulty climbing into his seat. The driver also seemed to have been drinking because the vehicle moved only slowly and uncertainly along the dark streets. As it neared the hotel, Wiley was slumped half-asleep in his seat.

Slattery was just wondering once more what Graf was doing in the town when suddenly he heard the roar of an engine and the interior of the taxi was flooded with a yellow glow as the headlights of a car swung on to it. Turning, he saw a big black Dodge roaring towards them. As it drew nearer, he heard the crash of guns and the rear window fell in. Immediately, the taxi driver heaved on the brake and dived out of the door.

'Murder,' he screamed.

'Get out!' Slattery yelled at Wiley, and dived after the driver into the darkness of an alley. But Wiley was slow with the drink he had taken. He had just sat bolt upright when a flung grenade exploded and the taxi's petrol tank went up in a flare of flame. Horrified, Slattery heard the screams from the centre of the holocaust and he saw Wiley's clothes and hair were on fire. He struggled to open the door on Wiley's side to drag him out but the explosion had jammed it shut and as Wiley collapsed a policeman came pounding up in his shabby uniform, spats and képi.

'There's a man in there,' Slattery yelled.

Though they tried to reach the reporter, the door remained jammed and the heat forced them back, their faces and clothes scorched, their hands blistered. By the time the fire brigade arrived it was too late. Burning tyres were sending up thick columns of black smoke and the

371

interior of the vehicle was only a red glow in the centre of which they could see Wiley's shrivelled body.

Slattery had assumed the attack had been over some private dispute involving the taxi driver, something to do with the poaching of fares, but as he watched from the darkness of a doorway he became aware of a group of men who had appeared in the roadway. He recognized them at once as Germans.

'Who was he?' the policeman asked, indicating the shrunken shape in the rear seat of the burning vehicle.

One of the men stepped forward. 'His name was Slattery,' he said. 'An English agent and a murderer. He was stirring up trouble in Mexico. He won't be much missed.'

Throughout the night, Slattery was occupied with wondering what Graf had been up to in Torreón and why he had been so thorough in his attempt to have him murdered. He made sure his door was locked and with daylight sent for a cab to take him to the police station where he sorted out the identification of the victim of the fire.

'It would be easy to make the mistake,' the police sergeant said with a shrug. 'There's not much left of him.'

Taking the taxi to the station, Slattery kept well to the back of the dusty waiting room as he waited for the train north, sitting where he could see everyone who appeared.

There was a strong wind blowing when he reached Chihuahua city, sweeping clouds of red dust from the slopes of the Sierra Madre. Murguía had arrived just ahead of him and the station staff had it that Villa was close by.

Despite Carranza's claim to have the country under control, he had never completely tamed Morelos and Chihuahua. In Morelos the fierce attempts to quell Zapata had always resulted in him striking back with equal ferocity. There had been no more success with Villa, who was steadily building up his strength yet again. He had an incredible ability to conjure armies out of the earth, and an attack on Ojinaga had once more driven the government garrison across the border into Texas in a panic-stricken flight. Now it seemed that, newly reinforced and newly armed, he was about to show Carranza just how little tamed he was.

The station forecourt was full of Murguía's soldiers and the last of their waggons were just leaving the station. Magdalena was surprised to see him but overjoyed at his appearance. She was just on the point of going to the Cathedral.

'To kneel for a few minutes to pray for our happiness,' she said. 'I'm going to tell Hermann to call off New York. There are more important things in life than success as a singer.'

She was in a strange mood and she sensed that as usual she was talking to hide some anxiety. He said nothing of his meeting with her brother and stood beside her in the Cathedral, in an atmosphere of ancient stone and decaying incense. As she prayed, her hand reached out to his and pulled him to his knees beside her.

A cab took them back to the house. Victoria, the housekeeper, eyed Slattery nervously. Magdalena still seemed uneasy and worried and eventually he pulled her to him.

'Magdalena,' he said sharply. 'What is it? Something's troubling you.'

'No.'

'I've known you long enough to know that's not the truth. What is it?'

It took her a long time to tell him.

'Fausto came.'

Slattery was alert at once. 'To this house?'

'Yes.'

'What did he want?'

'I don't know. I was out. Victoria was alone at the time.'

Slattery was suspicious at once. With Villa at nearby Carrizal and Graf in Chihuahua, something was brewing and if Graf was prepared to go as far as murder it was probably important.

'He tried to kill me, Magdalena,' he said bluntly.

'Again?'

373

He showed her his bandaged hands and explained what had happened. Her face showed her shock and horror.

'Are you hurt?'

'No. But I suspect he thinks I'm dead. What did he want here? He's not in this part of the country for nothing. Get Victoria in.'

The housekeeper cringed as Slattery questioned her but she swore she didn't know what Graf had wanted. 'He asked for Doña Magdalena,' she wailed. 'When I said she wasn't here, he left.'

'Jesús.'

'Sir?'

'I'm going to the telegraph office. Take care of Doña Magdalena.'

It was just growing dark as he found a cab. Graf's appearance close to the border at a time when Villa was expected could only mean trouble and, in view of what they had learned of German plans, he knew Horrocks would want to be warned of any movement of German agents.

He had just finished sending the wire when he heard the crack of a small cannon, a burst of musketry and wild yells. Then a car full of men in wide sombreros and festooned with cartridge-belts roared past outside. They were shooting wildly and a bullet struck the window alongside him, knocking out the glass.

'*Qué viva Villa!*' they were yelling as they disappeared.

'Oh, God' – Slattery spoke out loud – 'not *him*!'

9

It soon became clear that the attack on Chihuahua City was being led by Villa in person. The major thrust seemed to be along the Avenida Colon and it seemed very much as if the whole of the invading force was between Slattery and Magdalena's house.

The attack couldn't have come at a more inconvenient time and he knew he mustn't become involved. Horrocks would need him back in Mexico City where the biggest coup that had come out of the war still awaited their attention.

Making his way down a side street through the hurrying people seeking shelter, he found himself surrounded by a crowd which jammed the narrow alley to its walls. They were mostly youngsters itching to get into the fight, and there was the sound of glass being broken as windows were knocked in. But then a car drew up and the crowd scattered like mist in a wind. The man in the car was General Murguía, and behind him appeared a regiment of Federal troops. As he stepped to the pavement, he saw Slattery at once.

'What are you doing here?'

It was obvious he suspected treachery but Slattery managed to explain.

'So you are to marry La Graf?' Murguía said, nodding. 'You are a lucky man. But I'd advise you to stay off the streets or she might find herself widowed even before you have put the ring on her finger.' He gestured to the north. 'It's Villa. Pancho the Pistol. I was warned. If you see him, tell him Pancho the Rope is coming.'

As he vanished, Slattery allowed himself to be borne along by the press of people. One of Murguía's officers advanced, pistol in hand, accompanied by a couple of soldiers, and the crowd backed away silently, unwilling to give ground. Chihuahua was Villa's state and always had been, and Chihuahua City had always been his capital. The two soldiers spotted Slattery among the shoving people and as they moved towards him, he stood still, raising his hands to indicate he wasn't armed.

As he did so, the crowd surged forward and the officer started lashing out with his pistol. An infuriated workman hit back with a spade and, as the officer staggered back, Slattery brought his arms round to sweep the two soldiers together with a crash. Their heads clicked like billiard balls, and, as they sank at his feet, the crowd surged forward. The rifles were snatched up and he saw the officer's kepi fly into the air, then the shouting became the baying of wild dogs scenting a prey. As the officer's body was dragged away, already half-stripped and covered with blood, the crowd surrounded Slattery and tried to hoist him to their shoulders. Shocked by the sudden bloody violence that had resulted from what had been no more than an attempt to escape, he pushed them away, and they started to chip with pickaxes at the cobbles, lifting them for brickbats. The bodies of the two soldiers already hung from a tree, one by its feet. The officer lay in the gutter and an old woman with a hole in her stocking ground her heel in the dead face, then ran off in a hurried scuttle, her expression full of shame and guilt and hatred.

The shouting had died now, and there was the sort of hush that comes before a tumult, so that the creak of a shutter above their heads seemed to have an extra significance. Then Slattery heard the tramp of disciplined feet and the crowd, which was beginning to gather again, started to panic. They all seemed to be pushing different ways at once, then a man stumbled and fell, a girl fell on top of him and, as they heard the clatter of musketry, the group began to splinter as men and women flung themselves down.

For a moment the noise died then Slattery heard a machine-gun firing and saw plaster falling as bullets chinked against the walls. As he scrambled to his feet, he saw Murguía moving with his men up the Avenida Independencia. They tramped forward in silence and, in the distance, lit by flames, he saw sombreros and stetsons and guessed Villa had dug himself in.

Swinging into the Calle Jiménez, he headed for the railway station in an attempt to reach Magdalena's house by a roundabout route. The din was tremendous now and the sky was red with flames. Engine sheds were on fire and box-cars standing in the sidings were blazing furiously. The Villistas were at the end of the Avenida Pacheca but he managed to slip between them, and Magdalena's house appeared at last, lit up by the glare.

There was a motor car outside, its engine running, and as he hurried forward he heard a shout – 'No! No! You can't come in!' He recognized Jesús's voice at once and the sudden alarm in his mind set him running.

'You snivelling Indian filth! Get out of the way!'

The door was wide open and Jesús, holding his gun, was standing in front of the stairs, Magdalena behind him, her face shocked and horrified. At first Slattery thought the Villistas had invaded the house but, as he burst inside, he saw the intruder was Fausto Graf and he was also holding a gun. As he saw Slattery, he whirled on his heel and fired blindly, without thought, without aiming. The bullet struck the fleshy part of the calf of Slattery's injured leg, knocking it from under him and spinning him round to fling him to the ground. As he fell, he heard another shot and a cry, then Magdalena's shriek as she flung herself between them.

Then the shooting at the end of the street swelled up and there were shouts and, as he struggled to sit up, Slattery just managed to catch a glimpse of Graf by the door before he vanished. Finding he wasn't badly hurt, he tried to get to his feet and, as he did so, he saw Victoria with her hands to her face, her eyes wide with horror. Turning, he saw Jesús stretched on the floor. His chest was covered with blood and he realized where Graf's second shot had gone.

Struggling across to the boy, Slattery bent over him. As he did so, his eyes opened.

'I tried, sir,' he whispered.

'Yes, you did, Jesús.'

'I tried to stop him.'

'You did stop him, Jesús. He's gone. Doña Magdalena is safe.'

As Slattery looked up, Magdalena, her face chalk white, was just pushing Victoria out of the door.

'I've sent for the doctor,' she said.

Slattery reached out two fingers to close the boy's eyelids. 'There's no need for a doctor, Magdalena,' he said quietly, 'Jesús is dead.'

When the doctor arrived, Magdalena, hardly able to see for tears, had succeeded in staunching the bleeding in Slattery's leg. They had carried Jesús into the salon and laid him on a chaise longue but the doctor wasted no time over him before turning to Slattery's injury.

'You're alive,' he said bluntly. 'He isn't. This is nothing serious. You'll live, and there'll be plenty worse than this today.' He straightened up and glanced at Jesús. 'I'll write a certificate. But you'll not need it. There'll be many more.'

As he left, Slattery rose to his feet, his trouser leg slit to the knee. It was possible to stand, even to walk. Magdalena lifted her eyes to him, her expression agonized. Though she allowed him to put his arms round her, she remained fiercely in control.

'He was like a son,' she whispered. 'And he was so proud that he had made something of himself.'

As he held her, Slattery's eyes were moving about the room. Through his grief for the boy, he felt something was wrong. There were things that needed explaining. 'Where's Victoria?' he asked abruptly.

Grey-faced, her eyes rolling, the housekeeper was found hiding in the pantry. As Slattery dragged her out, she collapsed into a paroxysm of wailing and he had to slap her to bring her to her senses. Watched by a shocked and silent Magdalena, he began to question her.

'Don Fausto! Why did he come here?'

'To see Doña Magdalena, your honour.'

'I don't believe it. He was in too much of a hurry. There has to be a better reason than that. Why?'

It required another slap to make her go on.

378

'It was the suitcase, your honour.'

'Which suitcase?'

'He left it here when Doña Magdalena went to Carrizal. I was alone and he made me take it. He said he was being followed by an American agent and had to get rid of it for a while. I put it in the cupboard in my room.'

'Where's this suitcase now?'

'It's still there, your honour. Jesús wouldn't let him in the house for it.'

'Fetch it,'

It was an old and battered suitcase, with straps round it and a plethora of labels, as though Graf had enjoyed boasting about his travels. As Slattery forced it open, he saw it was full of files and papers, and immediately realized it contained the secrets of the German diplomatic campaign in Mexico. Everything seemed to be there – the involvement at Veracruz, at Santa Ysabela, at Columbus, at Carrizal, all set out and listed for Eckhardt, the German Minister in Mexico City.

He pushed the case aside and turned to find Magdalena sitting silently in a chair, her brows down, her eyes far away. He had no idea what she was thinking.

'We must arrange for Jesús to be buried,' she said in a flat voice.

'I can attend to that.'

'He was murdered. They can hang Fausto for this.'

'He's been asking for it for a long time.'

He poured her a brandy and handed it to her.

'Let me think,' she said. 'I need to be alone for a little while. I'll go to my room.'

Still rigidly in control, she disappeared and he turned again to the suitcase. Horrocks would need some sort of summary of its contents. But everything was there, clear and undeniable, for everyone to see. It all seemed to be contained in two large files headed *Deutschland, Carranza Und Die Mexikanische Revolution* and *Die Deutsche Politik in Mexiko*. It was all set out, even the German attempts to involve the Japanese, in a third, smaller file entitled *Die Gelbe Gefahr*. There were documents of the Iron Cross

Society and the Union of German Citizens in Mexico, and a list of funds passed to them from Berlin. It contained names, memos, and copies of instructions to German officers in Nuevo Laredo to organize Mexican raids into US territory, of supplies bought for the Mexicans by the German consul in Chihuahua who had crossed and recrossed the border between El Paso and Ciudad Juárez about his business. From San Salvador there were reports of German ex-officers and details of exactly where they were, of the hotels where they stayed in Mexico City, Torreón and Monterrey, of the Carrancista officers with whom they associated.

There were reports of attempts to persuade the Mexicans that Wilson was anti-Catholic, of Germans buying ships' coal on the west coast, of the Germans behind Carranza's call for an embargo on all war supplies to the Allies in Europe. There were details of the German-inspired revolt in Cuba which had bothered Slattery; of the influx of German reservists from North and South America into Mexico. There were even notes that revealed that Graf's patriotism hadn't been sufficient on its own for what he'd been involved in. He had been cheating Berlin of cash. Finally, there was a blue notebook which seemed to be some sort of signal log because it itemized every telegram Graf had handled – instructions concerning Columbus and Santa Ysabel, even the train disaster that had so worried Villa. And there, at the end, was an item that leapt out at Slattery as he read. 'Telegram seen and noted. Passed to Wertz for action and returned to Minister Eckhardt.' Following was a gleeful note. 'Enough to start a war on this side of the Atlantic.'

The contents of the case were dynamite. It was obvious that it should be taken at once to Horrocks and shown by Horrocks to Midwinter. Slattery sat back, frowning, aware that he had to return to Mexico City as soon as possible. By this time Atty ought to have pushed Turner's brother into action. What Slattery had found would add indisputable confirmation.

As he shovelled the documents back into the case and

380

locked it, he became aware that the house had become silent. He could hear Victoria in the kitchen, sniffing back her tears, but from Magdalena there was no sound and, suddenly alarmed, he ran up the stairs to her room. It was empty.

Tumbling down the stairs again to the kitchen, he snatched at Victoria's wrist. 'Where is she?'

The housekeeper began to wail again and this time he sent her reeling with the ferocity of the slap he gave her.

'She went out, your honour.'

'Where to?'

'She said she was going to find Don Fausto.'

Frustrated and angry, feeling he was being betrayed all along the line – now even by Magdalena – he thrust the woman aside. As she disappeared he went to where Jesús lay to take his gun. But it had disappeared. The holster was empty and he could only assume Victoria had stolen it.

Locking the suitcase in one of the bedrooms, he slipped the key into his pocket and left the house. It was empty now apart from Jesús. Poor Jesús, he thought. With all his promise, with all his pride in himself, it had been his misfortune to come face to face with someone as tough and bigoted and fanatic as Fausto Graf who, for all he knew, had been pushed just over the top by Slattery's taunts in Torreón.

He went to the room where the boy lay. For a moment he stared down at the still figure then, leaving the house and closing the door behind him, he headed into the street. Walking was difficult. His leg was always painful at the end of the day and the wound, slight as it was, added to his problems. At least, he thought, it was the same leg.

He could think of no reason for Magdalena's disappearance beyond a hope of smuggling her brother away. Why in the name of God couldn't she realize he was beyond saving? He was a swindler, a killer, a traitor to his adopted country. Christ, he thought, with Jesús dead and himself wounded, wasn't it enough to convince her Fausto was a dangerous lunatic?

The night sky was crimson with flames. The shooting all seemed to be along the Avenida Colon and round the

381

neighbouring park but there was no sign of Murguía's men in this area, only the tall hats of Villa's desperadoes.

The trees threw shadows over the streets that seemed to move in the flickering of the flames. There were a few men about carrying weapons but none of them showed any interest in Slattery. Eventually he came on a car and immediately recognized the figure standing alongside it as Villa. Hands went to guns and a man appeared from the shadows and stuck a rifle in Slattery's back.

'Do we shoot him, Don Pancho?'

Villa peered closely, then he gestured. 'Put up your gun,' he said. He stared at Slattery. 'What are you doing in Chihuahua, inglés? Did you know the German has betrayed me?'

'I know now, Panchito.'

'He told Murguía I was coming. If I find him I shall kill him.'

The firing was still going on and Villa stared down the Avenida Colon with its low overhanging trees.

'A lot of people have died, Panchito,' Slattery said.

'There'll be a lot more before long. Thanks to the German, three hundred of my gente have been cut off down there. Monserrat's with them and I shall have to abandon them.' Villa's voice was heavy and tired, his words like plodding footsteps. 'I shall give up the fight now, inglés,' he went on. 'It's time to stop. I want peace to educate my children. The revolution is finished. It's time now for the law-makers. Yesterday's heroes are out of date. Great visions were painted on my heart once, but there were too many ambitious men. I asked nothing from the revolution but others were different. I shall discharge my army. There is just this one last thing I have to do. If you see the German, tell him I want him and I shall find him.'

As he turned away, Slattery was at a loss where to head next. He had been on his feet a long time and his leg was painful. He had no idea where Graf had gone, and no idea where Magdalena might be in her search for him. The whole city seemed to be throbbing with the gunfire now and the park was lit by flames rising high in the sky and

382

showering the place with sparks. For a long time he moved among the trees then, suddenly, unexpectedly, he saw Magdalena.

She was standing quite still, staring into the shadows. Beyond her, also standing quite still, was her brother. For a moment Slattery wondered what she intended, then he realized that in her hand she held Jesús's gun, the gun the boy had carried to protect her, the gun Slattery had assumed had been taken by Victoria as she had bolted, and he finally understood why she was there, and what she intended.

Graf's head was turned away to stare into the darkness and it dawned on Slattery that he was totally unaware of his sister's presence and was staring in a different direction entirely. Magdalena's hand lifted but, as Slattery waited for the report, a different gun went off. He saw the flash and saw Graf stagger, then Consuela Lidgett stepped out from among the trees. The gun she held, the one she had shown him in her bag at the station, was still smoking.

Graf was gazing at her, his mouth open, holding his right arm with his left hand. He tried to lift his weapon but his arm dangled as if it were broken, and his face twisted with pain and rage.

'Hure!' he said, the words quite plain. 'Matze!'

He stared at her with hatred and Consuela dropped her gun and put her hands to her face.

'Bitch!' Graf shouted. 'Whore! *Puta*! You've shot me!'

Vaguely Slattery was conscious of movement near him and the throb of a car's engine, then as Graf turned to stumble away, another gun roared out. Twice. It was of a much heavier calibre than Consuela's and it sent Graf staggering several yards before he came up against a tree. He had dropped his gun and was sprawled against the trunk, his arms outstretched to support himself. Slowly he turned, his back to the tree, and he was searching for his new assailant as the gun roared twice more. Chips of wood flew and Slattery saw wisps of smoke come from Graf's clothes. He was flung back against the tree this time as if he were crucified, his mouth open, his eyes wide, his arms extended, then he slid down to a sitting position. For a moment or two longer he stared across his feet into the shadows, then slowly rolled on to his side.

Slattery had his arms round Magdalena, but she was silent and dry-eyed. 'Don't cry,' he whispered.

'I'm not crying,' she said firmly. 'He isn't worth the tears.'

As he led her back to the road, they passed Consuela, who was still standing with her hands to her face, and Magdalena put her arm round the distraught woman. As they reached the road, they saw the big black Dodge and behind it tall-hatted men with horses. Villa was among them, his face grim. He had his pistol in his hand and slowly he replaced it in its holster. 'He stayed alive long enough, I think, inglés,' he said, 'to remember me.'

10

There was clear satisfaction in Mexico City at Villa's defeat. Villa had always been the maverick, unpredictable and murderous. Even Zapata was never so full of dangerous plans.

The two days he had spent in Chihuahua had left Slattery spent. Villa's raid had been a disaster. As he had told Slattery, many of his men had been cut off in the Avenida Colon and the grim-faced Murguía had rounded up two hundred and fifty-six of them, Monserrat, the last of the Holy Trinity, among them, and strung them from the trees in what looked like huge bunches of human grapes. The bodies were still moving slowly in the breeze, feet dangling among the tangled ropes, and already the people of Chihuahua were calling the Avenida Colon the Avenue of Hanging Men.

The station sheds and the box-cars were charred skeletons and Slattery wondered if somehow Scheele had been responsible. Among the things which had gone up in the flames were the properties from the Opera House in Mexico City. Stutzmann had tried to save them and was now in his hotel with badly burned hands. With the properties, the costumes and their manager gone, there had been no alternative but to cancel the whole tour and when an American agent appeared from El Paso with contracts for a different date, Magdalena simply brushed him aside. Pushing Consuela aboard a train for the border, they buried Jesús quickly and prepared to return to Mexico City. The country was living up to its reputation for misery, murder and anarchy.

'Poor Jesús,' Magdalena kept whispering. 'Poor Hermann.'

They closed the house and boarded the train among the blackened buildings and burned-out box-cars. For most of

385

the journey south, Magdalena sat in silence, staring through the window as if she were shell-shocked. As they slid into the station in the capital, Slattery called a taxi and directed it to the house in the Avenida Versailles. When they arrived, Pilar was on the doorstep with Atty, who seemed to know exactly what had happened.

It was some time before Slattery felt he could leave her, but she insisted she was all right and that Pilar could do everything that was needed. Taking a cab to his office, Slattery was confronted by Horrocks as he placed the suitcase on the desk.

'I got your wire,' he said. 'Is this the case?'

'It's all there. As much proof as you need.'

Horrocks shrugged. 'Was Graf behind it all?'

'He was behind a lot of it.'

'We'll get Midwinter to pick him up if he tries to stick his nose over the border.'

'There's no need,' Slattery said. 'He's dead.'

Horrocks' eyebrows rose. 'Did you kill him?'

'No. Villa did.'

There was a long silence. 'Funny we should be in debt to Villa,' Horrocks said eventually. 'When you think of it, it all started with Villa, didn't it? How is Magdalena taking it?' For once there was a trace of compassion in the cold voice.

'She'll be all right,' Slattery said.

Horrocks waited for more but, realizing nothing further was forthcoming, he shrugged and pressed on. 'Our friend, Turner, did his stuff,' he said. 'Atty brought along a copy of the telegram we wanted. A photograph of it's gone to Washington.' He indicated the stick Slattery was still using. 'Heard you got hurt, by the way.'

'Nothing I can't handle.'

'That's the spirit, old chap. *Dulce et decorum est.* Stiff upper lip, play the game and all that.'

'Christ, sometimes I detest you!'

Horrocks sighed. 'A lot of people do,' he said. 'It's one of the hazards of command, as you'll discover.'

'What do you mean?'

386

'Midwinter's coming in two days' time. You'll enjoy explaining everything to him.'

'Me?'

'It's all yours, old boy.' Horrocks beamed. 'The rebel's become the satrap. The symbol of independence's suddenly the keeper of the keys.'

'What the hell are you talking about?'

Horrocks seemed tickled by his own words. 'You're in charge. Isn't that a surprise? I've been summoned to Washington, and they've given you my job. Little Unwilling is now the Boss.'

'I don't want to be the bloody boss!'

'No choice, old boy. I recommended you months ago. That's why they gave it to you. I told them I knew no one so well versed in treachery, and that you'd experienced it from every angle and at every level. I said you knew everybody likely to be involved and had more experience of the Germans than anyone south of the border save yours truly. That's why you were let into the secret of the telegram. It was known then that you'd probably have to handle it.'

'Me?' Slattery was still startled.

'You! You've got the appointment. And, if I may say so, you'd be a bloody fool to turn it down. There are a lot of things that go with it. Secure future. Good pay. Prestige. Probably a decoration after you've finished your time at the oars. Gives you a touch of class, a decoration. And class counts. Opens doors. Opens hearts. Good for tick at the grocer's.'

He realized Slattery was still looking a bit bewildered. 'What's so odd about it, damn it?' he went on. 'It's not a very difficult job, so even a bog Irishman like you ought to be able to cope. You know every name in the files, and, if you don't, Atty does.'

As Slattery stared, staggered, he went on cheerfully. 'Full status. Rise in pay. House, car and servants supplied. The ear of the ambassador whenever you want it. Just what the doctor ordered. Especially married to Magdalena Graf. She'll grace any diplomatic function you have to go to and

387

you'll be going to a few. It's always useful to have a beautiful wife. I envy you.'

Slattery was still staring and he went on cheerfully.

'She's even intelligent enough to be an asset to you. More than you could say for some wives. You could be here another twenty years – more if you want. Revolutions don't come to an end overnight.'

He paused, smiling. 'Of course,' he went on, 'on big occasions you'll have to wear a morning suit and top hat but, that should be no hardship. Atty takes your job. He's a damn funny choice but it's wartime and everybody else is in uniform. Though I don't ever see him as a future ambassador, I suspect he'll be better than some of the funny little men from the right schools they might have sent out.' Rising from his chair, he gestured at the desk. 'So you'd better get stuck into things, hadn't you? You'll need to be on top of the job when Midwinter appears.'

Despite her grief, Magdalena was impressed by Slattery's new importance. 'I'm proud,' she said quietly.

She was careful to attend to his clothes, chivvying Pilar to sponge and clean them, and provided linen to go with them, almost as if it were what she needed to take her mind off what had happened. Her eyes slowly became alight again and he knew it was the thought that he was being made to settle down after years of doing as he pleased.

She was recovering a little now from Jesús's death, though she had been stunned by the contents of her brother's suitcase. She was refusing to quit the house or receive visitors but Slattery left her alone, feeling that time would eventually heal her wounds, and he and Atty concentrated on adding to the contents of the suitcase with a few more discoveries of their own.

'German activity in Guatemala, me dear,' Atty said 'A nice little gunpowder train of revolutions in Central America, with all the régimes friendly to the United States to be overthrown for a new federated state of Central America with a German president.'

When Midwinter arrived, he looked like a bull trying to make up its mind which china shop to attack.

Slattery was ready for him. He had known what Horrocks had been up to since 1913 and had worked with him for three years far more closely than he had ever intended. And the delay before Midwinter had arrived had given him time to get on top of things. It had even helped him to get over what had happened in Chihuahua. The amount of work with which he had found himself faced had left him no time for brooding.

'What's goin' on?' Midwinter demanded. 'Somethin' is, because I keep hearin' rumours. There's talk of some telegram. There is one, I know, because Under-Secretary Polk in Washington's demanding it from Western Union and they're refusin' to let him have it. Are you Limeys thinkin' of negotiatin' with the Germans for peace, after all?'

Slattery smiled. 'Not on your life,' he said.

'Never mind "Not on your life",' Midwinter snarled. 'If I didn't know he'd been called to Washington, I'd suspect that long streak of whitewash, Horrocks, had disappeared so he wouldn't have to face me. Somethin's goin' to bust wide open soon. Up north it's like you took the wire off a champagne bottle but haven't popped the cork.'

The following day he was in possession of further information. 'There *is* a telegram,' he said. 'A German telegram. I've seen a copy. It's a fraud, of course.'

'Is it?' Slattery carefully cultivated Horrocks's disconcerting vagueness.

'All that stuff about an alliance and offering the Mexes New Mexico, Texas and Arizona?' Midwinter gestured derisively. 'Nobody would be that mad. It's eyewash.'

'Is it?' Slattery said again.

As he spoke, he realized he was starting to act like Horrocks. My God, he thought, it goes with the job!

Midwinter was staring at him with narrowed eyes as if he, too, had noticed the difference. 'Isn't it?' he said.

'Do you think that London would lay themselves wide open to an accusation of fraud at a time like this?'

'There are some goddam stupid rumours about it coming through on the State Department cable. Our own cable.'

'The statement to the press says it was received by a means which Washington isn't prepared to disclose.'

Midwinter stopped dead. 'By God,' he breathed. 'It *did*!'

'It would certainly make it authentic, wouldn't it?' Slattery said and Midwinter scowled, almost as if he found himself confronting another Horrocks.

The newspapers had already got wind of something big about to break and those which came down on the train from the north were screaming of German plots. The United States Congress was suddenly noisy with patriotic oratory and objections that the telegram had been planted by the British.

'I bet London's rollin' on the floor laughin',' Atty grinned.

Hardly able to believe their eyes, they saw in the next day's papers that Zimmermann, the German Foreign Minister, had been forced to admit sending the telegram.

'Was it a plant?' Midwinter asked.

Slattery quietly pushed across the blue notebook he had found in the suitcase in Chihuahua. One item was ringed in red ink.

' "Telegram seen and noted," ' he quoted. ' "Passed to Wertz for action and returned to Minister Eckhardt. Enough to start another war on this side of the Atlantic." '

'Where did you get this?'

'Fausto Graf's papers.'

'I want a copy.'

When Midwinter had gone, Slattery looked up at Atty. 'Of course,' he said. 'Though the date's about right, there's no proof at all that the telegram he refers to is telegram 158. It might be a reference to something else entirely. Still, it'll suffice. We're not exactly amateurs at dirty tricks ourselves.'

Atty grinned. ''Orrocks would approve,' he said.

When Midwinter reappeared two days later, he looked as though he didn't know whether to cheer or commit suicide.

'It's out,' he said. 'The full story.'

390

He placed a sheet of paper on the desk. It was a copy of the headlines in the Washington newspapers. *'Germany Seeks Alliance Against US,'* they said. *'Japan and Mexico Asked to Attack US.'*

The indifference with which three-quarters of the United States had regarded the war in Europe was shattered. The uproar over the sinking of the *Lusitania* was nothing compared with the new wave of indignation. Germany was actually proposing to attack the United States itself, setting a neighbour to stab her in the back, and the German-Americans who had been against the war suddenly decided they were American after all, and that they couldn't be loyal to both countries. Those newspapers with German owners and German names, which had come down heavily against the telegram, now actually began to consider changing their titles, while the shout of fury that came out of the threatened territories in the south and west even drowned the indignation in the north. The picture of hordes of Mexicans and Japanese led by German officers was enough to give people nightmares.

For the first time America was one nation and war fever suddenly began to sweep the country. Parades, with torches and brassy martial music, beat through the streets into the night. Churches prepared special military services and their choirs marched behind huge Stars and Stripes as preachers extolled the virtues of a 'holy crusade' until they seemed half-witted.

The United States seemed to be rolling up its sleeves, and the news put out by the New York and Washington newspapers was all repeated in the journals of the Mexican capital. It was possible to see men standing on corners engrossed in what the papers said, gossiping, arguing, even quarrelling. Mexico had never sided with the gringos but they were well aware that they were now witnessing a shattering event.

Packed into the chamber, Congress heard President Wilson declare that the world must be made safe for democracy and that America must fight for the principles that gave her birth. The uproar that greeted the words could be heard in Europe.

'Though she might not know it yet,' Slattery observed, 'Germany's just lost the war.'

The office was quiet as they digested what had occurred. Rising from his chair, Slattery opened a bottle of champagne. What had happened was a world-shaking thing. America, who had always isolated herself from Europe, could never, try as she might, claim isolation again.

Midwinter was the first to leave. As he vanished, Slattery took a cab to the Avenida Versailles. It was a month now since he had returned from Chihuahua, a month since Jesús's death. It had not been an easy month.

The house was silent and the street was deserted except for an old man begging with a few halting tunes on a trumpet. As Slattery entered there was no sign of Magdalena. Then Pilar crept from the kitchen and lifted her eyes to the stairs.

Magdalena's door was open and she was sitting on the bed. On the floor alongside her was a newspaper. Her face was expressionless and Slattery could see the headlines, bold against the white sheet. *'America Joins The Allies. US Decides To Fight Germany.'* She was mourning a lost heritage, a lost history, a lost background. Though she knew at last what she was, what her future was, she suddenly no longer had a past because the country she had been taught to revere was now an enemy. What had happened had made her someone else, a different person with different traditions, different hopes different ambitions, a different way of life.

Without a word, Slattery sat on the bed alongside her and gathered her in his arms. The room was silent except for the ticking of a clock. Then a door slammed downstairs and, unexpectedly, the old beggar with the trumpet opened up just outside. The sound came, high and thin like all Mexican trumpets, shattering the stillness. He was playing *'La Cucaracha'* and Slattery was suddenly reminded of old Apolinario Gomez García and all that had gone before.

> *'La Cucaracha, la cucaracha,*
> *Ya no pueda caminar*
> *Porque la falte, porque no tiene*
> *Marijuana que fumar.'*

Even played by a tattered old man with no skill, it evoked a flood of memories and had a brazen shout that suddenly seemed like a rallying call to thousands of fresh young men with dreams of glory to go and die in a new war. Magdalena seemed to sense what he felt and clutched him more tightly.

He sighed deeply. 'It's been decided for us, Magdalena,' he said quietly. 'For better or worse, America's in.'

Epilogue

Though it was over for the Germans in Mexico, the turmoil was by no means over for the Mexicans.

Orozco was dead. Huerta died in 1916, still a prisoner of the Americans. With treachery reaching a fine point of ingenuity, Zapata was assassinated for Carranza in 1919 by an officer who gained his confidence by pretending to desert the First Chief. He offered proof by sending his men against their unsuspecting Carrancista comrades at the town of Jonacatepec, and, as further proof, he had all his prisoners shot. Impressed, Zapata turned up for a meeting but, as the bugles blared, at the command 'Present arms' the guard of honour raised their rifles not to salute but to murder Zapata and his escort.

Carranza himself was assassinated in 1920. Finding himself running out of friends, he set out by train for Veracruz, the coaches stuffed with treasure stolen from the National Palace. Forced to take to horses, in a primitive village called San Antonio Tlaxcalantongo, he bedded down for the night in a one-room hut, and just before dawn his own escort murdered him and stole everything he possessed, even his blue-tinted spectacles.

Villa followed him in 1923. He had arranged an amnesty for himself and his followers and, engaged in farming in Canutillo, was working as he had promised to improve methods and provide education in the nearest town, Parral. After attending a christening, he was returning home when his car was ambushed. His widow claimed Obregón was behind it.

Obregón, the agnostic who had permitted the sacking of churches, did well for Mexico. After one term of office as president, he was succeeded by one of his followers and was re-elected himself in 1928. Unfortunately, he had not allowed for the hatred of the country's religious fanatics whose lives had become so heavily restricted, or for the fact that one of them might be prepared to give his life for Christ. He was attending a political banquet in a suburb of Mexico City when a young artist, pretending to be sketching the notables gathered there, showed him his drawings and asked him to pose for him. As he turned and smiled, he was shot five times in the face and died in his seat, only sixteen days after he had been re-elected.

The question of the peasants' land and the foreign holdings which had concentrated the minds of so many leaders was not settled until the late thirties when the then president grasped the nettle all the preceding leaders had feared, and declared the peasants could have their land and that all oil and minerals in Mexico belonged to the Mexicans. It turned out to be easier than expected.

The Germans returned in the thirties with their Nazi organizations but they were no luckier than their predecessors, though, when in 1942 the Mexican government declared war on the Axis, it left the Mexicans thunderstruck. What, they wondered, were they doing pointing their guns with the Yanquis instead of *at* them?